Emile Zola

Abbe Mouret´s Transgression

Outlook

Emile Zola

Abbe Mouret´s Transgression

1. Auflage | ISBN: 978-3-73261-764-7

Erscheinungsort: Paderborn, Deutschland

Erscheinungsjahr: 2018

Outlook Verlag GmbH, Paderborn.

Emile Zola

Abbe Mouret´s Transgression

Outlook

ABBE MOURET'S TRANSGRESSION

By Emile Zola

Edited with an Introduction by Ernest Alfred Vizetelly

CONTENTS

1

XIII

2

INTRODUCTION

'LA FAUTE DE L'ABBE MOURET' was, with respect to the date of publication, the fourth volume of M. Zola's 'Rougon-Macquart' series; but in the amended and final scheme of that great literary undertaking, it occupies the ninth place. It proceeds from the sixth volume of the series, 'The Conquest of Plassans;' which is followed by the two works that deal with the career of Octave Mouret, Abbe Serge Mouret's elder brother. In 'The Conquest of Plassans,' Serge and his half-witted sister, Desiree, are seen in childhood at their home in Plassans, which is wrecked by the doings of a certain Abbe Faujas and his relatives. Serge Mouret grows up, is called by an instinctive vocation to the priesthood, and becomes parish priest of Les Artaud, a well-nigh pagan hamlet in one of those bare, burning stretches of country with which Provence abounds. And here it is that 'La Faute de l'Abbe Mouret' opens in the old ruinous church, perched upon a hillock in full view of the squalid village, the arid fields, and the great belts of rock which shut in the landscape all around.

There are two elements in this remarkable story, which, from the standpoint of literary style, has never been excelled by anything that M. Zola has since written; and one may glance at it therefore from two points of view. Taking it under its sociological and religious aspect, it will be found to be an indirect indictment of the celibacy of the priesthood; that celibacy, contrary to Nature's fundamental law, which assuredly has largely influenced the destinies of the Roman Catholic Church. To that celibacy, and to all the evils that have sprang from it, may be ascribed much of the irreligion current in France to-day. The periodical reports on criminality issued by the French Ministers of Justice since the foundation of the Republic in 1871, supply materials for a most formidable indictment of that vow of perpetual chastity which Rome exacts from her clergy. Nowadays it is undoubtedly too late for Rome to go back upon that vow and thereby transform the whole of her sacerdotal organisation; but, perhaps, had she done so in past times, before the spirit of inquiry and free examination came into being, she might have assured herself many more centuries of supremacy than have fallen to her lot. But she has ever sought to dissociate the law of the Divinity from the law of Nature, as though indeed the latter were but the invention of the Fiend.

Abbe Mouret, M. Zola's hero, finds himself placed between the law of the Divinity and the law of Nature: and the struggle waged within him by those two forces is a terrible one. That which training has implanted in his mind proves the stronger, and, so far as the canons of the Church can warrant it, he saves his soul. But the problem is not quite frankly put by M. Zola; for if Abbe Mouret transgresses he does so unwittingly, at a time when he is unconscious of his priesthood and has no memory of any vow. When the truth flashes upon him he is horrified with himself, and forthwith returns to the Church. A further struggle between the contending forces then certainly ensues, and ends in the final victory of the Church. But it must at least be said that in the lapses which occur in real life among the Roman priesthood, the circumstances are altogether different from those which M. Zola has selected for his story.

The truth is that in 'La Faute de l'Abbe Mouret,' betwixt lifelike glimpses of French rural life, the author transports us to a realm of poesy and imagination. This is, indeed, so true that he has introduced into his work all the ideas on which he had based an early unfinished poem called 'Genesis.' He carries us to an enchanted garden, the Paradou—a name which one need hardly say is Provencal for Paradise*—and there Serge Mouret, on recovering from brain fever, becomes, as it were, a new Adam by the side of a new Eve, the fair and winsome Albine. All this part of the book, then, is poetry in prose. The author has remembered the ties which link Rousseau to the realistic school of fiction, and, as in the pages of Jean-Jacques, trees, springs, mountains, rocks, and flowers become animated beings and claim their place in the world's mechanism. One may indeed go back far beyond Rousseau, even to Lucretius himself; for more than once we are irresistibly reminded of Lucretian scenes, above which through M. Zola's pages there seems to hover the pronouncement of Sophocles:

```
No ordinance of man shall override
   The settled laws of Nature and of God;
   Not written these in pages of a book,
   Nor were they framed to-day, nor yesterday;
   We know not whence they are; but this we know,
   That they from all eternity have been,
   And shall to all eternity endure.
* There is a village called Paradou in Provence, between
  Les Baux and Arles.
```

And if we pass to the young pair whose duo of love is sung amidst the varied voices of creation, we are irresistibly reminded of the Paul and Virginia of St. Pierre, and the Daphnis and Chloe of Longus. Beside them, in their marvellous garden, lingers a memory too of Manon and Des Grieux, with a suggestion of Lauzun and a glimpse of the art of Fragonard. All combine, all contribute— from the great classics to the eighteenth century *petits maitres*— to build up a story of love's rise in the human breast in answer to Nature's promptings.

M. Zola wrote 'La Faute de l'Abbe Mouret' one summer under the trees of his garden, mindful the while of gardens that he had known in childhood: the flowery expanse which had stretched before his grandmother's home at Pont-au-Beraud and the wild estate of Galice, between Roquefavour and Aix-en-Provence, through which he had roamed as a lad with friends then boys like himself: Professor Baille and Cezanne, the painter. And into his description of the wondrous Paradou he has put all his remembrance of the gardens and woods of Provence, where many a plant and flower thrive with a luxuriance unknown to England. True, in order to refresh his memory and avoid mistakes, he consulted various horticultural manuals whilst he was writing; of which circumstance captious critics have readily laid hold, to proclaim that the description of the Paradou is a mere florist's catalogue.

But it is nothing of the kind. The florist who might dare to offer such a catalogue to the public would be speedily assailed by all the horticultural journalists of England and all the customers of villadom. For M. Zola avails himself of a poet's license to crowd marvel upon marvel, to exaggerate nature's forces, to transform the tiniest blooms into giant examples of efflorescence, and to mingle even the seasons one with the other. But all this was premeditated; there was a picture before his mind's eye, and that picture he sought to trace with his pen, regardless of all possible objections. It is the poet's privilege to do this and even to be admired for it. It would be easy for some leaned botanist, some expert zoologist, to demolish Milton from the standpoint of their respective sciences, but it would be absurd to do so. We ask of the poet the flowers of his imagination, and the further he carries us from the sordid realities, the limited possibilities of life, the more are we grateful to him.

And M. Zola's Paradou is a flight of fancy, even as its mistress, the fair, loving, guileless Albine, whose smiles and whose tears alike go to our hearts, is the daughter of imagination. She is a flower—the very flower of life's youth—in the midst of all the blossoms of her garden. She unfolds to life and to love even as they unfold; she loves rapturously even as they do under the sun and the azure; and she dies with them when the sun's caress is gone and the chill of winter has fallen. At the thought of her, one instinctively remembers Malherbe's 'Ode A Du Perrier:'

```
She to this earth belonged, where beauty fast
    To direst fate is borne:
A rose, she lasted, as the roses last,
    Only for one brief morn.
```

French painters have made subjects of many episodes in M. Zola's works, but none has been more popular with them than Albine's pathetic, perfumed death amidst the flowers. I know several paintings of great merit which that touching incident has inspired.

Albine, if more or less unreal, a phantasm, the spirit as it were of Nature

7

incarnate in womanhood, is none the less the most delightful of M. Zola's heroines. She smiles at us like the vision of perfect beauty and perfect love which rises before us when our hearts are yet young and full of illusions. She is the ideal, the very quintessence of woman.

In Serge Mouret, her lover, we find a man who, in more than one respect, recalls M. Zola's later hero, the Abbe Froment of 'Lourdes' and 'Rome.' He has the same loving, yearning nature; he is born—absolutely like Abbe Froment—of an unbelieving father and a mother of mystical mind. But unlike Froment he cannot shake off the shackles of his priesthood. Reborn to life after his dangerous illness, he relapses into the religion of death, the religion which regards life as impurity, which denies Nature's laws, and so often wrecks human existence, as if indeed that had been the Divine purpose in setting man upon earth. His struggles suggest various passages in 'Lourdes' and 'Rome.' In fact, in writing those works, M. Zola must have had his earlier creation in mind. There are passages in 'La Faute de l'Abbe Mouret' culled from the writings of the Spanish Jesuit Fathers and the 'Imitation' of Thomas a Kempis that recur almost word for word in the Trilogy of the Three Cities. Some might regard this as evidence of the limitation of M. Zola's powers, but I think differently. I consider that he has in both instances designedly taken the same type of priest in order to show how he may live under varied circumstances; for in the earlier instance he has led him to one goal, and in the later one to another. And the passages of prayer, entreaty, and spiritual conflict simply recur because they are germane, even necessary, to the subject in both cases.

Of the minor characters that figure in 'La Faute de l'Abbe Mouret' the chief thing to be said is that they are lifelike. If Serge is almost wholly spiritual, if Albine is the daughter of poesy, they, the others, are of the earth earthy. As a result of their appearance on the scene, there are some powerful contrasting passages in the book. Archangias, the coarse and brutal Christian Brother who serves as a foil to Abbe Mouret; La Teuse, the priest's garrulous old housekeeper; Desiree, his 'innocent' sister, a grown woman with the mind of a child and an almost crazy affection for every kind of bird and beast, are all admirably portrayed. Old Bambousse, though one sees but little of him, stands out as a genuine type of the hard-headed French peasant, who invariably places pecuniary considerations before all others. And Fortune and Rosalie, Vincent and Catherine, and their companions, are equally true to nature. It need hardly be said that there is many a village in France similar to Les Artaud. That hamlet's shameless, purely animal life has in no wise been over-pictured by M. Zola. Those who might doubt him need not go as far as Provence to find such communities. Many Norman hamlets are every whit as bad, and, in Normandy, conditions are aggravated by a marked predilection for the bottle, which, as French social-scientists have been pointing out for some years now, is fast hastening the degenerescence of the peasantry, both morally and physically.

With reference to the English version of 'La Faute de l'Abbe Mouret' herewith presented, I may just say that I have subjected it to considerable revision and have retranslated all the more important passages myself.

MERTON, SURREY.   E. A. V.

ABBE MOURET'S TRANSGRESSION

BOOK I

I

As La Teuse entered the church she rested her broom and feather-brush against the altar. She was late, as she had that day began her half-yearly wash. Limping more than ever in her haste and hustling the benches, she went down the church to ring the *Angelus*. The bare, worn bell-rope dangled from the ceiling near the confessional, and ended in a big knot greasy from handling. Again and again, with regular jumps, she hung herself upon it; and then let her whole bulky figure go with it, whirling in her petticoats, her cap awry, and her blood rushing to her broad face.

Having set her cap straight with a little pat, she came back breathless to give a hasty sweep before the altar. Every day the dust persistently settled between the disjoined boards of the platform. Her broom rummaged among the corners with an angry rumble. Then she lifted the altar cover and was sorely vexed to find that the large upper cloth, already darned in a score of places, was again worn through in the very middle, so as to show the under cloth, which in its turn was so worn and so transparent that one could see the consecrated stone, embedded in the painted wood of the altar. La Teuse dusted the linen, yellow from long usage, and plied her feather-brush along the shelf against which she set the liturgical altar-cards. Then, climbing upon a chair, she removed the yellow cotton covers from the crucifix and two of the candlesticks. The brass of the latter was tarnished.

'Dear me!' she muttered, 'they really want a clean! I must give them a polish up!'

Then hopping on one leg, swaying and stumping heavily enough to drive in the flagstones, she hastened to the sacristy for the Missal, which she placed unopened on the lectern on the Epistle side, with its edges turned towards the middle of the altar. And afterwards she lighted the two candles. As she went off with her broom, she gave a glance round her to make sure that the abode of the Divinity had been put in proper order. All was still, save that the bell-rope near the confessional still swung between roof and floor with a sinuous sweep.

Abbe Mouret had just come down to the sacristy, a small and chilly apartment, which a passage separated from his dining-room.

'Good morning, Monsieur le Cure,' said La Teuse, laying her broom aside. 'Oh! you have been lazy this morning! Do you know it's a quarter past six?' And without allowing the smiling young priest sufficient time to reply, she added 'I've a scolding to give you. There's another hole in the cloth again.

There's no sense in it. We have only one other, and I've been ruining my eyes over it these three days in trying to mend it. You will leave our poor Lord quite bare, if you go on like this.'

Abbe Mouret was still smiling. 'Jesus does not need so much linen, my good Teuse,' he cheerfully replied. 'He is always warm, always royally received by those who love Him well.'

Then stepping towards a small tap, he asked: 'Is my sister up yet? I have not seen her.'

'Oh, Mademoiselle Desiree has been down a long time,' answered the servant, who was kneeling before an old kitchen sideboard in which the sacred vestments were kept. 'She is already with her fowls and rabbits. She was expecting some chicks to be hatched yesterday, and it didn't come off. So you can guess her excitement.' Then the worthy woman broke off to inquire: 'The gold chasuble, eh?'

The priest, who had washed his hands and stood reverently murmuring a prayer, nodded affirmatively. The parish possessed only three chasubles: a violet one, a black one, and one in cloth-of-gold. The last had to be used on the days when white, red, or green was prescribed by the ritual, and it was therefore an all important garment. La Teuse lifted it reverently from the shelf covered with blue paper, on which she laid it after each service; and having placed it on the sideboard, she cautiously removed the fine cloths which protected its embroidery. A golden lamb slumbered on a golden cross, surrounded by broad rays of gold. The gold tissue, frayed at the folds, broke out in little slender tufts; the embossed ornaments were getting tarnished and worn. There was perpetual anxiety, fluttering concern, at seeing it thus go off spangle by spangle. The priest had to wear it almost every day. And how on earth could it be replaced—how would they be able to buy the three chasubles whose place it took, when the last gold threads should be worn out?

Upon the chasuble La Teuse next laid out the stole, the maniple, the girdle, alb and amice. But her tongue still wagged while she crossed the stole with the maniple, and wreathed the girdle so as to trace the venerated initial of Mary's holy name.

'That girdle is not up to much now,' she muttered; 'you will have to make up your mind to get another, your reverence. It wouldn't be very hard; I could plait you one myself if I only had some hemp.'

Abbe Mouret made no answer. He was dressing the chalice at a small table. A large old silver-gilt chalice it was with a bronze base, which he had just taken from the bottom of a deal cupboard, in which the sacred vessels and linen, the Holy Oils, the Missals, candlesticks, and crosses were kept. Across

13

the cup he laid a clean purificator, and on this set the silver-gilt paten, with the host in it, which he covered with a small lawn pall. As he was hiding the chalice by gathering together the folds in the veil of cloth of gold matching the chasuble, La Teuse exclaimed:

'Stop, there's no corporal in the burse. Last night I took all the dirty purificators, palls, and corporals to wash them—separately, of course—not with the house-wash. By-the-bye, your reverence, I didn't tell you: I have just started the house-wash. A fine fat one it will be! Better than the last.'

Then while the priest slipped a corporal into the burse and laid the latter on the veil, she went on quickly:

'By-the-bye, I forgot! that gadabout Vincent hasn't come. Do you wish me to serve your mass, your reverence?'

The young priest eyed her sternly.

'Well, it isn't a sin,' she continued, with her genial smile. 'I did serve a mass once, in Monsieur Caffin's time. I serve it better, too, than ragamuffins who laugh like heathens at seeing a fly buzzing about the church. True I may wear a cap, I may be sixty years old, and as round as a tub, but I have more respect for our Lord than those imps of boys whom I caught only the other day playing at leap-frog behind the altar.'

The priest was still looking at her and shaking his head.

'What a hole this village is!' she grumbled. 'Not a hundred and fifty people in it! There are days, like to-day, when you wouldn't find a living soul in Les Artaud. Even the babies in swaddling clothes are gone to the vineyards! And goodness knows what they do among such vines—vines that grow under the pebbles and look as dry as thistles! A perfect wilderness, three miles from any highway! Unless an angel comes down to serve your mass, your reverence, you've only got me to help you, on my honour! or one of Mademoiselle Desiree's rabbits, no offence to your reverence!'

Just at that moment, however, Vincent, the Brichets' younger son, gently opened the door of the sacristy. His shock of red hair and his little, glistening, grey eyes exasperated La Teuse.

'Oh! the wretch!' she cried. 'I'll bet he's just been up to some mischief! Come on, you scamp, since his reverence is afraid I might dirty our Lord!'

On seeing the lad, Abbe Mouret had taken up the amice. He kissed the cross embroidered in the centre of it, and for a second laid the cloth upon his head; then lowering it over the collar-band of his cassock, he crossed it and fastened the tapes, the right one over the left. He next donned the alb, the symbol of purity, beginning with the right sleeve. Vincent stooped and turned around him, adjusting the alb, in order that it should fall evenly all round him to a couple of inches from the ground. Then he presented the girdle to the priest, who fastened it tightly round his loins, as a reminder of the bonds wherewith the Saviour was bound in His Passion.

La Teuse remained standing there, feeling jealous and hurt and struggling to keep silence; but so great was the itching of her tongue, that she soon broke out once more: 'Brother Archangias has been here. He won't have a single child at school to-day. He went off again like a whirlwind to pull the brats' ears in the vineyards. You had better see him. I believe he has got something to say to you.'

Abbe Mouret silenced her with a wave of the hand. Then he repeated the usual prayers while he took the maniple—which he kissed before slipping it over his left forearm, as a symbol of the practice of good works—and while crossing on his breast the stole, the symbol of his dignity and power. La Teuse had to help Vincent in the work of adjusting the chasuble, which she fastened together with slender tapes, so that it might not slip off behind.

'Holy Virgin! I had forgotten the cruets!' she stammered, rushing to the cupboard. 'Come, look sharp, lad!'

Thereupon Vincent filled the cruets, phials of coarse glass, while she hastened to take a clean finger-cloth from a drawer. Abbe Mouret, holding the chalice by its stem with his left hand, the fingers of his right resting meanwhile on the burse, then bowed profoundly, but without removing his biretta, to a black wooden crucifix, which hung over the side-board. The lad bowed too, and, bearing the cruets covered with the finger-cloth, led the way out of the sacristy, followed by the priest, who walked on with downcast eyes, absorbed in deep and prayerful meditation.

II

The empty church was quite white that May morning. The bell-rope near the confessional hung motionless once more. The little bracket light, with its stained glass shade, burned like a crimson splotch against the wall on the right of the tabernacle. Vincent, having set the cruets on the credence, came back and knelt just below the altar step on the left, while the priest, after rendering homage to the Holy Sacrament by a genuflexion, went up to the altar and there spread out the corporal, on the centre of which he placed the chalice. Then, having opened the Missal, he came down again. Another bend of the knee followed, and, after crossing himself and uttering aloud the formula, 'In the name of the Father, the Son, and the Holy Ghost,' he raised his joined hands to his breast, and entered on the great divine drama, with his countenance blanched by faith and love.

'*Introibo ad altare Dei.*'

'*Ad Deum qui loetificat juventutem meam,*' gabbled Vincent, who, squatting on his heels, mumbled the responses of the antiphon and the psalm, while watching La Teuse as she roved about the church.

The old servant was gazing at one of the candles with a troubled look. Her anxiety seemed to increase while the priest, bowing down with hands joined again, recited the *Confiteor*. She stood still, in her turn struck her breast, her head bowed, but still keeping a watchful eye on the taper. For another minute the priest's grave voice and the server's stammers alternated:

'*Dominus vobiscum.*'

'*Et cum spiritu tuo.*'

Then the priest, spreading out his hands and afterwards again joining them, said with devout compunction: '*Oremus*' (Let us pray).

La Teuse could now stand it no longer, but stepped behind the altar, reached the guttering candle, and trimmed it with the points of her scissors. Two large blobs of wax had already been wasted. When she came back again putting the benches straight on her way, and making sure that there was holy-water in the fonts, the priest, whose hands were resting on the edge of the altar-cloth, was praying in subdued tones. And at last he kissed the altar.

Behind him, the little church still looked wan in the pale light of early morn. The sun, as yet, was only level with the tiled roof. The *Kyrie Eleisons* rang quiveringly through that sort of whitewashed stable with flat ceiling and bedaubed beams. On either side three lofty windows of plain glass, most of them cracked or smashed, let in a raw light of chalky crudeness.

The free air poured in as it listed, emphasising the naked poverty of the God of that forlorn village. At the far end of the church, above the big door which was never opened and the threshold of which was green with weeds, a boarded gallery—reached by a common miller's ladder—stretched from wall to wall. Dire were its creakings on festival days beneath the weight of wooden shoes. Near the ladder stood the confessional, with warped panels, painted a lemon yellow. Facing it, beside the little door, stood the font—a former holy- water stoup resting on a stonework pedestal. To the right and to the left, halfway down the church, two narrow altars stood against the wall, surrounded by wooden balustrades. On the left-hand one, dedicated to the Blessed Virgin, was a large gilded plaster statue of the Mother of God, wearing a regal gold crown upon her chestnut hair; while on her left arm sat the Divine Child, nude and smiling, whose little hand raised the star-spangled orb of the universe. The Virgin's feet were poised on clouds, and beneath them peeped the heads of winged cherubs. Then the right-hand altar, used for the masses for the dead, was surmounted by a crucifix of painted papier- mache—a pendant, as it were, to the Virgin's effigy. The figure of Christ, as large as a child of ten years old, showed Him in all the horror of His death- throes, with head thrown back, ribs projecting, abdomen hollowed in, and limbs distorted and splashed with blood. There was a pulpit, too—a square box reached by a five-step block—near a clock with running weights, in a walnut case, whose thuds shook the whole church like the beatings of some huge heart concealed, it might be, under the stone flags. All along the nave the fourteen Stations of the Cross, fourteen coarsely coloured prints in narrow black frames, bespeckled the staring whiteness of the walls with the yellow, blue, and scarlet of scenes from the Passion.

'*Deo Gratias,*' stuttered out Vincent at the end of the Epistle.

The mystery of love, the immolation of the Holy Victim, was about to begin. The server took the Missal and bore it to the left, or Gospel-side, of the altar, taking care not to touch the pages of the book. Each time he passed before the tabernacle he made a genuflexion slantwise, which threw him all askew. Returning to the right-hand side once more, he stood upright with crossed arms during the reading of the Gospel. The priest, after making the sign of the cross upon the Missal, next crossed himself: first upon his forehead—to declare that he would never blush for the divine word; then on his mouth—to show his unchanging readiness to confess his faith; and finally on his heart—to mark that it belonged to God alone.

'*Dominus vobiscum,*' said he, turning round and facing the cold white church.

'*Et cum spiritu tuo*,' answered Vincent, who once more was on his knees.

The Offertory having been recited, the priest uncovered the chalice. For a moment he held before his breast the paten containing the host, which he offered up to God, for himself, for those present, and for all the faithful, living and dead. Then, slipping it on to the edge of the corporal without touching it with his fingers, he took up the chalice and carefully wiped it with the purificator. Vincent had in the meanwhile fetched the cruets from the credence table, and now presented them in turn, first the wine and then the water. The priest then offered up on behalf of the whole world the half-filled chalice, which he next replaced upon the corporal and covered with the pall. Then once again he prayed, and returned to the side of the altar where the server let a little water dribble over his thumbs and forefingers to purify him from the slightest sinful stain. When he had dried his hands on the finger-cloth, La Teuse—who stood there waiting—emptied the cruet-salver into a zinc pail at the corner of the altar.

'*Orate, fratres*,' resumed the priest aloud as he faced the empty benches, extending and reclasping his hands in a gesture of appeal to all men of good-will. And turning again towards the altar, he continued his prayer in a lower tone, while Vincent began to mutter a long Latin sentence in which he eventually got lost. Now it was that the yellow sunbeams began to dart through the windows; called, as it were, by the priest, the sun itself had come to mass, throwing golden sheets of light upon the left-hand wall, the confessional, the Virgin's altar, and the big clock.

A gentle creak came from the confessional; the Mother of God, in a halo, in the dazzlement of her golden crown and mantle smiled tenderly with tinted lips upon the infant Jesus; and the heated clock throbbed out the time with quickening strokes. It seemed as if the sun peopled the benches with the dusty motes that danced in his beams, as if the little church, that whitened stable, were filled with a glowing throng. Without, were heard the sounds that told of the happy waking of the countryside, the blades of grass sighed out content, the damp leaves dried themselves in the warmth, the birds pruned their feathers and took a first flit round. And indeed the countryside itself seemed to enter with the sun; for beside one of the windows a large rowan tree shot up, thrusting some of its branches through the shattered panes and stretching out leafy buds as if to take a peep within; while through the fissures of the great door the weeds on the threshold threatened to encroach upon the nave. Amid all this quickening life, the big Christ, still in shadow, alone displayed signs of death, the sufferings of ochre-daubed and lake-bespattered flesh. A sparrow raised himself up for a moment at the edge of a hole, took a glance, then flew away; but only to reappear almost immediately when with noiseless wing he dropped between the benches before the Virgin's altar. A second sparrow followed; and soon from all the boughs of the rowan tree came others that calmly hopped about the flags.

'*Sanctus, Sanctus, Sanctus, Dominus Deus Sabaoth,*' said the priest in a low tone, whilst slightly stooping.

Vincent rang the little bell thrice; and the sparrows, scared by the sudden tinkling, flew off with such a mighty buzz of wings that La Teuse, who had just gone back into the sacristy, came out again, grumbling; 'The little rascals! they will mess everything. I'll bet that Mademoiselle Desiree has been here again to scatter bread-crumbs for them.'

The dread moment was at hand. The body and the blood of a God were about to descend upon the altar. The priest kissed the altar-cloth, clasped his hands, and multiplied signs of the cross over host and chalice. The prayers of the canon of the mass now fell from his lips in a very ecstasy of humility and gratitude. His attitude, his gestures, the inflections of his voice, all expressed his consciousness of his littleness, his emotion at being selected for so great a task. Vincent came and knelt beside him, lightly lifted the chasuble with his left hand, the bell ready in his right; and the priest, his elbows resting on the edge of the altar, holding the host with the thumbs and forefingers of both hands, pronounced over it the words of consecration: *Hoc est enim corpus meum.* Then having bowed the knee before it, he raised it slowly as high as his hands could reach, following it upwards with his eyes, while the kneeling server rang the bell thrice. Then he consecrated the wine—*Hic est enim calix* —leaning once more upon his elbows, bowing, raising the cup aloft, his right hand round the stem, his left holding its base, and his eyes following it aloft. Again the server rang the bell three times. The great mystery of the Redemption had once more been repeated, once more had the adorable Blood flowed forth.

'Just you wait a bit,' growled La Teuse, as she tried to scare away the sparrows with outstretched fist.

But the sparrows were now fearless. They had come back even while the bell was ringing, and, unabashed, were fluttering about the benches. The repeated tinklings even roused them into liveliness, and they answered back with little chirps which crossed amid the Latin words of prayer, like the rippling laughs of free urchins. The sun warmed their plumage, the sweet poverty of the church captivated them. They felt at home there, as in some barn whose shutters had been left open, and screeched, fought, and squabbled over the crumbs they found upon the floor. One flew to perch himself on the smiling Virgin's golden veil; another, whose daring put the old servant in a towering rage, made a hasty reconnaissance of La Teuse's skirts. And at the altar, the priest, with every faculty absorbed, his eyes fixed upon the sacred host, his thumbs and forefingers joined, did not even hear this invasion of the warm May morning, this rising flood of sunlight, greenery and birds, which overflowed even to the foot of the Calvary where doomed nature was wrestling in the death-throes.

'*Per omnia soecula soeculorum,*' he said.

'Amen,' answered Vincent.

The *Pater* ended, the priest, holding the host over the chalice, broke it in the centre. Detaching a particle from one of the halves, he dropped it into the precious blood, to symbolise the intimate union into which he was about to enter with God. He said the *Agnus Dei* aloud, softly recited the three prescribed prayers, and made his act of unworthiness, and then with his elbows resting on the altar, and with the paten beneath his chin, he partook of both portions of the host at once. After a fervent meditation, with his hands clasped before his face, he took the paten and gathered from the corporal the sacred particles of the host that had fallen, and dropped them into the chalice. One particle which had adhered to his thumb he removed with his forefinger. And, crossing himself, chalice in hand, with the paten once again below his chin, he drank all the precious blood in three draughts, never taking his lips from the cup's rim, but imbibing the divine Sacrifice to the last drop.

Vincent had risen to fetch the cruets from the credence table. But suddenly the door of the passage leading to the parsonage flew open and swung back against the wall, to admit a handsome child-like girl of twenty-two, who carried something hidden in her apron.

'Thirteen of them,' she called out. 'All the eggs were good.' And she opened out her apron and revealed a brood of little shivering chicks, with sprouting down and beady black eyes. 'Do just look,' said she; 'aren't they sweet little pets, the darlings! Oh, look at the little white one climbing on the others' backs! and the spotted one already flapping his tiny wings! The eggs were a splendid lot; not one of them unfertile.'

La Teuse, who was helping to serve the mass in spite of all prohibitions, and was at that very moment handing the cruets to Vincent for the ablutions, thereupon turned round and loudly exclaimed: 'Do be quiet, Mademoiselle Desiree! Don't you see we haven't finished yet?'

Through the open doorway now came the strong smell of a farmyard, blowing like some generative ferment into the church amidst the warm sunlight that was creeping over the altar. Desiree stood there for a moment delighted with the little ones she carried, watching Vincent pour, and her brother drink, the purifying wine, in order that nought of the sacred elements should be left within his mouth. And she stood there still when he came back to the side of the altar, holding the chalice in both hands, so that Vincent might pour over his forefingers and thumbs the wine and water of ablution, which he likewise drank. But when the mother hen ran up clucking with alarm to seek her little ones, and threatened to force her way into the church, Desiree went off, talking maternally to her chicks, while the priest, after pressing the purificator to his lips, wiped first the rim and next the interior of the chalice.

Then came the end, the act of thanksgiving to God. For the last time the server removed the Missal, and brought it back to the right-hand side. The priest replaced the purificator, paten, and pall upon the chalice; once more pinched the two large folds of the veil together, and laid upon it the burse containing the corporal. His whole being was now one act of ardent thanksgiving. He besought from Heaven the forgiveness of his sins, the grace of a holy life, and the reward of everlasting life. He remained as if overwhelmed by this miracle of love, the ever-recurring immolation, which sustained him day by day with the blood and flesh of his Savior.

Having read the final prayers, he turned and said: '*Ite, missa est.*'

'*Deo gratias,*' answered Vincent.

And having turned back to kiss the altar, the priest faced round anew, his left hand just below his breast, his right outstretched whilst blessing the church, which the gladsome sunbeams and noisy sparrows filled.

'*Benedicat vos omnipotens Deus, Pater et Filius, et Spiritus Sanctus.*'

'*Amen,*' said the server, as he crossed himself.

The sun had risen higher, and the sparrows were growing bolder. While the priest read from the left-hand altar-card the passage of the Gospel of St. John, announcing the eternity of the Word, the sunrays set the altar ablaze, whitened the panels of imitation marble, and dimmed the flame of the two candles, whose short wicks were now merely two dull spots. The victorious orb enveloped with his glory the crucifix, the candlesticks, the chasuble, the veil of the chalice—all the gold work that paled beneath his beams. And when at last the priest, after taking the chalice in his hands and making a genuflexion, covered his head and turned from the altar to follow the server, laden with the cruets and finger-cloth, to the sacristy, the planet remained sole master of the church. Its rays in turn now rested on the altar-cloth, irradiating the tabernacle-door with splendour, and celebrating the fertile powers of May. Warmth rose from the stone flags. The daubed walls, the tall Virgin, the huge Christ, too, all seemed to quiver as with shooting sap, as if death had been conquered by the earth's eternal youth.

III

Le Teuse hastily put out the candles, but lingered to make one last attempt to drive away the sparrows, and so when she returned to the sacristy with the Missal she no longer found Abbe Mouret there. Having washed his hands and put away the sacred vessels and vestments, he was now standing in the dining room, breakfasting off a cup of milk.

'You really ought to prevent your sister from scattering bread in the church,' said La Teuse on coming in. 'It was last winter she hit upon that pretty prank. She said the sparrows were cold, and that God might well give them some food. You see, she'll end by making us sleep with all her fowls and rabbits.'

'We should be all the warmer,' pleasantly replied the young priest. 'You are always grumbling, La Teuse. Do let our poor Desiree pet her animals. She has no other pleasure, poor innocent!'

The servant took her stand in the centre of the room.

'I do believe you yourself wouldn't mind a bit if the magpies actually built their nests in the church. You never can see anything, everything seems just what it ought to be to you. Your sister is precious lucky in having had you to take charge of her when you left the seminary. No father, no mother. I should like to know who would let her mess about as she does in a farmyard.'

Then softening, she added in a gentler tone: 'To be sure, it would be a pity to cross her. She hasn't a touch of malice in her. She's like a child of ten, although she's one of the finest grown girls in the neighbourhood. And I have to put her to bed, as you know, every night, and send her to sleep with stories, just like a little child.'

Abbe Mouret had remained standing, finishing the cup of milk he held between his fingers, which were slightly reddened by the chill atmosphere of the dining-room—a large room with painted grey walls, a floor of square tiles, and having no furniture beyond a table and a few chairs. La Teuse picked up a napkin which she had laid at a corner of the table in readiness for breakfast.

'It isn't much linen you dirty,' she muttered. 'One would think you could never sit down, that you are always just about to start off. Ah! if you had known Monsieur Caffin, the poor dead priest whose place you have taken! What a man he was for comfort! Why, he couldn't have digested his food, if he had eaten standing. A Norman he was, from Canteleu, like myself. I don't thank him, I tell you, for having brought me to such a wild-beast country as this. When first we came, O, Lord! how bored we were! But the poor priest had had some uncomfortable tales going about him at home…. Why, sir, didn't you sweeten your milk, then? Aren't those the two lumps of sugar?'

The priest put down his cup.

'Yes, I must have forgotten, I believe,' he said.

La Teuse stared at him and shrugged her shoulders. She folded up inside the napkin a slice of stale home-made bread which had also been left untouched on the table. Then just as the priest was about to go out, she ran after him and knelt down at his feet, exclaiming: 'Stop, your shoe-laces are not even fastened. I cannot imagine how your feet can stand those peasant shoes, you're such a little, tender man and look as if you had been preciously spoilt! Ah, the bishop must have known a deal about you, to go and give you the poorest living in the department.'

'But it was I who chose Les Artaud,' said the priest, breaking into another smile. 'You are very bad-tempered this morning, La Teuse. Are we not happy here? We have got all we want, and our life is as peaceful as if in paradise.'

She then restrained herself and laughed in her turn, saying: 'You are a holy man, Monsieur le Cure. But come and see what a splendid wash I have got. That will be better than squabbling with one another.'

The priest was obliged to follow, for she might prevent him going out at all if he did not compliment her on her washing. As he left the dining-room he stumbled over a heap of rubbish in the passage.

'What is this?' he asked.

Oh, nothing,' said La Teuse in her grimest tone. 'It's only the parsonage coming down. However, you are quite content, you've got all you want. Good heavens! there are holes and to spare. Just look at that ceiling, now. Isn't it cracked all over? If we don't get buried alive one of these days, we shall owe a precious big taper to our guardian angel. However, if it suits you—It's like the church. Those broken panes ought to have been replaced these two years. In winter our Lord gets frozen with the cold. Besides, it would keep out those rascally sparrows. I shall paste paper over the holes. You see if I don't.'

'A capital idea,' murmured the priest, 'they might very well be pasted over. As to the walls, they are stouter than we think. In my room, the floor has only given way slightly in front of the window. The house will see us all buried.'

On reaching the little open shed near the kitchen, in order to please La Teuse he went into ecstasies over the washing; he even had to dip his fingers into it and feel it. This so pleased the old woman that her attentions became quite motherly. She no longer scolded, but ran to fetch a clothes-brush, saying: 'You surely are not going out with yesterday's mud on your cassock! If you had left it out on the banister, it would be clean now—it's still a good one. But do lift it up well when you cross any field. The thistles tear everything.'

While speaking she kept turning him round like a child, shaking him from head to foot with her energetic brushing.

'There, there, that will do,' he said, escaping from her at last. 'Take care of Desiree, won't you? I will tell her I am going out.'

But at this minute a fresh clear voice called to him: 'Serge! Serge!'

Desiree came flying up, her cheeks ruddy with glee, her head bare, her black locks twisted tightly upon her neck, and her hands and arms smothered up to the elbows with manure. She had been cleaning out her poultry house. When she caught sight of her brother just about to go out with his breviary under his arm, she laughed aloud, and kissed him on his mouth, with her arms thrown back behind her to avoid soiling him.

'No, no,' she hurriedly exclaimed, 'I should dirty you. Oh! I am having such fun! You must see the animals when you come back.'

Thereupon she fled away again. Abbe Mouret then said that he would be back about eleven for luncheon, and as he started, La Teuse, who had followed him to the doorstep, shouted after him her last injunctions.

'Don't forget to see Brother Archangias. And look in also at the Brichets'; the wife came again yesterday about that wedding. Just listen, Monsieur le Cure! I met their Rosalie. She'd ask nothing better than to marry big Fortune. Have a talk with old Bambousse; perhaps he will listen to you now. And don't come back at twelve o'clock, like the other day. Come, say you'll be back at eleven, won't you?'

But the priest turned round no more. So she went in again, growling between her teeth:

'When does he ever listen to me? Barely twenty-six years old and does just as he likes. To be sure, he's an old man of sixty for holiness; but then he has never known life; he knows nothing, it's no trouble to him to be as good as a cherub!'

IV

When Abbe Mouret had got beyond all hearing of La Teuse he stopped, thankful to be alone at last. The church was built on a hillock, which sloped down gently to the village. With its large gaping windows and bright red tiles, it stretched out like a deserted sheep-cote. The priest turned round and glanced at the parsonage, a greyish building springing from the very side of the church; but as if fearful that he might again be overtaken by the interminable chatter that had been buzzing in his ears ever since morning, he turned up to the right again, and only felt safe when he at last stood before the great doorway, where he could not be seen from the parsonage. The front of the church, quite bare and worn by the sunshine and rain of years, was crowned by a narrow open stone belfry, in which a small bell showed its black silhouette, whilst its rope disappeared through the tiles. Six broken steps, on one side half buried in the earth, led up to the lofty arched door, now cracked, smothered with dust and rust and cobwebs, and so frailly hung upon its outwrenched hinges that it seemed as if the first slight puff would secure free entrance to the winds of heaven. Abbe Mouret, who had an affection for this dilapidated door, leaned against one of its leaves as he stood upon the steps. Thence he could survey the whole country round at a glance. And shading his eyes with his hands he scanned the horizon.

In the month of May exuberant vegetation burst forth from that stony soil. Gigantic lavenders, juniper bushes, patches of rank herbage swarmed over the church threshold, and scattered clumps of dark greenery even to the very tiles. It seemed as if the first throb of shooting sap in the tough matted underwood might well topple the church over. At that early hour, amid all the travail of nature's growth, there was a hum of vivifying warmth, and the very rocks quivered as with a long and silent effort. But the Abbe failed to comprehend the ardour of nature's painful labour; he simply thought that the steps were tottering, and thereupon leant against the other side of the door.

The countryside stretched away for a distance of six miles, bounded by a wall of tawny hills speckled with black pine-woods. It was a fearful landscape of arid wastes and rocky spurs rending the soil. The few patches of arable ground were like scattered pools of blood, red fields with rows of lean almond trees, grey-topped olive trees and long lines of vines, streaking the soil with their brown stems. It was as if some huge conflagration had swept by there, scattering the ashes of forests over the hill-tops, consuming all the grass of the meadow lands, and leaving its glare and furnace-like heat behind in the hollows. Only here and there was the softer note of a pale green patch of growing corn. The landscape generally was wild, lacking even a threadlet of water, dying of thirst, and flying away in clouds of dust at the least breath of wind. But at the farthest point where the crumbling hills on the horizon had left a breach one espied some distant fresh moist greenery, a stretch of the neighbouring valley fertilised by the Viorne, a river flowing down from the gorges of the Seille.

The priest lowered his dazzled glance upon the village, whose few scattered houses straggled away below the church—wretched hovels they were of rubble and boards strewn along a narrow path without sign of streets. There were about thirty of them altogether, some squatting amidst muck- heaps, and black with woeful want; others roomier and more cheerful-looking with their roofs of pinkish tiles. Strips of garden, victoriously planted amidst stony soil, displayed plots of vegetables enclosed by quickset hedges. At this hour Les Artaud was empty, not a woman was at the windows, not a child was wallowing in the dust; parties of fowls alone went to and fro, ferreting among the straw, seeking food up to the very thresholds of the houses, whose open doors gaped in the sunlight. A big black dog seated on his haunches at the entrance to the village seemed to be mounting guard over it.

Languor slowly stole over Abbe Mouret. The rising sun steeped him in such warmth that he leant back against the church door pervaded by a feeling of happy restfulness. His thoughts were dwelling on that hamlet of Les Artaud, which had sprung up there among the stones like one of the knotty growths of the valley. All its inhabitants were related, all bore the same name, so that from their very cradle they were distinguished among themselves by nicknames. An Artaud, their ancestor, had come hither and settled like a pariah in this waste. His family had grown with all the wild vitality of the herbage that sucked life from the rocky boulders. It had at last become a tribe, a rural community, in which cousin-ships were lost in the mists of centuries. They intermarried with shameless promiscuity. Not an instance could be cited of any Artaud taking himself a wife from any neighbouring village; only some of the girls occasionally went elsewhere. The others were born and died fixed to that spot, leisurely increasing and multiplying on their dunghills with the irreflectiveness of trees, and with no definite notion of the world that lay beyond the tawny rocks, in whose midst they vegetated. And yet there were already rich and poor among them; fowls having at times disappeared, the fowl-houses were now closed at night with stout padlocks; moreover one Artaud had killed another Artaud one evening behind the mill. These folk, begirt by that belt of desolate hills, were truly a people apart—a race sprung from the soil, a miniature replica of mankind, three hundred souls all told, beginning the centuries yet once again.

Over the priest the sombre shadows of seminary life still hovered. For years he had never seen the sun. He perceived it not even now, his eyes closed and gazing inwards on his soul, and with no feeling for perishable nature, fated to damnation, save contempt. For a long time in his hours of devout thought he had dreamt of some hermit's desert, of some mountain hole, where no living thing—neither being, plant, nor water—should distract him from the contemplation of God. It was an impulse springing from the purest love, from a loathing of all physical sensation. There, dying to self, and with his back turned to the light of day, he would have waited till he should cease to be, till nothing should remain of him but the sovereign whiteness of the soul. To him heaven seemed all white, with a luminous whiteness as if lilies there snowed down upon one, as if every form of purity, innocence, and chastity there blazed. But his confessor reproved him whenever he related his longings for solitude, his cravings for an existence of Godlike purity; and recalled him to the struggles of the Church, the necessary duties of the priesthood. Later on, after his ordination, the young priest had come to Les Artaud at his own request, there hoping to realise his dream of human annihilation. In that desolate spot, on that barren soil, he might shut his ears to all worldly sounds, and live the dreamy life of a saint. For some months past, in truth, his existence had been wholly undisturbed, rarely had any thrill of the village-life disturbed him; and even the sun's heat scarcely brought him any glow of feeling as he walked the paths, his whole being wrapped in heaven, heedless of the unceasing travail of life amidst which he moved.

The big black dog watching over Les Artaud had determined to come up to Abbe Mouret, and now sat upon its haunches at the priest's feet; but the unconscious man remained absorbed amidst the sweetness of the morning. On the previous evening he had begun the exercises of the Rosary, and to the intercession of the Virgin with her Divine Son he attributed the great joy which filled his soul. How despicable appeared all the good things of the earth! How thankfully he recognised his poverty! When he entered into holy orders, after losing on the same day both his father and his mother through a tragedy the fearful details of which were even now unknown to him,* he had relinquished all his share of their property to an elder brother. His only remaining link with the world was his sister; he had undertaken the care of her, stirred by a kind of religious affection for her feeble intelligence. The dear innocent was so childish, such a very little girl, that she recalled to him the poor in spirit to whom the Gospel promises the kingdom of heaven. Of late, however, she had somewhat disturbed him; she was growing too lusty, too full of health and life. But his discomfort was yet of the slightest. His days were spent in that inner life he had created for himself, for which he had relinquished all else. He closed the portals of his senses, and sought to free

28

himself from all bodily needs, so that he might be but a soul enrapt in contemplation. To him nature offered only snares and abominations; he gloried in maltreating her, in despising her, in releasing himself from his human slime. And as the just man must be a fool according to the world, he considered himself an exile on this earth; his thoughts were solely fixed upon the favours of Heaven, incapable as he was of understanding how an eternity of bliss could be weighed against a few hours of perishable enjoyment. His reason duped him and his senses lied; and if he advanced in virtue it was particularly by humility and obedience. His wish was to be the last of all, one subject to all, in order that the divine dew might fall upon his heart as upon arid sand; he considered himself overwhelmed with reproach and with confusion, unworthy of ever being saved from sin. He no longer belonged to himself—blind, deaf, dead to the world as he was. He was God's thing. And from the depth of the abjectness to which he sought to plunge, Hosannahs suddenly bore him aloft, above the happy and the mighty into the splendour of never-ending bliss.

* This forms the subject of M. Zola's novel, *The Conquest of Plassans*. ED.

Thus, at Les Artaud, Abbe Mouret had once more experienced, each time he read the 'Imitation,' the raptures of the cloistered life which he had longed for at one time so ardently. As yet he had not had to fight any battle. From the moment that he knelt down, he became perfect, absolutely oblivious of the flesh, unresisting, undisturbed, as if overpowered by the Divine grace. Such ecstasy at God's approach is well known to some young priests: it is a blissful moment when all is hushed, and the only desire is but a boundless craving for purity. From no human creature had he sought his consolations. He who believes a certain thing to be all in all cannot be troubled: and he did believe that God was all in all, and that humility, obedience, and chastity were everything. He could remember having heard temptation spoken of as an abominable torture that tries the holiest. But he would only smile: God had never left him. He bore his faith about him thus like a breast-plate protecting him from the slightest breath of evil. He could recall how he had hidden himself and wept for very love; he knew not whom he loved, but he wept for love, for love of some one afar off. The recollection never failed to move him. Later on he had decided on becoming a priest in order to satisfy that craving for a superhuman affection which was his sole torment. He could not see where greater love could be. In that state of life he satisfied his being, his inherited predisposition, his youthful dreams, his first virile desires. If temptation must come, he awaited it with the calmness of the seminarist ignorant of the world. He felt that his manhood had been killed in him: it gladdened him to feel himself a creature set apart, unsexed, turned from the usual paths of life, and, as became a lamb of the Lord, marked with the tonsure.

V

While the priest pondered the sun was heating the big church-door. Gilded flies buzzed round a large flower that was blooming between two of the church-door steps. Abbe Mouret, feeling slightly dazed, was at last about to move away, when the big black dog sprang, barking violently, towards the iron gate of the little graveyard on the left of the church. At the same time a harsh voice called out: 'Ah! you young rascal! So you stop away from school, and I find you in the graveyard! Oh, don't say no: I have been watching you this quarter of an hour.'

As the priest stepped forward he saw Vincent, whom a Brother of the Christian Schools was clutching tightly by the ear. The lad was suspended, as it were, over a ravine skirting the graveyard, at the bottom of which flowed the Mascle, a mountain torrent whose crystal waters plunged into the Viorne, six miles away.

'Brother Archangias!' softly called the priest, as if to appease the fearful man.

The Brother, however, did not release the boy's ear.

'Oh, it's you, Monsieur le Cure?' he growled. 'Just fancy, this rascal is always poking his nose into the graveyard. I don't know what he can be up to here. I ought to let go of him and let him smash his skull down there. It would be what he deserves.'

The lad remained dumb, with his cunning eyes tight shut as he clung to the bushes.

'Take care, Brother Archangias,' continued the priest, 'he might slip.'

And he himself helped Vincent to scramble up again.

'Come, my young friend, what were you doing there?' he asked. 'You must not go playing in graveyards.'

The lad had opened his eyes, and crept away, fearfully, from the Brother, to place himself under the priest's protection.

'I'll tell you,' he said in a low voice, as he raised his bushy head. 'There is a tomtit's nest in the brambles there, under that rock. For over ten days I've been watching it, and now the little ones are hatched, so I came this morning after serving your mass.'

'A tomtit's nest!' exclaimed Brother Archangias. 'Wait a bit! wait a bit!'

Thereupon he stepped aside, picked a clod of earth off a grave and flung it into the brambles. But he missed the nest. Another clod, however, more skilfully thrown upset the frail cradle, and precipitated the fledglings into the torrent below.

'Now, perhaps,' he continued, clapping his hands to shake off the earth that soiled them, 'you won't come roaming here any more, like a heathen; the dead will pull your feet at night if you go walking over them again.'

Vincent, who had laughed at seeing the nest dive into the stream, looked round him and shrugged his shoulders like one of strong mind.

'Oh, I'm not afraid,' he said. 'Dead folk don't stir.'

The graveyard, in truth, was not a place to inspire fear. It was a barren piece of ground whose narrow paths were smothered by rank weeds. Here and there the soil was bossy with mounds. A single tombstone, that of Abbe Caffin, brand-new and upright, could be perceived in the centre of the ground. Save this, all around there were only broken fragments of crosses, withered tufts of box, and old slabs split and moss-eaten. There were not two burials a year. Death seemed to make no dwelling in that waste spot, whither La Teuse came every evening to fill her apron with grass for Desiree's rabbits. A gigantic cypress tree, standing near the gate, alone cast shadow upon the desert field. This cypress, a landmark visible for nine miles around, was known to the whole countryside as the Solitaire.

'It's full of lizards,' added Vincent, looking at the cracks of the church- wall. 'One could have a fine lark—'

But he sprang out with a bound on seeing the Brother lift his foot. The latter proceeded to call the priest's attention to the dilapidated state of the gate, which was not only eaten up with rust, but had one hinge off, and the lock broken.

'It ought to be repaired,' said he.

Abbe Mouret smiled, but made no reply. Addressing Vincent, who was romping with the dog: 'I say, my boy,' he asked, 'do you know where old Bambousse is at work this morning?'

The lad glanced towards the horizon. 'He must be at his Olivettes field now,' he answered, pointing towards the left. 'But Voriau will show your reverence the way. He's sure to know where his master is.' And he clapped his hands and called: 'Hie! Voriau! hie!'

The big black dog paused a moment, wagging his tail, and seeking to read the urchin's eyes. Then, barking joyfully, he set off down the slope to the village. Abbe Mouret and Brother Archangias followed him, chatting. A hundred yards further Vincent surreptitiously bolted, and again glided up towards the church, keeping a watchful eye upon them, and ready to dart behind a bush if they should look round. With adder-like suppleness, he once more glided into the graveyard, that paradise full of lizards, nests, and flowers.

Meantime, while Voriau led the way before them along the dusty road, Brother Archangias was angrily saying to the priest: 'Let be! Monsieur le Cure, they're spawn of damnation, those toads are! They ought to have their backs broken, to make them pleasing to God. They grow up in irreligion, like their fathers. Fifteen years have I been here, and not one Christian have I been able to turn out. The minute they quit my hands, good-bye! They think of nothing but their land, their vines, their olive-trees. Not one ever sets foot in church. Brute beasts they are, struggling with their stony fields! Guide them with the stick, Monsieur le Cure, yes, the stick!'

Then, after drawing breath, he added with a terrific wave of his hands:

'Those Artauds, look you, are like the brambles over-running these rocks. One stem has been enough to poison the whole district. They cling on, they multiply, they live in spite of everything. Nothing short of fire from heaven, as at Gomorrha, will clear it all away.'

'We should never despair of sinners,' said Abbe Mouret, all inward peacefulness, as he leisurely walked on.

'But these are the devil's own,' broke in the Brother still more violently. 'I've been a peasant, too. Up to eighteen I dug the earth; and later on, when I was at the Training College, I had to sweep, pare vegetables, do all the heavy work. It's not their toilsome labour I find fault with. On the contrary, for God prefers the lowly. But the Artauds live like beasts! They are like their dogs, they never attend mass, and make a mock of the commandments of God and of the Church. They think of nothing but their plots of lands, so sweet they are on them!'

Voriau, his tail wagging, kept stopping and moving on again as soon as he saw that they still followed him.

'There certainly are some grievous things going on,' said Abbe Mouret. 'My predecessor, Abbe Caffin—'

'A poor specimen,' interrupted the Brother. 'He came here to us from Normandy owing to some disreputable affair. Once here, his sole thought was good living; he let everything go to rack and ruin.'

'Oh, no, Abbe Caffin certainly did what he could; but I must own that his efforts were all but barren in results. My own are mostly fruitless.'

Brother Archangias shrugged his shoulders. He walked on for a minute in silence, swaying his tall bony frame, which looked as if it had been roughly fashioned with a hatchet. The sun beat down upon his neck, shadowing his hard, sword-edged peasant's face.

'Listen to me, Monsieur le Cure,' he said at last. 'I am too much beneath you to lecture you; but still, I am almost double your age, I know this part, and therefore I feel justified in telling you that you will gain nothing by gentleness. The catechism, understand, is enough. God has no mercy on the wicked. He burns them. Stick to that.'

Then, as Abbe Mouret, whose head remained bowed, did not open his mouth, he went on: 'Religion is leaving the country districts because it is made over indulgent. It was respected when it spoke out like an unforgiving mistress. I really don't know what they can teach you now in the seminaries. The new priests weep like children with their parishioners. God no longer seems the same. I dare say, Monsieur le Cure, that you don't even know your catechism by heart now?'

But the priest, wounded by the imperiousness with which the Brother so roughly sought to dominate him, looked up and dryly rejoined:

'That will do, your zeal is very praiseworthy. But haven't you something to tell me? You came to the parsonage this morning, did you not?'

Thereupon Brother Archangias plumply answered: 'I had to tell you just what I have told you. The Artauds live like pigs. Only yesterday I learned that Rosalie, old Bambousse's eldest daughter, is in the family way. It happens with all of them before they get married. And they simply laugh at reproaches, as you know.'

'Yes,' murmured Abbe Mouret, 'it is a great scandal. I am just on my way to see old Bambousse to speak to him about it; it is desirable that they should be married as soon as possible. The child's father, it seems, is Fortune, the Brichets' eldest son. Unfortunately the Brichets are poor.'

'That Rosalie, now,' continued the Brother, 'is just eighteen. Not four years since I still had her under me at school, and she was already a gadabout. I have now got her sister Catherine, a chit of eleven, who seems likely to become even worse than her elder. One comes across her in every corner with that little scamp, Vincent. It's no good, you may pull their ears till they bleed, the woman always crops up in them. They carry perdition about with them and are only fit to be thrown on a muck-heap. What a splendid riddance if all girls were strangled at their birth!'

His loathing, his hatred of woman made him swear like a carter. Abbe Mouret, who had been listening to him with unmoved countenance, smiled at last at his rabid utterances. He called Voriau, who had strayed into a field close by.

'There, look there!' cried Brother Archangias, pointing to a group of children playing at the bottom of a ravine, 'there are my young devils, who play the truant under pretence of going to help their parents among the vines! You may be certain that jade of a Catherine is among them.... There, didn't I tell you! Till to-night, Monsieur le Cure. Oh, just you wait, you rascals!'

Off he went at a run, his dirty neckband flying over his shoulder, and his big greasy cassock tearing up the thistles. Abbe Mouret watched him swoop down into the midst of the children, who scattered like frightened sparrows. But he succeeded in seizing Catherine and one boy by the ears and led them back towards the village, clutching them tightly with his big hairy fingers, and overwhelming them with abuse.

The priest walked on again. Brother Archangias sometimes aroused strange scruples in his mind. With his vulgarity and coarseness the Brother seemed to him the true man of God, free from earthly ties, submissive in all to Heaven's will, humble, blunt, ready to shower abuse upon sin. He, the priest, would then feel despair at his inability to rid himself more completely of his body; he regretted that he was not ugly, unclean, covered with vermin like some of the saints. Whenever the Brother had wounded him by some words of excessive coarseness, or by some over-hasty churlishness, he would blame himself for his refinement, his innate shrinking, as if these were really faults. Ought he not to be dead to all the weaknesses of this world? And this time also he smiled sadly as he thought how near he had been to losing his temper at the Brother's roughly put lesson. It was pride, it seemed to him, seeking to work his perdition by making him despise the lowly. However, in spite of himself, he felt relieved at being alone again, at being able to walk on gently, reading his breviary, free at last from the grating voice that had disturbed his dream of heavenly love.

VI

The road wound on between fallen rocks, among which the peasants had succeeded here and there in reclaiming six or seven yards of chalky soil, planted with old olive trees. Under the priest's feet the dust in the deep ruts crackled lightly like snow. At times, as he felt a warmer puff upon his face, he would raise his eyes from his book, as if to seek whence came this soft caress; but his gaze was vacant, straying without perception over the glowing horizon, over the twisted outlines of that passion-breathing landscape as it stretched out in the sun before him, dry, barren, despairing of the fertilisation for which it longed. And he would lower his hat over his forehead to protect himself against the warm breeze and tranquilly resume his reading, his cassock raising behind him a cloudlet of dust which rolled along the surface of the road.

'Good morning, Monsieur le Cure,' a passing peasant said to him.

Sounds of digging alongside the cultivated strips of ground again roused him from his abstraction. He turned his head and perceived big knotty-limbed old men greeting him from among the vines. The Artauds were eagerly satisfying their passion for the soil, in the sun's full blaze. Sweating brows appeared from behind the bushes, heaving chests were slowly raised, the whole scene was one of ardent fructification, through which he moved with the calm step born of ignorance. No discomfort came to him from the great travail of love that permeated that splendid morning.

'Steady! Voriau, you mustn't eat people!' some one gaily shouted in a powerful voice by way of silencing the dog's loud barks.

Abbe Mouret looked up.

'Oh! it's you. Fortune?' he said, approaching the edge of the field in which the young peasant was at work. 'I was just on my way to speak to you.'

Fortune was of the same age as the priest: a bigly built, bold-looking young fellow, with skin already hardened. He was clearing a small plot of stony heath.

'What about, Monsieur le Cure?' he asked.

'About Rosalie and you,' replied the priest.

Fortune began to laugh. Perhaps he thought it droll that a priest should interest himself in such a matter.

'Well,' he muttered, 'I'm not to blame in it nor she either. So much the worse if old Bambousse refuses to let me have her. You saw yourself how his dog was trying to bite me just now; he sets him on me.'

Then, as Abbe Mouret was about to continue, old Artaud, called Brichet, whom he had not previously perceived, emerged from the shadow of a bush behind which he and his wife were eating. He was a little man, withered by age, with a cringing face.

'Your reverence must have been told a pack of lies,' he exclaimed. 'The youngster is quite ready to marry Rosalie. What's happened isn't anybody's fault. It has happened to others who got on all right just the same. The matter doesn't rest with us. You ought to speak to Bambousse. He's the one who looks down on us because he's got money.'

'Yes, we are very poor,' whined his wife, a tall lachrymose woman, who also rose to her feet. 'We've only this scrap of ground where the very devil seems to have been hailing stones. Not a bite of bread from it, even. Without you, your reverence, life would be impossible.'

Brichet's wife was the one solitary devotee of the village. Whenever she had been to communion, she would hang about the parsonage, well knowing that La Teuse always kept a couple of loaves for her from her last baking. At times she was even able to carry off a rabbit or a fowl given her by Desiree.

'There's no end to the scandals,' continued the priest. 'The marriage must take place without delay.'

'Oh! at once! as soon as the others are agreeable,' said the old woman, alarmed about her periodical presents. 'What do you say, Brichet? we are not such bad Christians as to go against his reverence?'

Fortune sniggered.

'Oh, I'm quite ready,' he said, 'and so is Rosalie. I saw her yesterday at the back of the mill. We haven't quarrelled. We stopped there to have a bit of a laugh.'

But Abbe Mouret interrupted him: 'Very well, I am now going to speak to Bambousse. He is over there, at Les Olivettes, I believe.'

The priest was going off when the mother asked him what had become of her younger son Vincent, who had left in the early morning to serve mass. There was a lad now who badly needed his reverence's admonitions. And she walked by the priest's side for another hundred yards, bemoaning her poverty, the failure of the potato crop, the frost which had nipped the olive trees, the hot weather which threatened to scorch up the scanty corn. Then, as she left him, she solemnly declared that her son Fortune always said his prayers, both morning and evening.

Voriau now ran on in front, and suddenly, at a turn in the road, he bolted across the fields. The priest then struck into a small path leading up a low hill. He was now at Les Olivettes, the most fertile spot in the neighbourhood, where the mayor of the commune, Artaud, otherwise Bambousse, owned several fields of corn, olive plantations, and vines. The dog was now romping round the skirts of a tall brunette, who burst into a loud laugh as she caught sight of the priest.

'Is your father here, Rosalie?' the latter asked.

'Yes, just across there,' she said, pointing with her hand and still smiling.

Leaving the part of the field she had been weeding, she walked on before him with the vigorous springiness of a hard-working woman, her head unshielded from the sun, her neck all sunburnt, her hair black and coarse like a horse's mane. Her green-stained hands exhaled the odour of the weeds she had been pulling up.

'Father,' she called out, 'here's Monsieur le Cure asking for you.'

And there she remained, bold, unblushing, with a sly smile still hovering over her features. Bambousse, a stout, sweating, round-faced man, left his work and gaily came towards the priest.

'I'd take my oath you are going to speak to me about the repairs of the church,' he exclaimed, as he clapped his earthy hands. 'Well, then, Monsieur le Cure, I can only say no, it's impossible. The commune hasn't got the coin. If the Lord provides plaster and tiles, we'll provide the workmen.'

At this jest of his the unbelieving peasant burst into a loud guffaw, slapped his thighs, coughed, and almost choked himself.

'It was not for the church I came,' replied the Abbe Mouret. 'I wanted to speak to you about your daughter Rosalie.'

'Rosalie? What has she done to you, then?' inquired Bambousse, his eyes blinking.

The girl was boldly staring at the young priest, scrutinising his white hands and slender, feminine neck, as if trying to make him redden. He, however, bluntly and with unruffled countenance, as if speaking of something quite indifferent, continued:

'You know what I mean, Bambousse. She must get married.'

'Oh, that's it, is it?' muttered the old man, with a bantering look. 'Many thanks for the message. The Brichets sent you, didn't they? Mother Brichet goes to mass, and so you give her a helping hand to marry her son—it's all very fine. But, I've got nothing to do with that. It doesn't suit me. That's all.'

Thereupon the astonished priest represented to him that the scandal must be stopped, and that he ought to forgive Fortune, as the latter was willing to make reparation for his transgression, and that, lastly, his daughter's reputation demanded a speedy marriage.

'Ta, ta, ta,' replied Bambousse, what a lot of words! I shall keep my daughter, please understand it. All that's got nothing to do with me. That Fortune is a beggarly pauper, without a brass farthing. What an easy job, if one could marry a girl like that! At that rate we should have all the young things marrying off morning and night. Thank Heaven! I'm not worried about Rosalie: everybody knows what has happened; but it makes no difference. She can marry any one she chooses in the neighbourhood.'

'But the child?' interrupted the priest.

'The child indeed! There'll be time enough to think of that when it's born.'

Rosalie, perceiving the turn the priest's application was taking, now thought it proper to ram her fists into her eyes and whimper. And she even let herself fall upon the ground.

'Shut up, will you, you hussy!' howled her father in a rage. And he proceeded to revile her in the coarsest terms, which made her laugh silently behind her clenched fists.

'You won't shut up? won't you? Just wait a minute then, you jade!' continued old Bambousse. And thereupon he picked up a clod of earth and flung it at her. It burst upon her knot of hair, crumbling down her neck and smothering her in dust. Dizzy from the blow, she bounded to her feet and fled, sheltering her head between her hands. But Bambousse had time to fling two more clods at her, and if the first only grazed her left shoulder, the next caught her full on the base of the spine, with such force that she fell upon her knees.

'Bambousse!' cried the priest, as he wrenched from the peasant's hand a number of stones which he had just picked up.

'Let be, Monsieur le Cure,' said the other. 'It was only soft earth. I ought to have thrown these stones at her. It's easy to see that you don't know girls. Hard as nails, all of them. I might duck that one in the well, I might break all her bones with a cudgel, and she'd still be just the same. But I've got my eye on her, and if I catch her!... Ah! well, they are all like that.'

He was already comforted. He took a good pull at a big flat bottle of wine, encased in wicker-work, which lay warming on the hot ground. And breaking once more into a laugh, he said: 'If I only had a glass, Monsieur le Cure, I would offer you some with pleasure.'

'So then,' again asked the priest, 'this marriage?'

'No, it can't be; I should get laughed at. Rosalie is a stout wench. She's worth a man to me. I shall have to hire a lad the day she goes off.... We can have another talk about it after the vintage. Besides, I don't want to be robbed. Give and take, say I. That's fair. What do you think?'

Nevertheless for another long half-hour did the priest remain there preaching to Bambousse, speaking to him of God, and plying him with all the reasons suited to the circumstances. But the old man had resumed his work; he shrugged his shoulders, jested, and grew more and more obstinate. At last, he broke out: 'But if you asked me for a sack of corn, you would give me money, wouldn't you? So why do you want me to let my daughter go for nothing?'

Much discomfited, Abbe Mouret left him. As he went down the path he saw Rosalie rolling about under an olive tree with Voriau, who was licking her face. With her arms whirling, she kept on repeating: 'You tickle me, you big stupid. Leave off!'

When she perceived the priest, she made an attempt at a blush, settled her clothes, and once more raised her fists to her eyes. He, on his part, sought to console her by promising to attempt some fresh efforts with her father, adding that, in the meantime, she should do nothing to aggravate her sin. And then, as she impudently smiled at him, he pictured hell, where wicked women burn in torment. And afterwards he left her, his duty done, his soul once more full of the serenity which enabled him to pass undisturbed athwart the corruptions of the world.

VII

The morning was becoming terribly hot. In that huge rocky amphitheatre the sun kindled a furnace-like glare from the moment when the first fine weather began. By the planet's height in the sky Abbe Mouret now perceived that he had only just time to return home if he wished to get there by eleven o'clock and escape a scolding from La Teuse. Having finished reading his breviary and made his application to Bambousse, he swiftly retraced his steps, gazing as he went at his church, now a grey spot in the distance, and at the black rigid silhouette which the big cypress-tree, the Solitaire, set against the blue sky. Amidst the drowsiness fostered by the heat, he thought of how richly that evening he might decorate the Lady chapel for the devotions of the month of Mary. Before him the road offered a carpet of dust, soft to the tread and of dazzling whiteness.

At the Croix-Verte, as the Abbe was about to cross the highway leading from Plassans to La Palud, a gig coming down the hill compelled him to step behind a heap of stones. Then, as he crossed the open space, a voice called to him: 'Hallo, Serge, my boy!'

The gig had pulled up and from it a man leant over. The priest recognised him—he was an uncle of his, Doctor Pascal Rougon, or Monsieur Pascal, as the poor folk of Plassans, whom he attended for nothing, briefly styled him. Although barely over fifty, he was already snowy white, with a big beard and abundant hair, amidst which his handsome regular features took an expression of shrewdness and benevolence.*

* See M. Zola's novels, *Dr. Pascal* and *The Fortune of the Rougons*.— ED.

'So you potter about in the dust at this hour of the day?' he said gaily, as he stooped to grasp the Abbe's hands. 'You're not afraid of sunstroke?'

'No more than you are, uncle,' answered the priest, laughing.

'Oh, I have the hood of my trap to shield me. Besides, sick folks won't wait. People die at all times, my boy.' And he went on to relate that he was now on his way to old Jeanbernat, the steward of the Paradou, who had had an apoplectic stroke the night before. A neighbour, a peasant on his way to Plassans market, had summoned him.

'He must be dead by this time,' the doctor continued. 'However, we must make sure…. Those old demons are jolly tough, you know.'

He was already raising his whip, when Abbe Mouret stopped him.

'Stay! what o'clock do you make it, uncle?'

'A quarter to eleven.'

The Abbe hesitated; he already seemed to hear La Teuse's terrible voice bawling in his ears that his luncheon was getting cold. But he plucked up courage and added swiftly: 'I'll go with you, uncle. The unhappy man may wish to reconcile himself to God in his last hour.'

Doctor Pascal could not restrain a laugh.

'What, Jeanbernat!' he said; 'ah, well! if ever you convert him! Never mind, come all the same. The sight of you is enough to cure him.'

The priest got in. The doctor, apparently regretting his jest, displayed an affectionate warmth of manner, whilst from time to time clucking his tongue by way of encouraging his horse. And out of the corner of his eye he inquisitively observed his nephew with the keenness of a scientist bent on taking notes. In short kindly sentences he inquired about his life, his habits, and the peaceful happiness he enjoyed at Les Artaud. And at each satisfactory reply he murmured, as if to himself in a tone of reassurance: 'Come, so much the better; that's just as it should be!'

He displayed peculiar anxiety about the young priest's state of health. And Serge, greatly surprised, assured him that he was in splendid trim, and had neither fits of giddiness or of nausea, nor headaches whatsoever.

'Capital, capital,' reiterated his uncle Pascal. 'In spring, you see, the blood is active. But you are sound enough. By-the-bye, I saw your brother Octave at Marseilles last month. He is off to Paris, where he will get a fine berth in a high-class business. The young beggar, a nice life he leads.'

'What life?' innocently inquired the priest.

To avoid replying the doctor chirruped to his horse, and then went on: 'Briefly, everybody is well—your aunt Felicite, your uncle Rougon, and the others. Still, that does not hinder our needing your prayers. You are the saint of the family, my lad; I rely upon you to save the whole lot.'

He laughed, but in such a friendly, good-humoured way that Serge himself began to indulge in jocularity.

'You see,' continued Pascal, 'there are some among the lot whom it won't be easy to lead to Paradise. Some nice confessions you'd hear if all came in turn. For my part, I can do without their confessions; I watch them from a distance; I have got their records at home among my botanical specimens and medical notes. Some day I shall be able to draw up a wondrously interesting diagram. We shall see; we shall see!'

He was forgetting himself, carried away by his enthusiasm for science. A glance at his nephew's cassock pulled him up short.

'As for you, you're a parson,' he muttered; 'you did well; a parson's a very happy man. The calling absorbs you, eh? And so you've taken to the good path. Well! you would never have been satisfied otherwise. Your relatives, starting like you, have done a deal of evil, and still they are unsatisfied. It's all logically perfect, my lad. A priest completes the family. Besides, it was inevitable. Our blood was bound to run to that. So much the better for you; you have had the most luck.' Correcting himself, however, with a strange smile, he added: 'No, it's your sister Desiree who has had the best luck of all.'

He whistled, whipped up his horse, and changed the conversation. The gig, after climbing a somewhat steep slope, was threading its way through desolate ravines; at last it reached a tableland, where the hollow road skirted an interminable and lofty wall. Les Artaud had disappeared; they found themselves in the heart of a desert.

'We are getting near, are we not?' asked the priest.

'This is the Paradou,' replied the doctor, pointing to the wall. 'Haven't you been this way before, then? We are not three miles from Les Artaud. A splendid property it must have been, this Paradou. The park wall this side alone is quite a mile and a half long. But for over a hundred years it's all been running wild.'

'There are some fine trees,' observed the Abbe, as he looked up in astonishment at the luxuriant mass of foliage which jutted over.

'Yes, that part is very fertile. In fact, the park is a regular forest amidst the bare rocks which surround it. The Mascle, too, rises there; I have heard four or five springs mentioned, I fancy.'

In short sentences, interspersed with irrelevant digressions, he then related the story of the Paradou, according to the current legend of the countryside. In the time of Louis XV., a great lord had erected a magnificent palace there, with vast gardens, fountains, trickling streams, and statues—a miniature Versailles hidden away among the stones, under the full blaze of the southern sun. But he had there spent but one season with a lady of bewitching beauty, who doubtless died there, as none had ever seen her leave. Next year the mansion was destroyed by fire, the park doors were nailed up, the very loopholes of the walls were filled with mould; and thus, since that remote time, not a glance had penetrated that vast enclosure which covered the whole of one of the plateaux of the Garrigue hills.

'There can be no lack of nettles there,' laughingly said Abbe Mouret.

'Don't you find that the whole wall reeks of damp, uncle?'

A pause followed, and he asked:

'And whom does the Paradou belong to now?'

'Why, nobody knows,' the doctor answered. 'The owner did come here once, some twenty years ago. But he was so scared by the sight of this adders' nest that he has never turned up since. The real master is the caretaker, that old oddity, Jeanbernat, who has managed to find quarters in a lodge where the stones still hang together. There it is, see—that grey building yonder, with its windows all smothered in ivy.'

The gig passed by a lordly iron gate, ruddy with rust, and lined inside with a layer of boards. The wide dry throats were black with brambles. A hundred yards further on was the lodge inhabited by Jeanbernat. It stood within the park, which it overlooked. But the old keeper had apparently blocked up that side of his dwelling, and had cleared a little garden by the road. And there he lived, facing southwards, with his back turned upon the Paradou, as if unaware of the immensity of verdure that stretched away behind him.

The young priest jumped down, looking inquisitively around him and questioning the doctor, who was hurriedly fastening the horse to a ring fixed in the wall.

'And the old man lives all alone in this out-of-the-way hole?' he asked.

'Yes, quite alone,' replied his uncle, adding, however, the next minute: 'Well, he has with him a niece whom he had to take in, a queer girl, a regular savage. But we must make haste. The whole place looks death-like.'

VIII

The house with its shutters closed seemed wrapped in slumber as it stood there in the midday sun, amidst the hum of the big flies that swarmed all up the ivy to the roof tiles. The sunlit ruin was steeped in happy quietude. When the doctor had opened the gate of the narrow garden, which was enclosed by a lofty quickset hedge, there, in the shadow cast by a wall, they found Jeanbernat, tall and erect, and calmly smoking his pipe, as in the deep silence he watched his vegetables grow.

'What, are you up then, you humbug?' exclaimed the astonished doctor.

'So you were coming to bury me, were you?' growled the old man harshly. 'I don't want anybody. I bled myself.'

He stopped short as he caught sight of the priest, and assumed so threatening an expression that the doctor hastened to intervene.

'This is my nephew,' he said; 'the new Cure of Les Artaud—a good fellow, too. Devil take it, we haven't been bowling over the roads at this hour of the day to eat you, Jeanbernat.'

The old man calmed down a little.

'I don't want any shavelings here,' he grumbled. 'They're enough to make one croak. Mind, doctor, no priests, and no physics when I go off, or we shall quarrel. Let him come in, however, as he is your nephew.'

Abbe Mouret, struck dumb with amazement, could not speak a word. He stood there in the middle of the path scanning that strange solitaire, with scorched, brick-tinted face, and limbs all withered and twisted like a bundle of ropes, who seemed to bear the burden of his eighty years with a scornful contempt for life. When the doctor attempted to feel his pulse, his ill-humour broke out afresh.

'Do leave me in peace! I bled myself with my knife, I tell you. It's all over, now. Who was the fool of a peasant who disturbed you? The doctor here, and the priest as well, why not the mutes too! Well, it can't be helped, people will be fools. It won't prevent us from having a drink, eh?'

He fetched a bottle and three glasses, and stood them on an old table which he brought out into the shade. Then, having filled the glasses to the brim, he insisted on clinking them. His anger had given place to jeering cheerfulness.

'It won't poison you, Monsieur le Cure,' he said. 'A glass of good wine isn't a sin. Upon my word, however, this is the first time I ever clinked a glass

46

with a cassock, but no offence to you. That poor Abbe Caffin, your predecessor, refused to argue with me. He was afraid.'

Jeanbernat gave vent to a hearty laugh, and then went on: 'Just fancy, he had pledged himself that he would prove to me that God exists. So, whenever I met him, I defied him to do it; and he sloped off crestfallen, I can tell you.'

'What, God does not exist!' cried Abbe Mouret, roused from his silence.

'Oh! just as you please,' mockingly replied Jeanbernat. 'We'll begin together all over again, if it's any pleasure to you. But I warn you that I'm a tough hand at it. There are some thousands of books in one of the rooms upstairs, which were rescued from the fire at the Paradou: all the philosophers of the eighteenth century, a whole heap of old books on religion. I've learned some fine things from them. I've been reading them these twenty years. Marry! you'll find you've got some one who can talk, Monsieur le Cure.'

He had risen, slowly waving his hand towards the surrounding horizon, to the earth and to the sky, and repeating solemnly: 'There's nothing, nothing, nothing. When the sun is snuffed out, all will be at an end.'

Doctor Pascal nudged Abbe Mouret with his elbow. With blinking eyes he was curiously observing the old man and nodding approvingly in order to induce him to talk. 'So you are a materialist, Jeanbernat?' he said.

'Oh, I am only a poor man,' replied the old fellow, relighting his pipe. 'When Count de Corbiere, whose foster-brother I was, died from a fall from his horse, his children sent me here to look after this park of the Sleeping Beauty, in order to get rid of me. I was sixty years old then, and I thought I was about done. But death forgot me; and I had to make myself a burrow. If one lives all alone, look you, one gets to see things in rather a queer fashion. The trees are no longer trees, the earth puts on the ways of a living being, the stones seem to tell you tales. A parcel of rubbish, eh? But I know some secrets that would fairly stagger you. Besides, what do you think there is to do in this devilish desert? I read the old books; it was more amusing than shooting. The Count, who used to curse like a heathen, was always saying to me: "Jeanbernat, my boy, I fully expect to meet you again in the hot place, so that you will be able to serve me there as you have up here."'

Once more he waved his hand to the horizon and added: 'You hear, nothing; there's nothing. It's all foolery.'

Dr. Pascal began to laugh.

'A pleasant piece of foolery, at any rate,' he said. 'Jeanbernat, you are a deceiver. I suspect you are in love, in spite of your affectation of being *blase*. You were speaking very tenderly of the trees and stones just now.'

'Oh, no, I assure you,' murmured the old man, 'I have done with that. At one time, it's true, when I first knew you and used to go herborising with you, I was stupid enough to love all sorts of things I came across in that huge liar, the country. Fortunately, the old volumes have killed all that. I only wish my garden was smaller; I don't go out into the road twice a year. You see that bench? That's where I spend all my time, just watching my lettuces grow.'

'And what about your rounds in the park?' broke in the doctor.

'In the park!' repeated Jeanbernat, with a look of profound surprise. 'Why, it's more than twelve years since I set foot in it! What do you suppose I could do inside that cemetery? It's too big. It's stupid, what with those endless trees and moss everywhere and broken statues, and holes in which one might break one's neck at every step. The last time I went in there, it was so dark under the trees, there was such a stink of wild flowers, and such queer breezes blew along the paths, that I felt almost afraid. So I have shut myself up to prevent the park coming in here. A patch of sunlight, three feet of lettuce before me, and a big hedge shutting out all the view, why, that's more than enough for happiness. Nothing, that's what I'd like, nothing at all, something so tiny that nothing from outside could come to disturb me. Seven feet of earth, if you like, just to be able to croak on my back.'

He struck the table with his fist, and suddenly raised his voice to call out to Abbe Mouret: 'Come, just another glass, your reverence. The old gentleman isn't at the bottom of the bottle, you know.'

The priest felt ill at ease. To lead back to God that singular old man, whose reason seemed to him to be strangely disordered, appeared a task beyond his powers. He now remembered certain bits of gossip he had heard from La Teuse about the Philosopher, as the peasants of Les Artaud dubbed Jeanbernat. Scraps of scandalous stories vaguely floated in his memory. He rose, making a sign to the doctor that he wished to leave this house, where he seemed to inhale an odour of damnation. But, in spite of his covert fears, a strange feeling of curiosity made him linger. He simply walked to the end of the garden, throwing a searching glance into the vestibule, as if to see beyond it, behind the walls. All he could perceive, however, through the gaping doorway, was the black staircase. So he came back again, and sought for some hole, some glimpse of that sea of foliage which he knew was near by the mighty murmur that broke upon the house, like the sound of waves.

'And is the little one well?' asked the doctor, taking up his hat.

'Pretty well,' answered Jeanbernat. 'She's never here. She often disappears all day long—still, she may be in the upstair rooms.'

He raised his head and called: 'Albine! Albine!' Then with a shrug of his shoulders, he added: 'Yes, my word, she is a nice hussy…. Well, till next time, Monsieur le Cure. I'm always at your disposal.'

Abbe Mouret, however, had no time to accept the Philosopher's challenge. A door suddenly opened at the end of the vestibule; a dazzling breach was made in the black darkness of the wall, and through the breach came a vision of a virgin forest, a great depth of woodland, beneath a flood of sunbeams. In that sudden blaze of light the priest distinctly perceived certain far-away things: a large yellow flower in the middle of a lawn, a sheet of water falling from a lofty rock, a colossal tree filled with a swarm of birds; and all this steeped, lost, blazing in such a tangle of greenery, such riotous luxuriance of vegetation, that the whole horizon seemed one great burst of shooting foliage. The door banged to, and everything vanished.

'Ah! the jade!' cried Jeanbernat, 'she was in the Paradou again!'

Albine was now laughing on the threshold of the vestibule. She wore an orange-coloured skirt, with a large red kerchief fastened round her waist, thus looking like some gipsy in holiday garb. And she went on laughing, her head thrown back, her bosom swelling with mirth, delighted with her flowers, wild flowers which she had plaited into her fair hair, fastened to her neck, her bodice, and her bare slender golden arms. She seemed like a huge nosegay, exhaling a powerful perfume.

'Ay, you are a beauty!' growled the old man. 'You smell of weeds enough to poison one—would any one think she was sixteen, that doll?'

Albine remained unabashed, however, and laughed still more heartily. Doctor Pascal, who was her great friend, let her kiss him.

'So you are not frightened in the Paradou?' he asked.

'Frightened? What of?' she said, her eyes wide open with astonishment. 'The walls are too high, no one can get in. There's only myself. It is my garden, all my very own. A fine big one, too. I haven't found out where it ends yet.'

'And the animals?' interrupted the doctor.

'The animals? Oh! they don't hurt; they all know me well.'

'But it is very dark under the trees?'

'Course! there's shade: if there were none, the sun would burn my face up. It is very pleasant in the shade among the leaves.'

She flitted about, filling the little garden with the rustling sweep of her skirts, and scattering round the pungent odour of wild flowers which clung to her. She had smiled at Abbe Mouret without trace of shyness, without heed of the astonished look with which he observed her. The priest had stepped aside. That fair-haired maid, with long oval face, glowing with life, seemed to him to be the weird mysterious offspring of the forest of which he had caught a glimpse in a sheet of sunlight.

'I say, I have got some blackbird nestlings; would you like them?' Albine asked the doctor.

'No, thanks,' he answered, laughing. 'You should give them to the Cure's sister; she is very fond of pets. Good day, Jeanbernat.'

Albine, however, had fastened on the priest.

'You are the vicar of Les Artaud, aren't you? You have a sister? I'll go and see her. Only you must not speak to me about God. My uncle will not have it.'

'You bother us, be off,' exclaimed Jeanbernat, shrugging his shoulders. Then bounding away like a goat, dropping a shower of flowers behind her, she disappeared. The slam of a door was heard, and from behind the house came bursts of laughter, which died away in the distance like the scampering rush of some mad animal let loose among the grass.

'You'll see, she will end by sleeping in the Paradou,' muttered the old man with indifference.

And as he saw his visitors off, he added: 'If you should find me dead one of these fine days, doctor, just do me the favour of pitching me into the muck-pit there, behind my lettuces. Good evening, gentlemen.'

He let the wooden gate which closed the hedge fall to again, and the house assumed once more its aspect of happy peacefulness in the noonday sunlight, amidst the buzzing of the big flies that swarmed all up the ivy even to the roof tiles.

IX

The gig once more rolled along the road skirting the Paradou's interminable wall. Abbe Mouret, still silent, scanned with upturned eyes the huge boughs which stretched over that wall, like the arms of giants hidden there. All sorts of sounds came from the park: rustling of wings, quivering of leaves, furtive bounds at which branches snapped, mighty sighs that bowed the young shoots —a vast breath of life sweeping over the crests of a nation of trees. At times, as he heard a birdlike note that seemed like a human laugh, the priest turned his head, as if he felt uneasy.

'A queer girl!' said his uncle as he eased the reins a little. 'She was nine years old when she took up her quarters with that old heathen. Some brother of his had ruined himself, though in what I can't remember. The little one was at school somewhere when her father killed himself. She was even quite a little lady, up to reading, embroidery, chattering, and strumming on the piano. And such a coquette too! I saw her arrive with open-worked stockings, embroidered skirts, frills, cuffs, a heap of finery. Ah, well! the finery didn't last long!'

He laughed. A big stone nearly upset the gig.

'It will be lucky if I don't leave a wheel in this cursed road!' he muttered. 'Hold on, my boy.'

The wall still stretched beside them: the priest still listened.

'As you may well imagine,' continued the doctor, 'the Paradou, what with its sun, its stones, and its thistles, would wreck a whole outfit every day. Three or four mouthfuls, that's all it made of all the little one's beautiful dresses. She used to come back naked. Now she dresses like a savage. To-day she was rather presentable; but sometimes she has scarcely anything on beyond her shoes and chemise. Did you hear her? The Paradou is hers. The very day after she came she took possession of it. She lives in it; jumps out of the window when Jeanbernat locks the door, bolts off in spite of all, goes nobody knows whither, buries herself in some invisible burrows known only to herself. She must have a fine time in that wilderness.'

'Hark, uncle!' interrupted Abbe Mouret. 'Isn't that some animal running behind the wall?'

Uncle Pascal listened.

'No,' he said after a minute's silence, 'it is the rattle of the trap on the stones. No, the child doesn't play the piano now. I believe she has even forgotten how to read. Just picture to yourself a young lady gone back to a state of primevalness, turned out to play on a desert island. My word, if ever you get to know of a girl who needs proper bringing up, I advise you not to entrust her to Jeanbernat. He has a most primitive way of letting nature alone. When I ventured to speak to him about Albine he answered me that he must not prevent trees from growing as they pleased. He says he is for the normal development of temperaments.... All the same, they are very interesting, both of them. I never come this way without paying them a visit.'

The gig was now emerging from the hollowed road. At this point the wall of the Paradou turned and wound along the crest of the hills as far as one could see. As Abbe Mouret turned to take a last look at that grey-hued barrier, whose impenetrable austerity had at last begun to annoy him, a rustling of shaken boughs was heard and a clump of young birch trees seemed to bow in greeting from above the wall.

'I knew some animal was running behind,' said the priest.

But, although nobody could be seen, though nothing was visible in the air above save the birches rocking more and more violently, they heard a clear, laughing voice call out: 'Good-bye, doctor! good-bye, Monsieur le Cure! I am kissing the tree, and the tree is sending you my kisses.'

'Why! it is Albine,' exclaimed Doctor Pascal. 'She must have followed the trap at a run. Jumping over bushes is mere play to her, the little elf!'

And he in his turn shouted out:

'Good-bye, my pet! How tall you must be to bow like that.'

The laughter grew louder, the birches bowed still lower, scattering their leaves around even on the hood of the gig.

'I am as tall as the trees; all the leaves that fall are kisses,' replied the voice now mellowed by distance, so musical, so merged into the rippling whispers of the park, that the young priest was thrilled.

The road grew better. On coming down the slope Les Artaud reappeared in the midst of the scorched plain. When the gig reached the turning to the village, Abbe Mouret would not let his uncle drive him back to the vicarage. He jumped down, saying:

'No, thanks, I prefer to walk: it will do me good.'

'Well, just as you like,' at last answered the doctor. And with a clasp of the hand, he added: 'Well, if you only had such parishioners as that old brute Jeanbernat, you wouldn't often be disturbed. However, you yourself wanted to come. And mind you keep well. At the slightest ache, night or day, send for me. You know I attend all the family gratis…. There, good-bye, my boy.'

X

Abbe Mouret felt more at ease when he found himself again alone, walking along the dusty road. The stony fields brought him back to his dream of austerity, of an inner life spent in a desert. From the trees all along the sunken road disturbing moisture had fallen on his neck, which now the burning sun was drying. The sight of the lean almond trees, the scanty corn crops, the weak vines, on either side of the way, soothed him, delivered him from the perturbation into which the lusty atmosphere of the Paradou had thrown him. Amid the blinding glare that flowed from heaven over the bare land, Jeanbernat's blasphemies no longer cast even a shadow. A thrill of pleasure ran through the priest as he raised his head and caught sight of the solitaire's motionless bar-like silhouette and the pink patch of tiles on the church.

But, as he walked on, fresh anxiety beset the Abbe. La Teuse would give him a fine reception; for his luncheon must have been waiting nearly two hours for him. He pictured her terrible face, the flood of words with which she would greet him, the angry clatter of kitchen ware which he would hear the whole afternoon. When he had got through Les Artaud, his fear became so lively that he hesitated, full of trepidation, and wondered if it would not be better to go round and reach the parsonage by way of the church. But, while he deliberated, La Teuse herself appeared on the doorstep of the parsonage, her cap all awry, and her hands on her hips. With drooping head he had perforce to climb the slope under her storm-laden gaze, which he could feel weighing upon his shoulders.

'I believe I am rather late, my good Teuse,' he stammered, as he turned the path's last bend.

La Teuse waited till he stood quite close before her. She then gave him a furious glance, and, without a word, turned and stalked before him into the dining-room, banging her big heels upon the floor-tiles and so rigid with ire that she hardly limped at all.

'I have had so many things to do,' began the priest, scared by this dumb reception. 'I have been running about all the morning.'

But she cut him short with another look, so fixed, so full of anger, that he felt his legs give way under him. He sat down, and began to eat. She waited on him in the sharp, mechanical manner of an automaton, all but breaking the plates with the violence with which she set them down. The silence became so awful that, choking with emotion, he was unable to swallow his third mouthful.

'My sister has had her luncheon?' he asked. 'Quite right of her. Luncheon should always be served whenever I am kept out.'

No answer came. La Teuse stood there waiting to remove his plate as soon as he should have emptied it. Thereupon, feeling that he could not possibly eat with those implacable eyes crushing him, he pushed his plate away. This angry gesture acted on La Teuse like a whip stroke, rousing her from her obstinate stiffness. She fairly jumped.

'Ah! that's how it is!' she exclaimed. 'There you are again, losing your temper! Very well, I am off; you can pay my fare, so that I may go back home. I have had enough of Les Artaud, and your church, and everything else!'

She took off her apron with trembling hands.

'You must have seen that I didn't wish to say anything to you. A nice life, indeed! Only mountebanks do such things, Monsieur le Cure! This is eleven o'clock, ain't it! Aren't you ashamed of sitting at table when it's almost two o'clock? It's not like a Christian, no, it is not like a Christian!'

And, taking her stand before him, she went on: 'Well, where do you come from? whom have you seen? what business can have kept you? If only you were a child you would have the whip. It isn't the place for a priest to be, on the roads in the blazing sun like a tramp without a roof to put over his head. A fine state you are in, with your shoes all white and your cassock smothered in dust! Who will brush your cassock for you? Who will buy you another one? Speak out, will you; tell me what you have been doing! My word! if everybody didn't know you, they would end by thinking queer things about you. And shall I tell you? Why, I won't say but what you may have been up to something wrong. When folks lunch at such hours they are capable of anything!'

Abbe Mouret let the storm blow over him. At the old servant's wrathful words he experienced a kind of relief.

'Come, my good Teuse,' he said, 'you will first put your apron on again.'

'No, no,' she cried, 'it's all over, I am going.'

But he got up and, laughing, tied her apron round her waist. She struggled against him and stuttered: 'I tell you no! You are a wheedler. I can see through your game, I see you want to come it over me with your honeyed words. Where did you go? We'll see afterwards.'

He gaily sat down to table again like a man who has gained a victory.

'First, I must be allowed to eat. I am dying with hunger,' said he.

'No doubt,' she murmured, her pity moved. 'Is there any common sense in it? Would you like me to fry you a couple of eggs? It would not take long. Well, if you have enough. But everything is cold! And I had taken such pains with your aubergines! Nice they are now! They look like old shoe-leather. Luckily you haven't got a tender tooth like poor Monsieur Caffin. Yes, you have some good points, I don't deny it.'

Thus chattering, she waited on him with all a mother's care. After he had finished she ran to the kitchen to see if the coffee was still warm. She frisked about and limped most outrageously in her delight at having made things up with him. As a rule Abbe Mouret fought shy of coffee, which always upset his nervous system; but on this occasion, to ratify the conclusion of peace, he took the cup she brought him. And as he lingered at table she sat down opposite him and repeated gently, like a woman tortured by curiosity:

'Where have you been, Monsieur le Cure?'

'Well,' he answered with a smile, 'I have seen the Brichets, I have spoken to Bambousse.'

Thereupon he had to relate to her what the Brichets had said, what Bambousse had decided, and how they looked, and where they were at work. When he repeated to her the answer of Rosalie's father, 'Of course!' she exclaimed, 'if the child should die her mishap would go for nothing.' And clasping her hands with a look of envious admiration she added, 'How you must have chattered, your reverence! More than half the day spent to obtain such a fine result! You took it easy coming home? It must have been very hot on the road?'

The Abbe, who by this time had risen, made no answer. He had been on the point of speaking about the Paradou, and asking for some information concerning it. But a fear of being flooded with eager questions, and a kind of vague unavowed shame, made him keep silence respecting his visit to Jeanbernat. He cut all further questions short by asking:

'Where is my sister? I don't hear her.'

'Come along, sir,' said La Teuse, beginning to laugh, and raising her finger to her lips.

They went into the next room, a country drawing-room, hung with faded wall-paper showing large grey flowers, and furnished with four armchairs and a sofa, covered with horse-hair. On the sofa now slept Desiree, stretched out at full length, with her head resting on her clenched hands. The pronounced curve of her bosom was raised somewhat by her upstretched arms, bare to the elbows. She was breathing somewhat heavily, her red lips parted, and thus showing her teeth.

'Lord! isn't she sleeping sound!' whispered La Teuse. 'She didn't even hear you pitching into me just now. Well, she must be precious tired. Just fancy, she was cleaning up her yard till nearly noon. And when she had eaten something, she came and dropped down there like a shot. She has not stirred since.'

For a moment the priest gazed lovingly at her. 'We must let her have as much rest as she wants,' he said.

'Of course. Isn't it a pity she's such an innocent? Just look at those big arms! Whenever I dress her I always think what a fine woman she would have made. Ay, she would have brought you some splendid nephews, sir. Don't you think she is like that stone lady in Plassans corn-market?'

She spoke thus of a Cybele stretched upon sheaves of wheat, the work of one of Puget's pupils, which was carved on the frontal of the market building. Without replying, however, Abbe Mouret gently pushed her out of the room, and begged her to make as little noise as possible. Till evening, therefore, perfect silence settled on the parsonage. La Teuse finished her washing in the shed. The priest, seated at the bottom of the little garden, his breviary fallen on his lap, remained absorbed in pious thoughts, while all around him rosy petals rained from the blossoming peach-trees.

XI

About six o'clock there came a sudden wakening. A noise of doors opening and closing, accompanied by bursts of laughter, shook the whole house. Desiree appeared, her hair all down and her arms still half bare.

'Serge! Serge!' she called.

And catching sight of her brother in the garden, she ran up to him and sat down for a minute on the ground at his feet, begging him to follow her:

'Do come and see the animals! You haven't seen the animals yet, have you? If you only knew how beautiful they are now!'

She had to beg very hard, for the yard rather scared him. But when he saw tears in Desiree's eyes, he yielded. She threw herself on his neck in a sudden puppy-like burst of glee, laughing more than ever, without attempting to dry her cheeks.

'Oh! how nice you are!' she stammered, as she dragged him off. 'You shall see the hens, the rabbits, the pigeons, and my ducks which have got fresh water, and my goat, whose room is as clean as mine now. I have three geese and two turkeys, you know. Come quick. You shall see all.'

Desiree was then twenty-two years old. Reared in the country by her nurse, a peasant woman of Saint-Eutrope, she had grown up anyhow. Her brain void of all serious thoughts, she had thriven on the fat soil and open air of the country, developing physically but never mentally, growing into a lovely animal—white, with rosy blood and firm skin. She was not unlike a high-bred donkey endowed with the power of laughter. Although she dabbled about from morning till night, her delicate hands and feet, the supple outlines of her hips, the bourgeois refinement of her maiden form remained unimpaired; so that she was in truth a creature apart—neither lady nor peasant—but a girl nourished by the soil, with the broad shoulders and narrow brow of a youthful goddess.

Doubtless it was by reason of her weak intellect that she was drawn towards animals. She was never happy save with them; she understood their language far better than that of mankind, and looked after them with motherly affection. Her reasoning powers were deficient, but in lieu thereof she had an instinct which put her on a footing of intelligence with them. At their very first cry of pain she knew what ailed them; she would choose dainties upon which they would pounce greedily. A single gesture from her quelled their squabbles. She seemed to know their good or their evil character at a glance;

and related such long tales about the tiniest chick, with such an abundance and minuteness of detail, as to astound those to whom one chicken was exactly like any other. Her farmyard had thus become a country, as it were, over which she reigned; a country complex in its organisation, disturbed by rebellions, peopled by the most diverse creatures whose records were known to her alone. So accurate was her instinct that she detected the unfertile eggs in a sitting, and foretold the number of a litter of rabbits.

When, at sixteen, Desiree became a young woman, she retained all her wonted health; and rapidly developed, with round, free-swaying bust, broad hips like those of an antique statue, the full growth indeed of a vigorous animal. One might have thought that she had sprung from the rich soil of her poultry-yard, that she absorbed the sap with her sturdy legs, which were as firm as young trees. And nought disturbed her amidst all this plenitude. She found continuous satisfaction in being surrounded by birds and animals which ever increased and multiplied, their fruitfulness filling her with delight. Nothing could have been healthier. She innocently feasted on the odour and warmth of life, knowing no depraved curiosity, but retaining all the tranquillity of a beautiful animal, simply happy at seeing her little world thus multiply, feeling as if she thereby became a mother, the common natural mother of one and all.

Since she had been living at Les Artaud, she had spent her days in complete beatitude. At last she was satisfying the dream of her life, the only desire which had worried her amidst her weak-minded puerility. She had a poultry- yard, a nook all to herself, where she could breed animals to her heart's content. And she almost lived there, building rabbit-hutches with her own hands, digging out a pond for the ducks, knocking in nails, fetching straw, allowing no one to assist her. All that La Teuse had to do was to wash her afterwards. The poultry-yard was situated behind the cemetery; and Desiree often had to jump the wall, and run hither and thither among the graves after some fowl whom curiosity had led astray. Right at the end was a shed giving accommodation to the fowls and the rabbits; to the right was a little stable for the goat. Moreover, all the animals lived together; the rabbits ran about with the fowls, the nanny-goat would take a footbath in the midst of the ducks; the geese, the turkeys, the guinea-fowls, and the pigeons all fraternised in the company of three cats. Whenever Desiree appeared at the wooden fence which prevented her charges from making their way into the church, a deafening uproar greeted her.

'Eh! can't you hear them?' she said to her brother, as they reached the dining-room door.

But, when she had admitted him and closed the gate behind them, she was assailed so violently that she almost disappeared. The ducks and the geese, opening and shutting their beaks, tugged at her skirts; the greedy hens sprang up and pecked her hands; the rabbits squatted on her feet and then bounded up to her knees; whilst the three cats leapt upon her shoulders, and the goat bleated in its stable at being unable to reach her.

'Leave me alone, do! all you creatures!' she cried with a hearty sonorous laugh, feeling tickled by all the feathers, claws, and beaks and paws rubbing against her.

However, she did not attempt to free herself. As she often said, she would have let herself be devoured; it seemed so sweet to feel all this life cling to her and encompass her with the warmth of eider-down. At last only one cat persisted in remaining on her back.

'It's Moumou,' she said. 'His paws are like velvet.' Then, calling her brother's attention to the yard, she proudly added: 'See, how clean it is!'

The yard had indeed been swept out, washed, and raked over. But the disturbed water and the forked-up litter exhaled so fetid and powerful an odour that Abbe Mouret half choked. The dung was heaped against the graveyard wall in a huge smoking mound.

'What a pile, eh?' continued Desiree, leading her brother into the pungent vapour, 'I put it all there myself, nobody helped me. Go on, it isn't dirty. It cleans. Look at my arms.'

As she spoke she held out her arms, which she had merely dipped into a pail of water—regal arms they were, superbly rounded, blooming like full white roses amidst the manure.

'Yes, yes,' gently said the priest, 'you have worked hard. It's very nice now.'

Then he turned towards the wicket, but she stopped him.

'Do wait a bit. You shall see them all. You have no idea—' And so saying, she dragged him to the rabbit house under the shed.

'There are young ones in all the hutches,' she said, clapping her hands in glee.

Then at great length she proceeded to explain to him all about the litters. He had to crouch down and come close to the wire netting, whilst she gave him minute details. The mother does, with big restless ears, eyed him askance, panting and motionless with fear. Then, in one hutch, he saw a hairy cavity wherein crawled a living heap, an indistinct dusky mass heaving like a single body. Close by some young ones, with enormous heads, ventured to the edge of the hole. A little farther were yet stronger ones, who looked like young rats, ferreting and leaping about with their raised rumps showing their white scuts. Others, white ones with pale ruby eyes, and black ones with jet eyes, galloped round their hutches with playful grace. Now a scare would make them bolt off swiftly, revealing at every leap their slender reddened paws. Next they would squat down all in a heap, so closely packed that their heads could no longer be seen.

'It is you they are frightened at,' Desiree kept on saying. 'They know me well.'

She called them and drew some bread-crust from her pocket. The little rabbits then became more confident, and, with puckered noses, kept sidling up, and rearing against the netting one by one. She kept them like that for a minute to show her brother the rosy down upon their bellies, and then gave her crust to the boldest one. Upon this the whole of them flocked up, sliding forward and squeezing one another, but never quarreling. At one moment three little ones were all nibbling the same piece of crust, but others darted away, turning to the wall so as to eat in peace, while their mothers in the rear remained snuffing distrustfully and refused the crusts.

'Oh! the greedy little things!' exclaimed Desiree. 'They would eat like that till to-morrow morning! At night, even, you can bear them crunching the leaves they have overlooked in the day-time.'

The priest had risen as if to depart, but she never wearied of smiling on her dear little ones.

'You see the big one there, that's all white, with black ears—Well! he dotes on poppies. He is very clever at picking them out from the other weeds. The other day he got the colic. So I took him and kept him warm in my pocket. Since then he has been quite frisky.'

She poked her fingers through the wire netting and stroked the rabbits' backs.

'Wouldn't you say it was satin?' she continued. 'They are dressed like princes. And ain't they coquettish! Look, there's one who is always cleaning himself. He wears the fur off his paws.... If only you knew how funny they are! I say nothing, but I see all their little games. That grey one looking at us, for instance, used to hate a little doe, which I had to put somewhere else. There were terrible scenes between them. It would take too long to tell you all, but the last time he gave her a drubbing, when I came up in a rage, what do you think I saw? Why that rascal huddled up at the back there as if he was just at his last gasp. He wanted to make me believe that it was he who had to complain of her.'

Then Desiree paused to apostrophise the rabbit. 'Yes, you may listen to me; you're a rogue!' And turning towards her brother, 'He understands all I say,' she added softly, with a wink.

But Abbe Mouret could stand it no longer. He was perturbed by the heat that emanated from the litters, the life that crawled under the hair plucked from the does' bellies, exhaling powerful emanations. On the other hand, Desiree, as if slowly intoxicated, was growing brighter and pinker.

'But there's nothing to take you away!' she cried; 'you always seem anxious to go off. You must see my little chicks! They were born last night.'

She took some rice and threw a handful before her. The hen gravely drew near, clucking to the little band of chickens that followed her chirping and scampering as if in bewilderment. When they were fairly in the middle of the scattered rice the hen eagerly pecked at it, and threw down the grains she cracked, while her little ones hastily began to feed. All the charm of infancy was theirs. Half-naked as it were, with round heads, eyes sparkling like steel needles, beaks so queerly set, and down so quaintly ruffled up, they looked like penny toys. Desiree laughed with enjoyment at sight of them.

'What little loves they are!' she stammered.

She took up two of them, one in each hand, and smothered them with eager kisses. And then the priest had to inspect them all over, while she coolly said to him:

'It isn't easy to tell the cocks. But I never make a mistake. This one is a hen, and this one is a hen too.'

Then she set them on the ground again. Other hens were now coming up to eat the rice. A large ruddy cock with flaming plumage followed them, lifting his large feet with majestic caution.

'Alexander is getting splendid,' said the Abbe, to please his sister.

Alexander was the cock's name. He looked up at the young girl with his fiery eye, his head turned round, his tail outspread, and then installed himself close by her skirts.

'He is very fond of me,' she said. 'Only I can touch him. He is a good bird. There are fourteen hens, and never do I find a bad egg in the nests. Do I, Alexander?'

She stooped; the bird did not fly from her caress. A rush of blood seemed to set his comb aflame; flapping his wings, and stretching out his neck, he burst into a long crow which rang out like a blast from a brazen throat. Four times did he repeat his crow while all the cocks of Les Artaud answered in the distance. Desiree was greatly amused by her brother's startled looks.

'He deafens one, eh?' she said. 'He has a splendid voice. But he's not vicious, I assure you, though the hens are—You remember the big speckled one, that used to lay yellow eggs? Well, the day before yesterday she hurt her foot. When the others saw the blood they went quite mad. They all followed her, pecking at her and drinking her blood, so that by the evening they had eaten up her foot. I found her with her head behind a stone, like an idiot, saying nothing, and letting herself be devoured.'

The remembrance of the fowls' voracity made her laugh. She calmly related other cruelties of theirs: young chickens devoured, of which she had only found the necks and wings, and a litter of kittens eaten up in the stable in a few hours.

'You might give them a human being,' she continued, 'they'd finish him. And aren't they tough livers! They get on with a broken limb even. They may have wounds, big holes in their bodies, and still they'll gobble their victuals. That's what I like them for; their flesh grows again in two days; they are always as warm as if they had a store of sunshine under their feathers. When I want to give them a treat, I cut them up some raw meat. And worms too! Wait, you'll see how they love them.'

She ran to the dungheap, and unhesitatingly picked up a worm she found there. The fowls darted at her hands; but to amuse herself with the sight of their greediness she held the worm high above them. At last she opened her fingers, and forthwith the fowls hustled one another and pounced upon the worm. One of them fled with it in her beak, pursued by the others; it was thus taken, snatched away, and retaken many times until one hen, with a mighty gulp, swallowed it altogether. At that they all stopped short with heads thrown back, and eyes on the alert for another worm. Desiree called them by their names, and talked pettingly to them; while Abbe Mouret retreated a few steps from this display of voracious life.

'No, I am not at all comfortable,' he said to his sister, when she tried to make him feel the weight of a fowl she was fattening. 'It always makes me uneasy to touch live animals.'

He tried to smile, but Desiree taxed him with cowardice.

'Ah well, what about my ducks, and geese, and turkeys?' said she. 'What would you do if you had all those to look after? Ducks are dirty, if you like. Do you hear them shaking their bills in the water? And when they dive, you can only see their tails sticking straight up like ninepins. Geese and turkeys, too, are not easy to manage. Isn't it fun to see them walking along with their long necks, some quite white and others quite black? They look like ladies and gentlemen. And I wouldn't advise you to trust your finger to them. They would swallow it at a gulp. But my fingers, they only kiss—see!'

Her words were cut short by a joyous bleat from the goat, which had at last forced the door of the stable open. Two bounds and the animal was close to her, bending its forelegs, and affectionately rubbing its horns against her. To the priest, with its pointed beard and obliquely set eyes, it seemed to wear a diabolical grin. But Desiree caught it round the neck, kissed its head, played and ran with it, and talked about how she liked to drink its milk. She often did so, she said, when she was thirsty in the stable.

'See, it has plenty of milk,' she added, pointing to the animal's udder.

The priest lowered his eyes. He could remember having once seen in the cloister of Saint-Saturnin at Plassans a horrible stone gargoyle, representing a goat and a monk; and ever since he had always looked on goats as dissolute creatures of hell. His sister had only been allowed to get one after weeks of begging. For his part, whenever he came to the yard, he shunned all contact with the animal's long silky coat, and carefully guarded his cassock from the touch of its horns.

'All right, I'll let you go now,' said Desiree, becoming aware of his growing discomfort. 'But you must just let me show you something else first. Promise not to scold me, won't you? I have not said anything to you about it, because you wouldn't have allowed it…. But if you only knew how pleased I am!'

As she spoke she put on an entreating expression, clasped her hands, and laid her head upon her brother's shoulder.

'Another piece of folly, no doubt,' he murmured, unable to refrain from smiling.

'You won't mind, will you?' she continued, her eyes glistening with delight. 'You won't be angry?—He is so pretty!'

Thereupon she ran to open the low door under the shed, and forthwith a little pig bounded into the middle of the yard.

'Oh! isn't he a cherub?' she exclaimed with a look of profound rapture as she saw him leap out.

The little pig was indeed charming, quite pink, his snout washed clean by the greasy slops placed before him, though incessant routing in his trough had left a ring of dirt about his eyes. He trotted about, hustled the fowls, rushing to gobble up whatever was thrown them, and upsetting the little yard with his sudden turns and twists. His ears flapped over his eyes, his snout went snorting over the ground, and with his slender feet he resembled a toy animal on wheels. From behind, his tail looked like a bit of string that served to hang him up by.

'I won't have this beast here!' exclaimed the priest, terribly put out.

'Oh, Serge, dear old Serge,' begged Desiree again, 'don't be so unkind. See, what a harmless little thing he is! I'll wash him, I'll keep him very clean. La Teuse went and had him given her for me. We can't send him back now. See, he is looking at you; he wants to smell you. Don't be afraid, he won't eat you.'

But she broke off, seized with irresistible laughter. The little pig had blundered in a dazed fashion between the goat's legs, and tripped her up. And he was now madly careering round, squeaking, rolling, scaring all the denizens of the poultry-yard. To quiet him Desiree had to get him an earthen pan full of dish-water. In this he wallowed up to his ears, splashing and grunting, while quick quivers of delight coursed over his rosy skin. And now his uncurled tail hung limply down.

The stirring of this foul water put a crowning touch to Abbe Mouret's disgust. Ever since he had been there, he had choked more and more; his hands and chest and face were afire, and he felt quite giddy. The odour of the fowls and rabbits, the goat, and the pig, all mingled in one pestilential stench. The atmosphere, laden with the ferments of life, was too heavy for his maiden shoulders. And it seemed to him that Desiree had grown taller, expanding at the hips, waving huge arms, sweeping the ground with her skirts, and stirring up all that powerful odour which overpowered him. He had only just time to open the wicket. His feet clung to the stone flags still dank with manure, in such wise that it seemed as if he were held there by some clasp of the soil. And suddenly, despite himself, there came back to him a memory of the Paradou, with its huge trees, its black shadows, its penetrating perfumes.

'There, you are quite red now,' Desiree said to him as she joined him outside the wicket. 'Aren't you pleased to have seen everything? Do you hear the noise they are making?'

On seeing her depart, the birds and animals had thrown themselves against the trellis work emitting piteous cries. The little pig, especially, gave vent to prolonged whines that suggested the sharpening of a saw. Desiree, however, curtsied to them and kissed her finger-tips to them, laughing at seeing them all huddled together there, like so many lovers of hers. Then, hugging her brother, as she accompanied him to the garden, she whispered into his ear with a blush: 'I should so like a cow.'

He looked at her, with a ready gesture of disapproval.

'No, no, not now,' she hurriedly went on. 'We'll talk about it again later on —— But there would be room in the stable. A lovely white cow with red spots. You'd soon see what nice milk we should have. A goat becomes too little in the end. And when the cow has a calf!'

At the mere thought of this she skipped and clapped her hands with glee; and to the priest she seemed to have brought the poultry-yard away with her in her skirts. So he left her at the end of the garden, sitting in the sunlight on the ground before a hive, whence the bees buzzed like golden berries round her neck, along her bare arms and in her hair, without thought of stinging her.

XII

Brother Archangias dined at the parsonage every Thursday. As a rule he came early so as to talk over parish matters. It was he who, for the last three months, had kept the Abbe informed of all the affairs of the valley. That Thursday, while waiting till La Teuse should call them, they strolled about in front of the church. The priest, on relating his interview with Bambousse, was surprised to find that the Brother thought the peasant's reply quite natural.

'The man's right,' said the Ignorantin.* 'You don't give away chattels like that. Rosalie is no great bargain, but it's always hard to see your own daughter throw herself away on a pauper.'

* A popular name in France for a Christian Brother.—ED.

'Still,' rejoined Abbe Mouret, 'a marriage is the only way of stopping the scandal.'

The Brother shrugged his big shoulders and laughed aggravatingly. 'Do you think you'll cure the neighbourhood with that marriage?' he exclaimed. 'Before another two years Catherine will be following her sister's example. They all go the same way, and as they end by marrying, they snap their fingers at every one. These Artauds flourish in it all, as on a congenial dungheap. There is only one possible remedy, as I have told you before: wring all the girls' necks if you don't want the country to be poisoned. No husbands, Monsieur le Cure, but a good thick stick!'

Then calming down a bit, he added: 'Let every one do with their own as they think best.'

He went on to speak about fixing the hours for the catechism classes; but Abbe Mouret replied in an absent-minded way, his eyes dwelling on the village at his feet in the setting sun. The peasants were wending their way homewards, silently and slowly, with the dragging steps of wearied oxen returning to their sheds. Before the tumble-down houses stood women calling to one another, carrying on bawling conversations from door to door, while bands of children filled the roadway with the riot of their big clumsy shoes, grovelling and rolling and pushing each other about. A bestial odour ascended from that heap of tottering houses, and the priest once more fancied himself in Desiree's poultry-yard, where life ever increased and multiplied. Here, too, was the same incessant travail, which so disturbed him. Since morning his mind had been running on that episode of Rosalie and Fortune, and now his thoughts returned to it, to the foul features of existence, the incessant, fated task of Nature, which sowed men broadcast like grains of wheat. The Artauds were a herd penned in between four ranges of hills, increasing, multiplying, spreading more and more thickly over the land with each successive generation.

'See,' cried Brother Archangias, interrupting his discourse to point to a tall girl who was letting her sweetheart snatch a kiss, 'there is another hussy over there!'

He shook his long black arms at the couple and made them flee. In the distance, over the crimson fields and the peeling rocks, the sun was dying in one last flare. Night gradually came on. The warm fragrance of the lavender became cooler on the wings of the light evening breeze which now arose. From time to time a deep sigh fell on the ear as if that fearful land, consumed by ardent passions, had at length grown calm under the soft grey rain of twilight. Abbe Mouret, hat in hand, delighted with the coolness, once more felt quietude descend upon him.

'Monsieur le Cure! Brother Archangias!' cried La Teuse. 'Come quick! The soup is on the table.'

It was cabbage soup, and its odoriferous steam filled the parsonage dining-room. The Brother seated himself and fell to, slowly emptying the huge plate that La Teuse had put down before him. He was a big eater, and clucked his tongue as each mouthful descended audibly into his stomach. Keeping his eyes on his spoon, he did not speak a word.

'Isn't my soup good, then, Monsieur le Cure?' the old servant asked the priest. 'You are only fiddling with your plate.'

'I am not a bit hungry, my good Teuse,' Serge replied, smiling.

'Well! how can one wonder at it when you go on as you do! But you would have been hungry, if you hadn't lunched at past two o'clock.'

Brother Archangias, tilting into his spoon the last few drops of soup remaining in his plate, said gravely: 'You should be regular in your meals, Monsieur le Cure.'

At this moment Desiree, who also had finished her soup, sedately and in silence, rose and followed La Teuse to the kitchen. The Brother, then left alone with Abbe Mouret, cut himself some long strips of bread, which he ate while waiting for the next dish.

'So you made a long round to-day?' he asked the priest. But before the other could reply a noise of footsteps, exclamations, and ringing laughter, arose at the end of the passage, in the direction of the yard. A short altercation apparently took place. A flute-like voice which disturbed the Abbe rose in vexed and hurried accents, which finally died away in a burst of glee.

'What can it be?' said Serge, rising from his chair.

But Desiree bounded in again, carrying something hidden in her gathered-up skirt. And she burst out excitedly: 'Isn't she queer? She wouldn't come in at all. I caught hold of her dress; but she is awfully strong; she soon got away from me.'

'Whom on earth is she talking about?' asked La Teuse, running in from the kitchen with a dish of potatoes, across which lay a piece of bacon.

The girl sat down, and with the greatest caution drew from her skirt a blackbird's nest in which three wee fledglings were slumbering. She laid it on her plate. The moment the little birds felt the light, they stretched out their feeble necks and opened their crimson beaks to ask for food. Desiree clapped her hands, enchanted, seized with strange emotion at the sight of these hitherto unknown creatures.

'It's that Paradou girl!' exclaimed the Abbe suddenly, remembering everything.

La Teuse had gone to the window. 'So it is,' she said. 'I might have known that grasshopper's voice—— Oh! the gipsy! Look, she's stopped there to spy on us.'

Abbe Mouret drew near. He, too, thought that he could see Albine's orange-coloured skirt behind a juniper bush. But Brother Archangias, in a towering passion, raised himself on tiptoe behind him, and, stretching out his fist and wagging his churlish head, thundered forth: 'May the devil take you, you brigand's daughter! I will drag you right round the church by your hair if ever I catch you coming and casting your evil spells here!'

A peal of laughter, fresh as the breath of night, rang out from the path, followed by light hasty footsteps and the swish of a dress rustling through the grass like an adder. Abbe Mouret, standing at the window, saw something golden glide through the pine trees like a moonbeam. The breeze, wafted in from the open country, was now laden with that penetrating perfume of verdure, that scent of wildflowers, which Albine had scattered from her bare arms, unfettered bosom, and streaming tresses at the Paradou.

'An accursed soul! a child of perdition!' growled Brother Archangias, as he reseated himself at the dinner table. He fell greedily upon his bacon, and swallowed his potatoes whole instead of bread. La Teuse, however, could not persuade Desiree to finish her dinner. That big baby was lost in ecstasy over the nestlings, asking questions, wanting to know what food they ate, if they laid eggs, and how the cockbirds could be known.

The old servant, however, was troubled by a suspicion, and taking her stand on her sound leg, she looked the young cure in the face.

'So you know the Paradou people?' she said.

Thereupon he simply told the truth, relating the visit he had paid to old Jeanbernat. La Teuse exchanged scandalised glances with Brother Archangias. At first she answered nothing, but went round and round the table, limping frantically and stamping hard enough with her heels to split the flooring.

'You might have spoken to me of those people these three months past,' said the priest at last. 'I should have known at any rate what sort of people I was going to call upon.'

La Teuse stopped short as if her legs had just broken.

'Don't tell falsehoods, Monsieur le Cure,' she stuttered, 'don't tell them; you will only make your sin still worse. How dare you say I haven't spoken to you of the Philosopher, that heathen who is the scandal of the whole neighbourhood? The truth is, you never listen to me when I talk. It all goes in at one ear and out at the other. Ah, if you did listen to me, you'd spare yourself a good deal of trouble!'

'I, too, have spoken to you about those abominations,' affirmed the Brother.

Abbe Mouret lightly shrugged his shoulders. 'Well, I didn't remember it,' he said. It was only when I found myself at the Paradou that I fancied I recollected certain tales. Besides, I should have gone to that unhappy man all the same as I thought him in danger of death.'

Brother Archangias, his mouth full, struck the table violently with his knife, and roared: 'Jeanbernat is a dog; he ought to die like a dog.' Then seeing the priest about to protest he cut him short: 'No, no, for him there is no God, no penitence, no mercy. It would be better to throw the host to the pigs than carry it to that scoundrel.'

Then he helped himself to more potatoes, and with his elbows on the table, his chin in his plate, began chewing furiously. La Teuse, her lips pinched, quite white with anger, contented herself with saying dryly: 'Let it be, his reverence will have his own way. He has secrets from us now.'

Silence reigned. For a moment one only heard the working of Brother Archangias's jaws, and the extraordinary rumbling of his gullet. Desiree, with her bare arms round the nest in her plate, smiled to the little ones, talking to them slowly and softly in a chirruping of her own which they seemed to understand.

'People say what they have done when they have nothing to hide,' suddenly cried La Teuse.

And then silence reigned again. What exasperated the old servant was the mystery the priest seemed to make about his visit to the Paradou. She deemed herself a woman who had been shamefully deceived. Her curiosity smarted. She again walked round the table, not looking at the Abbe, not addressing anybody, but comforting herself with soliloquy.

'That's it; that's why we have lunch so late! We go gadding about till two o'clock in the afternoon. We go into such disreputable houses that we don't even dare to tell what we've done. And then we tell lies, we deceive everybody.'

'But nobody,' gently interrupted Abbe Mouret, who was forcing himself to eat a little more, so as to prevent La Teuse from getting crosser than ever, 'nobody asked me if I had been to the Paradou. I have not had to tell any lies.'

La Teuse, however, went on as if she had never heard him.

'Yes, we go ruining our cassock in the dust, we come home rigged up like a thief. And if some kind person takes an interest in us, and questions us for our own good, we push her about and treat her like a good-for-nothing woman, whom we can't trust. We hide things like a slyboots, we'd rather die than breathe a word; we're not even considerate enough to enliven our home by relating what we've seen.'

She turned to the priest, and looked him full in the face.

'Yes, you take that to yourself. You are a close one, you're a bad man!'

Thereupon she fell to crying and the Abbe had to soothe her.

'Monsieur Caffin used to tell me everything,' she moaned out.

However, she soon grew calmer. Brother Archangias was finishing a big piece of cheese, apparently quite unruffled by the scene. In his opinion Abbe Mouret really needed being kept straight, and La Teuse was right in making him feel the reins. Having drunk a last glassful of the weak wine, the Brother threw himself back in his chair to digest his meal.

'Well now,' finally asked the old servant, 'what did you see at the Paradou? Tell us, at any rate.'

Abbe Mouret smiled and related in a few words how strangely Jeanbernat had received him. La Teuse, after overwhelming him with questions, broke out into indignant exclamations, while Brother Archangias clenched his fists and brandished them aloft.

'May Heaven crush him!' said he, 'and burn both him and his witch!'

In his turn the Abbe then endeavoured to elicit some fresh particulars about the people at the Paradou, and listened intently to the Brother's monstrous narrative.

'Yes, that little she-devil came and sat down in the school. It's a long time ago now, she might then have been about ten. Of course, I let her come; I thought her uncle was sending her to prepare for her first communion. But for two months she utterly revolutionised the whole class. She made herself worshipped, the minx! She knew all sorts of games, and invented all sorts of finery with leaves and shreds of rags. And how quick and clever she was, too, like all those children of hell! She was the top one at catechism. But one fine morning the old man burst in just in the middle of our lessons. He was going to smash everything, and shouted that the priests had taken his child from him. We had to get the rural policeman to turn him out. As to the little one, she bolted. I could see her through the window, in a field opposite, laughing at her uncle's frenzy. She had been coming to school for the last two months without his even suspecting it. He had regularly scoured the country after her.'

'She's never taken her first communion,' exclaimed La Teuse below her breath with a slight shudder.

'No, never,' rejoined Brother Archangias. 'She must be sixteen now. She's growing up like a brute beast. I have seen her running on all fours in a thicket near La Palud.'

'On all fours,' muttered the servant, turning towards the window with superstitious anxiety.

Abbe Mouret attempted to express some doubt, but the Brother burst out: 'Yes, on all fours! And she jumped like a wild cat. If I had only had a gun I could have put a bullet in her. We kill creatures that are far more pleasing to God than she is. Besides, every one knows she comes caterwauling every night round Les Artaud. She howls like a beast. If ever a man should fall into her clutches, she wouldn't leave him a scrap of skin on his bones, I know.'

The Brother's hatred of womankind was boiling over. He banged the table with his fist, and poured forth all his wonted abuse.

'The devil's in them. They reek of the devil! And that's what bewitches fools.'

The priest nodded approvingly. Brother Archangias's outrageous violence and La Teuse's loquacious tyranny were like castigation with thongs, which it often rejoiced him to find lashing his shoulders. He took a pious delight in sinking into abasement beneath their coarse speech. He seemed to see the peace of heaven behind contempt of the world and degradation of his whole being. It was delicious to inflict mortification upon his body, to drag his susceptible nature through a gutter.

'There is nought but filth,' he muttered as he folded up his napkin.

La Teuse began to clear the table and wished to remove the plate on which Desiree had laid the blackbird's nest. You are not going to bed here, I suppose, mademoiselle,' she said. 'Do leave those nasty things.'

Desiree, however, defended her plate. She covered the nest with her bare arms, no longer gay, but cross at being disturbed.

'I hope those birds are not going to be kept,' exclaimed Brother Archangias. 'It would bring bad luck. You must wring their necks.'

And he already stretched out his big hands; but the girl rose and stepped back quivering, hugging the nest to her bosom. She stared fixedly at the Brother, her lips curling upwards, like those of a wolf about to bite.

'Don't touch the little things,' she stammered. 'You are ugly.'

With such singular contempt did she emphasise that last word that Abbe Mouret started as if the Brother's ugliness had just struck him for the first time. The latter contented himself with growling. He had always felt a covert hatred for Desiree, whose lusty physical development offended him. When she had left the room, still walking backwards, and never taking her eyes from him, he shrugged his shoulders and muttered between his teeth some coarse abuse which no one heard.

'She had better go to bed,' said La Teuse. 'She would only bore us by-and-by in church.'

'Has any one come yet?' asked Abbe Mouret.

'Oh, the girls have been outside a long time with armfuls of boughs. I am just going to light the lamps. We can begin whenever you like.'

A few seconds later she could be heard swearing in the sacristy because the matches were damp. Brother Archangias, who remained alone with the priest, sourly inquired: 'For the month of Mary, eh?'

'Yes,' replied Abbe Mouret. 'The last few days the girls about here were hard at work and couldn't come as usual to decorate the Lady Chapel. So the ceremony was postponed till to-night.'

'A nice custom,' muttered the Brother. 'When I see them all putting up their boughs I feel inclined to knock them down and make them confess their misdeeds before touching the altar. It's a shame to allow women to rustle their dresses so near the holy relics.'

The Abbe made an apologetic gesture. He had only been at Les Artaud a little while, he must follow the customs.

'Whenever you like, Monsieur le Cure, we're ready!' now called out La Teuse.

But Brother Archangias detained him a minute. 'I am off,' he said. 'Religion isn't a prostitute that it should be decorated with flowers and laces.'

He walked slowly to the door. Then once more he stopped, and lifting one of his hairy fingers added: 'Beware of your devotion to the Virgin.'

XIII

On entering the church Abbe Mouret found nine or ten big girls awaiting him with boughs of ivy, laurel, and rosemary. Few garden flowers grew on the rocks of Les Artaud, so the custom was to decorate the Lady altar with a greenery which might last throughout the month of May. Thereto La Teuse would add a few wallflowers whose stems were thrust into old decanters.

'Will you let me do it, Monsieur le Cure?' she asked. 'You are not used to it —— Come, stand there in front of the altar. You can tell me if the decorations please you.'

He consented, and it was she who really directed the arrangements. Having climbed upon a pair of steps she bullied the girls as they came up to her in turn with their leafy contributions.

'Not so fast, now! You must give me time to fix the boughs. We can't have all these bundles coming down on his reverence's head—— Come on, Babet, it's your turn. What's the good of staring at me like that with your big eyes? Fine rosemary yours is, my word! as yellow as a thistle. You next, La Rousse. Ah, well, that is splendid laurel! You got that out of your field at Croix-Verte, I know.'

The big girls laid their branches on the altar, which they kissed; and there they lingered for a while, handing up the greenery to La Teuse. The sly look of devotion they had assumed on stepping on to the altar steps was quickly set aside, and soon they were laughing, digging each other with their knees, swaying their hips against the altar's edge, and thrusting their bosoms against the tabernacle itself. Over them the tall Virgin in gilded plaster bent her tinted face, and smiled with her rosy lips upon the naked Jesus she bore upon her left arm.

'That's it, Lisa!' cried La Teuse; 'why don't you sit on the altar while you're about it? Just pull your petticoats straight, will you? Aren't you ashamed of behaving like that?—If any one of you lolls about I'll lay her boughs across her face.—Can't you hand me the things quietly?'

Then turning round, she asked:

'Do you like it, sir? Do you think it will do?'

She had converted the space behind the Virgin's statue into a verdant niche, whence leafy sprays projected on either side, forming a bower, and drooping over in front like palm leaves. The priest expressed his approval, but ventured to remark: 'I think there ought to be a cluster of more delicate foliage up above.'

'No doubt,' grumbled La Teuse. 'But they only bring me laurel and rosemary—I should like to know who has brought an olive branch. Not one, you bet! They are afraid of losing a single olive, the heathens!'

At this, however, Catherine came up laden with an enormous olive bough which completely hid her.

'Oh, you've got some, you minx!' continued the old servant.

'Of course,' one of the other girls exclaimed, 'she stole it. I saw Vincent breaking it off while she kept a look-out.'

But Catherine flew into a rage and swore it was not true. She turned, and thrusting her auburn head through the greenery, which she still tightly held, she started lying with marvellous assurance, inventing quite a long story to prove that the olive bough was really hers.

'Besides,' she added, 'all the trees belong to the Blessed Virgin.'

Abbe Mouret was about to intervene, but La Teuse sharply inquired if they wanted to make game of her and keep her arms up there all night. At last she proceeded to fasten the olive bough firmly, while Catherine, holding on to the steps behind her, mimicked the clumsy manner in which she turned her huge person about with the help of her sound leg. Even the priest could not forbear to smile.

'There,' said La Teuse, as she came down and stood beside him to get a good view of her work, 'there's the top done. Now we will put some clumps between the candlesticks, unless you would prefer a garland all along the altar shelf.'

The priest decided in favour of some big clumps.

'Very good; come on, then,' continued the old servant, once more clambering up the steps. 'We can't go to bed here. Just kiss the altar, will you, Miette? Do you fancy you are in your stable? Monsieur le Cure, do just see what they are up to over there! I can hear them laughing like lunatics.'

On raising one of the two lamps the dark end of the church was lit up and three of the girls were discovered romping about under the gallery; one of them had stumbled and pitched head foremost into the holy water stoup, which mishap had so tickled the others that they were rolling on the ground to laugh at their ease. They all came back, however, looking at the priest sheepishly, with lowered eyelids, but with their hands swinging against their hips as if a scolding rather pleased them than otherwise.

However, the measure of La Teuse's wrath was filled when she suddenly perceived Rosalie coming up to the altar like the others with a bundle of boughs in her arms.

'Get down, will you?' she cried to her. 'You are a cool one, and no mistake, my lass!—Hurry up, off you go with your bundle.'

'What for, I'd like to know?' said Rosalie boldly. 'You can't say I have stolen it.'

The other girls drew closer, feigning innocence and exchanging sparkling glances.

'Clear out,' repeated La Teuse, 'you have no business here, do you hear?'

Then, quite losing her scanty patience, she gave vent to a very coarse epithet, which provoked a titter of delight among the peasant girls.

'Well, what next?' said Rosalie. 'Mind your own business. Is it any concern of yours?'

Then she burst into a fit of sobbing and threw down her boughs, but let the Abbe lead her aside and give her a severe lecture. He had already tried to silence La Teuse; for he was beginning to feel uneasy amidst the big shameless hussies who filled the church with their armfuls of foliage. They were pushing right up to the altar step, enclosing him with a belt of woodland, wafting in his face a rank perfume of aromatic shoots.

'Let us make haste, be quick!' he exclaimed, clapping his hands lightly.

'Goodness knows I would rather be in my bed,' grumbled La Teuse. 'It's not so easy as you think to fasten all these bits of stuff.'

Finally, however, she succeeded in setting some lofty plumes of foliage between the candlesticks. Next she folded the steps, which were laid behind the high altar by Catherine. And then she only had to arrange two clumps of greenery at the sides of the altar table. The last boughs sufficed for this, and indeed there were some left which the girls strewed over the sanctuary floor up to the wooden rails. The Lady altar now looked like a grove, a shrubbery with a verdant lawn before it.

At present La Teuse was willing to make way for Abbe Mouret, who ascended the altar steps, and, again lightly clapping his hands, exclaimed: 'Young ladies, to-morrow we will continue the devotions of the month of Mary. Those who may be unable to come ought at least to say their Rosary at home.'

He knelt, and the peasant girls, with a mighty rustle of skirts, sank down and settled themselves on their heels. They followed his prayer with a confused muttering, through which burst here and there a giggle. One of them, on being pinched from behind, burst into a scream, which she attempted to stifle with a sudden fit of coughing; and this so diverted the others that for a moment after the Amen they remained writhing with merriment, their noses close to the stone flags.

La Teuse dismissed them; while the priest, after crossing himself, remained absorbed before the altar, no longer hearing what went on behind him.

'Come, now, clear out,' muttered the old woman. 'You're a pack of good-for-nothings, who can't even respect God. It's shameful, it's unheard of, for girls to roll about on the floor in church like beasts in a meadow—— What are you doing there, La Rousse? If I see you pinching any one, you'll have to deal with me! Oh, yes, you may put out your tongue at me; I'll tell his reverence about it. Out you get; out you get, you minxes!'

She drove them slowly towards the door, while running and bobbling round them frantically. And she had succeeded, as she thought, in getting every one of them outside, when she caught sight of Catherine and Vincent calmly installed in the confessional, where they were eating something with an air of great enjoyment. She drove them away; and as she popped her head outside the church, before closing the door, she espied Rosalie throwing her arm over the shoulder of Fortune, who had been waiting for her. The pair of them vanished in the darkness amid a faint sound of kisses.

'To think that such creatures dare to come to our Lady's altar!' La Teuse stuttered as she shot the bolts. 'The others are no better, I am sure. If they came to-night with their boughs, it was only for a bit of fun and to get kissed by the lads on going off! Not one of them will put herself out of the way to- morrow; his reverence will have to say his *Aves* by himself—— We shall only see the jades who have got assignations.'

Thus soliloquising, she thrust the chairs back into their places, and looked round to see if anything suspicious was lying about before going off to bed. In the confessional she picked up a handful of apple-parings, which she threw behind the high altar. And she also found a bit of ribbon torn from some cap, and a lock of black hair, which she made up into a small parcel, with the view of opening an inquiry into the matter. With these exceptions the church seemed to her tidy. There was oil enough for the night in the bracket-lamp of the sanctuary, and as to the flags of the choir, they could do without washing till Saturday.

'It's nearly ten o'clock, Monsieur le Cure,' she said, drawing near the priest, who was still on his knees. 'You might as well come up now.'

He made no answer, but only bowed his head.

'All right, I know what that means,' continued La Teuse. 'In another hour he will still be on the stones there, giving himself a stomach-ache. I'm off, as I shall only bore him. All the same, I can't see much sense in it, eating one's lunch when others are at dinner, and going to bed when the fowls get up!—— I worry you, don't I, your reverence? Good-night. You're not at all reasonable!'

She made ready to go, but suddenly came back to put out one of the two lamps, muttering the while that such late prayers spelt ruination in oil. Then, at last, she did go off, after passing her sleeve brushwise over the cloth of the high altar, which seemed to her grey with dust. Abbe Mouret, his eyes uplifted, his arms tightly clasped against his breast, then remained alone.

XIV

With only one lamp burning amid the verdure on the altar of the Virgin, huge floating shadows filled the church at either end. From the pulpit a sheet of gloom projected to the rafters of the ceiling. The confessional looked quite black under the gallery, showing strange outlines suggestive of a ruined sentry-box. All the light, softened and tinted as it were by the green foliage, rested slumberingly upon the tall gilded Virgin, who seemed to descend with queenly mien, borne upon the cloud round which gambolled the winged cherubim. At sight of that round lamp gleaming amid the boughs one might have thought the pallid moon was rising on the verge of a wood, casting its light upon a regal apparition, a princess of heaven, crowned and clothed with gold, who with her nude and Divine Infant had come to stroll in the mysterious woodland avenues. Between the leaves, along the lofty plumes of greenery, within the large ogival arbour, and even along the branches strewing the flagstones, star-like beams glided drowsily, like the milky rain of light that filters through the bushes on moonlit nights. Vague sounds and creakings came from the dusky ends of the church; the large clock on the left of the chancel throbbed slowly, with the heavy breathing of a machine asleep. And the radiant vision, the Mother with slender bands of chestnut hair, as if reassured by the nocturnal quiet of the nave, came lower and lower, scarce bending the blades of grass in the clearings beneath the gentle flight of her cloudy chariot.

Abbe Mouret gazed at her. This was the hour when he most loved the church. He forgot the woeful figure on the cross, the Victim bedaubed with carmine and ochre, who gasped out His life behind him, in the chapel of the Dead. His thoughts were no longer distracted by the garish light from the windows, by the gayness of morning coming in with the sun, by the irruption of outdoor life—the sparrows and the boughs invading the nave through the shattered panes. At that hour of night Nature was dead; shadows hung the whitewashed walls with crape; a chill fell upon his shoulders like a salutary penance-shirt. He could now wholly surrender himself to the supremest love, without fear of any flickering ray of light, any caressing breeze or scent, any buzzing of an insect's wing disturbing him amidst the delight of loving. Never had his morning mass afforded him the superhuman joys of his nightly prayers.

With quivering lips Abbe Mouret now gazed at the tall Virgin. He could see her coming towards him from the depths of her green bower in ever- increasing splendour. No longer did a flood of moonlight seem to float across the tree-tops. She seemed to him clothed with the sun; she advanced majestically, glorious, colossal, and so all-powerful that he was tempted at times to cast himself face downwards to shun the flaming splendour of that gate opening into heaven. Then, amidst the adoration of his whole being, which stayed his words upon his lips, he remembered Brother Archangias's final rebuke, as he might have remembered words of blasphemy. The Brother often reproved him for his devotion to the Virgin, which he declared was veritable robbery of devotion due to God. In the Brother's opinion it enervated the soul, put religion into petticoats, created and fostered a state of sentimentalism quite unworthy of the strong. He bore the Virgin a grudge for her womanhood, her beauty, her maternity; he was ever on his guard against her, possessed by a covert fear of feeling tempted by her gracious mien, of succumbing to her seductive sweetness. 'She will lead you far!' he had cried one day to the young priest, for in her he saw the commencement of human passion. From contemplating her one might glide to delight in lovely chestnut hair, in large bright eyes, and the mystery of garments falling from neck to toes. His was the blunt rebellion of a saint who roughly parted the Mother from the Son, asking as He did: 'Woman, what have we in common, thou and I?'

But Abbe Mouret thrust away such thoughts, prostrated himself, endeavoured to forget the Brother's harsh attacks. His rapture in the immaculate purity of Mary alone raised him from the depths of lowliness in which he sought to bury himself. Whenever, alone before the tall golden Virgin, he so deceived himself as to imagine that he could see her bending down for him to kiss her braided locks, he once more became very young, very good, very strong, very just, full of tenderness.

Abbe Mouret's devotion to the Virgin dated from his early youth. Already when he was quite a child, somewhat shy and fond of shrinking into corners, he took pleasure in the thought that a lovely lady was watching over him: that two blue eyes, so sweet, ever followed him with their smile. When he felt at night a breath of air glide across his hair, he would often say that the Virgin had come to kiss him. He had grown up beneath this womanly caress, in an atmosphere full of the rustle of divine robes. From the age of seven he had satisfied the cravings of his affection by expending all the pence he received as pocket money in the purchase of pious picture-cards, which he jealously concealed that he alone might feast on them. But never was he tempted by the pictures of Jesus and the Lamb, of Christ on the Cross, of God the Father, with a mighty beard, stooping over a bank of clouds; his preference was always for the winning portraits of Mary, with her tiny smiling mouth and delicate outstretched hands. By degrees he had made quite a collection of them all—of Mary between a lily and a distaff, Mary carrying her child as if she were his elder sister, Mary crowned with roses, and Mary crowned with stars. For him they formed a family of lovely young maidens, alike in their attractiveness, in the grace, kindliness, and sweetness of their countenances, so youthful beneath their veils, that although they bore the name of 'Mother of God,' he had felt no awe of them as he had often felt for grown-up persons.

They seemed to him of his own age, little girls such as he wished to meet with, little girls of heaven such as the little boys who die when seven years old have for eternal playmates in some nook of Paradise. But even at this early age he was self-contained; and full of the exquisite bashfulness of adolescence he grew up without betraying the secret of his religious love. Mary grew up with him, being invariably a year or two older than himself, as should always be the case with one's chiefest friend. When he was eighteen, she was twenty; she no longer kissed his forehead at night time, but stood a little further from him with folded arms, chastely smiling, ravishingly sweet. And he—he only named her now in a whisper, feeling as if he would faint each time the well-loved name passed his lips in prayer. No more did he dream of childish games within the garden of heaven, but of continual contemplation before that white figure, whose perfect purity he feared to sully with his breath. Even from his own mother did he conceal the fervour of his love for Mary.

Then, a few years later, at the seminary, his beautiful affection for her, seemingly so just, so natural, was disturbed by inward qualms. Was the cult of Mary necessary for salvation? Was he not robbing God by giving Mary a part, the greater part, of his love, his thoughts, his heart, his entire being? Perplexing questions were these, provoking an inward struggle which increased his passion, riveted his bonds. For he dived into all the subtleties of his affection, found unknown joys in discussing the lawfulness of his feelings. The books treating of devotion to the Virgin brought him excuses, joyful raptures, a wealth of arguments which he repeated with prayerful fervour. From them he learned how, in Mary, to be the slave of Jesus. He went to Jesus through Mary. He cited all kinds of proofs, he discriminated, he drew inferences. Mary, whom Jesus had obeyed on earth, should be obeyed by all mankind; Mary still retained her maternal power in heaven, where she was the great dispenser of God's treasures, the only one who could beseech Him, the only one who allotted the heavenly thrones; and thus Mary, a mere creature before God, but raised up to Him, became the human link between heaven and earth, the intermediary of every grace, of every mercy; and his conclusion always was that she should be loved above all else in God himself. Another time he was attracted by more complicated theological curiosities: the marriage of the celestial spouse, the Holy Ghost sealing the Vase of Election, making of the Virgin Mary an everlasting miracle, offering her inviolable purity to the devotion of mankind. She was the Virgin overcoming all heresies, the irreconcilable foe of Satan, the new Eve of whom it had been foretold that she should crush the Serpent's head, the august Gate of Grace, by which the Saviour had already entered once and through which He would come again at the Last Day—a vague prophecy, allotting a yet larger future role to Mary, which threw Serge into a dreamy imagining of some immense expansion of divine love.

This entry of woman into the jealous, cruel heaven depicted by the Old Testament, this figure of whiteness set at the feet of the awesome Trinity, appeared to him the very grace itself of religion, the one consolation for all the dread inspired by things of faith, the one refuge when he found himself lost amidst the mysteries of dogma. And when he had thus proved to himself, point by point, that she was the way to Jesus—easy, short, perfect, and certain —he surrendered himself anew to her, wholly and without remorse: he strove to be her true devotee, dead to self and steeped in submission.

It was an hour of divine voluptuousness! The books treating of devotion to the Virgin burned his hands. They spoke to him in a language of love, warm, fragrant as incense. Mary no longer seemed a young maiden veiled in white, standing with crossed arms, a foot or two away from his pillow. She came surrounded by splendour, even as John saw her, clothed with the sun, crowned with twelve stars, and having the moon beneath her feet. She perfumed him with her fragrance, inflamed him with longing for heaven, ravished him even with the ardent glow of the planets flaming on her brow. He threw himself before her and called himself her slave. No word could have been sweeter than that word of slave, which he repeated, which he relished yet more and more as it trembled on his stammering tongue, whilst casting himself at her feet—to become her thing, her mite, the dust lightly scattered by the waving of her azure robe. With David he exclaimed: 'Mary is made for me,' and with the Evangelist he added: 'I have taken her for my all.' He called her his 'beloved mistress,' for words failed him, and he fell into the prattle of child or lover, his breath breaking with intensity of passion. She was the Blessed among women, the Queen of Heaven glorified by the nine Choirs of Angels, the Mother of Predilection, the Treasure of the Lord. All the vivid imagery of her cult unrolled itself before him comparing to her an earthly paradise of virgin soil, with beds of flowering virtues, green meadows of hope, impregnable towers of strength, and smiling dwellings of confidence. Again she was a fountain sealed by the Holy Ghost, a shrine and dwelling-place of the Holy Trinity, the Throne of God, the City of God, the Altar of God, the Temple of God, and the World of God. And he walked in that garden, in its shade, its sunlight, beneath its enchanting greenery; he sighed after the water of that Fountain; he dwelt within Mary's beauteous precincts—resting, hiding, heedlessly straying there, drinking in the milk of infinite love that fell drop by drop from her virginal bosom.

Every morning, on rising at the seminary, he greeted Mary with a hundred bows, his face turned towards the strip of sky visible from his window. And at night in like fashion he bade her farewell with his eyes fixed upon the stars. Often, when he thus gazed out on fine bright nights, when Venus gleamed golden and dreamy through the warm atmosphere, he forgot himself, and then, like a soft song, would fall from his lips the *Ave maris Stella*, that tender hymn which set before his eyes a distant azure land, and a tranquil sea, scarce wrinkled by a caressing quiver, and illuminated by a smiling star, a very sun in size. He recited, too, the *Salve Regina*, the *Regina Coeli*, the *O gloriosa Domina*, all the prayers and all the canticles. He would read the Office of the Virgin, the holy books written in her honour, the little Psalter of St. Bonaventura, with such devout tenderness, that he could not turn the leaves for tears. He fasted and mortified himself, that he might offer up to her his bruised and wounded flesh. Ever since the age of ten he had worn her livery —the holy scapular, the twofold image of Mary sewn on squares of cloth, whose warmth upon his chest and back thrilled him with delight. Later on, he also took to wearing the little chain in token of his loving slavery. But his greatest act of love was ever the Angelic Salutation, the *Ave Maria*, his heart's perfect prayer. 'Hail, Mary——' and he saw her advancing towards him, full of grace, blessed amongst women; and he cast his heart at her feet for her to tread on it in sweetness. He multiplied and repeated that salutation in a hundred different ways, ever seeking some more efficacious one. He would say twelve *Aves* to commemorate the crown of twelve stars that encircled Mary's brow; he would say fourteen in remembrance of her fourteen joys; at another time he would recite seven decades of them in honour of the years she lived on earth. For hours the beads of his Rosary would glide between his fingers. Then, again, on certain days of mystical assignation he would launch into the endless muttering of the Rosary.

When, alone in his cell, with time to give to his love, he knelt upon the floor, the whole of Mary's garden with its lofty flowers of chastity blossomed around him. Between his fingers glided the Rosary's wreath of *Aves*, intersected by *Paters*, like a garland of white roses mingled with the lilies of the Annunciation, the blood-hued flowers of Calvary, and the stars of the Coronation. He would slowly tread those fragrant paths, pausing at each of the fifteen dizains of *Aves*, and dwelling on its corresponding mystery; he was beside himself with joy, or grief, or triumph, according as the mystery belonged to one or other of the three series—the joyful, the sorrowful, or the glorious. What an incomparable legend it was, the history of Mary, a complete human life, with all its smiles and tears and triumph, which he lived over again from end to end in a single moment! And first he entered into joy with the five glad Mysteries, steeped in the serene calm of dawn. First the Archangel's salutation, the fertilising ray gliding down from heaven, fraught with the spotless union's adorable ecstasy; then the visit to Elizabeth on a bright hope-laden morn, when the fruit of Mary's womb for the first time stirred and thrilled her with the shock at which mothers blench; then the birth in a stable at Bethlehem, and the long string of shepherds coming to pay homage to her Divine Maternity; then the new-born babe carried into the Temple on the arms of his mother who smiled, still weary, but already happy at offering her child to God's justice, to Simeon's embrace, to the desires of the world; and lastly, Jesus at a later age revealing Himself before the doctors, in whose midst He is found by His anxious mother, now proud and comforted.

But, after that tender radiant dawn, it seemed to Serge as if the sky were suddenly overcast. His feet now trod on brambles, the beads of the Rosary pricked his fingers; he cowered beneath the horror of the five Sorrowful Mysteries: Mary, agonising in her Son in the garden of Olives, suffering with Him from the scourging, feeling on her own brow the wounds made by the crown of thorns, bearing the fearful weight of His Cross, and dying at his feet on Calvary. Those inevitable sufferings, that harrowing martyrdom of the queen he worshipped, and for whom he would have shed his blood like Jesus, roused in him a feeling of shuddering repulsion which ten years' practice of the same prayers and the same devotions had failed to weaken. But as the beads flowed on, light suddenly burst upon the darkness of the Crucifixion, and the resplendent glory of the five last Mysteries shone forth in all the brightness of a cloudless sun. Mary was transfigured, and sang the hallelujah of the Resurrection, the victory over Death and the eternity of life. With outstretched hands, and dazed with admiration, she beheld the triumph of her Son ascending into heaven on golden clouds, fringed with purple. She gathered the Apostles round her, and, as on the day of her conception, participated in the glow of the Spirit of Love, descending now in tongues of fire. She, too, was carried up to heaven by a flight of angels, borne aloft on their white wings like a spotless ark, and tenderly set down amid the splendour of the heavenly thrones; and there, in her supreme glory, amidst a splendour so dazzling that the light of the sun was quenched, God crowned her with the stars of the firmament. Impassioned love has but one word. In reciting a hundred and fifty *Aves* Serge had not once repeated himself. The monotonous murmur, the ever recurring words, akin to the 'I love you' of lovers, assumed each time a deeper and deeper meaning; and he lingered over it all, expressed everything with the aid of the one solitary Latin sentence, and learned to know Mary through and through, until, as the last bead of his

Rosary slipped from his hand, his heart grew faint with the thought of parting from her.

Many a night had the young man spent in this way. Daybreak had found him still murmuring his prayers. It was the moon, he would say to cheat himself, that was making the stars wane. His superiors had to reprove him for those vigils, which left him languid and pale as if he had been losing blood. On the wall of his cell had long hung a coloured engraving of the Sacred Heart of Mary, an engraving which showed the Virgin smiling placidly, throwing open her bodice, and revealing a crimson fissure, wherein glowed her heart, pierced with a sword, and crowned with white roses. That sword tormented him beyond measure, brought him an intolerable horror of suffering in woman, the very thought of which scattered his pious submissiveness to the winds. He erased the weapon, and left only the crowned and flaming heart which seemed to be half torn from that exquisite flesh, as if tendered as an offering to himself. And it was then he felt beloved: Mary was giving him her heart, her living heart, even as it throbbed in her bosom, dripping with her rosy blood.

In all this there was no longer the imagery of devout passion, but a material entity, a prodigy of affection which impelled him, when he was praying before the engraving, to open out his hands in order that he might reverently receive the heart that leaped from that immaculate bosom. He could see it, hear it beat; he was loved, that heart was beating for himself! His whole being quickened with rapture; he would fain have kissed that heart, have melted in it, have lain beside it within the depths of that open breast. Mary's love for him was an active one; she desired him to be near her, to be wholly hers in the eternity to come; her love was efficacious, too, she was ever solicitous for him, watching over him everywhere, guarding him from the slightest breach of his fidelity. She loved him tenderly, more than the whole of womankind together, with a love as azure, as deep, as boundless as the sky itself. Where could he ever find so delightful a mistress? What earthly caress could be compared to the air in which he moved, the breath of Mary? What mundane union or enjoyment could be weighed against that everlasting flower of desire which grew unceasingly, and yet was never over-blown? At this thought the *Magnificat* would exhale from his mouth, like a cloud of incense. He sang the joyful song of Mary, her thrill of joy at the approach of her Divine Spouse. He glorified the Lord who overthrew the mighty from their thrones, and who sent Mary to him, poor destitute child that he was, dying of love on the cold tiled floor of his cell.

And when he had given all up to Mary—his body, his soul, his earthly goods, and spiritual chattels—when he stood before her stripped, bare, with all his prayers exhausted, there welled from his burning lips the Virgin's litanies, with their reiterated, persistent, impassioned appeals for heavenly succour. He fancied himself climbing a flight of pious yearnings, which he ascended step by step at each bound of his heart. First he called her 'Holy.' Next he called her 'Mother,' most pure, most chaste, amiable, and admirable. And with fresh ardour he six times proclaimed her maidenhood; his lips cooled and freshened each time that he pronounced that name of 'Virgin,' which he coupled with power, goodness, and fidelity. And as his heart drew him higher up the ladder of light, a strange voice from his veins spoke within him, bursting into dazzling flowers of speech. He yearned to melt away in fragrance, to be spread around in light, to expire in a sigh of music. As he named her 'Mirror of Justice,' 'Seat of Wisdom,' and 'Source of Joy,' he could behold himself pale with ecstasy in that mirror, kneeling on the warmth of the divine seat, quaffing intoxication in mighty draughts from the holy Source.

Again he would transform her, throwing off all restraint in his frantic love, so as to attain to a yet closer union with her. She became a 'Vessel of Honour,' chosen of God, a 'Bosom of Election,' wherein he desired to pour his being, and slumber for ever.* She was the 'Mystical Rose'—a great flower which bloomed in Paradise, with petals formed of the angels clustering round their queen, a flower so fresh, so fragrant, that he could inhale its perfume from the depths of his unworthiness with a joyful dilation of his sides which stretched them to bursting. She became changed into a 'House of Gold,' a 'Tower of David,' and a 'Tower of Ivory,' of inestimable richness, of a whiteness that swans might envy, and of lofty, massive, rounded form, which he would fain have encircled with his outstretched arms as with a girdle of submissiveness. She stood on the distant skyline as the 'Gate of Heaven,' a glimpse of which he caught behind her shoulders when a puff of wind threw back the folds of her veil. She rose in splendour from behind the mountain in the waning hour of night, like the 'Morning Star' to help all travellers astray, like the very dawn of Love. And when he had ascended to this height—scant of breath, yet still unsatiated—he could only further glorify her with the title of 'Queen,' with which he nine times hailed her, as with nine parting salutations from the censer of his soul. His canticle died joyfully away in those last ejaculations of triumph: 'Queen of virgins, Queen of all saints. Queen conceived without sin!' She, ever before him, shone in splendour; and he, on the topmost step, only reached by Mary's intimates, remained there yet another moment, swooning amidst the subtle atmosphere around him; still too far away to kiss the edge of her azure robe, already feeling that he was about to fall, but ever possessed by a desire to ascend again and again, and seek that superhuman felicity.

How many times had not the Litany of the Virgin, recited in common in the
seminary chapel, left the young man with broken limbs and void head, as if
from some great fall! And since his departure from the seminary, Abbe Mouret
had grown to love the Virgin still more. He gave to her that impassioned cult
which to Brother Archangias savoured of heresy. In his opinion it was she who
would save the Church by some matchless prodigy whose near appearance
would entrance the world. She was the only miracle of our impious age—the
blue-robed lady that showed herself to little shepherdesses, the whiteness that
gleamed at night between two clouds, her veil trailing over the low thatched
roofs of peasant homes. When Brother Archangias coarsely asked him if he
had ever espied her, he simply smiled and tightened his lips as if to keep his
secret. Truth to say, he saw her every night. She no longer seemed a playful
sister or a lovely pious maiden; she wore a bridal robe, with white flowers in
her hair; and from beneath her drooping eyelids fell moist glances of hopeful
promise that set his cheeks aglow. He could feel that she was coming, that she
was promising to delay no longer; that she said to him, 'Here I am, receive
me!' Thrice a day when the *Angelus* rang out—at break of dawn, in the fulness
of midday, and at the gentle fall of twilight—he bared his head and said an *Ave*
with a glance around him as if to ascertain whether the bell were not at last
announcing Mary's coming. He was five-and-twenty. He awaited her.

During the month of May the young priest's expectation was fraught with
joyful hope. To La Teuse's grumblings he no longer paid the slightest attention.
If he remained so late praying in the church, it was because he entertained the
mad idea that the great golden Virgin would at last come down from her
pedestal. And yet he stood in awe of that Virgin, so like a princess in her mien.
He did not love all the Virgins alike, and this one inspired him with supreme
respect. She was, indeed, the Mother of God, she showed the fertile
development of form, the majestic countenance, the strong arms of the Divine
Spouse bearing Jesus. He pictured her thus, standing in the midst of the
heavenly court, the train of her royal mantle trailing among the stars; so far
above him, and of such exceeding might, that he would be shattered into dust
should she deign to cast her eyes upon him. She was the Virgin of his days of
weakness, the austere Virgin who restored his inward peace by an awesome
glimpse of Paradise.

That night Abbe Mouret remained for over an hour on his knees in the empty
church. With folded hands and eyes fixed on the golden Virgin rising planet-
like amid the verdure, he sought the drowsiness of ecstasy, the

appeasement of the strange discomfort he had felt that day. But he failed to find the semi-somnolence of prayer with the delightful ease he knew so well. However glorious and pure Mary might reveal herself, her motherhood, the maturity of her charms, and the bare infant she bore upon her arm, disquieted him. It seemed as if in heaven itself there were a repetition of the exuberant life, through which he had been moving since the morning. Like the vines of the stony slopes, like the trees of the Paradou, like the human troop of Artauds, Mary suggested the blossoming, the begetting of life. Prayer came but slowly to his lips; fancies made his mind wander. He perceived things he had never seen before—the gentle wave of her chestnut hair, the rounded swell of her rosy throat. She had to assume a sterner air and overwhelm him with the splendour of her sovereign power to bring him back to the unfinished sentences of his broken prayer. At last the sight of her golden crown, her golden mantle, all the golden sheen which made of her a mighty princess, reduced him once more to slavish submission, and his prayer again flowed evenly, and his mind became wrapped in worship.

In this ecstatic trance, half asleep, half awake, he remained till eleven o'clock, heedless of his aching knees, fancying himself suspended in mid air, rocked to and fro like a child, and yielding to restful slumber, though conscious of some unknown weight that oppressed his heart. Meanwhile the church around him filled with shadows, the lamp grew dim, and the lofty sprays of leafage darkened the tall Virgin's varnished face.

When the clock, about to strike, gave out a rending whine, a shudder passed through Abbe Mouret. He had not hitherto felt the chill of the church upon his shoulders, but now he was shivering from head to foot. As he crossed himself a memory swiftly flashed through the stupor of his wakening
—the chattering of his teeth recalled to him the nights he had spent on the floor of his cell before the Sacred Heart of Mary, when his whole frame would quiver with fever. He rose up painfully, displeased with himself. As a rule, he would leave the altar untroubled in his flesh and with Mary's sweet breath still fresh upon his brow. That night, however, as he took the lamp to go up to his room he felt as if his throbbing temples were bursting. His prayer had not profited him; after a transient alleviation he still experienced the burning glow which had been rising in his heart and brain since morning. When he reached the sacristy door, he turned and mechanically raised the lamp to take a last look at the tall Virgin. But she was now shrouded in the deep shadows falling from the rafters, buried in the foliage around her whence only the golden cross upon her crown emerged.

XV

Abbe Mouret's bedroom, which occupied a corner of the vicarage, was a spacious one, having two large square windows; one of which opened above Desiree's farmyard, whilst the other overlooked the village, the valley beyond, the belt of hills, the whole landscape. The yellow-curtained bed, the walnut chest of drawers, and the three straw-bottomed chairs seemed lost below that lofty ceiling with whitewashed joists. A faint tartness, the somewhat musty odour of old country houses, ascended from the tiled and ruddled floor that glistened like a mirror. On the chest of drawers a tall statuette of the Immaculate Conception rose greyly between some porcelain vases which La Teuse had filled with white lilac.

Abbe Mouret set his lamp on the edge of the chest of drawers before the Virgin. He felt so unwell that he determined to light the vine-stem fire which was laid in readiness. He stood there, tongs in hand, watching the kindling wood, his face illuminated by the flame. The house beneath slumbered in unbroken stillness. The silence filled his ears with a hum, which grew into a sound of whispering voices. Slowly and irresistibly these voices mastered him and increased the feeling of anxiety which had almost choked him several times that day. What could be the cause of such mental anguish? What could be the strange trouble which had slowly grown within him and had now become so unbearable? He had not fallen into sin. It seemed as if but yesterday he had left the seminary with all his ardent faith, and so fortified against the world that he moved among men beholding God alone. And, suddenly, he fancied himself in his cell at five o'clock in the morning, the hour for rising. The deacon on duty passed his door, striking it with his stick, and repeating the regulation summons—

'*Benedicamus Domino!*'

'*Deo gratias!*' he answered half asleep, with his eyes still swollen with slumber.

And he jumped out upon his strip of carpet, washed himself, made his bed, swept his room, and refilled his little pitcher. He enjoyed this petty domestic work while the morning air sent a thrilling shiver throughout his frame. He could hear the sparrows in the plane-trees of the court-yard, rising at the same time as himself with a deafening noise of wings and notes—their way of saying their prayers, thought he. Then he went down to the meditation room, and stayed there on his knees for half an hour after prayers, to con that reflection of St. Ignatius: 'What profit be it to a man to gain the whole world if he lose his soul?' A subject, this, fertile in good resolutions, which impelled him to renounce all earthly goods, and dwell on that fond dream of a desert life, beneath the solitary wealth and luxury of a vast blue sky. When ten minutes had passed, his bruised knees became so painful that his whole being slowly swooned into ecstasy, in which he pictured himself as a mighty conqueror, the master of an immense empire, flinging down his crown, breaking his sceptre, trampling under foot unheard-of wealth, chests of gold, floods of jewels, and rich stuffs embroidered with precious stones, before going to bury himself in some Thebais, clothed in rough drugget that rasped his back. Mass, however, snatched him from these heated fancies, upon which he looked back as upon some beautiful reality which might have been his lot in ancient times; and then, his communion made, he chanted the psalm for the day unconscious of any other voice than his own, which rang out with crystal purity, flying upward till it reached the very ear of the Lord.

When he returned to his room he ascended the stairs step by step, as advised by St. Bonaventura and St. Thomas Aquinas. His gait was slow, his mien grave; he kept his head bowed as he walked along, finding ineffable delight in complying with the most trifling regulations. Next came breakfast. It was pleasant in the refectory to see the hunks of bread and the glasses of white wine, set out in rows. He had a good appetite, and was of a joyous mood. He would say, for instance, that the wine was truly Christian—a daring allusion to the water which the bursar was taxed with putting in the bottles. Still his gravity at once returned to him on going in to lectures. He took notes on his knees, while the professor, resting his hands on the edge of his desk, talked away in familiar Latin, interspersed with an occasional word in French, when he was at fault for a better. A discussion would then follow in which the students argued in a strange jargon, with never a smile upon their faces. Then, at ten o'clock, there came twenty minutes' reading of Holy Writ. He fetched the Sacred Book, a volume richly bound and gilt-edged. Having kissed it with especial reverence, he read it out bare-headed, bowing every time he came upon the name of Jesus, Mary, or Joseph. And with the arrival of the second meditation he was ready to endure for love of God another and even longer spell of kneeling than the first. He avoided resting on his heels for a second even. He delighted in that examination of conscience which lasted for three-quarters of an hour. He racked his memory for sins, and at times even fancied himself damned for forgetting to kiss the pictures on his scapular the night before, or for having gone to sleep upon his left side—abominable faults which he would have willingly redeemed by wearing out his knees till night; and yet happy faults, in that they kept him busy, for without them he would have no occupation for his unspotted heart, steeped in a life of purity.

He would return to the refectory, as if relieved of some great crime. The seminarists on duty, wearing blue linen aprons, and having their cassock sleeves tucked up, brought in the vermicelli soup, the boiled beef cut into little squares, and the helps of roast mutton and French beans. Then followed a terrific rattling of jaws, a gluttonous silence, a desperate plying of forks, only broken by envious greedy glances at the horseshoe table, where the heads of the seminary ate more delicate meats and drank ruddier wines. And all the while above the hubbub some strong-lunged peasant's son, with a thick voice and utter disregard for punctuation, would hem and haw over the perusal of some letters from missionaries, some episcopal pastoral, or some article from a religious paper. To this he listened as he ate. Those polemical fragments, those narratives of distant travels, surprised, nay, even frightened him, with their revelations of bustling, boundless fields of action, of which he had never dreamt, beyond the seminary walls. Eating was still in progress when the wooden clapper announced the recreation hour. The recreation- ground was a sandy yard, in which stood eight plane-trees, which in summer cast cool shadows around. On the south side rose a wall, seventeen feet high, and bristling with broken glass, above which all that one saw of Plassans was the steeple of St. Mark, rising like a stony needle against the blue sky. To and fro he slowly paced the court with a row of fellow-students; and each time he faced the wall he eyed that spire which to him represented the whole town, the whole earth spread beneath the scudding clouds. Noisy groups waxed hot in disputation round the plane-trees; friends would pair off in the corners under the spying glance of some director concealed behind his window-blind. Tennis and skittle matches would be quickly organised to the great discomfort of quiet loto players who lounged on the ground before their cardboard squares, which some bowl or ball would suddenly smother with sand. But when the bell sounded the noise ceased, a flight of sparrows rose from the plane-trees, and the breathless students betook themselves to their lesson in plain-chant with folded arms and hanging heads. And thus Serge's day closed in peacefulness; he returned to his work; then, at four o'clock, he partook of his afternoon snack, and renewed his everlasting walk in sight of St. Mark's spire. Supper was marked by the same rattling of jaws and the same droning perusal as the midday meal. And when it was over Serge repaired to the chapel to attend prayers, and finally betook himself to bed at a quarter past eight, after first sprinkling his pallet with holy water to ward off all evil dreams.

How many delightful days like these had he not spent in that ancient convent of old Plassans, where abode the aroma of centuries of piety! For five years had the days followed one another, flowing on with the unvarying murmur of limpid water. In this present hour he recalled a thousand little incidents which moved him. He remembered going with his mother to purchase his first outfit, his two cassocks, his two waist sashes, his half-dozen bands, his eight pairs of socks, his surplice, and his three-cornered hat. And how his heart had beaten that mild October evening when the seminary door had first closed behind him! He had gone thither at twenty, after his school years, seized with a yearning to believe and love. The very next day he had forgotten all, as if he had fallen into a long sleep in that big silent house. He once more saw the narrow cell in which he had lived through his two years as student of philosophy—a little hutch with only a bed, a table, and a chair, divided from the other cells by badly fitted partitions, in a vast hall containing about fifty similar little dens. And he again saw the cell he had dwelt in three years longer while in the theology class—a larger one, with an armchair, a dressing-table, and a bookcase—a happy room full of the dreams which his faith had evoked. Down those endless passages, up those stairs of stone, in all sorts of nooks, sudden inspirations, unexpected aid had come to him. From the lofty ceilings fell the voices of guardian angels. There was not a flagstone in the halls, not an ashlar of the walls, not a bough of the plane-trees, but it spoke to him of the delights of his contemplative life, his lispings of tenderness, his gradual initiation, the favours vouchsafed him in return for self-bestowal, all that happiness of divine first love.

On such and such a day, on awaking, he had beheld a bright flood of light which had steeped him in joy. On such and such an evening as he closed the door of his cell he had felt warm hands clasping his neck so lovingly that he had lost consciousness, and had afterwards found himself on the floor weeping and choked by sobs. Again, at other times, especially in the little archway leading to the chapel, he had surrendered himself to supple arms which raised him from the ground. All heaven had then been concerned in him, had moved round him, and imparted to his slightest actions a peculiar sense, an astonishing perfume, which seemed to cling faintly to his clothes, to his very skin. And again, he remembered the Thursday walks. They started at two o'clock for some verdant nook about three miles from Plassans. Often they sought a meadow on the banks of the Viorne, where the gnarled willows steeped their leaves in the stream. But he saw nothing—neither the big yellow flowers in the meadow, nor the swallows sipping as they flew by, with wings lightly touching the surface of the little river. Till six o'clock, seated in groups beneath the willows, his comrades and himself recited the Office of the Virgin in common, or read in pairs the 'Little Hours,' the book of prayers recommended to young seminarists, but not enjoined on them.

Abbe Mouret smiled as he stirred the burning embers of his vine-stock fire. In all that past he only found great purity and perfect obedience. He had been a lily whose sweet scent had charmed his masters. He could not recall a single bad action. He had never taken advantage of the absolute freedom of those walks, when the two prefects in charge would go off to have a chat with a parish priest in the neighbourhood, or to have a smoke behind a hedge, or to drink beer with a friend. Never had he hidden a novel under his mattress, nor a bottle of *anisette* in a cupboard. For a long time, even, he had had no suspicion of the sinfulness around him—of the wings of chicken and the cakes smuggled into the seminary in Lent, of the guilty letters brought in by servers, of the abominable conversations carried on in whispers in certain corners of the courtyard. He had wept hot tears when he first perceived that few among his fellows loved God for His own sake. There were peasants' sons there who had taken orders simply through their terror of conscription, sluggards who dreamed of a career of idleness, and ambitious youths already agitated by a vision of the staff and the mitre. And when he found the world's wickedness reappearing at the altar's very foot, he had withdrawn still further into himself, giving himself still more to God, to console Him for being forsaken.

He did recollect, however, that he had crossed his legs one day in class, and that, when the professor reproved him for it, his face had become fiery red, as if he had committed some abominable action. He was one of the best students, never arguing, but learning his texts by heart. He established the existence and eternity of God by proofs drawn from Holy Writ, the opinions of the fathers of the Church, the universal consensus of all mankind. This kind of reasoning filled him with an unshakeable certainty. During his first year of philosophy, he had worked at his logic so earnestly that his professor had checked him, remarking that the most learned were not the holiest. In his second year, therefore, he had carried out his study of metaphysics as a regulation task, constituting but a small fraction of his daily duties. He felt a growing contempt for science; he wished to remain ignorant, in order to preserve the humility of his faith. Later on, he only followed the course of Rohrbacher's 'Ecclesiastical History' from submission; he ventured as far as Gousset's arguments, and Bouvier's 'Theological Course,' without daring to take up Bellarmin, Liguori, Suarez, or St. Thomas Aquinas. Holy Writ alone impassioned him. Therein he found all desirable knowledge, a tale of infinite love which should be sufficient instruction for all men of good-will. He simply adopted the dicta of his teachers, casting on them the care of inquiry, needing nought of such rubbish to know how to love, and accusing books of stealing away the time which should be devoted to prayer. He even succeeded in forgetting his years of college life. He no longer knew anything, but was simplicity itself, a child brought back to the lispings of his catechism.

Such was the manner in which he had ascended step by step to the priesthood. And here his recollections thronged more quickly on him, softer, still warm with heavenly joy. Each year he had drawn nearer to God. His vacations had been spent in holy fashion at an uncle's, in confessions every day and communions twice a week. He would lay fasts upon himself, hide rock-salt inside his trunk, and kneel on it with bared knees for hours together. At recreation time he remained in chapel, or went up to the room of one of the directors, who told him pious and extraordinary stories. Then, as the fast of the Holy Trinity drew nigh, he was rewarded beyond all measure, overwhelmed by the stirring emotion which pervades all seminaries on the eve of ordinations. This was the great festival of all, when the sky opened to allow the elect to rise another step nearer unto God. For a fortnight in advance he imposed a bread and water diet on himself. He closed his window blinds so that he might not see the daylight at all, and he prostrated himself in the gloom to implore Jesus to accept his sacrifice. During the last four days he suffered torturing pangs, terrible scruples, which would force him from his bed in the middle of the night to knock at the door of some strange priest giving the Retreat—some barefooted Carmelite, or often a converted Protestant respecting whom some wonderful story was current. To him he would make at great length a general confession of his whole life in a voice choking with sobs. Absolution alone quieted him, refreshed him, as if he had enjoyed a bath of grace.

On the morning of the great day he felt wholly white; and so vividly was he conscious of his whiteness that he seemed to himself to shed light around him. The seminary bell rang out in clear notes, while all the scents of June— the perfume of blossoming stocks, of mignonette and of heliotropes—came over the lofty courtyard wall. In the chapel relatives were waiting in their best attire, so deeply moved that the women sobbed behind their veils. Next came the procession—the deacons about to receive their priesthood in golden chasubles, the sub-deacons in dalmatics, those in minor orders and the tonsured with their surplices floating on their shoulders and their black birettas in their hands. The organ rolled diffusing the flutelike notes of a canticle of joy. At the altar, the bishop officiated, staff in hand, assisted by two canons. All the Chapter were there, the priests of all the parishes thronged thick amid a dazzling wealth of apparel, a flaring of gold beneath a broad ray of sunlight falling from a window in the nave. The epistle over, the ordination began.

At this very hour Abbe Mouret could remember the chill of the scissors when he was marked with the tonsure at the beginning of his first year of theology. It had made him shudder slightly. But the tonsure had then been very small, hardly larger than a penny. Later, with each fresh order conferred on him, it had grown and grown until it crowned him with a white spot as large as a big Host. The organ's hum grew softer, and the censers swung with a silvery tinkling of their slender chains, releasing a cloudlet of white smoke, which unrolled in lacelike folds. He could see himself, a tonsured youth in a surplice, led to the altar by the master of ceremonies; there he knelt and bowed his head down low, while the bishop with golden scissors snipped off three locks—one over his forehead, and the other two near his ears. Yet another twelvemonth, and he could again see himself in the chapel amid the incense, receiving the four minor orders. Led by an archdeacon, he went to the main doorway, closed the door with a bang, and opened it again, to show that to him was entrusted the care of churches; next he rang a small bell with his right hand, in token that it was his duty to call the faithful to the divine offices; then he returned to the altar, where fresh privileges were conferred upon him by the bishop—those of singing the lessons, of blessing the bread, of catechising children, of exorcising evil spirits, of serving the deacons, of lighting and extinguishing the candles of the altars.

Next came back the memory of the ensuing ordination, more solemn and more dread, amid the same organ strains which sounded now like God's own thunder: this time he wore a sub-deacon's dalmatic upon his shoulders, he bound himself for ever by the vow of chastity, he trembled in every pore, despite his faith, at the terrible *Accedite* from the bishop, which put to flight two of his companions, blanching by his side. His new duties were to serve the priest at the altar, to prepare the cruets, sing the epistle, wipe the chalice, and carry the cross in processions. And, at last, he passed once more, and for the last time, into the chapel, in the radiance of a June sun: but this time he walked at the very head of the procession, with alb girdled about his waist, with stole crossed over his breast, and chasuble falling from his neck. All but fainting from emotion, he could perceive the pallid face of the bishop giving him the priesthood, the fulness of the ministry, by the threefold laying of his hands. And after taking the oath of ecclesiastical obedience, he felt himself uplifted from the stone flags, when the prelate in a full voice repeated the Latin words: '*Accipe Spiritum Sanctum…. Quorum remiseris peccata, remittuntur eis, et quorum retinueris, retenta sunt.*'—'Receive the Holy Ghost…. Whose sins thou dost forgive they are forgiven; and whose sins thou dost retain, they are retained.'

XVI

This evocation of the deep joys of his youth had given Abbe Mouret a touch of feverishness. He no longer felt the cold. He put down the tongs and walked towards the bedstead as if about to go to bed, but turned back and pressed his forehead to a window-pane, looking out into the night with sightless eyes. Could he be ill? Why did he feel such languor in all his limbs, why did his blood burn in every vein? On two occasions, while at the seminary, he had experienced similar attacks—a sort of physical discomfort which made him most unhappy; one day, indeed, he had gone to bed in raving delirium. Then he bethought himself of a young girl possessed by evil spirits, whom Brother Archangias asserted he had cured with a simple sign of the cross, one day when she fell down before him. This reminded him of the spiritual exorcisms which one of his teachers had formerly recommended to him: prayer, a general confession, frequent communion, the choosing of a wise confessor who should have great authority on his mind. And then, without any transition, with a suddenness which astonished himself, he saw in the depths of his memory the round face of one of his old friends, a peasant, who had been a choir boy at eight years old, and whose expenses at the seminary were defrayed by a lady who watched over him. He was always laughing, he rejoiced beforehand at the anticipated emoluments of his career; twelve hundred francs of stipend, a vicarage at the end of a garden, presents, invitations to dinners, little profits from weddings, and baptismal and burial fees. That young fellow must indeed be happy in his parish.

The feeling of melancholy regret evoked by this recollection surprised Abbe Mouret extremely. Was he not happy, too? Until that day he had regretted nothing, wished for nothing, envied nothing. Even as he searched himself at that very moment he failed to find any cause for bitterness. He believed himself the same as in the early days of his deaconship, when the obligatory perusal of his breviary at certain stated hours had filled his days with continuous prayer. No doubts had tormented him; he had prostrated himself before the mysteries he could not understand; he had sacrificed his reason, which he despised, with the greatest ease. When he left the seminary, he had rejoiced at finding himself a stranger among his fellowmen, no longer walking like them, carrying his head differently, possessed of the gestures, words, and opinions of a being apart. He had felt emasculated, nearer to the angels, cleansed of sexuality. It had almost made him proud to belong no longer to his species, to have been brought up for God and carefully purged of all human grossness by a jealously watchful training. Again, it had seemed to him as if for years he had been dwelling in holy oil, prepared with all due rites, which had steeped his flesh in beatification. His limbs, his brain, had lost material substance to gain in soulfulness, impregnated with a subtle vapour which, at times, intoxicated him and dizzied him as if the earth had suddenly failed beneath his feet. He displayed the fears, the unwittingness, the open candour of a cloistered maiden. He sometimes remarked with a smile that he was prolonging his childhood, under the impression that he was still quite little, retaining the same sensations, the same ideas, the same opinions as in the past. At six years old, for instance, he had known as much of God as he knew at twenty-five; in prayer the inflexions of his voice were still the same, and he yet took a childish pleasure in folding his hands quite correctly. The world too seemed to him the same as he had seen in former days when his mother led him by the hand. He had been born a priest, and a priest he had grown up. Whenever he displayed before La Teuse some particularly gross ignorance of life, she would stare him in the face, astounded, and remark with a strange smile that 'he was Mademoiselle Desiree's brother all over.'

In all his existence he could only recall one shock of shame. It had happened during his last six months at the seminary, between his deaconship and priesthood. He had been ordered to read the work of Abbe Craisson, the superior of the great seminary at Valence: '*De rebus Veneris ad usum confessariorum.*' And he had risen from this book terrified and choking with sobs. That learned casuistry, dealing so fully with the abominations of mankind, descending to the most monstrous examples of vice, violated, as it were, all his virginity of body and mind. He felt himself for ever befouled. Yet every time he heard confessions he inevitably recurred to that catechism of shame. And though the obscurities of dogma, the duties of his ministry, and the death of all free will within him left him calm and happy at being nought but the child of God, he retained, in spite of himself, a carnal taint of the horrors he must needs stir up; he was conscious of an ineffaceable stain, deep down somewhere in his being, which might some day grow larger and cover him with mud.

The moon was rising behind the Garrigue hills. Abbe Mouret, still more and more feverish, opened the window and leaned out upon his elbows, that he might feel upon his face the coolness of the night. He could no longer remember at what time exactly this illness had come upon him. He recollected, however, that in the morning, while saying mass, he had been quite calm and restful. It must have been later, perhaps during his long walk in the sun, or while he shivered under the trees of the Paradou, or while stifling in Desiree's poultry-yard. And then he lived through the day again.

Before him stretched the vast plain, more direful still beneath the pallid light of the oblique moonbeams. The olive and almond trees showed like grey spots amid the chaos of rocks spreading to the sombre row of hills on the horizon. There were big splotches of gloom, bumpy ridges, blood-hued earthy pools in which red stars seemed to contemplate one another, patches of chalky light, suggestive of women's garments cast off and disclosing shadowy forms which slumbered in the hollow folds of ground. At night that glowing landscape weltered there strangely, passionately, slumbering with uncovered bosom, and outspread twisted limbs, whilst heaving mighty sighs, and exhaling the strong aroma of a sweating sleeper. It was as if some mighty Cybele had fallen there beneath the moon, intoxicated with the embraces of the sun. Far away, Abbe Mouret's eyes followed the path to Les Olivettes, a narrow pale ribbon stretching along like a wavy stay-lace. He could hear Brother Archangias whipping the truant schoolgirls, and spitting in the faces of their elder sisters. He could see Rosalie slyly laughing in her hands while old Bambousse hurled clods of earth after her and smote her on her hips. Then, too, he thought, he had still been well, his neck barely heated by the lovely morning sunshine. He had felt but a quivering behind him, that confused hum of life, which he had faintly heard since morning when the sun, in the midst of his mass, had entered the church by the shattered windows. Never, then, had the country disturbed him, as it did at this hour of night, with its giant bosom, its yielding shadows, its gleams of ambery skin, its lavish goddess-like nudity, scarce hidden by the silvery gauze of moonlight.

The young priest lowered his eyes, and gazed upon the village of Les Artaud. It had sunk into the heavy slumber of weariness, the soundness of peasants' sleep. Not a light: the battered hovels showed like dusky mounds intersected by the white stripes of cross lanes which the moonbeams swept. Even the dogs were surely snoring on the thresholds of the closed doors. Had the Artauds poisoned the air of the parsonage with some abominable plague? Behind him gathered and swept the gust whose approach filled him with so much anguish. Now he could detect a sound like the tramping of a flock, a whiff of dusty air, which reached him laden with the emanations of beasts. Again came back his thoughts of a handful of men beginning the centuries over again, springing up between those naked rocks like thistles sown by the winds. In his childhood nothing had amazed and frightened him more than those myriads of insects which gushed forth when he raised certain damp stones. The Artauds disturbed him even in their slumber; he could recognise their breath in the air he inhaled. He would have liked to have had the rocks alone below his window. The hamlet was not dead enough; the thatched roofs bulged like bosoms; through the gaping cracks in the doors came low faint sounds which spoke of all the swarming life within. Nausea came upon him. Yet he had often faced it all without feeling any other need than that of refreshing himself in prayer.

His brow perspiring, he proceeded to open the other window, as if to seek cooler air. Below him, to his left, lay the graveyard with the Solitaire erect like a bar, unstirred by the faintest breeze. From the empty field arose an odour like that of a newly mown meadow. The grey wall of the church, that wall full of lizards and planted with wall-flowers, gleamed coldly in the moonlight, and the panes of one of the windows glistened like plates of steel. The sleeping church could now have no other life within it than the extra- human life of the Divinity embodied in the Host enclosed in the tabernacle. He thought of the bracket lamp's yellow glow peeping out of the gloom, and was tempted to go down once more to try to ease his ailing head amid those deep shadows. But a strange feeling of terror held him back; he suddenly fancied, while his eyes were fixed upon the moonlit panes, that he saw the church illumined by a furnace-like glare, the blaze of a festival of hell, in which whirled the Month of May, the plants, the animals, and the girls of Les Artaud, who wildly encircled trees with their bare arms. Then, as he leaned over, he saw beneath him Desiree's poultry-yard, black and steaming. He could not clearly distinguish the rabbit-hutches, the fowls' roosting-places, or the ducks' house. The place was all one big mass heaped up in stench, still exhaling in its sleep a pestiferous odour. From under the stable-door came the acrid smell of the nanny-goat; while the little pig, stretched upon his back, snorted near an empty porringer. And suddenly with his brazen throat Alexander, the big yellow cock, raised a crow, which awoke in the distance impassioned calls from all the cocks of the village.

Then all at once Abbe Mouret remembered: The fever had struck him in Desiree's farmyard, while he was looking at the hens still warm from laying, the rabbit-does plucking the down from under them. And now the feeling that some one was breathing on his neck became so distinct that he turned at last to see who was behind him. And then he recalled Albine bounding out of the Paradou, and the door slamming upon the vision of an enchanted garden; he recalled the girl racing alongside the interminable wall, following the gig at a run, and throwing birch leaves to the breeze as kisses; he recalled her, again, in the twilight, laughing at the oaths of Brother Archangias, her skirts skimming over the path like a cloudlet of dust bowled along by the evening breeze. She was sixteen; how strange she looked, with her rather elongated face! she savoured of the open air, of the grass, of mother earth. And so accurate was his recollection of her that he could once more see a scratch upon one of her supple wrists, a rosy scar on her white skin. Why did she laugh like that when she looked at him with her blue eyes? He was engulfed in her laugh as in a sonorous wave which resounded and pressed close to him on every side; he inhaled it, he felt it vibrate within him. Yes, all his evil came from that laugh of hers which he had quaffed.

Standing in the middle of the room, with both windows open, he remained shivering, seized with a fright which made him hide his face in his hands. So this was the ending of the whole day; this evocation of a fair girl, with a somewhat long face and eyes of blue. And the whole day came in through the open windows. In the distance—the glow of those red lands, the ardent passion of the big rocks, of the olive-trees springing up amid the stones, of the vines twisting their arms by the roadside. Nearer—the steam of human sweat borne in upon the air from Les Artaud, the musty odour of the cemetery, the fragrance of incense from the church, tainted by the scent of greasy-haired wenches. And there was also the steaming muck-heap, the fumes of the poultry-yard, the oppressing ferment of animal germs. And all these vapours poured in at once, in one asphyxiating gust, so offensive, so violent, as to choke him. He tried to close his senses, to subdue and annihilate them. But Albine reappeared before him like a tall flower that had sprung and grown beautiful in that soil. She was the natural blossom of that corruption, delicate in the sunshine, her white shoulders expanding in youthfulness, her whole being so fraught with the gladness of life, that she leaped from her stem and darted upon his mouth, scenting him with her long ripple of laughter.

A cry burst from the priest. He had felt a burning touch upon his lips. A stream as of fire coursed through his veins. And then, in search of refuge, he threw himself on his knees before the statuette of the Immaculate Conception, exclaiming, with folded hands:

'Holy Virgin of Virgins, pray for me!'

XVII

The Immaculate Conception, set on the walnut chest of drawers, was smiling softly, with her slender lips, marked by a dash of carmine. Her form was small and wholly white. Her long white veil, falling from head to foot, had but an imperceptible thread of gold around its edge. Her gown, draped in long straight folds over a sexless figure, was fastened around her flexible neck. Not a single lock of her chestnut hair peeped forth. Her countenance was rosy, with clear eyes upturned to heaven: her hands were clasped—rosy, childlike hands, whose finger-tips appeared beneath the folds of her veil, above the azure scarf which seemed to girdle her waist with two streaming ends of the firmament. Of all her womanly charms not one was bared, except her feet, adorable feet which trod the mystical eglantine. And from those nude feet sprang golden roses, like the natural efflorescence of her twofold purity of flesh.

'Virgin most faithful, pray for me,' the priest despairingly pleaded.

This Virgin had never distressed him. She was not a mother yet; she did not offer Jesus to him, her figure did not yet present the rounded outlines of maternity. She was not the Queen of Heaven descending, crowned with gold and clothed in gold like a princess of the earth, borne in triumph by a flight of cherubim. She had never assumed an awesome mien; had never spoken to him with the austere severity of an all-powerful mistress, the very sight of whom must bow all foreheads to the dust. He could dare to look on her and love her, without fear of being moved by the gentle wave of her chestnut hair; her bare feet alone excited his affection, those feet of love which blossomed like a garden of chastity in too miraculous a manner for him to seek to cover them with kisses. She scented his room with lily-like fragrance. She was indeed the silver lily planted in a golden vase, she was precious, eternal, impeccable purity. Within the white veil, so closely drawn round her, there could be nothing human—only a virgin flame, burning with ever even glow. At night when he went to bed, in the morning when he woke, he could see her there, still and ever wearing that same ecstatic smile.

'Mother most pure, Mother most chaste, Mother ever-virgin, pray for me!' he stammered in his fear, pressing close to the Virgin's feet, as if he could hear Albine's sonorous footfalls behind him. 'You are my refuge, the source of my joy, the seat of my wisdom, the tower of ivory in which I have shut up my purity. I place myself in your spotless hands, I beseech you to take me, to cover me with a corner of your veil, to hide me beneath your innocence, behind the hallowed rampart of your garment—so that no fleshly breath may reach me. I need you, I die without you, I shall feel for ever parted from you, if you do not bear me away in your helpful arms, far hence into the glowing whiteness wherein you dwell. O Mary, conceived without sin, annihilate me in the depths of the immaculate snow that falls from your every limb. You are the miracle of eternal chastity. Your race has sprung from a very beam of grace, like some wondrous tree unsown by any germ. Your son, Jesus, was born of the breath of God; you yourself were born without defilement of your mother's womb, and I would believe that this virginity goes back thus from age to age in endless unwittingness of flesh. Oh! to live, to grow up outside the pale of the senses! Oh! to perpetuate life solely by the contact of a celestial kiss!'

This despairing appeal, this cry of purified longing, calmed the young priest's fears. The Virgin—wholly white, with eyes turned heavenward, appeared to smile more tenderly with her thin red lips. And in a softened voice he went on:

'I should like to be a child once more. I should like to be always a child, walking in the shadow of your gown. When I was quite little, I clasped my hands when I uttered the name of Mary. My cradle was white, my body was white, my every thought was white. I could see you distinctly, I could hear you calling me, I went towards you in the light of a smile over scattered rose- petals. And nought else did I feel or think, I lived but just enough to be a flower at your feet. No one should grow up. You would have around you none but fair young heads, a crowd of children who would love you with pure hands, unsullied lips, tender limbs, stainless as if fresh from a bath of milk. To kiss a child's cheek is to kiss its soul. A child alone can say your name without befouling it. In later years our lips grow tainted and reek of our passions. Even I, who love you so much, and have given myself to you, I dare not at all times call on you, for I would not let you come in contact with the impurities of my manhood. I have prayed and chastised my flesh, I have slept in your keeping, and lived in chastity; and yet I weep to see that I am not yet dead enough to this world to be your betrothed. O Mary! adorable Virgin, why can I not be only five years old—why could I not remain the child who pressed his lips to your pictures? I would take you to my heart, I would lay you by my side, I would clasp and kiss you like a friend—like a girl of my own age. Your close hanging garments, your childish veil, your blue scarf— all that youthfulness which makes you like an elder sister would be mine. I would not try to kiss your locks, for hair is a naked thing which should not be seen; but I would kiss your bare feet, one after the other, for nights and nights together, until my lips should have shred the petals of those golden roses, those mystical roses of our veins.'

He stopped, waiting for the Virgin to look down upon him and touch his forehead with the edges of her veil. But she remained enwrapped in muslin to her neck and finger-nails and ankles, so slim, so etherealised, that she already seemed to be above earth, to be wholly heaven's own.

'Well, then,' he went on more wildly still, 'grant that I become a child again, O kindly Virgin! Virgin most powerful. Grant that I may be only five years old. Rid me of my senses, rid me of my manhood. Let a miracle sweep away all the man that has grown up within me. You reign in heaven, nothing is easier to you than to change me, to rid me of all my strength so that evermore I may be unable to raise my little finger without your leave. I wish never more to feel either nerve, or muscle, or the beating of my heart. I long to be simply a thing— a white stone at your feet, on which you will leave but a perfume; a stone that will not move from where you cast it, but will remain earless and eyeless, content to lie beneath your heel, unable to think of foulness! Oh! then what bliss for me! I shall reach without an effort and at a bound my dream of perfection. I shall at last proclaim myself your true priest. I shall become what all my studies, my prayers, my five years of initiation have been unable to make me. Yes, I reject life; I say that the death of mankind is better than abomination. Everything is stained; everywhere is love tainted. Earth is steeped in impurity, whose slightest drops yield growths of shame. But that I may be perfect, O Queen of angels, hearken to my prayer, and grant it! Make me one of those angels that have only two great wings behind their cheeks; I shall then no longer have a body, no longer have any limbs; I will fly to you if you call me. I shall be but a mouth to sing your praises, a pair of spotless wings to cradle you in your journeys through the heavens. O death! death! Virgin, most venerable, grant me the death of all! I will love you for the death of my body, the death of all that lives and multiplies. I will consummate with you the sole marriage that my heart desires. I will ascend, ever higher and higher, till I have reached the brasier in which you shine in splendour. There one beholds a mighty planet, an immense white rose, whose every petal glows like a moon, a silver throne whence you beam with such a blaze of innocence that heaven itself is all illumined by the gleam of your veil alone. All that is white, the early dawns, the snow on inaccessible peaks, the lilies barely opening, the water of hidden, unknown springs, the milky sap of the plants untouched by the sun, the smiles of maidens, the souls of children dead in their cradles—all rains upon your white feet. And I will rise to your mouth like a subtle flame; I will enter into you by your parted lips, and the bridal will be fulfilled, while the archangels are thrilled by our joyfulness. Oh, to be maiden, to love in maidenhood, to preserve amid the sweetest kisses one's maiden whiteness! To possess all love, stretched on the wings of swans, in a sky of purity, in the arms of a mistress of light, whose caresses are but raptures of the soul! Oh, there lies the perfection, the super-human dream, the yearning which shatters my very bones, the joy which bears me up to heaven! O Mary, Vessel of Election, rid me of all that is human in me, so that you may fearlessly surrender to me the treasure of your maidenhood!'

And then Abbe Mouret, felled by fever, his teeth chattering, swooned away on the floor.

BOOK II

I

Through calico curtains, carefully drawn across the two large windows, a pale white light like that of breaking day filtered into the room. It was a lofty and spacious room, fitted up with old Louis XV. furniture, the woodwork painted white, the upholstery showing a pattern of red flowers on a leafy ground. On the piers above the doors on either side of the alcove were faded paintings still displaying the rosy flesh of flying Cupids, whose games it was now impossible to follow. The wainscoting with oval panels, the folding doors, the rounded ceiling (once sky-blue and framed with scrolls, medallions, and bows of flesh-coloured ribbons), had all faded to the softest grey. Opposite the windows the large alcove opened beneath banks of clouds which plaster Cupids drew aside, leaning over, and peeping saucily towards the bed. And like the windows, the alcove was curtained with coarsely hemmed calico, whose simplicity seemed strange in this room where lingered a perfume of whilom luxury and voluptuousness.

Seated near a pier table, on which a little kettle bubbled over a spirit-lamp, Albine intently watched the alcove curtains. She was gowned in white, her hair gathered up in an old lace kerchief, her hands drooping wearily, as she kept watch with the serious mien of youthful womanhood. A faint breathing, like that of a slumbering child, could be heard in the deep silence. But she grew restless after a few minutes, and could not restrain herself from stepping lightly towards the alcove and raising one of the curtains. On the edge of the big bed lay Serge, apparently asleep, with his head resting on his bent arm. During his illness his hair had lengthened, and his beard had grown. He looked very white, with sunken eyes and pallid lips.

Moved by the sight Albine was about to let the curtain fall again. But Serge faintly murmured, 'I am not asleep.'

He lay perfectly still with his head on his arm, without stirring even a finger, as if overwhelmed by delightful weariness. His eyes had slowly opened, and his breath blew lightly on one of his hands, raising the golden down on his fair skin.

'I heard you,' he murmured again. 'You were walking very gently.'*

---

* From this point in the original Serge and Albine thee and thou one another; but although this *tutoiement* has some bearing on the development of the story, it was impossible to preserve it in an English translation.—ED.

His voice enchanted her. She went up to his bed and crouched beside it to bring her face on a level with his own. 'How are you?' she asked, and then continued: 'Oh! you are well now. Do you know, I used to cry the whole way home when I came back from over yonder with bad news of you. They told me you were delirious, and that if your dreadful fever did spare your life, it would destroy your reason. Oh, didn't I kiss your uncle Pascal when he brought you here to recruit your health!'

Then she tucked in his bed-clothes like a young mother.

'Those burnt-up rocks over yonder, you see, were no good to you. You need trees, and coolness, and quiet. The doctor hasn't even told a soul that he was hiding you away here. That's a secret between himself and those who love you. He thought you were lost. Nobody will ever disturb you, you may be sure of that! Uncle Jeanbernat is smoking his pipe by his lettuce bed. The others will get news of you on the sly. Even the doctor isn't coming back any more. I am to be your doctor now. You don't want any more physic, it seems. What you now want is to be loved; do you see?'

He did not seem to hear her, his brain as yet was void. His eyes, although his head remained motionless, wandered inquiringly round the room, and it struck her that he was wondering where he might be.

'This is my room,' she said. 'I have given it to you. Isn't it a pretty one? I took the finest pieces of furniture out of the lumber attic, and then I made those calico curtains to prevent the daylight from dazzling me. And you're not putting me out a bit. I shall sleep on the second floor. There are three or four empty rooms there.'

Still he looked anxious.

'You're alone?' he asked.

'Yes; why do you ask that?'

He made no answer, but muttered wearily: 'I have been dreaming, I am always dreaming. I hear bells ringing, and they tire me.'

And after a pause he went on: 'Go and shut the door, bolt it; I want you to be alone, quite alone.'

When she came back, bringing a chair with her, and sat down by his pillow, he looked as gleeful as a child, and kept on saying: 'Nobody can come in now. I shall not hear those bells any more. When you are talking to me, it rests me.'

'Would you like something to drink?' she asked.

He made a sign that he was not thirsty. He looked at Albine's hands as if so astonished, so delighted to see them, that with a smile she laid one on the edge of his pillow. Then he let his head glide down, and rested his cheek

111

against that small, cool hand, saying, with a light laugh: 'Ah! it's as soft as silk. It is just as if it were sending a cool breeze through my hair. Don't take it away, please.'

Then came another long spell of silence. They gazed on one another with loving kindliness—Albine calmly scanning herself in the convalescent's eyes, Serge apparently listening to some faint whisper from the small, cool hand.

'Your hand is so nice,' he said once more. 'You can't fancy what good it does me. It seems to steal inside me, and take away all the pain in my limbs. It's as if I were being soothed all over, relieved, cured.'

He gently rubbed his cheek against it, with growing animation, as if he were at last coming back to life.

'You won't give me anything nasty to drink, will you? You won't worry me with all sorts of physic? Your hand is quite enough for me. I have come here for you to put it there under my head.'

'Dear Serge,' said Albine softly, 'how you must have suffered.'

'Suffered! yes, yes; but it's a long time ago. I slept badly, I had such frightful dreams. If I could, I would tell you all about it.'

He closed his eyes for a moment and strove hard to remember.

'I can see nothing but darkness,' he stammered. 'It is very odd, I have just come back from a long journey. I don't even know now where I started from. I had fever, I know, a fever that raced through my veins like a wild beast. That was it—now I remember. The whole time I had a nightmare, in which I seemed to be crawling along an endless underground passage; and every now and then I had an attack of intolerable pain, and then the passage would be suddenly walled up. A shower of stones fell from overhead, the side walls closed in, and there I stuck, panting, mad to get on; and then I bored into the obstacle and battered away with feet and fists, and skull, despairing of ever being able to get through the ever increasing mound of rubbish. At other times, I only had to touch it with my finger and it vanished: I could then walk freely along the widened gallery, weary only from the pangs of my attack.'

Albine tried to lay a hand upon his lips.

'No,' said he, 'it doesn't tire me to talk. I can whisper to you here, you see. I feel as if I were thinking and you could hear me. The queerest point about that underground journey of mine was that I hadn't the faintest idea of turning back again; I got obstinate, although I had the thought before me that it would take me thousands of years to clear away a single heap of wreckage. It seemed a fated task, which I had to fulfil under pain of the greatest misfortunes. So, with my knees all bruised, and my forehead bumping against the hard rock, I set myself to work with all my might, so that I might get to the end as quickly as possible. The end? What was it?... Ah! I do not know, I do not know.'

He closed his eyes and pondered dreamily. Then, with a careless pout, he again sank upon Albine's hand and said laughing: 'How silly of me! I am a child.'

But the girl, to ascertain if he were wholly hers, questioned him and led him back to the confused recollections he had tried to summon up. He could remember nothing, however; he was truly in a happy state of childhood. He fancied that he had been born the day before.

'Oh! I am not strong enough yet,' he said. 'My furthest recollection is of a bed which burned me all over, my head rolled about on a pillow like a pan of live coals, and my feet wore away with perpetual rubbing against each other. I was very bad, I know. It seemed as if I were having my body changed, as if I were being taken all to pieces, and put together again like some broken machine.'

He laughed at this simile, and continued: 'I shall be all new again. My illness has given me a fine cleaning. But what was it you were asking me? No, nobody was there. I was suffering all by myself at the bottom of a black hole. Nobody, nobody. And beyond that, nothing—I can see nothing.... Let me be your child, will you? You shall teach me to walk. I can see nothing else but you now. I care for nothing but you.... I can't remember, I tell you. I came, you took me, and that is all.'

And restfully, pettingly, he said once more: 'How warm your hand is now! it is as nice as the sun. Don't let us talk any more. It makes me hot.'

A quivering silence fell from the blue ceiling of the large room. The spirit lamp had just gone out, and from the kettle came a finer and finer thread of steam. Albine and Serge, their heads side by side upon the pillow, gazed at the large calico curtains drawn across the windows. Serge's eyes, especially, were attracted to them as to the very source of light, in which he sought to steep himself, as in diluted sunshine fitted to his weakness. He could tell that the sun lay behind that yellower gleam upon one corner of the curtain, and that sufficed to make him feel himself again. Meanwhile a far-off rustle of leaves came upon his listening ear, and against the right-hand window the clean-cut greenish shadow of a lofty bough brought him disturbing thoughts of the forest which he could feel to be near him.

'Would you like me to open the curtains?' asked Albine, misunderstanding his steady gaze.

'No, no,' he hastily replied.

'It's a fine day; you would see the sunlight and the trees.'

'No, please don't…. I don't want to see anything outside. That bough there tires me with its waving and its rising, as if it was alive. Leave your hand here, I will go to sleep. All is white now. It's so nice.'

And then he calmly fell asleep, while Albine watched beside him and breathed upon his face to make his slumber cool.

II

The fine weather broke up on the morrow, and it rained heavily. Serge's fever returned, and he spent a day of suffering, with his eyes despairingly fixed upon the curtains through which the light now fell dim and ashy grey as in a cellar. He could no longer see a trace of sunshine, and he looked in vain for the shadow that had scared him, the shadow of that lofty bough which had disappeared amid the mist and the pouring rain, and seemed to have carried away with it the whole forest. Towards evening he became slightly delirious and cried out to Albine that the sun was dead, that he could hear all the sky, all the country bewailing the death of the sun. She had to soothe him like a child, promising him the sun, telling him that it would come back again, that she would give it to him. But he also grieved for the plants. The seeds, he said, must be suffering underground, waiting for the return of light; they had nightmares, they also dreamed that they were crawling along an underground passage, hindered by mounds of ruins, struggling madly to reach the sunshine. And he began to weep and sob out in low tones that winter was a disease of the earth, and that he should die with the earth, unless the springtide healed them both.

For three days more the weather was truly frightful. The downpour burst over the trees with the awful clamour of an overflowing river. Gusts of wind rolled by and beat against the windows with the violence of enormous waves. Serge had insisted on Albine closing the shutters. By lamplight he was no longer troubled by the gloom of the pallid curtains, he no longer felt the greyness of the sky glide in through the smallest chinks, and flow up to him like a cloud of dust intent on burying him. However, increasing apathy crept upon him as he lay there with shrunken arms and pallid features; his weakness augmented as the earth grew more ailing. At times, when the clouds were inky black, when the bending trees cracked, and the grass lay limp beneath the downpour like the hair of a drowned woman, he all but ceased to breathe, and seemed to be passing away, shattered by the hurricane. But at the first gleam of light, at the tiniest speck of blue between two clouds, he breathed once more and drank in the soothing calm of the drying leaves, the whitening paths, the fields quaffing their last draught of water. Albine now also longed for the sun; twenty times a day would she go to the window on the landing to scan the sky, delighted at the smallest scrap of white that she espied, but perturbed when she perceived any dusky, copper-tinted, hail-laden masses, and ever dreading lest some sable cloud should kill her dear patient. She talked of sending for Doctor Pascal, but Serge would not have it.

'To-morrow there will be sunlight on the curtains,' he said, 'and then I shall be well again.'

One evening when his condition was most alarming, Albine again gave him her hand to rest his cheek upon. But when she saw that it brought him no relief she wept to find herself powerless. Since he had fallen into the lethargy of winter she had felt too weak to drag him unaided from the nightmare in which he was struggling. She needed the assistance of spring. She herself was fading away, her arms grew cold, her breath scant; she no longer knew how to breathe life into him. For hours together she would roam about the spacious dismal room, and as she passed before the mirror and saw herself darkening in it, she thought she had become hideous.

One morning, however, as she raised his pillows, not daring to try again the broken spell of her hands, she fancied that she once more caught the first day's smile on Serge's lips.

'Open the shutters,' he said faintly.

She thought him still delirious, for only an hour previously she had seen but a gloomy sky on looking out from the landing.

'Hush, go to sleep,' she answered sadly; 'I have promised to wake you at the very first ray—— Sleep on, there's no sun out yet.'

'Yes, I can feel it, its light is there…. Open the shutters.'

III

And there, indeed, the sunlight was. When Albine had opened the shutters, behind the large curtains, the genial yellow glow once more warmed a patch of the white calico. But that which impelled Serge to sit up in bed was the sight of the shadowy bough, the branch that for him heralded the return of life. All the resuscitated earth, with its wealth of greenery, its waters, and its belts of hills, was in that greenish blur that quivered with the faintest breath of air. It no longer disturbed him; he greedily watched it rocking, and hungered for the fortified powers of the vivifying sap which to him it symbolised. Albine, happy once more, exclaimed, as she supported him in her arms: 'Ah! my dear Serge, the winter is over. Now we are saved.'

He lay down again, his eyes already brighter, and his voice clearer. 'To-morrow I shall be very strong,' he said. 'You shall draw back the curtains. I want to see everything.'

But on the morrow he was seized with childish fear. He would not hear of the windows being opened wide. 'By-and-by,' he muttered, 'later on.' He was fearful, he dreaded the first beam of light that would flash upon his eyes. Evening came on, and still he had been unable to make up his mind to look upon the sun. He remained thus all day long, his face turned towards the curtains, watching on their transparent tissue the pallor of morn, the glow of noon, the violet tint of twilight, all the hues, all the emotions of the sky. There were pictured even the quiverings of the warm air at the light stroke of a bird's wing, even the delight of earth's odours throbbing in a sunbeam. Behind that veil, behind that softened phantasm of the mighty life without, he could hear the rise of spring. He even felt stifled at times when in spite of the curtains' barrier the rush of the earth's new blood came upon him too strongly.

The following morning he was still asleep when Albine, to hasten his recovery, cried out to him:

'Serge! Serge! here's the sun!'

She swiftly drew back the curtains and threw the windows wide open. He raised himself and knelt upon his bed, oppressed, swooning, his hands tightly pressed against his breast to keep his heart from breaking. Before him stretched the broad sky, all blue, a boundless blue; and in it he washed away his sufferings, surrendering himself to it, and drinking from it sweetness and purity and youth. The bough whose shadow he had noted jutted across the window and alone set against the azure sea its vigorous growth of green; but even this was too much for his sickly fastidiousness; it seemed to him that the very swallows flying past besmeared the purity of the azure. He was being born anew. He raised little involuntary cries, as he felt himself flooded with light, assailed by waves of warm air, while a whirling, whelming torrent of life flowed within him. As last with outstretched hands he sank back upon his pillow in a swoon of joy.

What a happy, delicious day that was! The sun came in from the right, far away from the alcove. Throughout the morning Serge watched it creeping onward. He could see it coming towards him, yellow as gold, perching here and there on the old furniture, frolicking in corners, at times gliding along the ground like a strip of ribbon. It was a slow deliberate march, the approach of a fond mistress stretching her golden limbs, drawing nigh to the alcove with rhythmic motion, with voluptuous lingering, which roused intense desire. At length, towards two o'clock, the sheet of sunlight left the last armchair, climbed along the coverlet, and spread over the bed like loosened locks of hair. To its glowing fondling Serge surrendered his wasted hands: with his eyes half-closed, he could feel fiery kisses thrilling each of his fingers; he lay in a bath of light, in the embrace of a glowing orb. And when Albine leaned over smiling, 'Let me be,' he stammered, his eyes now shut; 'don't hold me so tightly. How do you manage to hold me like this in your arms?'

But the sun crept down the bed again and slowly retreated to the left; and as Serge watched it bend once more and settle on chair after chair, he bitterly regretted that he had not kept it to his breast. Albine still sat upon the side of the bed, and the pair of them, an arm round each other's neck, watched the slow paling of the sky. At times a mighty thrill seemed to make it blanch. Serge's languid eyes now wandered over it more freely and detected in it exquisite tints of which he had never dreamed. It was not all blue, but rosy blue, lilac blue, tawny blue, living flesh, vast and spotless nudity heaving like a woman's bosom in the breeze. At every glance into space he found a fresh surprise—unknown nooks, coy smiles, bewitching rounded outlines, gauzy veils which were cast over the mighty, glorious forms of goddesses in the depths of peeping paradises. And with his limbs lightened by suffering he winged his way amid that shimmering silk, that stainless down of azure. The sun sank lower and lower, the blue melted into purest gold, the sky's living flesh gleamed fairer still, and then was slowly steeped in all the hues of gloom. Not a cloud—nought but gradual disappearance, a disrobing which left behind it but a gleam of modesty on the horizon. And at last the broad sky slumbered.

'Oh, the dear baby!' exclaimed Albine, as she looked at Serge, who had fallen asleep upon her neck at the same time as the heavens.

She laid him down in bed and shut the windows. Next morning, however, they were opened at break of day. Serge could no longer live without the sunlight. His strength was growing, he was becoming accustomed to the gusts of air which sent the alcove curtains flying. Even the azure, the everlasting azure, began to pall upon him. He grew weary of being white and swanlike, of ever swimming on heaven's limpid lake. He came to wish for a pack of black clouds, some crumbling of the skies, that would break upon the monotony of all that purity. And as his health returned, he hungered for keener sensations. He now spent hours in gazing at the verdant bough: he would have liked to see it grow, expand, and throw out its branches to his very bed. It no longer satisfied him, but only roused desires, speaking to him as it did of all the trees whose deep-sounding call he could hear although their crests were hidden from his sight. An endless whispering of leaves, a chattering as of running water, a fluttering as of wings, all blended in one mighty, long-drawn, quivering voice, resounded in his ears.

'When you are able to get up,' said Albine, 'you shall sit at the window. You will see the lovely garden!'

He closed his eyes and murmured gently:

'Oh! I can see it, I hear it; I know where the trees are, where the water runs, where the violets grow.'

And then he added: 'But I can't see it clearly, I see it without any light. I must be very strong before I shall be able to get as far as the window.'

At times when Albine thought him asleep, she would vanish for hours. And on coming in again, she would find him burning with impatience, his eyes gleaming with curiosity.

'Where have you been?' he would call to her, taking hold of her arms, and feeling her skirts, her bodice, and her cheeks. 'You smell of all sorts of nice things. Ah! you have been walking on the grass?'

At this she would laugh and show him her shoes wet with dew.

'You have been in the garden! you have been in the garden!' he then exclaimed delightedly. 'I knew it. When you came in you seemed like a large flower. You have brought the whole garden in your skirt.'

He would keep her by him, inhaling her like a nosegay. Sometimes she came back with briars, leaves, or bits of wood entangled in her clothes. These he would remove and hide under his pillow like relics. One day she brought him a bunch of roses. At the sight of them he was so affected that he wept. He kissed them and went to sleep with them in his arms. But when they faded, he felt so keenly grieved that he forbade Albine to gather any more. He preferred her, said he, for she was as fresh and as balmy; and she never faded, her hands, her hair, her cheeks were always fragrant. At last he himself would send her into the garden, telling her not to come back before an hour.

'In that way,' he said, 'I shall get sunlight, fresh air, and roses till to-morrow.'

Often, when he saw her coming in out of breath, he would cross-examine her. Which path had she taken? Had she wandered among the trees, or had she gone round the meadow side? Had she seen any nests? Had she sat down behind a bush of sweetbriar, or under an oak, or in the shade of a clump of poplars? But when she answered him and tried to describe the garden to him, he would put his hand to her lips.

'No, no,' he said gently. 'It is wrong of me. I don't want to know. I would rather see it myself.'

Then he would relapse into his favourite dream of all the greenery which he could feel only a step away. For several days he lived on that dream alone. At first, he said, he had perceived the garden much more distinctly. As he gained strength, the surging blood that warmed his veins seemed to blur his dreamy imaginings. His uncertainties multiplied. He could no longer tell whether the trees were on the right, whether the water flowed at the bottom of the garden, or whether some great rocks were not piled below his windows. He talked softly of all this to himself. On the slightest indication he would rear wondrous plans, which the song of a bird, the creaking of a bough, the scent of a flower, would suddenly make him modify, impelling him to plant a thicket of lilac in one spot, and in another to place flower-beds where formerly there had been a lawn. Every hour he designed some new garden, much to the amusement of Albine, who, whenever she surprised him at it, would exclaim with a burst of laughter: 'That's not it, I assure you. You can't have any idea of it. It's more beautiful than all the beautiful things you ever saw. So don't go racking your head about it. The garden's mine, and I will give it to you. Be easy, it won't run away.'

Serge, who had already been so afraid of the light, felt considerable trepidation when he found himself strong enough to go and rest his elbows on the window-sill. Every evening he once more repeated, 'To-morrow,' and 'To-morrow.' He would turn away in his bed with a shudder when Albine came in, and would cry out that she smelt of hawthorn, that she had scratched her hands in burrowing a hole through a hedge to bring him all its odour. One morning, however, she suddenly took him up in her arms, and almost carrying him to the window, held him there and forced him to look out and see.

'What a coward you are!' she exclaimed with her fine ringing laugh.

And waving one hand all round the landscape, she repeated with an air of triumph, full of tender promise: 'The Paradou! The Paradou!'

Serge looked out upon it, speechless.

IV

A sea of verdure, in front, to right, to left, everywhere. A sea rolling its surging billows of leaves as far as the horizon, unhindered by house, or screen of wall, or dusty road. A desert, virgin, hallowed sea, displaying its wild sweetness in the innocence of solitude. The sun alone came thither, weltering in the meadows in a sheet of gold, threading the paths with the frolicsome scamper of its beams, letting its fine-spun, flaming locks droop through the trees, sipping from the springs with amber lips that thrilled the water. Beneath that flaming dust the vast garden ran riot like some delighted beast let loose at the world's very end, far from everything and free from everything. So prodigal was the luxuriance of foliage, so overflowing the tide of herbage, that from end to end it all seemed hidden, flooded, submerged. Nought could be seen but slopes of green, stems springing up like fountains, billowy masses, woodland curtains closely drawn, mantles of creepers trailing over the ground, and flights of giant boughs swooping down upon every side.

Amidst that tremendous luxuriance of vegetation even lengthy scrutiny could barely make out the bygone plan of the Paradou. In the foreground, in a sort of immense amphitheatre, must have lain the flower garden, whose fountains were now sunken and dry, its stone balustrades shattered, its flight of steps all warped, and its statues overthrown, patches of their whiteness gleaming amidst the dusky stretches of turf. Farther back, behind the blue line of a sheet of water, stretched a maze of fruit-trees; farther still rose towering woodland, its dusky, violet depths streaked with bands of light. It was a forest which had regained virginity, an endless stretch of tree-tops rising one above the other, tinged with yellowish green and pale green and vivid green, according to the variety of the species.

On the right, the forest scaled some hills, dotting them with little clumps of pine-trees, and dying away in straggling brushwood, while a huge barrier of barren rock, heaped together like the fallen wreckage of a mountain, shut out all view beyond. Flaming growths there cleaved the rugged soil, monstrous plants lay motionless in the heat, like drowsing reptiles; a silvery streak, a foamy splash that glistened in the distance like a cloud of pearls, revealed the presence of a waterfall, the source of those tranquil streams that lazily skirted the flower-garden. Lastly, on the left the river flowed through a vast stretch of meadowland, where it parted into four streamlets which winded fitfully beneath the rushes, between the willows, behind the taller trees. And far away into the distance grassy patches prolonged the lowland freshness, forming a landscape steeped in bluish haze, where a gleam of daylight slowly melted into the verdant blue of sunset. The Paradou—its flower-garden, forest, rocks, streams, and meadows—filled the whole breadth of sky.

'The Paradou!' stammered Serge, stretching out his arms as if to clasp the entire garden to his breast.

He tottered, and Albine had to seat him in an armchair. There he sat for two whole hours intently gazing, without opening his lips, his chin resting on his hands. At times his eyelids fluttered and a flush rose to his cheeks. Slowly he looked, profoundly amazed. It was all too vast, too complex, too overpowering.

'I cannot see, I cannot understand,' he cried, stretching out his hands to Albine with a gesture of uttermost weariness.

The girl came and leant over the back of his armchair. Taking his head between her hands, she compelled him to look again, and softly said:

'It's all our own. Nobody will ever come in. When you are well again, we will go for walks there. We shall have room enough for walking all our lives. We'll go wherever you like. Where would you like to go?'

He smiled.

'Oh! not far,' he murmured. 'The first day only two steps or so beyond the door. I should surely fall—— See, I'll go over there, under that tree close to the window.'

But she resumed: 'Would you like to go into the flower-garden, the parterre? You shall see the roses—they have over-run everything, even the old paths are all covered with them. Or would you like the orchard better? I can only crawl into it on my hands and knees, the boughs are so bowed down with fruit. But we'll go even farther if you feel strong enough. We'll go as far as the forest, right into the depths of shade, far, far away; so far that we'll sleep out there when night steals over us. Or else, some morning, we can climb up yonder to the summit of those rocks. You'll see the plants which make me quake; you'll see the springs, such a shower of water! What fun it will be to feel the spray all over our faces!... But if you prefer to walk along the hedges, beside a brook, we must go round by the meadows. It is so nice under the willows in the evening, at sunset. One can lie down on the grass and watch the little green frogs hopping about on the rushes.'

'No, no,' said Serge, 'you weary me, I don't want to go so far.... I will only go a couple of steps, that will be more than enough.'

'Even I,' she still continued, 'even I have not yet been able to go everywhere. There are many nooks I don't know. I have walked and walked in it for years, and still I feel sure there are unknown spots around, places where the shade must be cooler and the turf softer. Listen, I have always fancied there must be one especially in which I should like to live for ever. I know it's somewhere; I must have passed it by, or perhaps it's hidden so far away that I have never even got as far, with all my rambles. But we'll look for it together, Serge, won't we? and live there.'

'No, no, be quiet,' stammered the young man. 'I don't understand what you are saying. You're killing me.'

For a moment she let him sob in her arms. It troubled and grieved her that she could find no words to soothe him.

'Isn't the Paradou as beautiful, then, as you fancied it?' she asked at last.

He raised his face and answered:

'I don't know. It was quite little, and now it is ever growing bigger and bigger—— Take me away, hide me.'

She led him back to bed, soothing him like a child, lulling him with a fib.

'There, there! it's not true, there is no garden. It was only a story that I told you. Go, sleep in peace.'

V

Every day in this wise she made him sit at the window during the cool hours of morning. He would now attempt to take a few steps, leaning the while on the furniture. A rosy tint appeared upon his cheeks, and his hands began to lose their waxy transparency. But, while he thus regained health, his senses remained in a state of stupor which reduced him to the vegetative life of some poor creature born only the day before. Indeed, he was nothing but a plant; his sole perception was that of the air which floated round him. He lacked the blood necessary for the efforts of life, and remained, as it were, clinging to the soil, imbibing all the sap he could. It was like a slow hatching in the warm egg of springtide. Albine, remembering certain remarks of Doctor Pascal, felt terrified at seeing him remain in this state, 'innocent,' dull- witted like a little boy. She had heard it said that certain maladies left insanity behind them. And she spent hours in gazing at him and trying her utmost, as mothers do, to make him smile. But as yet he had not laughed. When she passed her hand across his eyes, he never saw, he never followed the shadow. Even when she spoke to him, he barely turned his head in the direction whence the sound came. She had but one consolation: he thrived splendidly, he was quite a handsome child.

For another whole week she lavished the tenderest care on him. She patiently waited for him to grow. And as she marked various symptoms of awakening perception, her fears subsided and she began to think that time might make a man of him. When she touched him now he started slightly. Another time, one night, he broke into a feeble laugh. On the morrow, when she had seated him at the window, she went down into the garden, and ran about in it, calling to him the while. She vanished under the trees, flitted across the sunny patches, and came back breathless and clapping her hands. At first his wavering eyes failed to perceive her. But as she started off again, perpetually playing at hide-and-seek, reappearing behind every other bush, he was at last able to follow the white gleam of her skirt; and when she suddenly came forward and stood with upraised face below his window, he stretched out his arms and seemed anxious to go down to her. But she came upstairs again, and embraced him proudly: 'Ah! you saw me, you saw me!' she cried. 'You would like to come into the garden with me, would you not?—— If you only knew how wretched you have made me these last few days, with your stupid ways, never seeing me or hearing me!'

He listened to her, but apparently with some slight sensation of pain that made him bend his neck in a shrinking way.

'You are better now, however,' she went on. 'Well enough to come down whenever you like—— Why don't you say anything? Have you lost your tongue? Oh, what a baby! Why, I shall have to teach him how to talk!'

And thereupon she really did amuse herself by telling him the names of the things he touched. He could only stammer, reiterating the syllables, and failing to utter a single word plainly. However, she began to walk him about the room, holding him up and leading him from the bed to the window—quite a long journey. Two or three times he almost fell on the way, at which she laughed. One day he fairly sat down on the floor, and she had all the trouble in the world to get him up on his feet again. Then she made him undertake the round of the room, letting him rest by the way on the sofa and the chairs—a tour round a little world which took up a good hour. At last he was able to venture on a few steps alone. She would stand before him with outstretched hands, and move backwards, calling him, so that he should cross the room in search of her supporting arms. If he sulked and refused to walk, she would take the comb from her hair and hold it out to him like a toy. Then he would come to her and sit still in a corner for hours, playing with her comb, and gently scratching his hands with its teeth.

At last one morning she found him up. He had already succeeded in opening one of the shutters, and was attempting to walk about without leaning on the furniture.

'Good gracious, we are active this morning!' she exclaimed gleefully. 'Why, he will be jumping out of the window to-morrow if he has his own way —— So you are quite strong now, eh?'

Serge's answer was a childish laugh. His limbs were regaining the strength of adolescence, but more perceptive sensations remained unroused. He spent whole afternoons in gazing out on the Paradou, pouting like a child that sees nought but whiteness and hears but the vibration of sounds. He still retained the ignorance of urchinhood—his sense of touch as yet so innocent that he failed to tell Albine's gown from the covers of the old armchairs. His eyes still stared wonderingly; his movements still displayed the wavering hesitation of limbs which scarce knew how to reach their goal; his state was one of incipient, purely instinctive existence into which entered no knowledge of surroundings. The man was not yet born within him.

'That's right, you'll act the silly, will you?' muttered Albine. 'We'll see.'

She took off her comb, and held it out to him.

'Will you have my comb?' she said. 'Come and fetch it.'

When she had got him out of the room, by retreating before him all the way, she put her arm round his waist and helped him down each stair, amusing him while she put her comb back, even tickling his neck with a lock of her hair, so that he remained unaware that he was going downstairs. But when he was in the hall, he became frightened at the darkness of the passage.

'Just look!' she cried, throwing the door wide open.

It was like a sudden dawn, a curtain of shadow snatched aside, revealing the joyousness of early day. The park spread out before them verdantly limpid, freshly cool and deep as a spring. Serge, entranced, lingered upon the threshold, with a hesitating desire to feel that luminous lake with his foot.

'One would think you were afraid of wetting yourself,' said Albine. 'Don't be frightened, the ground is safe enough.'

He had ventured to take one step, and was astonished at encountering the soft resistance of the gravel. The first touch of the soil gave him a shock; life seemed to rebound within him and to set him for a moment erect, with expanding frame, while he drew long breaths.

'Come now, be brave,' insisted Albine. 'You know you promised me to take five steps. We'll go as far as the mulberry tree there under the window —— There you can rest.'

It took him a quarter of an hour to make those five steps. After each effort he stopped as if he had been obliged to tear up roots that held him to the ground.

The girl, pushing him along, said with a laugh: 'You look just like a walking tree.'

Having placed him with his back leaning against the mulberry tree, in the rain of sunlight falling from its boughs, she bounded off and left him, calling out to him that he must not stir. Serge, standing there with drooping hands, slowly turned his head towards the park. Terrestrial childhood met his gaze. The pale greenery was steeped in the very milk of youth, flooded with golden brightness. The trees were still in infancy, the flowers were as tender-fleshed as babes, the streams were blue with the artless blue of lovely infantile eyes. Beneath every leaf was some token of a delightful awakening.

Serge had fixed his eyes upon a yellow breach which a wide path made in front of him amidst a dense mass of foliage. At the very end, eastward, some meadows, steeped in gold, looked like the luminous field upon which the sun would descend, and he waited for the morn to take that path and flow towards him. He could feel it coming in a warm breeze, so faint at first that it barely brushed across his skin, but rising little by little, and growing ever brisker till he was thrilled all over. He could also taste it coming with a more and more pronounced savour, bringing the healthful acridity of the open air, holding to his lips a feast of sugary aromatics, sour fruits, and milky shoots. Further, he could smell it coming with the perfumes which it culled upon its way—the scent of earth, the scent of the shady woods, the scent of the warm plants, the scent of living animals, a whole posy of scents, powerful enough to bring on dizziness. He could likewise hear it coming with the rapid flight of a bird skimming over the grass, waking the whole garden from silence, giving voice to all it touched, and filling his ears with the music of things and beings. Finally, he could see it coming from the end of the path, from the meadows steeped in gold—yes, he could see that rosy air, so bright that it lighted the way it took with a gleaming smile, no bigger in the distance than a spot of daylight, but in a few swift bounds transformed into the very splendour of the sun. And the morn flowed up and beat against the mulberry tree against which Serge was leaning. And he himself resuscitated amidst the childhood of the morn.

'Serge! Serge!' cried Albine, lost to sight behind the high shrubs of the flower garden. 'Don't be afraid, I am here.'

But Serge no longer felt frightened. He was being born anew in the sunshine, in that pure bath of light which streamed upon him. He was being born anew at five-and-twenty, his senses hurriedly unclosing, enraptured with the mighty sky, the joyful earth, the prodigy of loveliness spread out around him. This garden, which he knew not only the day before, now afforded him boundless delight. Everything filled him with ecstasy, even the blades of grass, the pebbles in the paths, the invisible puffs of air that flitted over his cheeks. His whole body entered into possession of this stretch of nature; he embraced it with his limbs, he drank it in with his lips, he inhaled it with his nostrils, he carried it in his ears and hid it in the depths of his eyes. It was his own. The roses of the flower garden, the lofty boughs of the forest, the resounding rocks of the waterfall, the meadows which the sun planted with blades of light, were his. Then he closed his eyes and slowly reopened them that he might enjoy the dazzle of a second wakening.

'The birds have eaten all the strawberries,' said Albine disconsolately, as she ran up to him. 'See, I have only been able to find these two!'

But she stopped short a few steps away, heart-struck and gazing at Serge with rapturous astonishment. 'How handsome you are!' she cried.

She drew a little nearer; then stood there, absorbed in her contemplation, and murmuring: 'I had never, never seen you before.'

He had certainly grown taller. Clothed in a loose garment, he stood erect, still somewhat slender, with finely moulded limbs, square chest, and rounded shoulders. His head, slightly thrown back, was poised upon a flexible and snowy neck, rimmed with brown behind. Health and strength and power were on his face. He did not smile, his expression was that of repose, with grave and tender mouth, firm cheeks, large nose, and grey, clear, commanding eyes. The long locks that thickly covered his head fell upon his shoulders in jetty curls; while a slender growth of hair, through which gleamed his white skin, curled upon his upper lip and chin.

'Oh! how handsome, how handsome you are!' lingeringly repeated Albine, crouching at his feet and gazing up at him with loving eyes. 'But why are you sulking with me? Why don't you speak to me?'

Still he stood there and made no answer. His eyes were far away; he never even saw that child at his feet. He spoke to himself in the sunlight, and said: 'How good the light is!'

That utterance sounded like a vibration of the sunlight itself. It fell amid the silence in the faintest of whispers like a musical sigh, a quiver of warmth and of life. For several days Albine had never heard his voice, and now, like himself, it had altered. It seemed to her to course through the park more sweetly than the melody of birds, more imperiously than the wind that bends the boughs. It reigned, it ruled. The whole garden heard it, though it had been but a faint and passing breath, and the whole garden was thrilled with the joyousness it brought.

'Speak to me,' implored Albine. 'You have never spoken to me like that. When you were upstairs in your room, when you were not dumb, you talked the silly prattle of a child. How is it I no longer know your voice? Just now I thought it had come down from the trees, that it reached me from every part of the garden, that it was one of those deep sighs that used to worry me at night before you came. Listen, everything is keeping silence to hear you speak again.'

But still he failed to recognise her presence. Tenderer grew her tones. 'No, don't speak if it tires you. Sit down beside me, and we will remain here on the grass till the sun wanes. And look, I have found two strawberries. Such trouble I had too! The birds eat up everything. One's for you, both if you like; or we can halve them, and taste each of them. You'll thank me, and then I shall hear you.'

But he would not sit down, he refused the strawberries, which Albine pettishly threw away. She did not open her lips again. She would rather have seen him ill, as in those earlier days when she had given him her hand for a pillow, and had felt him coming back to life beneath the cooling breath she blew upon his face. She cursed the returning health which now made him stand in the light like a young unheeding god. Would he be ever thus then, with never a glance for her? Would he never be further healed, and at last see her and love her? And she dreamed of once again being his healer, of accomplishing by the sole power of her little hands the cure of the second childhood in which he remained. She could clearly see that there was no spark in the depths of his grey eyes, that his was but a pallid beauty like that of the statues which had fallen among the nettles of the flower-garden. She rose and clasped him, breathing on his neck to rouse him. But that morning Serge never even felt the breath that lifted his silky beard. The sun got low, it was time to go indoors. On reaching his room, Albine burst into tears.

From that morning forward the invalid took a short walk in the garden every day. He went past the mulberry tree, as far as the edge of the terrace, where a wide flight of broken steps descended to the flowery parterre. He grew accustomed to the open air, each bath of sunlight brought him fresh vigour. A young chestnut tree, which had sprung from some fallen nut between two stones of the balustrade, burst the resin of its buds, and unfolded its leafy fans with far less vigour than he progressed. One day, indeed, he even attempted to descend the steps, but in this his strength failed him, and he sat down among the dane-wort which had grown up between the cracks in the stone flags. Below, to the left, he could see a small wood of roses. It was thither that he dreamt of going.

'Wait a little longer,' said Albine. 'The scent of the roses is too strong for you yet. I have never been able to sit long under the rose-trees without feeling exhausted, light-headed, with a longing to cry. Don't be afraid, I will some day lead you to the rose-trees, and I shall surely weep among them, for you make me very sad.'

VI

One morning she at last succeeded in helping him to the foot of the steps, trampling down the grass before him with her feet, and clearing a way for him through the briars, whose supple arms barred the last few yards. Then they slowly entered the wood of roses. It was indeed a very wood, with thickets of tall standard roses throwing out leafy clumps as big as trees, and enormous rose bushes impenetrable as copses of young oaks. Here, formerly, there had been a most marvellous collection of plants. But since the flower garden had been left in abandonment, everything had run wild, and a virgin forest had arisen, a forest of roses over-running the paths, crowded with wild offshoots, so mingled, so blended, that roses of every scent and hue seemed to blossom on the same stem. Creeping roses formed mossy carpets on the ground, while climbing roses clung to others like greedy ivy plants, and ascended in spindles of verdure, letting a shower of their loosened petals fall at the lightest breeze. Natural paths coursed through the wood—narrow footways, broad avenues, enchanting covered walks in which one strolled in the shade and scent. These led to glades and clearings, under bowers of small red roses, and between walls hung with tiny yellow ones. Some sunny nooks gleamed like green silken stuff embroidered with bright patterns; other shadier corners offered the seclusion of alcoves and an aroma of love, the balmy warmth, as it were, of a posy languishing on a woman's bosom. The rose bushes had whispering voices too. And the rose bushes were full of songbirds' nests.

'We must take care not to lose ourselves,' said Albine, as she entered the wood. 'I did lose myself once, and the sun had set before I was able to free myself from the rose bushes which caught me by the skirt at every step.'

They had barely walked a few minutes, however, before Serge, worn out with fatigue, wished to sit down. He stretched himself upon the ground, and fell into deep slumber. Albine sat musing by his side. They were on the edge of a glade, near a narrow path which stretched away through the wood, streaked with flashes of sunlight, and, through a small round blue gap at its far end, revealed the sky. Other little paths led from the clearing into leafy recesses. The glade was formed of tall rose bushes rising one above the other with such a wealth of branches, such a tangle of thorny shoots, that big patches of foliage were caught aloft, and hung there tent-like, stretching out from bush to bush. Through the tiny apertures in the patches of leaves, which were suggestive of fine lace, the light filtered like impalpable sunny dust. And from the vaulted roof hung stray branches, chandeliers, as it were, thick clusters suspended from green thread-like stems, armfuls of flowers that reached to the ground, athwart some rent in the leafy ceiling, which trailed around like a tattered curtain.

Albine meanwhile was gazing at Serge asleep. She had never seen him so utterly prostrated in body as now, his hands lying open on the turf, his face deathly. So dead indeed he was to her that she thought she could kiss his face without his even feeling it. And sadly, absently, she busied her hands with shredding all the roses within her reach. Above her head drooped an enormous cluster which brushed against her hair, set roses on her twisted locks, her ears, her neck, and even threw a mantle of the fragrant flowers across her shoulders. Higher up, under her fingers, other roses rained down with large and tender petals exquisitely formed, which in hue suggested the faintly flushing purity of a maiden's bosom. Like a living snowfall these roses already hid her feet in the grass. And they climbed her knees, covered her skirt, and smothered her to her waist; while three stray petals, which had fluttered on to her bodice, just above her bosom, there looked like three glimpses of her bewitching skin.

'Oh! the lazy fellow!' she murmured, feeling bored and picking up two handfuls of roses, which she flung in Serge's face to wake him.

He did not stir, however, but still lay there with the roses on his eyes and mouth. This made Albine laugh. She stooped down, and with her whole heart kissed both his eyes and his mouth, blowing as she kissed to drive the rose petals away; but they remained upon his lips, and she broke into still louder laughter, intensely amused at this flowery caressing.

Serge slowly raised himself. He gazed at her with amazement, as if startled at finding her there.

'Who are you? where do you come from? what are you doing here beside me?' he asked her. And still she smiled, transported with delight at marking this awakening of his senses. Then he seemed to remember something, and continued with a gesture of happy confidence:

'I know, you are my love, flesh of my flesh, you are waiting for me that we may be one for ever. I was dreaming of you. You were in my breast, and I gave you my blood, my muscles, my bones. I felt no pain. You took half my heart so tenderly that I experienced keen inward delight at thus dividing myself. I sought all that was best and most beautiful within me to give it to you. You might have carried off everything, and still I should have thanked you. And I woke when you went out of me. You left through my eyes and mouth; ay, I felt it. You were all warm, all fragrant, so sweet that it was the thrill from you that has made me awake.'

Albine listened to his words with ecstasy. At last he saw her; at last his birth was accomplished, his cure begun. With outstretched hands she begged him to go on.

'How have I managed to live without you?' he murmured. 'No, I did not live, I was like a slumbering animal. And now you are mine! and you are no one but myself! Listen, you must never leave me; for you are my very breath, and in leaving me you would rob me of my life. We will remain within ourselves. You will be mine even as I shall be yours. Should I ever forsake you, may I be accursed, may my body wither like a useless and noxious weed!'

He caught hold of her hands, and exclaimed in a voice quivering with admiration: 'How beautiful you are!'

In the falling dust of sunshine Albine's skin looked milky white, scarce gilded here and there by the sunny sheen. The shower of roses around and on her steeped her in pinkness.

Her fair hair, loosely held together by her comb, decked her head as with a setting planet whose last bright sparks shone upon the nape of her neck. She wore a white gown; her arms, her throat, her stainless skin bloomed unabashed as a flower, musky with a goodly fragrance. Her figure was slender, not too tall, but supple as a snake's, with softly rounded, voluptuously expanding outlines, in which the freshness of childhood mingled with womanhood's nascent charms. Her oval face, with its narrow brow and rather full mouth, beamed with the tender living light of her blue eyes. And yet she was grave, too, her cheeks unruffled, her chin plump—as naturally lovely as are the trees.

'And how I love you!' said Serge, drawing her to himself.

They were wholly one another's now, clasped in each other's arms! They did not kiss, but held each other round the waist, cheek to cheek, united, dumb, delighted with their oneness. Around them bloomed the roses with a mad, amorous blossoming, full of crimson and rosy and white laughter. The living, opening flowers seemed to bare their very bosoms. Yellow roses were there showing the golden skin of barbarian maidens: straw-coloured roses, lemon-coloured roses, sun-coloured roses—every shade of the necks which are ambered by glowing skies. Then there was skin of softer hue: among the tea roses, bewitchingly moist and cool, one caught glimpses of modest, bashful charms, with skin as fine as silk tinged faintly with a blue network of veins. Farther on all the smiling life of the rose expanded: there was the blush white rose, barely tinged with a dash of carmine, snowy as the foot of a maid dabbling in a spring; there was the silvery pink, more subdued than even the glow with which a youthful arm irradiates a wide sleeve; there was the clear, fresh rose, in which blood seemed to gleam under satin as in the bare shoulders of a woman bathed in light; and there was the bright pink rose with its buds like the nipples of virgin bosoms, and its opening flowers that suggested parted lips, exhaling warm and perfumed breath. And the climbing roses, the tall cluster roses with their showers of white flowers, clothed all these others with the lacework of their bunches, the innocence of their flimsy muslin; while, here and there, roses dark as the lees of wine, sanguineous, almost black, showed amidst the bridal purity like passion's wounds. Verily, it was like a bridal—the bridal of the fragrant wood, the virginity of May led to the fertility of July and August; the first unknowing kiss culled like a nosegay on the wedding morn. Even in the grass, moss roses, clad in close-fitting garments of green wool, seemed to be awaiting the advent of love. Flowers rambled all along the sun-streaked path, faces peeped out everywhere to court the passing breezes. Bright were the smiles under the spreading tent of the glade. Not a flower that bloomed the same: the roses differed in the fashion of their wooing. Some, shy and blushing, would show but a glimpse of bud, while others, panting and wide open, seemed consumed with infatuation for their persons. There were pert, gay little things that filed off, cockade in cap; there were huge ones, bursting with sensuous charms, like portly, fattened-up sultanas; there were impudent hussies, too, in coquettish disarray, on whose petals the white traces of the powder-puff could be espied; there were virtuous maids who had donned low-necked garb like demure *bourgeoises*; and aristocratic ladies, graceful and original, who contrived attractive deshabilles. And the cup-like roses offered their perfume as in precious crystal; the drooping, urn-shaped roses let it drip drop by drop; the round, cabbage-like roses exhaled it with the even breath of slumbering flowers; while the budding roses tightly locked their petals and only sent forth as yet the faint sigh of maidenhood.

'I love you, I love you,' softly repeated Serge.

Albine, too, was a large rose, a pallid rose that had opened since the morning. Her feet were white, her arms were rosy pink, her neck was fair of skin, her throat bewitchingly veined, pale and exquisite. She was fragrant, she proffered lips which offered as in a coral cup a perfume that was yet faint and cool. Serge inhaled that perfume, and pressed her to his breast. Albine laughed.

The ring of that laugh, which sounded like a bird's rhythmic notes, enraptured Serge.

'What, that lovely song is yours?' he said. 'It is the sweetest I ever heard. You are indeed my joy.'

Then she laughed yet more sonorously, pouring forth rippling scales of high-pitched, flute-like notes that melted into deeper ones. It was an endless laugh, a long-drawn cooing, then a burst of triumphant music celebrating the delight of awakening love. And everything—the roses, the fragrant wood, the whole of the Paradou—laughed in that laugh of woman just born to beauty and to love. Till now the vast garden had lacked one charm—a winning voice which should prove the living mirth of the trees, the streams, and the sunlight. Now the vast garden was endowed with that charm of laughter.

'How old are you?' asked Albine, when her song had ended in a faint expiring note.

'Nearly twenty-six,' Serge answered.

She was amazed. What! he was twenty-six! He, too, was astonished at having made that answer so glibly, for it seemed to him that he had not yet lived a day—an hour.

'And how old are you?' he asked in his turn.

'Oh, I am sixteen.'

Then she broke into laughter again, quivering from head to foot, repeating and singing her age. She laughed at her sixteen years with a fine-drawn laugh that flowed on with rhythmic trilling like a streamlet. Serge scanned her closely, amazed at the laughing life that transfigured her face. He scarcely knew her now with those dimples in her cheeks, those bow-shaped lips between which peeped the rosy moistness of her mouth, and those eyes blue like bits of sky kindling with the rising of the sun. As she threw back her head, she sent a glow of warmth through him.

He put out his hand, and fumbled mechanically behind her neck.

'What do you want?' she asked. And suddenly remembering, she exclaimed: 'My comb! my comb! that's it.'

She gave him her comb, and let fall her heavy tresses. A cloth of gold suddenly unrolled and clothed her to her hips. Some locks which flowed down upon her breast gave, as it were a finishing touch to her regal raiment. At the sight of that sudden blaze, Serge uttered an exclamation; he kissed each lock, and burned his lips amidst that sunset-like refulgence.

But Albine now relieved herself of her long silence, and chatted and questioned unceasingly.

'Oh, how wretched you made me! You no longer took any notice of me, and day after day I found myself useless and powerless, worried out of my wits like a good-for-nothing.... And yet the first few days I had done you good. You saw me and spoke to me.... Do you remember when you were

136

lying down, and went to sleep on my shoulder, and murmured that I did you good?'

'No!' said Serge, 'no, I don't remember it. I had never seen you before. I have only just seen you for the first time—lovely, radiant, never to be forgotten.'

She clapped her hands impatiently, exclaiming: 'And my comb? You must remember how I used to give you my comb to keep you quiet when you were a little child? Why, you were looking for it just now.'

'No, I don't remember. Your hair is like fine silk. I have never kissed your hair before.'

At this, with some vexation, she recounted certain particulars of his convalescence in the room with the blue ceiling. But he only laughed at her, and at last closed her lips with his hand, saying with anxious weariness: 'No, be quiet, I don't know; I don't want to know any more…. I have only just woke up, and found you there, covered with roses. That is enough.'

And he drew her once more towards him and held her there, dreaming aloud, and murmuring: 'Perhaps I have lived before. It must have been a long, long time ago…. I loved you in a painful dream. You had the same blue eyes, the same rather long face, the same youthful mien. But your hair was carefully hidden under a linen cloth, and I never dared to remove that cloth, because your locks seemed to me fearsome and would have made me die. But to-day your hair is the very sweetness of yourself. It preserves your scent, and when I kiss it, when I bury my face in it like this, I drink in your very life.'

He kept on passing the long curls through his hands, and pressing them to his lips, as if to squeeze from them all Albine's blood. And after an interval of silence, he continued: 'It's strange, before one's birth, one dreams of being born…. I was buried somewhere. I was very cold. I could hear all the life of the world outside buzzing above me. But I shut my ears despairingly, for I was used to my gloomy den, and enjoyed some fearful delights in it, so that I never sought to free myself from all the earth weighing upon my chest. Where could I have been then? Who was it gave me light?'

He struggled to remember, while Albine now waited in fear and trembling lest he should really do so. Smiling, she took a handful of her hair and wound it round the young man's neck, thus fastening him to herself. This playful act roused him from his musings.

'You're right,' he said, 'I am yours, what does the rest matter? It was you, was it not, who drew me out of the earth? I must have been under this garden. What I heard were your steps rattling the little pebbles in the path. You were looking for me, you brought down upon my head the songs of the birds, the scent of the pinks, the warmth of the sun. I fancied that you would find me at last. I waited a long time for you. But I never expected that you would give yourself to me without your veil, with your hair undone—the terrible hair which has become so soft.'

He sat her on his lap, placing his face beside hers.

'Do not let us talk any more. We are alone for ever. We love each other.'

And thus in all innocence they lingered in each other's arms; for a long, long time did they remain there forgetfully. The sun rose higher; and the dust of light fell hotter from the lofty boughs. The yellow and white and crimson roses were now only a ray of their delight, a sign of their smiles to one another. They had certainly caused buds to open around them. The roses crowned their heads and threw garlands about their waists. And the scent of the roses became so penetrating, so strong with amorous emotion, that it seemed to be the scent of their own breath.

At last Serge put up Albine's hair. He raised it in handfuls with delightful awkwardness, and stuck her comb askew in the enormous knot that he had heaped upon her head. And as it happened she looked bewitching thus. Then, rising from the ground, he held out his hands to her, and supported her waist as she got up. They still smiled without speaking a word, and slowly they went down the path.

VII

Albine and Serge entered the flower garden. She was watching him with tender anxiety, fearing lest he should overtire himself; but he reassured her with a light laugh. He felt strong enough indeed to carry her whithersoever she listed. When he found himself once more in the full sunlight, he drew a sigh of content. At last he lived; he was no longer a plant subject to the terrible sufferings of winter. And how he was moved with loving gratitude! Had it been within his power, he would have spared Albine's tiny feet even the roughness of the paths; he dreamed of carrying her, clinging round his neck, like a child lulled to sleep by her mother. He already watched over her with a guardian's watchful care, thrusting aside the stones and brambles, jealous lest the breeze should waft a fleeting kiss upon those darling locks which were his alone. She on her side nestled against his shoulder and serenely yielded to his guidance.

Thus Albine and Serge strolled on together in the sunlight for the first time. A balmy fragrance floated in their wake, the very path on which the sun had unrolled a golden carpet thrilled with delight under their feet. Between the tall flowering shrubs they passed like a vision of such wondrous charm that the distant paths seemed to entreat their presence and hail them with a murmur of admiration, even as crowds hail long-expected sovereigns. They formed one sole, supremely lovely being. Albine's snowy skin was but the whiteness of Serge's browner skin. And slowly they passed along clothed with sunlight—nay, they were themselves the sun—worshipped by the low bending flowers.

A tide of emotion now stirred the Paradou to its depths. The old flower garden escorted them—that vast field bearing a century's untrammelled growth, that nook of Paradise sown by the breeze with the choicest flowers. The blissful peace of the Paradou, slumbering in the broad sunlight, prevented the degeneration of species. It could boast of a temperature ever equable, and a soil which every plant had long enriched to thrive therein in the silence of its vigour. Its vegetation was mighty, magnificent, luxuriantly untended, full of erratic growths decked with monstrous blossoming, unknown to the spade and watering-pot of gardeners. Nature left to herself, free to grow as she listed, in the depths of that solitude protected by natural shelters, threw restraint aside more heartily at each return of spring, indulged in mighty gambols, delighted in offering herself at all seasons strange nosegays not meant for any hand to pluck. A rabid fury seemed to impel her to overthrow whatever the effort of man had created; she rebelliously cast a straggling multitude of flowers over the paths, attacked the rockeries with an ever-rising tide of moss, and knotted round the necks of marble statues the flexible cords of creepers with which she threw them down; she shattered the stonework of the fountains, steps, and terraces with shrubs which burst through them; she slowly, creepingly, spread over the smallest cultivated plots, moulding them to her fancy, and planting on them, as ensign of rebellion, some wayside spore, some lowly weed which she transformed into a gigantic growth of verdure. In days gone by the parterre, tended by a master passionately fond of flowers, had displayed in its trim beds and borders a wondrous wealth of choice blossoms. And the same plants could still be found; but perpetuated, grown into such numberless families, and scampering in such mad fashion throughout the whole garden, that the place was now all helter-skelter riot to its very walls, a very den of debauchery, where intoxicated nature had hiccups of verbena and pinks.

Though to outward seeming Albine had yielded her weaker self to the guidance of Serge, to whose shoulder she clung, it was she who really led him. She took him first to the grotto. Deep within a clump of poplars and willows gaped a cavern, formed by rugged bits of rocks which had fallen over a basin where tiny rills of water trickled between the stones. The grotto was completely lost to sight beneath the onslaught of vegetation. Below, row upon row of hollyhocks seemed to bar all entrance with a trellis-work of red, yellow, mauve, and white-hued flowers, whose stems were hidden among colossal bronze-green nettles, which calmly exuded blistering poison. Above them was a mighty swarm of creepers which leaped aloft in a few bounds; jasmines starred with balmy flowers; wistarias with delicate lacelike leaves; dense ivy, dentated and resembling varnished metal; lithe honeysuckle, laden with pale coral sprays; amorous clematideae, reaching out arms all tufted with white aigrettes. And among them twined yet slenderer plants, binding them more and more closely together, weaving them into a fragrant woof. Nasturtium, bare and green of skin, showed open mouths of ruddy gold; scarlet runners, tough as whipcord, kindled here and there a fire of gleaming sparks; convolvuli opened their heart-shaped leaves, and with thousands of little bells rang a silent peal of exquisite colours; sweetpeas, like swarms of settling butterflies, folded tawny or rosy wings, ready to be borne yet farther away by the first breeze. It was all a wealth of leafy locks, sprinkled with a shower of flowers, straying away in wild dishevelment, and suggesting the head of some giantess thrown back in a spasm of passion, with a streaming of magnificent hair, which spread into a pool of perfume.

'I have never dared to venture into all that darkness,' Albine whispered to Serge.

He urged her on, carried her over the nettles; and as a great boulder barred the way into the grotto, he held her up for a moment in his arms so that she might be able to peer through the opening that yawned at a few feet from the ground.

'A marble woman,' she whispered, 'has fallen full length into the stream. The water has eaten her face away.'

Then he, too, in his turn wanted to look, and pulled himself up. A cold breeze played upon his cheeks. In the pale light that glided through the hole, he saw the marble woman lying amidst the reeds and the duckweed. She was naked to the waist. She must have been drowning there for the last hundred years. Some grief had probably flung her into that spring where she was slowly committing suicide. The clear water which flowed over her had worn her face into a smooth expanse of marble, a mere white surface without a feature; but her breasts, raised out of the water by what appeared an effort of her neck, were still perfect and lifelike, throbbing even yet with the joys of some old delight.

'She isn't dead yet,' said Serge, getting down again. 'One day we will come and get her out of there.'

But Albine shuddered and led him away. They passed out again into the sunlight and the rank luxuriance of beds and borders. They wandered through a field of flowers capriciously, at random. Their feet trod a carpet of lovely dwarf plants, which had once neatly fringed the walks, and now spread about in wild profusion. In succession they passed ankle-deep through the spotted silk of soft rose catchflies, through the tufted satin of feathered pinks, and the blue velvet of forget-me-nots, studded with melancholy little eyes. Further on they forced their way through giant mignonette, which rose to their knees like a bath of perfume; then they turned through a patch of lilies of the valley in order that they might spare an expanse of violets, so delicate-looking that they feared to hurt them. But soon they found themselves surrounded on all sides by violets, and so with wary, gentle steps they passed over their fresh fragrance inhaling the very breath of springtide. Beyond the violets, a mass of lobelias spread out like green wool gemmed with pale mauve. The softly shaded stars of globularia, the blue cups of nemophila, the yellow crosses of saponaria, the white and purple ones of sweet rocket, wove patches of rich tapestry, stretching onward and onward, a fabric of royal luxury, so that the young couple might enjoy the delights of that first walk together without fatigue. But the violets ever reappeared; real seas of violets that rolled all round them, shedding the sweetest perfumes beneath their feet and wafting in their wake the breath of their leaf-hidden flowerets.

Albine and Serge quite lost themselves. Thousands of loftier plants towered up in hedges around them, enclosing narrow paths which they found it delightful to thread. These paths twisted and turned, wandered maze-like through dense thickets. There were ageratums with sky-blue tufts of bloom; woodruffs with soft musky perfume; brazen-throated mimuluses, blotched with bright vermilion; lofty phloxes, crimson and violet, throwing up distaffs of flowers for the breezes to spin; red flax with sprays as fine as hair; chrysanthemums like full golden moons, casting short faint rays, white and violet and rose, around them. The young couple surmounted all the obstacles that lay in their path and continued their way betwixt the walls of verdure. To the right of them sprang up the slim fraxinella, the centranthus draped with snowy blossoms, and the greyish hounds-tongue, in each of whose tiny flowercups gleamed a dewdrop. To their left was a long row of columbines of every variety; white ones, pale rose ones, and some of deep violet hues, almost black, that seemed to be in mourning, the blossoms that drooped from their lofty, branching stems being plaited and goffered like crape. Then, as they advanced further on, the character of the hedges changed. Giant larkspurs thrust up their flower-rods, between the dentated foliage of which gaped the mouths of tawny snapdragons, while the schizanthus reared its scanty leaves and fluttering blooms, that looked like butterflies' wings of sulphur hue splashed with soft lake. The blue bells of campanulae swayed aloft, some of them even over the tall asphodels, whose golden stems served as their steeples. In one corner was a giant fennel that reminded one of a lace- dressed lady spreading out a sunshade of sea-green satin. Then the pair suddenly found their way blocked. It was impossible to advance any further; a mass of flowers, a huge sheaf of plants stopped all progress. Down below, a mass of brank-ursine formed as it were a pedestal, from the midst of which sprang scarlet geum, rhodanthe with stiff petals, and clarkia with great white carved crosses, that looked like the insignia of some barbarous order. Higher up still, bloomed the rosy viscaria, the yellow leptosiphon, the white colinsia, and the lagurus, whose dusty green bloom contrasted with the glowing colours around it. Towering over all these growths scarlet foxgloves and blue lupins, rising in slender columns, formed a sort of oriental rotunda gleaming vividly with crimson and azure; while at the very summit, like a surmounting dome of dusky copper, were the ruddy leaves of a colossal castor-bean.

As Serge reached out his hands to try to force a passage, Albine stopped him and begged him not to injure the flowers. 'You will break the stems and crush the leaves,' she said. 'Ever since I have been here, I have always taken care to hurt none of them. Come, and I will show you the pansies.'

She made him turn and led him from the narrow paths to the centre of the parterre, where, once upon a time, great basins had been hollowed out. But these had now fallen into ruin, and were nothing but gigantic *jardinieres*, fringed with stained and cracked marble. In one of the largest of them, the wind had sown a wonderful basketful of pansies. The velvety blooms seemed almost like living faces, with bands of violet hair, yellow eyes, paler tinted mouths, and chins of a delicate flesh colour.

When I was younger they used to make me quite afraid,' murmured Albine. 'Look at them. Wouldn't you think that they were thousands of little faces looking up at you from the ground? And they turn, too, all in the same direction. They might be a lot of buried dolls thrusting their heads out of the ground.'

She led him still further on. They went the round of all the other basins. In the next one a number of amaranthuses had sprung up, raising monstrous crests which Albine had always shrunk from touching, such was their resemblance to big bleeding caterpillars. Balsams of all colours, now straw-coloured, now the hue of peach-blossom, now blush-white, now grey like flax, filled another basin where their seed pods split with little snaps. Then in the midst of a ruined fountain, there flourished a colony of splendid carnations. White ones hung over the moss-covered rims, and flaked ones thrust a bright medley of blossom between the chinks of the marble; while from the mouth of the lion, whence formerly the water-jets had spurted, a huge crimson clove now shot out so vigorously that the decrepit beast seemed to be spouting blood. Near by, the principal piece of ornamental water, a lake, on whose surface swans had glided, had now become a thicket of lilacs, beneath whose shade stocks and verbenas and day-lilies screened their delicate tints, and dozed away, all redolent of perfume.

'But we haven't seen half the flowers yet,' said Albine, proudly. 'Over yonder there are such huge ones that I can quite bury myself amongst them like a partridge in a corn-field.'

They went thither. They tripped down some broad steps, from whose fallen urns still flickered the violet fires of the iris. All down the steps streamed gilliflowers, like liquid gold. The sides were flanked with thistles, that shot up like candelabra, of green bronze, twisted and curved into the semblance of birds' heads, with all the fantastic elegance of Chinese incense-burners. Between the broken balustrades drooped tresses of stonecrop, light greenish locks, spotted as with mouldiness. Then at the foot of the steps another parterre spread out, dotted over with box-trees that were vigorous as oaks; box-trees which had once been carefully pruned and clipped into balls and pyramids and octagonal columns, but which were now revelling in unrestrained freedom of untidiness, breaking out into ragged masses of greenery, through which blue patches of sky were visible.

And Albine led Serge straight on to a spot that seemed to be the graveyard of the flower-garden. There the scabious mourned, and processions of poppies stretched out in line, with deathly odour, unfolding heavy blooms of feverish brilliance. Sad anemones clustered in weary throngs, pallid as if infected by some epidemic. Thick-set daturas spread out purplish horns, from which insects, weary of life, sucked fatal poison. Marigolds buried with choking foliage their writhing starry flowers, that already reeked of putrefaction. And there were other melancholy flowers also: fleshy ranunculi with rusty tints, hyacinths and tuberoses that exhaled asphyxia and died from their own perfume. But the cinerarias were most conspicuous, crowding thickly in half-mourning robes of violet and white. In the middle of this gloomy spot a mutilated marble Cupid still remained standing, smiling beneath the lichens which overspread his youthful nakedness, while the arm with which he had once held his bow lay low amongst the nettles.

Then Albine and Serge passed on through a rank growth of peonies, reaching to their waists. The white flowers fell to pieces as they passed, with a rain of snowy petals which was as refreshing to their hands as the heavy drops of a thunder shower. And the red ones grinned with apoplectical faces which perturbed them. Next they passed through a field of fuchsias, forming dense, vigorous shrubs that delighted them with their countless bells. Then they went on through fields of purple veronicas and others of geraniums, blazing with all the fiery tints of a brasier, which the wind seemed to be ever fanning into fresh heat. And they forced their way through a jungle of gladioli, tall as reeds, which threw up spikes of flowers that gleamed in the full daylight with all the brilliance of burning torches. They lost themselves too in a forest of sunflowers, with stalks as thick as Albine's wrist, a forest darkened by rough leaves large enough to form an infant's bed, and peopled with giant starry faces that shone like so many suns. And thence they passed into another forest, a forest of rhododendrons so teeming with blossom that the branches and leaves were completely hidden, and nothing but huge nosegays, masses of soft calyces, could be seen as far as the eye could reach.

'Come along; we have not got to the end yet,' cried Albine. 'Let us push on.'

But Serge stopped. They were now in the midst of an old ruined colonnade. Some of the columns offered inviting seats as they lay prostrate amongst primroses and periwinkles. Further away, among the columns that still remained upright, other flowers were growing in profusion. There were expanses of tulips showing brilliant streaks like painted china; expanses of calceolarias dotted with crimson and gold; expanses of zinnias like great daisies; expanses of petunias with petals like soft cambric through which rosy flesh tints gleamed; and other fields, with flowers they could not recognise spreading in carpets beneath the sun, in a motley brilliance that was softened by the green of their leaves.

'We shall never be able to see it all,' said Serge, smiling and waving his hand. 'It would be very nice to sit down here, amongst all this perfume.'

Near them there was a large patch of heliotropes, whose vanilla-like breath permeated the air with velvety softness. They sat down upon one of the fallen columns, in the midst of a cluster of magnificent lilies which had shot up there. They had been walking for more than an hour. They had wandered on through the flowers from the roses to the lilies. These offered them a calm, quiet haven after their lovers' ramble amid the perfumed solicitations of luscious honeysuckle, musky violets, verbenas that breathed out the warm scent of kisses, and tuberoses that panted with voluptuous passion. The lilies, with their tall slim stems, shot up round them like a white pavilion and sheltered them with snowy cups, gleaming only with the gold of their slender pistils. And there they rested, like betrothed children in a tower of purity; an impregnable ivory tower, where all their love was yet perfect innocence.

Albine and Serge lingered amongst the lilies till evening. They felt so happy there, and seemed to break out into a new life. Serge felt the last trace of fever leave his hands, while Albine grew quite white, with a milky whiteness untinted by any rosy hue. They were unconscious that their arms and necks and shoulders were bare, and their straying unconfined hair in nowise troubled them. They laughed merrily one at the other, with frank open laughter. The expression of their eyes retained the limpid calmness of clear spring water. When they quitted the lilies, their feelings were but those of children ten years old; it seemed to them that they had just met each other in that garden so that they might be friends for ever and amuse themselves with perpetual play. And as they returned through the parterre, the very flowers bore themselves discreetly, as though they were glad to see their childishness, and would do nothing that might corrupt them. The forests of peonies, the masses of carnations, the carpets of forget-me-nots, the curtains of clematis now steeped in the atmosphere of evening, slumbering in childlike purity akin to their own, no longer spread suggestions of voluptuousness around them. The pansies looked up at them with their little candid faces, like playfellows; and the languid mignonette, as Albine's white skirt brushed by it, seemed full of compassion, and held its breath lest it should fan their love prematurely into life.

VIII

At dawn the next day it was Serge who called Albine. She slept in a room on the upper floor. He looked up at her window and saw her throw open the shutters just as she had sprung out of bed. They laughed merrily as their eyes met.

'You must not go out to-day,' said Albine, when she came down. 'We must stay indoors and rest. To-morrow I will take you a long, long way off, to a spot where we can have a very jolly time.'

'But sha'n't we grow tired of stopping here?' muttered Serge.

'Oh, dear no! I will tell you stories.'

They passed a delightful day. The windows were thrown wide open, and all the beauty of the Paradou came in and rejoiced with them in the room. Serge now really took possession of that delightful room, where he imagined he had been born. He insisted upon seeing everything, and upon having everything explained to him. The plaster Cupids who sported round the alcove amused him so much that he mounted upon a chair to tie Albine's sash round the neck of the smallest of them, a little bit of a man who was turning somersaults with his head downward. Albine clapped her hands, and said that he looked like a cockchafer fastened by a string. Then, as though seized by an access of pity, she said, 'No, no, unfasten him. It prevents him from flying.'

But it was the Cupids painted over the doors that more particularly attracted Serge's attention. He fidgeted at not being able to make out what they were playing at, for the paintings had grown very dim. Helped by Albine, he dragged a table to the wall, and when they both had climbed upon it, Albine began to explain things to him.

'Look, now, those are throwing flowers. Under the flowers you can only see some bare legs. It seems to me that when first I came here I could make out a lady reposing there. But she has been gone for a long time now.'

They examined all the panels in turn; but they had faded to such a degree that little more could be distinguished than the knees and elbows of infants. The details which had doubtless delighted the eyes of those whose old-time passion seemed to linger round the alcove, had so completely disappeared under the influence of the fresh air, that the room, like the park, seemed restored to pristine virginity beneath the serene glory of the sun.

'Oh! they are only some little boys playing,' said Serge, as he descended from the table. 'Do you know how to play at "hot cockles"?'

There was no game that Albine did not know how to play at. But, for 'hot cockles,' at least three players are necessary, and that made them laugh. Serge protested, however, that they got on too well together ever to desire a third there, and they vowed that they would always remain by themselves.

'We are quite alone here; one cannot hear a sound,' said the young man, lolling on the couch. 'And all the furniture has such a pleasant old-time smell. The place is as snug as a nest. We ought to be very happy in this room.'

The girl shook her head gravely.

'If I had been at all timid,' she murmured, 'I should have been very much frightened at first…. That is one of the stories I want to tell you. The people in the neighbourhood told it to me. Perhaps it isn't true, but it will amuse us, at any rate.'

Then she came and sat down by Serge's side.

'It is years and years since it all happened. The Paradou belonged to a rich lord, who came and shut himself up in it with a very beautiful lady. The gates of the mansion were kept so tightly closed, and the garden walls were built so very high, that no one ever caught sight even of the lady's skirts.'

'Ah! I know,' Serge interrupted; 'the lady was never seen again.'

Then, as Albine looked at him in surprise, somewhat annoyed to find that he knew her story already, he added in a low voice, apparently a little astonished himself: 'You told me the story before, you know.'

She declared that she had never done so; but all at once she seemed to change her mind, and allowed herself to be convinced. However, that did not prevent her from finishing her tale in these words: 'When the lord went away his hair was quite white. He had all the gates barricaded up, so that no one might get inside and disturb the lady. It was in this room that she died.'

'In this room!' cried Serge. 'You never told me that! Are you quite sure that it was really in this room she died?'

Albine seemed put out. She repeated to him what every one in the neighbourhood knew. The lord had built the pavilion for the reception of this unknown lady, who looked like a princess. The servants employed at the mansion afterwards declared that he spent all his days and nights there. Often, too, they saw him in one of the walks, guiding the tiny feet of the mysterious lady towards the densest coppices. But for all the world they would never have ventured to spy upon the pair, who sometimes scoured the park for weeks together.

'And it was here she died?' repeated Serge, who felt touched with sorrow.

'And you have taken her room; you use her furniture, and you sleep in her bed.'

Albine smiled.

'Ah! well, you know, I am not timid. Besides, it is so long since it all happened. You said what a delightful room it was.'

Then they both dropped into silence, and glanced, for a moment, towards the alcove, the lofty ceiling, and the corners, steeped in grey gloom. The faded furniture seemed to speak of long past love. A gentle sigh, as of resignation, passed through the room.

'No, indeed,' murmured Serge, 'one could not feel afraid here. It is too peaceful.'

But Albine came closer to him and said: 'There is something else that only a few people know, and that is that the lord and the lady discovered in the garden a certain spot where perfect happiness was to be found, and where they afterwards spent all their time. I have been told that by a very good authority. It is a cool, shady spot, hidden away in the midst of an impenetrable jungle, and it is so marvellously beautiful that anyone who reaches it forgets all else in the world. The poor lady must have been buried there.'

'Is it anywhere about the parterre?' asked Serge curiously.

'Ah! I cannot tell, I cannot tell,' said the young girl with an expression of discouragement. 'I know nothing about it. I have searched everywhere, but I have never been able to find the least sign of that lovely clearing. It is not amongst the roses, nor the lilies, nor the violets.'

'Perhaps it is hidden somewhere away amongst those mournful-looking flowers, where you showed me the figure of a boy standing with his arm broken off.'

'No, no, indeed.'

'Perhaps, then, it is in that grotto, near that clear stream, where the great marble woman, without a face, is lying.'

'No, no.'

Albine seemed to reflect for a moment. Then, as though speaking to herself, she went on: 'As soon as ever I came here, I began to hunt for it. I spent whole days in the Paradou, and ferreted about in all the out-of-the-way green corners, to have the pleasure of sitting for an hour in that happy spot. What mornings have I not wasted in groping under the brambles and peeping into the most distant nooks of the park! Oh! I should have known it at once, that enchanting retreat, with the mighty tree that must shelter it with a canopy of foliage, with its carpet of soft silky turf, and its walls of tangled greenery, which the very birds themselves cannot penetrate.

She raised her voice, and threw one of her arms round Serge's neck, as she continued: 'Tell me, now; shall we search for it together? We shall surely find it. You, who are strong, will push aside the heavy branches, while I crawl underneath and search the brakes. When I grow weary, you can carry me; you can help me to cross the streams; and if we happen to lose ourselves, you can climb the trees and try to discover our way again. Ah! and how delightful it will be for us to sit, side by side, beneath the green canopy in the centre of the clearing! I have been told that in one minute one may there live the whole of life. Tell me, my dear Serge, shall we set off to-morrow and scour the park, from bush to bush, until we have found what we want?'

Serge shrugged his shoulders, and smiled. 'What would be the use?' he said. 'Is it not pleasant in the parterre? Don't you think we ought to remain among the flowers, instead of seeking a greater happiness that lies so far away?'

'It is there that the dead lady lies buried,' murmured Albine, falling back into her reverie. 'It was the joy of being there that killed her. The tree casts a shade, whose charm is deathly.... I would willingly die so. We would clasp one another there, and we would die, and none would ever find us again.'

'Don't talk like that,' interrupted Serge. 'You make me feel so unhappy. I would rather that we should live in the bright sunlight, far away from that fatal shade. Your words distress me, as though they urged us to some irreparable misfortune. It must be forbidden to sit beneath a tree whose shade can thus affect one.'

'Yes,' Albine gravely declared, 'it is forbidden. All the folks of the countryside have told me that it is forbidden.'

Then silence fell. Serge rose from the couch where he had been lolling, and laughed, and pretended that he did not care about stories. The sun was setting, however, before Albine would consent to go into the garden for even a few minutes. She led Serge to the left, along the enclosing wall, to a spot strewn with fragments of stone, and woodwork, and ironwork, bristling too with briars and brambles. It was the site of the old mansion, still black with traces of the fire which had destroyed the building. Underneath the briars lay rotting timbers and fire-split masonry. The spot was like a little ravined, hillocky wilderness of sterile rocks, draped with rude vegetation, clinging creepers that twined and twisted through every crevice like green serpents. The young folks amused themselves by wandering across this chaos, groping about in the holes, turning over the debris, trying to reconstruct something of the past out of the ruins before them. They did not confess their curiosity as they chased one another through the midst of fallen floorings and overturned partitions; but they were indeed, all the time, secretly pondering over the legend of those ruins, and of that lady, lovelier than day, whose silken skirt had rustled down those steps, where now lizards alone were idly crawling.

Serge ended by climbing the highest of the ruinous masses; and, looking round at the park which unfolded its vast expanse of greenery, he sought the grey form of the pavilion through the trees. Albine was standing silent by his side, serious once more.

'The pavilion is yonder, to the right,' she said at last, without waiting for Serge to ask her. 'It is the only one of the buildings that is left. You can see it quite plainly at the end of that grove of lime-trees.'

They fell into silence again; and then Albine, as though pursuing aloud the reflections which were passing through their minds, exclaimed: 'When he went to see her, he must have gone down yonder path, then past those big chestnut trees, and then under the limes. It wouldn't take him a quarter of an hour.'

Serge made no reply. But as they went home, they took the path which Albine had pointed out, past the chestnuts and under the limes. It was a path that love had consecrated. And as they walked over the grass, they seemed to be seeking footmarks, or a fallen knot of ribbon, or a whiff of ancient perfume —something that would clearly satisfy them that they were really travelling along the path that led to the joy of union.

'Wait out here,' said Albine, when they once more stood before the pavilion; 'don't come up for three minutes.'

Then she ran off merrily, and shut herself up in the room with the blue ceiling. And when she had let Serge knock at the door twice, she softly set it ajar, and received him with an old-fashioned courtesy.

'Good morrow, my dear lord,' she said as she embraced him.

This amused them extremely. They played at being lovers with childish glee. In stammering accents they would have revived the passion which had once throbbed and died there. But it was like a first effort at learning a lesson. They knew not how to kiss each other's lips, but sought each other's cheeks, and ended by dancing around each other, with shrieks of laughter, from ignorance of any other way of showing the pleasure they experienced from their mutual love.

IX

The next morning Albine was anxious to start at sunrise upon the grand expedition which she had planned the night before. She tapped her feet gleefully on the ground, and declared that they would not come back before nightfall.

'Where are you going to take me?' asked Serge.

'You will see, you will see.'

But he caught her by the hands and looked her very earnestly in the face. 'You must not be foolish, you know. I won't have you hunting for that glade of yours, or for the tree, or for the grassy couch where one droops and dies. You know that it is forbidden.'

She blushed slightly, protesting that she had no such idea in her head. Then she added: 'But if we should come across them, just by chance, you know, and without really seeking them, you wouldn't mind sitting down, would you? Else you must love me very little.'

They set off, going straight through the parterre without stopping to watch the awakening of the flowers which were all dripping after their dewy bath. The morning had a rosy hue, the smile of a beautiful child, just opening its eyes on its snowy pillow.

'Where are you taking me?' repeated Serge.

But Albine only laughed and would not answer. Then, on reaching the stream which ran through the garden at the end of the flower-beds, she halted in great distress. The water was swollen with the late rains.

'We shall never be able to get across,' she murmured. 'I can generally manage it by taking off my shoes and stockings, but, to-day, the water would reach to our waists.'

They walked for a moment or two along the bank to find some fordable point; but the girl said it was hopeless; she knew the stream quite well. Once there had been a bridge across, but it had fallen in, and had strewn the river bed with great blocks of stone, between which the water rushed along in foaming eddies.

'Get on to my back, then,' said Serge.

'No, no; I'd rather not. If you were to slip, we should both of us get a famous wetting. You don't know how treacherous those stones are.'

'Get on to my back,' repeated Serge.

She was tempted to do so. She stepped back for a spring, and then jumped up, like a boy; but she felt that Serge was tottering; and crying out that she was not safely seated, she got down again. However, after two more attempts, she managed to settle herself securely on Serge's back.

'When you are quite ready,' said the young man, laughing, 'we will start. Now, hold on tightly. We are off.'

And, with three light strides, he crossed the stream, scarcely wetting even his toes. Midway, however, Albine thought that he was slipping. She broke out into a little scream, and hugged him tightly round his neck. But he sprang forward, and carried her at a gallop over the fine sand on the other side.

'Gee up!' she cried, quite calm again, and delighted with this novel game.

He ran along with her for some distance, she clucking her tongue, and guiding him to right or left by some locks of his hair.

'Here—here we are,' she said at last, tapping him gently on the cheeks.

Then she jumped to the ground; while he, hot and perspiring, leaned against a tree to draw breath. Albine thereupon began to scold him, and threatened that she would not nurse him if he made himself ill again.

'Stuff!' he cried, 'it's done me good. When I have grown quite strong again, I will carry you about all day. But where are you taking me?'

'Here,' she said, as she seated herself beneath a huge pear-tree.

They were in the old orchard of the park. A hawthorn hedge, a real wall of greenery with here and there a gap, separated it from everything else. There was quite a forest of fruit trees, which no pruning knife had touched for a century past. Some of the trees had been strangely warped and twisted by the storms which had raged over them; while others, bossed all over with huge knots and full of deep holes, seemed only to hold on to the soil with their bark. The high branches, bent each year by weight of fruit, stretched out like big rackets; and each tree helped to keep its fellows erect. The trunks were like twisted pillars supporting a roof of greenery; and sometimes narrow cloisters, sometimes light halls were formed, while now and again the verdure swept almost to the ground and left scarcely room to pass. Round each colossus a crowd of wild and self-sown saplings had grown up, thicket-like with the entanglement of their young shoots. In the greenish light which filtered like tinted water through the foliage, in the deep silence of the mossy soil, one only heard the dull thud of the fruit as it was culled by the wind.

And there were patriarchal apricot trees that bore their great age quite bravely. Though decayed on one side, where they showed a perfect scaffolding of dead wood, they were so youthful, so full of life, that, on the other, young shoots were ever bursting through their rough bark. There were cherry trees, that formed complete towns with houses of several stories, that threw out staircases and floors of branches, big enough for half a score of families. Then there were the apple trees, with their limbs twisted like old cripples, with bark gnarled and knotted, and all stained with lichen-growth. There were also smooth pear trees, that shot up mast-like with long slender spars. And there were rosy-blossomed peach-trees that won a place amid this teeming growth as pretty maids do amidst a human crowd by dint of bright smiles and gentle persistence. Some had been formerly trained as espaliers, but they had broken down the low walls which had once supported them, and now spread abroad in wild confusion, freed from the trammels of trellis work, broken fragments of which still adhered to some of their branches. They grew just as they listed, and resembled well-bred trees, once neat and prim, which, having gone astray, now flaunted but vestiges of whilom respectability. And from tree to tree, and from bough to bough, vine branches hung in confusion. They rose like wild laughter, twined for an instant round some lofty knot, then started off again with yet more sonorous mirth, splotching all the foliage with the merry ebriety of their tendrils. Their pale sun-gilt green set a glow of bacchanalianism about the weather-worn heads of the old orchard giants.

Then towards the left were trees less thickly planted. Thin-foliaged almonds allowed the sun's rays to pass and ripen the pumpkins, which looked like moons that had fallen to the earth. Near the edge of a stream which flowed through the orchard there also grew various kinds of melons, some rough with knotty warts, some smooth and shining, as oval as the eggs of ostriches. At every step, too, progress was barred by currant bushes, showing limpid bunches of fruit, rubies in one and all of which there sparkled liquid sunlight. And hedges of raspberry canes shot up like wild brambles, while the ground was but a carpet of strawberry plants, teeming with ripe berries which exhaled a slight odour of vanilla.

But the enchanted corner of the orchard was still further to the left, near a tier of rocks which there began to soar upwards. There you found yourself in a veritable land of fire, in a natural hot-house, on which the sun fell freely. At first, you had to make your way through huge, ungainly fig trees, which stretched out grey branches like arms weary of lying still, and whose villose leather-like foliage was so dense that in order to pass one constantly had to snap off twigs that had sprouted from the old wood. Next you passed on through groves of strawberry trees with verdure like that of giant box-plants, and with scarlet berries which suggested maize plants decked out with crimson ribbon. Then there came a jungle of nettle-trees, medlars and jujube trees, which pomegranates skirted with never-fading verdure. The fruit of the latter, big as a child's fist, was scarcely set as yet; and the purple blossoms, fluttering at the ends of the branches, looked like the palpitating wings of the humming birds, which do not even bend the shoots on which they perch. Lastly, there was a forest of orange and lemon trees growing vigorously in the open air. Their straight trunks stood like rows of brown columns, while their shiny leaves showed brightly against the blue of the sky, and cast upon the ground a network of light and shadow, figuring the palms of some Indian fabric. Here there was shade beside which that of the European orchard seemed colourless, insipid; the warm joy of sunlight, softened into flying gold-dust; the glad certainty of evergreen foliage; the penetrating perfume of blossom, and the more subdued fragrance of fruit; all helping to fill the body with the soft languor of tropical lands.

'And now let us breakfast,' cried Albine, clapping her hands. 'It must be at least nine o'clock, and I am very hungry.'

She had risen from the ground. Serge confessed that he, too, would find some food acceptable.

'You goose!' she said, 'you didn't understand, then, that I brought you here to breakfast. We sha'n't die of hunger here. We can help ourselves to all there is.'

They went along under the trees, pushing aside the branches and making their way to the thickest of the fruit. Albine, who went first, turned, and in her flute-like voice asked her companion: 'What do you like best? Pears, apricots, cherries, or currants? I warn you that the pears are still green; but they are very nice all the same.'

Serge decided upon having cherries, and Albine agreed it would be as well to start with them; but when she saw him foolishly beginning to scramble up the first cherry tree he found, she made him go on for another ten minutes through a frightful entanglement of branches. The cherries on this tree, she said, were small and good for nothing; those on that were sour; those on another would not be ripe for at least a week. She knew all the trees.

'Stop, climb this one,' she said at last, as she stopped at the foot of a tree, so heavily laden with fruit that clusters of it hung down to the ground, like strings of coral beads.

Serge settled himself comfortably between two branches and began his breakfast. He no longer paid attention to Albine. He imagined she was in another tree, a few yards away, when, happening to cast his eyes towards the ground, he saw her calmly lying on her back beneath him. She had thrown herself there, and, without troubling herself to use her hands, was plucking with her teeth the cherries which dangled over her mouth.

When she saw she was discovered, she broke out into a peal of laughter, and twisted about on the grass like a fish taken from the water. And finally, crawling along on her elbows, she gradually made the circuit of the tree, snapping up the plumpest cherries as she went along.

'They tickle me so,' she cried. 'See, there's a beauty just fallen on my neck. They are so deliciously fresh and juicy. They get into my ears, my eyes, my nose, everywhere. They are much sweeter down here than up there.'

'Ah!' said Serge, laughing, 'you say that because you daren't climb up.'

She remained for a moment silent with indignation. 'Daren't!—I!—' she stammered.

Then, having gathered up her skirts, she tightly grasped the tree and pulled herself up the trunk with a single effort of her strong wrists. And afterwards she stepped lightly along the branches, scarcely using her hands to steady herself. She had all the agile nimbleness of a squirrel, and made her way onward, maintaining her equilibrium only by the swaying poise of her body. When she was quite aloft at the end of a frail branch, which shook dangerously beneath her weight, she cried; 'Now you see whether I daren't climb.'

'Come down at once,' implored Serge, full of alarm for her. 'I beg of you to come down. You will be injuring yourself.'

But she, enjoying her triumph, began to mount still higher. She crawled along to the extreme end of a branch, grasping its leaves in her hands to maintain her hold.

'The branch will break!' cried Serge, thoroughly frightened.

'Let it break,' she answered, with a laugh; 'it will save me the trouble of getting down.'

And the branch did break, but only slowly, with such deliberation that, as it gradually settled towards the ground, it let Albine slip down in very gentle fashion. She did not appear in the least degree frightened; but gave herself a shake, and said: 'That was really nice. It was quite like being in a carriage.'

Serge had jumped down from the tree to catch her in his arms. As he stood there, quite pale from fright, she laughed at him. 'One tumbles down from trees every day,' she exclaimed, 'but there is never any harm done. Look more cheerful, you great stupid! Stay, just wet your finger and rub it upon my neck. I have scratched it.'

Serge wetted his finger and touched her neck with it.

'There, I am all right again now,' she cried, as she bounded off. 'Let us play at hide and seek, shall we?'

She was the first to hide. She disappeared, and presently from the depths of the greenery, which she alone knew, and where Serge could not possibly find her, she called, 'Cuckoo, cuckoo.' But this game of hide and seek did not put a stop to the onslaught upon the fruit trees. Breakfasting went on in all the nooks and corners where the two big children sought each other. Albine, while gliding beneath the branches, would stretch out her hand to pluck a green pear or fill her skirt with apricots. Then in some of her lurking-places she would come upon such rich discoveries as would make her careless of the game, content to sit upon the ground and remain eating. Once, however, she lost sound of Serge's movements. So, in her turn, she set about seeking him; and she was surprised, almost vexed, when she discovered him under a plum- tree, of whose existence she herself had been ignorant, and whose ripe fruit had a delicious musky perfume. She soundly rated him. Did he want to eat everything himself, that he hadn't called to her to come? He pretended to know nothing about the trees, but he evidently had a very keen scent to be able to find all the good things. She was especially indignant with the poor tree itself— a stupid tree which no one had known of, and which must have sprung up in the night on purpose to put people out. As she stood there pouting, refusing to pluck a single plum, it occurred to Serge to shake the tree violently. And then a shower, a regular hail, of plums came down. Albine, standing in the midst of the downfall, received plums on her arms, plums on her neck, plums on the very tip of her nose. At this she could no longer restrain her laughter; she stood in the midst of the deluge, crying 'More! more!' amused as she was by the round bullet-like fruit which fell around her as she squatted there, with hands and mouth open, and eyes closed.

It was a morning of childish play, of wild gambols in the Paradou. Albine and Serge spent hours, scampering up and down, shouting and sporting with each other, their thoughts still all innocence. And in what a delicious spot they found themselves! Depths of greenery, with undiscoverable hiding-places; paths, along whose windings it was never possible to be serious, such greedy laughter fell from the very hedges. In this happy orchard, there was such a playful straggling of bushes, such fresh and appetising shade, such a wealth of old trees laden like kindly grandfathers with sweet dainties. Even in the depths of the recesses green with moss, beneath the broken trunks which compelled them to creep the one behind the other, in the narrow leafy alleys, the young folks never succumbed to the perilous reveries of silence. No trouble touched them in that happy wood.

And when they had grown weary of the apricot-trees and the plum-trees and the cherry-trees, they ran beneath the slender almond-trees; eating green almonds, scarcely yet as big as peas, hunting for strawberries in the grassy carpet, and regretting that the melons were not already ripe. Albine finished by running as fast as she could go, pursued by Serge, who was unable to overtake her. She rushed amongst the fig-trees, leaping over their heavy branches, and pulling off the leaves to throw them behind her in her companion's face. In a few strides she had cleared the clumps of arbutus, whose red berries she tasted on her way; and it was in the jungle of nettle- trees, medlars, and jujube-trees that Serge lost her. At first he thought she was hiding behind a pomegranate; but found that he had mistaken two clustering blossoms for the rosy roundness of her wrists. Then he scoured the plantation of orange-trees, rejoicing in their beauty and perfume, and thinking that he must have reached the abode of the fairies of the sun. In the midst of them he caught sight of Albine, who, not believing him so near her, was peering inquisitively into the green depths.

'What are you looking for?' he cried. 'You know very well that is forbidden.'

She sprang up hastily, and slightly blushed for the first time that day. Then sitting down by the side of Serge, she told him of the fine times there would be when the oranges should be ripe. The wood would then be all golden, all bright with those round stars, dotting with yellow sparks the arching green.

When at last they really set off homeward she halted at every wild-growing fruit tree, and filled her pockets with sour pears and bitter plums, saying that they world be good to eat on their way. They would prove a hundred times more enjoyable than anything they had tasted before. Serge was obliged to swallow some of them, in spite of the grimaces he made at each bite. And eventually they found themselves indoors again, tired out but feeling very happy.

X

A week later there was another expedition to the park. They had planned to extend their rambles beyond the orchard, striking out to the left through the meadows watered by the four streams. They would travel several miles over the thick grass, and they might live on fish, if they happened to lose themselves.

'I will take my knife,' said Albine, holding up a broad-bladed peasant's knife.

She crammed all kinds of things into her pockets, string, bread, matches, a small bottle of wine, some rags, a comb, and some needles. Serge took a rug, but by the time they had passed the lime-trees and reached the ruins of the chateau, he found it such an encumbrance that he hid it beneath a piece of fallen wall.

The sun was hotter than before, Albine had delayed their departure by her extensive preparations. Thus in the heat of the morning they stepped along side by side, almost quietly. They actually managed to take twenty paces at a time without pushing one another or laughing. They began to talk.

'I never can wake up,' began Albine. 'I slept so soundly last night. Did you?'

'Yes, indeed, very soundly,' replied Serge.

'What does it mean when you dream of a bird that talks to you?' the girl resumed.

'I don't know. What did your bird say to you?'

'Oh, I have forgotten. But it said all kinds of things, and many of them sounded very comical. Stop, look at that big poppy over there. You sha'n't get it, you sha'n't get it!'

And then she sprang forward; but Serge, thanks to his long legs, outstripped her and plucked the poppy, which he waved about victoriously. She stood there with lips compressed, saying nothing, but feeling a strong inclination to cry. Serge threw down the flower. Nothing else occurred to him. Then, to make his peace with her, he asked: 'Would you like me to carry you as I did the other day?'

'No, no.'

She pouted a little, but she had not gone another thirty steps, when she turned round smiling. A bramble had caught hold of her dress.

'I thought it was you who were treading on my dress purposely. It won't let me go. Come and unfasten me.'

When she was released, they walked on again, side by side, very quietly. Albine pretended that it was much more amusing to stroll along in this fashion, like steady grown-up folks. They had just reached the meadows. Far away, in front of them, stretched grassy expanses scarce broken here and there by the tender foliage of willows. The grass looked soft and downy, like velvet. It was a deep green, subsiding in the distance into lighter tints, and on the horizon assuming a bright yellow glow beneath the flaring sun. The clumps of willows right over yonder seemed like pure gold, bathed in the tremulous brilliance of the sunshine. Dancing dust tipped the blades of grass with quivering light, and as the gentle breezes swept over the free expanse, moire-like reflections appeared on the caressed and quivering herbage. In the nearer fields a multitude of little white daisies, now in swarms, now straggling, and now in groups, like holiday makers at some public rejoicing, brightly peopled the dark grass. Buttercups showed themselves, gay like little brass bells which the touch of a fly's wing would set tinkling. Here and there big lonely poppies raised fiery cups, and others, gathered together further away, spread out like vats purple with lees of wine. Big cornflowers balanced aloft their light blue caps which looked as if they would fly away at every breath of air. Then under foot there were patches of woolly feather-grass and fragrant meadow-sweet, sheets of fescue, dog's-tail, creeping-bent, and meadow grass. Sainfoin reared its long fine filaments; clover unfurled its clear green leaves, plantains brandished forests of spears, lucerne spread out in soft beds of green satin broidered with purple flowers. And all these were seen, to right, to left, in front, everywhere, rolling over the level soil, showing like the mossy surface of a stagnant sea, asleep beneath the sky which ever seemed to expand. Here and there, in the vast expanse, the vegetation was of a limpid blue, as though it reflected the colour of the heavens.

Albine and Serge stepped along over the meadow-lands, with the grass reaching to their knees. It was like wading through a pool. Now and then, indeed, they found themselves caught by a current in which a stream of bending stalks seemed to flow away between their legs. Then there were placid-looking, slumbering lakes, basins of short grass, which scarcely reached their ankles. As they walked along together, their joy found expression not in wild gambols, as in the orchard a week before, but rather in loitering, with their feet caught among the supple arms of the herbage, tasting as it were the caresses of a pure stream which calmed the exuberance of their youth. Albine turned aside and slipped into a lofty patch of vegetation which reached to her chin. Only her head appeared. For a moment or two she stood there in silence. Then she called to Serge: 'Come here, it is just like a bath. It is as if one had green water all over one.'

Then she gave a jump and scampered off without waiting for him, and they both walked along the margin of the first stream which barred their onward course. It was a shallow tranquil brook between banks of wild cress. It flowed on so placidly and gently that its surface reflected like a mirror the smallest reed that grew beside it. Albine and Serge followed this stream, whose onward motion was slower than their own, for a long time before they came across a tree that flung a long shadow upon the idle waters. As far as their eyes could reach they saw the bare brook stretch out and slumber in the sunlight like a blue serpent half uncoiled. At last they reached a clump of three willows. Two had their roots in the stream; the third was set a little backward. Their trunks, rotten and crumbling with age, were crowned with the bright foliage of youth. The shadow they cast was so slight as scarcely to be perceptible upon the sunlit bank. Yet here the water, which, both above and below, was so unruffled, showed a transient quiver, a rippling of its surface, as though it were surprised to find even this light veil cast over it. Between the three willows the meadowland sloped down to the stream, and some crimson poppies had sprung up in the crevices of the decaying old trunks. The foliage of the willows looked like a tent of greenery fixed upon three stakes by the water's edge, beside a rolling prairie.

'This is the place,' cried Albine, 'this is the place;' and she glided beneath the willows.

Serge sat down by her side, his feet almost in the water. He glanced round him, and murmured: 'You know everything, you know all the best spots. One might almost think this was an island, ten feet square, right in the middle of the sea.'

'Yes, indeed, we are quite at home,' she replied, as she gleefully drummed the grass with her fists. 'It is altogether our own, and we are going to do everything ourselves.' Then, as if struck by a brilliant idea, she sprang towards him, and, with her face close to his, asked him joyously: 'Will you be my husband? I will be your wife.'

He was delighted at the notion, and replied that he would gladly be her husband, laughing even more loudly than she had done herself. Then Albine suddenly became grave, and assumed the anxious air of a housewife.

'You know,' she said, 'that it is I who will have to give the orders. We will have breakfast as soon as you have laid the table.'

She gave him her orders in an imperious fashion. He had to stow all the various articles which she extracted from her pockets into a hole in one of the willows, which bole she called the cupboard. The rags supplied the household linen, while the comb represented the toilette necessaries. The needles and string were to be used for mending the explorers' clothes. Provision for the inner man consisted of the little bottle of wine and a few crusts which she had saved from yesterday. She had, to be sure, some matches, by the aid of which she intended to cook the fish they were going to catch.

When Serge had finished laying the table, the bottle of wine in the centre, and three crusts grouped round it, he hazarded the observation that the fare seemed to be scanty. But Albine shrugged her shoulders with feminine superiority. And wading into the water, she said in a severe tone, 'I will catch the fish; you can watch me.'

For half an hour she strenuously exerted herself in trying to catch some of the little fishes with her hands. She had gathered up her petticoats and fastened them together with a piece of string. And she advanced quietly into the water, taking the greatest care not to disturb it. When she was quite close to some tiny fish, that lay lurking between a couple of pebbles, she thrust down her bare arm, made a wild grasp, and brought her hand up again with nothing in it but sand and gravel. Serge then broke out into noisy laughter which brought her back to the bank, indignant. She told him that he had no business to laugh at her.

'But,' he ended by asking, 'how are we going to cook your fish when you have caught it? There is no wood about.'

That put the finishing touch to her discouragement. However, the fish in that stream didn't seem to be good for much; so she came out of the water and ran through the long grass to get her feet dry.

'See,' she suddenly exclaimed, 'here is some pimpernel. It is very nice. Now we shall have a feast.'

Serge was ordered to gather a quantity of the pimpernel and place it on the table. They ate it with their crusts. Albine declared that it was much better than nuts. She assumed the position of mistress of the establishment, and cut Serge's bread for him, for she would not trust him with the knife. At last she made him store away in the 'cupboard' the few drops of wine that remained at the bottom of the bottle. He was also ordered to sweep the grass. Then Albine lay down at full length.

'We are going to sleep now, you know. You must lie down by my side.'

He did as he was ordered. They lay there stiffly staring into the air, and saying that they were asleep, and that it was very nice. After a while, however, they drew slightly away from one another, averting their heads as if they felt some discomfort. And at last breaking the silence which had fallen between them, Serge exclaimed: 'I love you very much.'

It was love such as it is without any sensual feeling; that instinctive love which wakens in the bosom of a little man ten years old at the sight of some white-robed baby-girl. The meadow-lands, spreading around them all open and free, dissipated the slight fear each felt of the other. They knew that they lay there, seen of all the herbage, that the blue sky looked down upon them through the light foliage of the willows, and the thought was pleasant to them. The willow canopy over their heads was a mere open screen. The shade it cast was so imperceptible that it wafted to them none of the languor that some dim coppice might have done. From the far-off horizon came a healthy breeze fraught with all the freshness of the grassy sea, swelling here and there into waves of flowers; while, at their feet, the stream, childlike as they were, flowed idly along with a gentle babbling that sounded to them like the laughter of a companion. Ah! happy solitude, so tranquil and placid, immensity wherein the little patch of grass serving as their couch took the semblance of an infant's cradle.

'There, that's enough; said Albine, getting up; 'we've rested long enough.'

Serge seemed a little surprised at this speedy termination of their sleep. He stretched out his arm and caught hold of Albine, as though to draw her near him again; and when she, laughing, dropped upon her knees he grasped her elbows and gazed up at her. He knew not to what impulse he was yielding. But when she had freed herself, and again had risen to her feet, he buried his face amongst the grass where she had lain, and which still retained the warmth of her body.

'Yes,' he said at last, 'it is time to get up,' and then he rose from the ground.

They scoured the meadow-lands until evening began to fall. They went on and on, inspecting their garden. Albine walked in front, sniffing like a young dog, and saying nothing, but she was ever in search of the happy glade, although where they found themselves there were none of the big trees of which her thoughts were full. Serge meanwhile indulged in all kinds of clumsy gallantry. He rushed forward so hastily to thrust the tall herbage aside, that he nearly tripped her up; and he almost tore her arm from her body as he tried to assist her over the brooks. Their joy was great when they came to the three other streams. The first flowed over a bed of pebbles, between two rows of willows, so closely planted that they had to grope between the branches with the risk of falling into some deep part of the water. It only rose to Serge's knees, however, and having caught Albine in his arms he carried her to the opposite bank, to save her from a wetting. The next stream flowed black with shade beneath a lofty canopy of foliage, passing languidly onward with the gentle rustling and rippling of the satin train of some lady, dreamily sauntering through the woodland depths. It was a deep, cold, and rather dangerous-looking stream, but a fallen tree that stretched from bank to bank served them as a bridge. They crossed over, bestriding the tree with dangling feet, at first amusing themselves by stirring the water which looked like a mirror of burnished steel, but then suddenly hastening, frightened by the strange eyes which opened in the depths of the sleepy current at the slightest splash. But it was the last stream which delayed them the most. It was sportive like themselves, it flowed more slowly at certain bends, whence it started off again with merry ripples, past piles of big stones, into the shelter of some clump of trees, and grew calmer once more. It exhibited every humour as it sped along over soft sand or rocky boulders, over sparkling pebbles or greasy clay, where leaping frogs made yellow puddles. Albine and Serge dabbled about in delight, and even walked homewards through the stream in preference to remaining on the bank. At every little island that divided the current they landed. They conquered the savage spot or rested beneath the lofty canes and reeds, which seemed to grow there expressly as shelter for shipwrecked adventurers. Thus they made a delightful progress, amused by the changing scenery of the banks, enlivened by the merry humour of the living current.

But when they were about to leave the river, Serge realised that Albine was still seeking something along the banks, on the island, even among the plants that slept on the surface of the water. He was obliged to go and pull her from the midst of a patch of water-lilies whose broad leaves set *collerettes* around her limbs. He said nothing, but shook his finger at her. And at last they went home, walking along, arm in arm, like young people after a day's outing. They looked at each other, and thought one another handsomer and stronger than before, and of a certainty their laughter had a different ring from that with which it had sounded in the morning.

XI

'Are we never going out again?' asked Serge some days later.

And when he saw Albine shrug her shoulders with a weary air, he added, in a teasing kind of way, 'You have got tired of looking for your tree, then?'

They joked about the tree all day and made fun of it. It didn't exist. It was only a nursery-story. Yet they both spoke of it with a slight feeling of awe. And on the morrow they settled that they would go to the far end of the park and pay a visit to the great forest-trees which Serge had not yet seen. Albine refused to take anything along with them. They breakfasted before starting and did not set off till late. The heat of the sun, which was then great, brought them a feeling of languor, and they sauntered along gently, side by side, seeking every patch of sheltering shade. They lingered neither in the garden nor the orchard, through which they had to pass. When they gained the shady coolness beneath the big trees, they dropped into a still slower pace; and, without a word, but with a deep sigh, as though it were welcome relief to escape from the glare of day, they pushed on into the forest's depths. And when they had nothing but cool green leaves about them, when no glimpse of the sunlit expanse was afforded by any gap in the foliage, they looked at each other and smiled, with a feeling of vague uneasiness.

'How nice it is here!' murmured Serge.

Albine simply nodded her head. A choking sensation in her throat prevented her from speaking. Their arms were not passed as usual round each other's waist, but swung loosely by their sides. They walked along without touching each other, and with their heads inclined towards the ground.

But Serge suddenly stopped short on seeing tears trickle down Albine's cheeks and mingle with the smile that played around her lips.

'What is the matter with you?' he exclaimed; 'are you in pain? Have you hurt yourself?'

'No, don't you see I'm smiling? I don't know how it is, but the scent of all these trees forces tears into my eyes.' She glanced at him, and then resumed: 'Why, you're crying too! You see you can't help it.'

'Yes,' he murmured, 'all this deep shade affects one. It seems so peaceful, so mournful here that one feels a little sad. But you must tell me, you know, if anything makes you really unhappy. I have not done anything to annoy you, have I? you are not vexed with me?'

She assured him that she was not. She was quite happy, she said.

'Then why are you not enjoying yourself more? Shall we have a race?'

'Oh! no, we can't race,' she said, disdainfully, with a pout. And when he went on to suggest other amusements, such as bird-nesting or gathering strawberries or violets, she replied a little impatiently: 'We are too big for that sort of thing. It is childish to be always playing. Doesn't it please you better to walk on quietly by my side?'

She stepped along so prettily, that it was, indeed, a pleasure to hear the pit-pat of her little boots on the hard soil of the path. Never before had he paid attention to the rhythmic motion of her figure, the sweep of her skirts that followed her with serpentine motion. It was happiness never to be exhausted, to see her thus walking sedately by his side, for he was ever discovering some new charm in the lissom suppleness of her limbs.

'You are right,' he said, 'this is really the best. I would walk by your side to the end of the world, if you wished it.'

A little further on, however, he asked her if she were not tired, and hinted that he would not be sorry to have a rest himself.

'We might sit down for a few minutes,' he suggested in a stammering voice.

'No,' she replied, 'I don't want to.'

'But we might lie down, you know, as we did in the meadows the other day. We should be quite comfortable.'

'No, no; I don't want to.'

And she suddenly sprang aside, as if scared by the masculine arms outstretched towards her. Serge called her a big stupid, and tried to catch her. But at the light touch of his fingers she cried out with such an expression of pain that he drew back, trembling.

'I have hurt you?' he said.

She did not reply for a moment, surprised, herself, at her cry of fear, and already smiling at her own alarm.

'No; leave me, don't worry me;' and she added in a grave tone, though she tried to feign jocularity: 'you know that I have my tree to look for.'

Then Serge began to laugh, and offered to help her in her search. He conducted himself very gently in order that he might not again alarm her, for he saw that she was even yet trembling, though she had resumed her slow walk beside him. What they were contemplating was forbidden, and could bring them no luck; and he, like her, felt a delightful awe, which thrilled him at each repeated sigh of the forest trees. The perfume of the foliage, the soft green light which filtered through the leaves, the soughing silence of the undergrowth, filled them with tremulous excitement, as though the next turn of the path might lead them to some perilous happiness.

And for hours they walked on under the cool trees. They retained their reserved attitude towards each other, and scarcely exchanged a word, though they never left each other's side, but went together through the darkest greenery of the forest. At first their way lay through a jungle of saplings with trunks no thicker than a child's wrist. They had to push them aside, and open a path for themselves through the tender shoots which threw a wavy lacework of foliage before their eyes. The saplings closed up again behind them, leaving no trace of their passage, and they struggled on and on at random, ignorant of where they might be, and leaving nothing behind them to mark their progress, save a momentary waving of shaken boughs. Albine, weary of being unable to see more than three steps in front of her, was delighted when they at last found themselves free of this jungle, whose end they had long tried to discover. They had now reached a little clearing, whence several narrow paths, fringed with green hedges, struck out in various directions, twisting hither and thither, intersecting one another, bending and stretching in the most capricious fashion. Albine and Serge rose on tip-toes to peep over the hedges; but they were in no haste, and would willingly have stayed where they were, lost in the mazy windings, without ever getting anywhere, if they had not seen before them the proud lines of the lofty forest trees. They passed at last beneath their shade, solemnly and with a touch of sacred awe, as when one enters some vaulted cathedral. The straight lichen-stained trunks of the mighty trees, of a dingy grey, like discoloured stone, towered loftily, line by line, like a far-reaching infinity of columns. Naves opened far away, with lower, narrower aisles; naves strangely bold in their proportions, whose supporting pillars were very slender, richly caned, so finely chiselled that everywhere they allowed a glimpse of the blue heavens. A religious silence reigned beneath the giant arches, the ground below lay hard as stone in its austere nakedness; not a blade of green was there, nought but a ruddy dust of dead leaves. And Serge and Albine listened to their ringing footsteps as they went on, thrilled by the majestic solitude of this temple.

Here, indeed, if anywhere, must be the much-sought tree, beneath whose shade perfect happiness had made its home. They felt that it was nigh, such was the delight which stole through them amidst the dimness of those mighty arches. The trees seemed to be creatures of kindliness, full of strength and silence and happy restfulness. They looked at them one by one, and they loved them all; and they awaited from their majestic tranquillity some

167

revelation whereby they themselves might grow, expand into the bliss of strong and perfect life. The maples, the ashes, the hornbeams, the cornels, formed a nation of giants, a multitude full of proud gentleness, who lived in peace, knowing that the fall of any one of them would have sufficed to wreck a whole corner of the forest. The elms displayed colossal bodies and limbs full of sap, scarce veiled by light clusters of little leaves. The birches and the alders, delicate as sylphs, swayed their slim figures in the breeze to which they surrendered the foliage that streamed around them like the locks of goddesses already half metamorphosed into trees. The planes shot up regularly with glossy tattooed bark, whence scaly fragments fell. Down a gentle slope descended the larches, resembling a band of barbarians, draped in *sayons* of woven greenery. But the oaks were the monarchs of all—the mighty oaks, whose sturdy trunks thrust out conquering arms that barred the sun's approach from all around them; Titan-like trees, oft lightning-struck, thrown back in postures like those of unconquered wrestlers, with scattered limbs that alone gave birth to a whole forest.

Could the tree which Serge and Albine sought be one of those colossal oaks? or was it one of those lovely planes, or one of those pale, maidenly birches, or one of those creaking elms? Albine and Serge still plodded on, unable to tell, completely lost amongst the crowding trees. For a moment they thought they had found the object of their quest in the midst of a group of walnut trees from whose thick foliage fell so cold a shadow that they shivered beneath it. Further on they felt another thrill of emotion as they came upon a little wood of chestnut trees, green with moss and thrusting out big strange- shaped branches, on which one might have built an aerial village. But further still Albine caught sight of a clearing, whither they both ran hastily. Here, in the midst of a carpet of fine turf, a locust tree had set a very toppling of greenery, a foliaged Babel, whose ruins were covered with the strangest vegetation. Stones, sucked up from the ground by the mounting sap, still remained adhering to the trunk. High branches bent down to earth again, and, taking root, surrounded the parent tree with lofty arches, a nation of new trunks which ever increased and multiplied. Upon the bark, seared with bleeding wounds, were ripening fruit-pods; the mere effort of bearing fruit strained the old monster's skin until it split. The young folks walked slowly round it, passing under the arched branches which formed as it were the streets of a city, and stared at the gaping cracks of the naked roots. Then they went off, for they had not felt there the supernatural happiness they sought.

'Where are we?' asked Serge.

Albine did not know. She had never before come to this part of the park. They were now in a grove of cytisus and acacias, from whose clustering blossoms fell a soft, almost sugary perfume. 'We are quite lost,' she laughed. 'I don't know these trees at all.'

'But the garden must come to an end somewhere,' said Serge. 'When we get to the end, you will know where you are, won't you?'

'No,' she answered, waving her hands afar.

They fell into silence; never yet had the vastness of the park filled them with such pleasure. They joyed at knowing that they were alone in so far- spreading a domain that even they themselves could not reach its limits.

'Well, we are lost,' said Serge, gaily; then humbly drawing near her he inquired: 'You are not afraid, are you?'

'Oh! no. There's no one except you and me in the garden. What could I be afraid of? The walls are very high. We can't see them, but they guard us, you know.'

Serge was now quite close to her, and he murmured, 'But a little time ago you were afraid of me.'

She looked him straight in the face, perfectly calm, without the least faltering in her glance. 'You hurt me,' she replied, 'but you are different now. Why should I be afraid of you?'

'Then you will let me hold you like this. We will go back under the trees.'

'Yes, you may put your arm around me, it makes me feel happy. And we'll walk slowly, eh? so that we may not find our way again too soon.'

He had passed his arm round her waist, and it was thus that they sauntered back to the shade of the great forest trees, under whose arching vaults they slowly went, with love awakening within them. Albine said that she felt a little tired, and rested her head on Serge's shoulder. The fabulous tree was now forgotten. They only sought to draw their faces nearer together that they might smile in one another's eyes. And it was the trees, the maples, the elms, the oaks, with their soft green shade, that whisperingly suggested to them the first words of love.

'I love you!' said Serge, while his breath stirred the golden hair that clustered round Albine's temples. He tried to think of other words, but he could only repeat, 'I love you! I love you!'

Albine listened with a delightful smile upon her face. The music of her heart was in accord with his.

'I love you! I love you!' she sighed, with all the sweetness of her soft young voice.

Then, lifting up her blue eyes, in which the light of love was dawning, she asked, 'How do you love me?'

Serge reflected for a moment. The forest was wrapped in solemn quietude, the lofty naves quivered only with the soft footsteps of the young pair.

'I love you beyond everything,' he answered. 'You are more beautiful than all else that I see when I open my window in the morning. When I look at you, I want nothing more. If I could have you only, I should be perfectly happy.'

She lowered her eyes, and swayed her head as if accompanying a strain of music. 'I love you,' he went on. 'I know nothing about you. I know not who you are, nor whence you came. You are neither my mother nor my sister; and yet I love you to a point that I have given you my whole heart and kept nought of it for others. Listen, I love those cheeks of yours, so soft and satiny; I love your mouth with its rose-sweet breath; I love your eyes, in which I see my own love reflected; I love even your eyelashes, even those little veins which blue the whiteness of your temples. Ah! yes, I love you, I love you, Albine.'

'And I love you, too,' she answered. 'You are strong, and tall, and handsome. I love you, Serge.'

For a moment or two they remained silent, enraptured. It seemed to them that soft, flute-like music went before them, that their own words came from some dulcet orchestra which they could not see. Shorter and shorter became their steps as they leaned one towards the other, ever threading their way amidst the mighty trees. Afar off through the long vista of the colonnades were glimpses of waning sunlight, showing like a procession of white-robed maidens entering church for a betrothal ceremony amid the low strains of an organ.

'And why do you love me?' asked Albine again.

He only smiled, and did not answer her immediately; then he said, 'I love you because you came to me. That expresses all.... Now we are together and we love one another. It seems to me that I could not go on living if I did not love you. You are the very breath of my life.'

He bent his head, speaking almost as though he were in a dream.

'One does not know all that at first. It grows up in one as one's heart grows. One has to grow, one has to get strong.... Do you remember how we loved one another though we didn't speak of it? One is childish and silly at first. Then, one fine day, it all becomes clear, and bursts out. You see, we have nothing to trouble about; we love one another because our love and our life are one.'

Albine's head was cast back, her eyes were tightly closed, and she scarce drew her breath. Serge's caressing words enraptured her: 'Do you really, really love me?' she murmured, without opening her eyes.

Serge remained silent, sorely troubled that he could find nothing further to say to prove to her the force of his love. His eyes wandered over her rosy face, which lay upon his shoulder with the restfulness of sleep. Her eyelids were soft as silk. Her moist lips were curved into a bewitching smile, her brow was pure white, with just a rim of gold below her hair. He would have liked to give his whole being with the word which seemed to be upon his tongue but which he could not utter. Again he bent over her, and seemed to consider on what sweet spot of that fair face he should whisper the supreme syllables. But he said nothing, he only breathed a little sigh. Then he kissed Albine's lips.

'Albine, I love you!'

'I love you, Serge!'

Then they stopped short, thrilled, quivering with that first love kiss. She had opened her eyes quite widely. He was standing with his lips protruding slightly towards hers. They looked at each other without a blush. They felt they were under the influence of some sovereign power. It was like the realisation of a long dreamt-of meeting, in which they beheld themselves grown, made one for the other, for ever joined. For a moment they remained wondering, raising their eyes to the solemn vault of greenery above them, questioning the tranquil nation of trees as if seeking an echo of their kiss. But, beneath the serene complacence of the forest, they yielded to prolonged, ringing lovers' gaiety, full of all the tenderness now born.

'Tell me how long you have loved me. Tell me everything. Did you love me that day when you lay sleeping upon my hand? Did you love me when I fell out of the cherry tree, and you stood beneath it, stretching out your arms to catch me, and looking so pale? Did you love me when you took hold of me round the waist in the meadows to help me over the streams?'

'Hush, let me speak. I have always loved you. And you, did you love me; did you?'

Until the evening closed round them they lived upon that one word 'love,' in which they ever seemed to find some new sweetness. They brought it into every sentence, ejaculated it inconsequentially, merely for the pleasure they found in pronouncing it. Serge, however, did not think of pressing a second kiss to Albine's lips. The perfume of the first sufficed them in their purity.

They had found their way again, or rather had stumbled upon it, for they had paid no attention to the paths they took. As they left the forest, twilight had fallen, and the moon was rising, round and yellow, between the black foliage. It was a delightful walk home through the park, with that discreet luminary peering at them through the gaps in the big trees. Albine said that the moon was surely following them. The night was balmy, warm too with stars. Far away a long murmur rose from the forest trees, and Serge listened, thinking: 'They are talking of us.'

When they reached the parterre, they passed through an atmosphere of sweetest perfumes; the perfume of flowers at night, which is richer, more caressing than by day, and seems like the very breath of slumber.

'Good night, Serge.'

'Good night, Albine.'

They clasped each other by the hand on the landing of the first floor, without entering the room where they usually wished each other good night. They did not kiss. But Serge, when he was alone, remained seated on the edge of his bed, listening to Albine's every movement in the room above. He was weary with happiness, a happiness that benumbed his limbs.

XII

For the next few days Albine and Serge experienced a feeling of embarrassment. They avoided all allusion to their walk beneath the trees. They had not again kissed each other, or repeated their confession of love. It was not any feeling of shame which had sealed their lips, but rather a fear of in any way spoiling their happiness. When they were apart, they lived upon the dear recollection of love's awakening, plunged into it, passed once more through the happy hours which they had spent, with their arms around each other's waist, and their faces close together. It all ended by throwing them both into a feverish state. They looked at each other with heavy eyes, and talked, in a melancholy mood, of things that did not interest them in the least. Then, after a long interval of silence, Serge would say to Albine in a tone full of anxiety: 'You are ill?'

But she shook her head as she answered, 'No, no. It is you who are not well; your hands are burning.'

The thought of the park filled them with vague uneasiness which they could not understand. They felt that danger lurked for them in some by-path, and would seize them and do them hurt. They never spoke about these disquieting thoughts, but certain timid glances revealed to them the mutual anguish which held them apart as though they were foes. One morning, however, Albine ventured, after much hesitation, to say to Serge: 'It is wrong of you to keep always indoors. You will fall ill again.'

Serge laughed in rather an embarrassed way. 'Bah!' he muttered, 'we have been everywhere, we know all the garden by heart.'

But Albine shook her head, and in a whisper replied, 'No, no, we don't know the rocks, we have never been to the springs. It was there that I warmed myself last winter. There are some nooks where the stones seem to be actually alive.'

The next morning, without having said another word on the subject, they set out together. They climbed up to the left behind the grotto where the marble woman lay slumbering; and as they set foot on the lowest stones, Serge remarked: 'We must see everything. Perhaps we shall feel quieter afterwards.'

The day was very hot, there was thunder in the air. They had not ventured to clasp each other's waist; but stepped along, one behind the other, glowing beneath the sunlight. Albine took advantage of a widening of the path to let

Serge go on in front; for the warmth of his breath upon her neck troubled her. All around them the rocks arose in broad tiers, storeys of huge flags, bristling with coarse vegetation. They first came upon golden gorse, clumps of sage, thyme, lavender, and other balsamic plants, with sour-berried juniper trees and bitter rosemary, whose strong scent made them dizzy. Here and there the path was hemmed in by holly, that grew in quaint forms like cunningly wrought metal work, gratings of blackened bronze, wrought iron, and polished copper, elaborately ornamented, covered with prickly *rosaces*. And before reaching the springs, they had to pass through a pine-wood. Its shadow seemed to weigh upon their shoulders like lead. The dry needles crackled beneath their feet, throwing up a light resinous dust which burned their lips.

'Your garden doesn't make itself very agreeable just here,' said Serge, turning towards Albine.

They smiled at each other. They were now near the edge of the springs. The sight of the clear waters brought them relief. Yet these springs did not hide beneath a covering of verdure, like those that bubble up on the plains and set thick foliage growing around them that they may slumber idly in the shade. They shot up in the full light of day from a cavity in the rock, without a blade of grass near by to tinge the clear water with green. Steeped in the sunshine they looked silvery. In their depths the sun beat against the sand in a breathing living dust of light. And they darted out of their basin like arms of purest white, they rebounded like nude infants at play, and then suddenly leapt down in a waterfall whose curve suggested a woman's breast.

'Dip your hands in,' cried Albine; 'the water is icy cold at the bottom.'

They were indeed able to refresh their hot hands. They threw water over their faces too, and lingered there amidst the spray which rose up from the streaming springs.

'Look,' cried Albine; 'look, there is the garden, and there are the meadows and the forest.'

For a moment they looked at the Paradou spread out beneath their feet.

'And you see,' she added, 'there isn't the least sign of any wall. The whole country belongs to us, right up to the sky.'

By this time, almost unawares, they had slipped their arms round each other's waist. The coolness of the springs had soothed their feverish disquietude. But just as they were going away, Albine seemed to recall something and led Serge back again, saying:

'Down there, below the rocks, a long time ago, I once saw the wall.'

'But there is nothing to be seen,' replied Serge, turning a little pale.

'Yes, yes; it must be behind that avenue of chestnut trees on the other side of those bushes.'

Then, on feeling Serge's arm tremble, she added: 'But perhaps I am mistaken.... Yet I seem to remember that I suddenly came upon it as I left the avenue. It stopped my way, and was so high that I felt a little afraid. And a few steps farther on, I came upon another surprise. There was a huge hole in it, through which I could see the whole country outside.'

Serge looked at her with entreaty in his eyes. She gave a little shrug of her shoulders to reassure him, and went on: 'But I stopped the hole up; I have told you that we are quite alone, and we are. I stopped it up at once. I had my knife with me, and I cut down some brambles and rolled up some big stones. I would defy even a sparrow to force its way through. If you like, we will go and look at it one of these days, and then you will be satisfied.'

But he shook his head. Then they went away together, still holding each other by the waist; but they had grown anxious once more. Serge gazed down askance at Albine's face, and she felt perturbed beneath his glance. They would have liked to go down again at once, and thus escape the uneasiness of a longer walk. But, in spite of themselves, as though impelled by some stronger power, they skirted a rocky cliff and reached a table-land, where once more they found the intoxication of the full sunlight. They no longer inhaled the soft languid perfumes of aromatic plants, the musky scent of thyme, and the incense of lavender. Now they were treading a foul-smelling growth under foot; wormwood with bitter, penetrating smell; rue that reeked like putrid flesh; and hot valerian, clammy with aphrodisiacal exudations. Mandragoras, hemlocks, hellebores, dwales, poured forth their odours, and made their heads swim till they reeled and tottered one against the other.

'Shall I hold you up?' Serge asked Albine, as he felt her leaning heavily upon him.

He was already pressing her in his arms, but she struggled out of his grasp, and drew a long breath.

'No; you stifle me,' she said. 'Leave me alone. I don't know what is the matter with me. The ground seems to give way under my feet. It is there I feel the pain.'

She took hold of his hand and laid it upon her breast. Then Serge turned quite pale. He was even more overcome than she. And both had tears in their eyes as they saw each other thus ill and troubled, unable to think of a remedy for the evil which had fallen upon them. Were they going to die here of that mysterious, suffocating faintness?

'Come and sit down in the shade,' said Serge. 'It is these plants which are poisoning us with their noxious odours.'

He led her gently along by her finger-tips, for she shivered and trembled when he but touched her wrist. It was beneath a fine cedar, whose level roof-like branches spread nearly a dozen yards around, that she seated herself. Behind grew various quaint conifers; cypresses, with soft flat foliage that looked like heavy lace; spruce firs, erect and solemn, like ancient druidical pillars, still black with the blood of sacrificed victims; yews, whose dark robes were fringed with silver; evergreen trees of all kinds, with thick-set foliage, dark leathery verdure, splashed here and there with yellow and red. There was a weird-looking araucaria that stood out strangely with large regular arms resembling reptiles grafted one on the other, and bristling with imbricated leaves that suggested the scales of an excited serpent. In this heavy shade, the warm air lulled one to voluptuous drowsiness. The atmosphere slept, breathless; and a perfume of Eastern love, the perfume that came from the painted lips of the Shunamite, was exhaled by the odorous trees.

'Are you not going to sit down?' said Albine.

And she slipped a little aside to make room for him; but Serge stepped back and remained standing. Then, as she renewed her request, he dropped upon his knees, a little distance away, and said, softly: 'No, I am more feverish even than you are; I should make you hot. If I wasn't afraid of hurting you, I would take you in my arms, and clasp you so tightly that we should no longer feel any pain.'

He dragged himself nearer to her on his knees.

'Oh! to have you in my arms! In the night I awake from dreams in which I see you near me; but, alas! you are ever far away. There seems to be some wall built up between us which I can never beat down. And yet I am now quite strong again; I could catch you up in my arms and swing you over my shoulder, and carry you off as though you belonged to me.'

He had let himself sink upon his elbows, in an attitude of deep adoration. And he breathed a kiss upon the hem of Albine's skirt. But at this the girl sprang up, as though it was she herself that had received the kiss. She hid her brow with her hands, perturbed, quivering, and stammering forth: 'Don't! don't! I beg of you. Let us go on.'

She did not hurry away, but let Serge follow her as she walked slowly on, stumbling against the roots of the plants, and with her hands still clasped round her head, as though to check the excitement that thrilled her. When they came out of the little wood, they took a few steps over ledges of rocks, on which a whole nation of ardent fleshy plants was squatting. It was like a crawling, writhing assemblage of hideous nameless monsters such as people a nightmare; monsters akin to spiders, caterpillars, and wood-lice, grown to gigantic proportions, some with bare glaucous skins, others tufted with filthy matted hairs, whilst many had sickly limbs—dwarf legs, and shrivelled, palsied arms—sprawling around them. And some displayed horrid dropsical bellies; some had spines bossy with hideous humps, and others looked like dislocated skeletons. Mamillaria threw up living pustules, a crawling swarm of greenish tortoises, bristling hideously with long hairs that were stiffer than iron. The echinocacti, which showed more flesh, suggested nests of young writhing, knotted vipers. The echinopses were mere excrescent red-haired growths that made one think of huge insects rolled into balls. The prickly-pears spread out fleshy leaves spotted with ruddy spikes that resembled swarms of microscopic bees. The gasterias sprawled about like big shepherd-spiders turned over on their backs, with long-speckled and striated legs. The cacti of the cereus family showed a horrid vegetation, huge polyps, the diseases of an overheated soil, the maladies of poisoned sap. But the aloes, languidly unfolding their hearts, were particularly numerous and conspicuous. Among them one found every possible tint of green, pale green and vivid, yellowish green and greyish, browny green, dashed with a ruddy tone, and deep green, fringed with pale gold. And the shapes of their leaves were as varied as their tints. Some were broad and heart-shaped, others were long and narrow like sword-blades; some bristled with spikey thorns, while yet others looked as though they had been cunningly hemmed at the edges. There were giant ones, in lonely majesty, with flower stalks that towered up aloft like poles wreathed with rosy coral; and there were tiny ones clustering thickly together on one and the same stem, and throwing forth on all sides leaves that gleamed and quivered like adders' tongues.

'Let us go back to the shade,' begged Serge. 'You can sit down there as you did just now, and I will lie at your feet and talk to you.'

Where they stood the sun rays fell like torrential rain. It was as if the triumphant orb seized upon the shadowless ground, and strained it to his blazing breast. Albine grew faint, staggered, and turned to Serge for support.

But the moment they felt each other's touch, they fell together without even a word. It was as though the very rock beneath them had opened, as though they were ever going down and down. Their hands sought each other caressingly, embracingly, but such keen anguish did they experience that they suddenly tore themselves apart, and fled, each in a different direction. Serge did not cease running till he had reached the pavilion, and had thrown himself upon his bed, his brain on fire, and despair in his heart. Albine did not return till nightfall, after hours of weeping in a corner of the garden. It was the first time that they had not returned home together, tired after their long wanderings. For three days they kept apart, feeling terribly unhappy.

XIII

Yet now the park was entirely their own. They had taken sovereign possession of it. There was not a corner of it that was not theirs to use as they willed. For them alone the thickets of roses put forth their blossoms, and the parterre exhaled its soft perfume, which lulled them to sleep as they lay at night with their windows open. The orchard provided them with food, filling Albine's skirts with fruits, and spread over them the shade of its perfumed boughs, under which it was so pleasant to breakfast in the early morning. Away in the meadows the grass and the streams were all theirs; the grass, which extended their kingdom to such boundless distance, spreading an endless silky carpet before them; and the streams, which were the best of their joys, emblematic of their own purity and innocence, ever offering them coolness and freshness in which they delighted to bathe their youth. The forest, too, was entirely theirs, from the mighty oaks, which ten men could not have spanned, to the slim birches which a child might have snapped; the forest, with all its trees, all its shade, all its avenues and clearings, its cavities of greenery, of which the very birds themselves were ignorant; the forest which they used as they listed, as if it were a giant canopy, beneath which they might shelter from the noontide heat their new-born love. They reigned everywhere, even among the rocks and the springs, even over that gruesome stretch of ground that teemed with such hideous growth, and which had seemed to sink and give way beneath their feet, but which they loved yet even more than the soft grassy couches of the garden, for the strange thrill of passion they had felt there.

Thus, now, in front of them, behind them, to the right of them and to the left, all was theirs. They had gained possession of the whole domain, and they walked through a friendly expanse which knew them, and smiled kindly greetings to them as they passed, devoting itself to their pleasure, like a faithful and submissive servitor. The sky, with its vast canopy of blue overhead, was also theirs to enjoy. The park walls could not enclose it, their eyes could ever revel in its beauty, and it entered into the joy of their life, at daytime with its triumphal sun, at night with its golden rain of stars. At every moment of the day it delighted them afresh, its expression ever varying. In the early morning it was pale as a maiden just risen from her slumber; at noon, it was flushed, radiant as with a longing for fruitfulness, and in the evening it became languid and breathless, as after keen enjoyment. Its countenance was constantly changing. Particularly in the evenings, at the hour of parting, did it delight them. The sun, hastening towards the horizon, ever found a fresh smile. Sometimes he disappeared in the midst of serene calmness, unflecked by a single cloud, sinking gradually beneath a golden sea. At other times he threw out crimson glories, tore his vaporous robe to shreds, and set amidst wavy flames that streaked the skies like the tails of gigantic comets, whose radiant heads lit up the crests of the forest trees. Then, again, extinguishing his rays one by one, he would softly sink to rest on shores of ruddy sand, far-reaching banks of blushing coral; and then, some other night, he would glide away demurely behind a heavy cloud that figured the grey hangings of some alcove, through which the eye could only detect a spark like that of a night-light. Or else he would rush to his couch in a tumult of passion, rolled round with white forms which gradually crimsoned beneath his fiery embraces, and finally disappeared with him below the horizon in a confused chaos of gleaming, struggling limbs.

It was only the plants which had not made their submission. Albine and Serge passed like monarchs through the kingdom of animals, who rendered them humble and loyal obeisance. When they crossed the parterre, flights of butterflies arose to delight their eyes, to fan them with quivering wings, and to follow in their train like living sunbeams or flying blossoms. In the orchard, they were greeted by the birds that banqueted in the fruit-trees. The sparrows, the chaffinches, the golden orioles, the bullfinches, showed them the ripest fruit scarred by their hungry beaks; and while they sat astride the branches and breakfasted, birds twittered and sported round them like children at play, and even purloined the fruit beneath their very feet. Albine found even more amusement in the meadows, where she caught the little green frogs with eyes of gold, that lay squatting amongst the reeds, absorbed in contemplation; while Serge, with a piece of straw, poked the crickets out of their hiding- places, or tickled the grasshoppers to make them sing. He picked up insects of all colours, blue ones, red ones, yellow ones, and set them creeping upon his sleeve, where they gleamed and glittered like buttons of sapphire and ruby and topaz.

Then there was all the mysterious life of the streams; the grey-backed fishes that threaded the dim waters, the eels whose presence was betrayed by a slight quivering of the water-plants, the young fry, which dispersed like blackish sand at the slightest sound, the long-legged flies and the water- beetles that ruffled into circling silvery ripples the stagnant surface of the pools; all that silent teeming life which drew them to the water and impelled them to dabble and stand in it, so that they might feel those millions of existences ever and ever gliding past their limbs. At other times, when the day was hot and languid, they would betake themselves beneath the voiceful shade of the forest and listen to the serenades of their musicians, the clear fluting of the nightingales, the silvery bugle-notes of the tomtits, and the far- off accompaniment of the cuckoos. They gazed with delight upon the swift flight of the pheasants, whose plumes gleamed like sudden sun rays amidst the branches, and with a smile they stayed their steps to let a troop of young roebucks bound past, or else a couple of grave stags that slackened their pace to look at them. Again, on other days they would climb up amongst the rocks, when the sun was blazing in the heavens, and find a pleasure in watching the swarms of grasshoppers which at the sound of their footsteps arose with a great crepitation of wings from the beds of thyme. The snakes that lay uncoiled beneath the parched bushes, or the lizards that sprawled over the red- hot stones, watched them with friendly eyes.

Of all the life that thus teemed round them in the park, Albine and Serge had only become really conscious since the day when a kiss had awakened them to life themselves. Now it deafened them at times, and spoke to them in a language which they did not understand. It was that life—all the voices of the animal creation, all the perfumes and soft shadows of the flowers and trees—which perturbed them to such a point as to make them angry with one another. And yet throughout the whole park they found nothing but loving familiarity. Every plant and every creature was their friend. All the Paradou was one great caress.

Before they had come thither, the sun had for a whole century reigned over it in lonely majesty. The garden, then, had known no other master; it had beheld him, every morning, scaling the boundary wall with his slanting rays, at noontide it had seen him pour his vertical heat upon the panting soil; and at evening it had seen him go off, on the other side, with a kiss of farewell upon its foliage. And so the garden had no shyness; it welcomed Albine and Serge, as it had so long welcomed the sun, as pleasant companions, with whom one puts on no ceremony. The animals, the trees, the streams, the rocks, all continued in an unrestrained state of nature, speaking aloud, living openly, without a secret, displaying the innocent shamelessness, the hearty tenderness of the world's first days. Serge and Albine, however, suffered from these voluptuous surroundings, and at times felt minded to curse the garden. On the afternoon when Albine had wept so bitterly after their saunter amongst the rocks, she had called out to the Paradou, whose intensity of life and passion filled her with distress:

'If you really be our friend, why, why do you make us so wretched?'

XIV

The next morning Serge barricaded himself in his room. The perfume from the garden irritated him. He drew the calico curtains closely across the window to shut out the sight of the park. Perhaps he thought he might recover all his old serenity and calm if he shut himself off from that greenery, whose shade sent such passionate thrills quivering through him.

During the long hours they spent together, Albine and he never now spoke of the rocks or the streams, the trees or the sky. The Paradou might no longer have been in existence. They strove to forget it. And yet they were all the time conscious of its presence on the other side of those slight curtains. Scented breezes forced their way in through the interstices of the window frame, the many voices of nature made the panes resound. All the life of the park laughed, chattered, and whispered in ambush beneath their window. As it reached them their cheeks would pale and they would raise their voices, seeking some occupation which might prevent them from hearing it.

'Have you noticed,' said Serge one morning during these uneasy intervals, 'there is a painting of a woman over the door there? She is like you.'

He laughed noisily as he finished speaking. They both turned to the paintings and dragged the table once more alongside the wall, with a nervous desire to occupy themselves.

'Oh! no,' murmured Albine. 'She is much fatter than I am. But one can't see her very well; her position is so queer.'

They relapsed into silence. From the decayed, faded painting a scene, which they had never before noticed, now showed forth. It was as if the picture had taken shape and substance again beneath the influence of the summer heat. You could sea a nymph with arms thrown back and pliant figure on a bed of flowers which had been strewn for her by young cupids, who, sickle in hand, ever added fresh blossoms to her rosy couch. And nearer, you could also see a cloven-hoofed faun who had surprised her thus. But Albine repeated, 'No, she is not like me, she is very plain.'

Serge said nothing. He looked at the girl and then at Albine, as though he were comparing them one with the other. Albine pulled up one of her sleeves, as if to show that her arm was whiter than that of the pictured girl. Then they subsided into silence again, and gazed at the painting; and for a moment Albine's large blue eyes turned to Serge's grey ones, which were glowing.

'You have got all the room painted again, then?' she cried, as she sprang from the table. 'These people look as though they were all coming to life again.'

They began to laugh, but there was a nervous ring about their merriment as they glanced at the nude and frisking cupids which started to life again on all the panels. They no longer took those survivals of voluptuous eighteenth century art to represent mere children at play. They were disturbed by the sight of them, and as Albine felt Serge's hot breath on her neck she started and left his side to seat herself on the sofa. 'They frighten me,' she murmured. 'The men are like robbers, and the women, with their dying eyes, look like people who are being murdered.'

Serge sat down in a chair, a little distance away, and began to talk of other matters. But they remained uneasy. They seemed to think that all those painted figures were gazing at them. It was as if the trooping cupids were springing out of the panelling, casting the flowers they held around them, and threatening to bind them together with the blue ribbons which already enchained two lovers in one corner of the ceiling. And the whole story of the nymph and her faun lover, from his first peep at her to his triumph among the flowers, seemed to burst into warm life. Were all those lovers, all those impudent shameless cupids about to step down from their panels and crowd around them? They already seemed to hear their panting sighs, and to feel their breath filling the spacious room with the perfume of voluptuousness.

'It's quite suffocating, isn't it?' sighed Albine. 'In spite of every airing I have given it, the room has always seemed close to me!

'The other night,' said Serge, 'I was awakened by such a penetrating perfume, that I called out to you, thinking you had come into the room. It was just like the soft warmth of your hair when you have decked it with heliotropes.... In the earlier times it seemed to be wafted to me from a distance, it was like the lingering memory of a perfume; but now I can't sleep for it, and it is so strong and penetrating that it quite stupefies me. The alcove grows so hot, too, at night that I shall be obliged to lie on the couch.'

Albine laid her fingers on her lips, and whispered, 'It is the dead girl—she who once lived here.'

They sniffed the odorous air with forced gaiety, but in reality feeling very troubled. Certainly never before had the room exhaled such a disquieting aroma. The very walls seemed to be still echoing the faint rustling of perfumed skirts; and the floor had retained the fragrance of satin slippers dropped by the bedside, and near the head of the bed itself Serge thought he could trace the imprint of a little hand, which had left behind it a clinging scent of violets. Over all the furniture the phantom presence of the dead girl still lingered fragrantly.

'See, this is the armchair where she used to sit,' cried Albine; 'there is the scent of her shoulders at the back of it yet.'

She sat down in it herself, and bade Serge drop upon his knees and kiss her hand.

'You remember the day when I first let you in and said, "Good morrow, my dear lord!" But that wasn't all, was it? He kissed her hands when the door was closed. There they are, my hands. They are yours.'

Then they tried to resume their old frolics in order that they might forget the Paradou, whose joyous murmur they heard ever rising outside, and that they might no longer think of the pictures nor yield to the languor-breathing influence of the room. Albine put on an affected manner, leant back in her chair, and finally laughed at the foolish figure which Serge made at her feet.

'You stupid!' she said, 'take me round the waist, and say pretty things to me, since you are supposed to be in love with me. Don't you know how to make love then?'

But as soon as she felt him clasp her with eager impetuosity, she began to struggle, and freed herself from his embrace.

'No, no; leave me alone. I can't bear it. I feel as though I were choking in this room.'

From that day forward they felt the same kind of fear for the room as they already felt for the garden. Their one remaining harbour of refuge was now a place to be shunned and dreaded, a spot where they could no longer find themselves together without watching each other furtively. Albine now scarcely ventured to enter it, but remained near the threshold, with the door wide open behind her so as to afford her an immediate retreat. Serge lived there in solitude, a prey to sickening restlessness, half-stifling, lying on the couch and vainly trying to close his ears to the sighs of the soughing park and his nostrils to the haunting fragrance of the old furniture. At night he dreamt wild passionate dreams, which left him in the morning nervous and disquieted. He believed that he was falling ill again, that he would never recover plenitude of health. For days and days he remained there in silence, with dark rings round his sleepy eyes, only starting into wakefulness when Albine came to visit him. They would remain face to face, gazing at one another sadly, and uttering but a few soft words, which seemed to choke them. Albine's eyes were even darker than Serge's, and were filled with an imploring gaze.

Then, after a week had gone by, Albine's visit never lasted more than a few

185

minutes. She seemed to shun him. When she came to the room, she appeared thoughtful, remained standing, and hurried off as soon as possible. When he questioned her about this change in her demeanour towards him, and reproached her for no longer being friendly, she turned her head away and avoided replying. He never could get her to tell him how she spent the mornings that she passed alone. She would only shake her head, and talk about being very idle. If he pressed her more closely, she bounded out of the room, just wishing him a hasty good-night as she disappeared through the doorway. He often noticed, however, that she had been crying. He observed, too, in her expression the phases of a hope that was never fulfilled, the perpetual struggling of a desire eager to be satisfied. Sometimes she seemed quite overwhelmed with melancholy, dragging herself about with an air of utter discouragement, like one who no longer had any pleasure in living. At other times she laughed lightly, her face shone with an expression of triumphant hope, of which, however, she would not yet speak, and her feet could not remain still, so eager was she to dart away to what seemed to her some last certainty. But on the following day, she would sink again into desperation, to soar afresh on the morrow on the pinions of renewed hope. One thing which she could not conceal from Serge was that she suffered from extreme lassitude. Even during the few moments they spent together she could not prevent her head from nodding, or keep herself from dozing off.

Serge, recognising that she was unwilling to reply, had ceased to question her; and, when she now entered his room, he contented himself with casting an anxious glance at her, fearful lest some evening she should no longer have strength enough to come to him. Where could she thus reduce herself to such exhaustion? What perpetual struggle was it that brought about those alternations of joy and despair? One morning he started at the sound of a light footfall beneath his window. It could not be a roe venturing abroad in that manner. Moreover he could recognise that light footfall. Albine was wandering about the Paradou without him. It was from the Paradou that she returned to him with all those hopes and fears and inward wrestlings, all that lassitude which was killing her. And he could well guess what she was seeking out there, alone in the woody depths, with all the silent obstinacy of a woman who has vowed to effect her purpose. After that he used to listen for her steps. He dared not draw aside the curtain and watch her as she hurried along through the trees; but he experienced strange, almost painful emotion, in listening to ascertain what direction she took, whether she turned to right or to left, whether she went straight on through the flower-beds, and how far her ramble extended. Amidst all the noisy life of the Paradou, amidst the soughing chorus of the trees, the rustling of the streams, and the ceaseless songs of the birds, he could distinguish the gentle pit-pat of her shoes so plainly that he could have told whether she was stepping over the gravel near the rivers, the crumbling mould of the forest, or the bare ledges of the rocks. In time he even learned to tell, from the sound of her nervous footfall, whether she came back hopeful or depressed. As soon as he heard her step on the staircase, he hurried from the window, and he never let her know that he had thus followed her from afar in her wanderings. But she must have guessed it, for with a glance she always afterwards told him where she had been.

'Stay indoors, and don't go out,' he begged her, with clasped hands, one morning when he saw her still unrecovered from the fatigue of the previous day. 'You drive me to despair.'

But she hastened away in irritation. The garden, now that it rang with Albine's footfalls, seemed to have a more depressing influence than ever upon Serge. The pit-pat of her feet was yet another voice that called him; an imperious voice that echoed ever more and more loudly within him. He closed his ears and tried to shut out the sound, but the distant footsteps still echoed to him in the throbbings of his heart. And when she came back, in the evening, it was the whole park that came back with her, with the memories of their walks together, and of the slow dawn of their love, in the midst of conniving nature. She seemed to have grown taller and graver, mellowed, matured by her solitary rambles. There was nothing left in her of the frolicsome child, and his teeth would suddenly set at times when he looked at her and beheld her so desirable.

One day, about noon, Serge heard Albine returning in hot haste. He had restrained himself from listening for her steps when she went away. Usually, she did not return till late, and he was amazed at her impetuosity as she sped along, forcing her way through the branches that barred her path. As she passed beneath his window, he heard her laugh; and as she mounted the stairway, she panted so heavily that he almost thought he could feel her hot breath streaming against his face. She threw the door wide open, and cried out: 'I have found it!'

Then she sat down and repeated softly, breathlessly: 'I have found it! I have found it!'

Serge, distracted, laid his fingers on her lips, and stammered: 'Don't tell me anything, I beg you. I want to know nothing of it. It will kill me, if you speak.'

Then she sank into silence with gleaming eyes and lips tightly pressed lest the words she kept back should spring out in spite of her. And she stayed in the room till evening, trying to meet Serge's glance, and imparting to him, each time that their eyes met, something of that which she had discovered. Her whole face beamed with radiance, she exhaled a delicious odour, she was full of life; and Serge felt that she permeated him through all his senses. Despairingly did he struggle against this gradual invasion of his being.

On the morrow she returned to his room as soon as she was up.

'Aren't you going out?' he asked, conscious that he would be vanquished should she remain there.

'No,' she said; she wasn't going out any more. As by degrees she recovered from her fatigue he felt her becoming stronger, more triumphant. She would soon be able to take him by the hand and drag him to that spot, whose charm her silence proclaimed so loudly. That day, however, she did not speak; she contented herself with keeping him seated on a cushion at her feet. It was not till the next morning that she ventured to say: 'Why do you shut yourself up here? It is so pleasant under the trees.'

He rose from her feet, and stretched out his arms entreatingly. But she laughed at him.

'Well, well, then, we won't go out, since you would rather not.... But this room has such a strange scent, and we should be much more comfortable in the garden. It is very wrong of you to have taken such a dislike to it.'

He had again settled himself at her feet in silence, his eyelids lowered, his features quivering with passionate emotion.

'We won't go out,' she repeated, 'so don't worry. But do you really prefer these pictures to the grass and flowers in the park? Do you remember all we saw together? It is these paintings which make us feel so unhappy. They are a nuisance, always looking and watching us as they do.'

As Serge gradually leant more closely against her, she passed her arm round his neck and laid his head upon her lap, while murmuring in yet a lower tone: 'There is a little corner there I know, where we might be so very happy. Nothing would trouble us there; the fresh air would cool your feverishness.'

Then she stopped, as she felt him quivering. She was afraid lest she might again revive his old fears. But she gradually conquered him merely by the caressing gaze of her blue eyes. His eyelids were now raised, and he rested there quietly, wholly hers, his tremor past.

'Ah! if you only knew!' she softly breathed; and seeing that he continued to smile, she went on boldly: 'It is all a lie; it is not forbidden. You are a man now and ought not to be afraid. If we went there, and any danger threatened me, you would protect me, you would defend me, would you not? You could carry me off on your back, couldn't you? I am never the least afraid when I have you with me. Look how strong your arms have grown. What is there for any one with such strong arms as yours to be afraid of?'

She caressed him beguilingly as she spoke, stroking his hair and neck and shoulders with her hand.

'No, it is not forbidden,' she resumed. 'That is only a story for stupids, and was invented, long ago, by some one who didn't want to be disturbed in the most charming spot in the whole garden. As soon as you sat down on that grassy carpet, you would be happy and well again. Listen, then, come with me.'

He shook his head but without any sign of vexation, as though indeed he liked thus being teased. Then after a short silence, grieved to see her pouting, and longing for a renewal of her caresses, he opened his lips and asked: 'Where is it?'

She did not answer him immediately. Her eyes seemed to be wandering far away: 'It is over yonder,' she murmured at last. 'I cannot explain to you clearly. One has to go down the long avenue, and then to turn to the left, and then again to the left. We must have passed it at least a score of times. You might look for it for ever without finding it, if I didn't go with you to show you. I could find my way to it quite straight, though I could never explain it to you.'

'And who took you there?'

'I don't know. That morning the trees and plants seemed to drive me there. The long branches pushed me on, the grass bent down before me invitingly, the paths seemed to open expressly for me to take them. And I believe the animals themselves helped to lead me there, for I saw a stag trotting on before me as though he wanted me to follow; while a company of bullfinches flitted on from tree to tree, and warned me with their cries whenever I was about to take a wrong direction.'

'And is it very beautiful?'

Again she did not reply. Deep ecstasy filled her eyes; at last, when she was able to speak again, she said: 'Ah! so beautiful, that I could never tell you of it. I was so charmed that I was conscious only of some supreme joy, which I could not name, falling from the leaves and slumbering amid the grass. And I ran back here to take you along with me that I might not be without you.'

Then she clasped her arms round his neck again, and entreated him passionately, her lips almost pressed to his own.

'Oh! you will come!' she stammered; 'you must come; you will make me so miserable if you don't. You can't want me to be miserable…. And even if you knew that you would die there, even if that shade should be fatal to both of us, would you hesitate or cast a regretful look behind? We should remain there, at the foot of the tree, and sleep on quietly for ever, in one anther's arms. Ah! would it not be bliss indeed?'

'Yes, yes!' he stammered, transported by her passionate entreaties.

'But we shall not die,' she continued, raising her voice, and laughing with the laugh which proclaims woman's victory; 'we shall live to love each other. It is a tree of life, a tree whose shadow will make us stronger, more perfect, more complete. You will see that all will now go happily. Some blessed joy will assuredly descend on us from heaven! Will you come?'

His face paled, and his eyelids quivered, as though too powerful a light were suddenly beating against them.

'Will you come? will you come?' she cried again, yet more passionately, and already half rising to her feet.

He sprang up and followed her, at first with tottering steps and then with his arm thrown round her waist, as if he could endure no separation from her. He went where she went, carried along in the warm fragrance that streamed from her hair. And as he thus remained slightly in the rear, she turned upon him a face so radiant with love, such tempting lips and eyes, which so imperiously bade him follow, that he would have gone with her anywhere, trusting and unquestioning, like a dog.

XV

They went down and out into the garden without the smile fading from Serge's face. All that he saw of the greenery around him was such as was reflected in the clear depths of Albine's eyes. As they approached, the garden smiled and smiled again, a murmur of content sped from leaf to leaf and from bough to bough to the furthest depths of the avenues. For days and days the garden must have been hoping and expecting to see them thus, clinging to one another, making their peace again with the trees and searching for their lost love on the grassy banks. A solemn warning breath sighed through the branches; the afternoon sky was drowsy with heat; the plants raised their bowing heads to watch them pass.

'Listen,' whispered Albine. 'They drop into silence as we come near them; but over yonder they are expecting us, they are telling each other the way they must lead us.... I told you we should have no trouble about the paths, the trees themselves will direct us with their spreading arms.'

The whole park did, indeed, appear to be impelling them gently onward. In their rear it seemed as if a barrier of brush-wood had bristled up to prevent them from retracing their steps; while, in front of them, the grassy lawns spread out so invitingly, that they glided along the soft slopes, without thought of choosing their way.

'And the birds are coming with us, too,' said Albine. 'It is the tomtits this time. Don't you see them? They are skimming over the hedges, and they stop at each turning to see that we don't lose our way.' Then she added: 'All the living things of the park are with us. Can't you hear them? There is a deep rustling close behind us. It is the birds in the trees, the insects in the grass, the roebucks and the stags in the coppices, and even the little fishes splashing the quiet water with their beating fins. Don't turn round, or you will frighten them. Ah! I am sure we have a rare train behind us.'

They still walked on, unfatigued. Albine spoke only to charm Serge with the music of her voice, while Serge obeyed the slightest pressure of her hand. They knew not what they passed, but they were certain that they were going straight towards their goal. And as they went along, the garden became gradually graver, more discreet; the soughing of the branches died away, the streams hushed their plashing waters, the birds, the beasts, and the insects fell into silence. All around them reigned solemn stillness.

Then Albine and Serge instinctively raised their heads. In front of them they beheld a colossal mass of foliage; and, as they hesitated for a moment, a roe, after gazing at them with its sweet soft eyes, bounded into the thickets.

'It is there,' said Albine.

She led the way, her face again turned towards Serge, whom she drew with her, and they disappeared amid the quivering leaves, and all grew quiet again. They were entering into delicious peace.

In the centre there stood a tree covered with so dense a foliage that one could not recognise its species. It was of giant girth, with a trunk that seemed to breathe like a living breast, and far-reaching boughs that stretched like protecting arms around it. It towered up there beautiful, strong, virile, and fruitful. It was the king of the garden, the father of the forest, the pride of the plants, the beloved of the sun, whose earliest and latest beams smiled daily on its crest. From its green vault poured all the joys of creation: fragrance of flowers, music of birds, gleams of golden light, wakeful freshness of dawn, slumbrous warmth of evening twilight. So strong was the sap that it burst through the very bark, bathing the tree with the powers of fruitfulness, making it the symbol of earth's virility. Its presence sufficed to give the clearing an enchanting charm. The other trees built up around it an impenetrable wall, which isolated it as in a sanctuary of silence and twilight. There was but greenery there, not a scrap of sky, not a glimpse of horizon; nothing but a swelling rotunda, draped with green silkiness of leaves, adorned below with mossy velvet. And one entered, as into the liquid crystal of a source, a greenish limpidity, a sheet of silver reposing beneath reflected reeds. Colours, perfumes, sounds, quivers, all were vague, indeterminate, transparent, steeped in a felicity amidst which everything seemed to faint away. Languorous warmth, the glimmer of a summer's night, as it fades on the bare shoulder of some fair girl, a scarce perceptible murmur of love sinking into silence, lingered beneath the motionless branches, unstirred by the slightest zephyr. It was hymeneal solitude, a chamber where Nature lay hidden in the embraces of the sun.

Albine and Serge stood there in an ecstasy of joy. As soon as the tree had received them beneath its shade, they felt eased of all the anxious disquiet which had so long distressed them. The fears which had made them avoid each other, the fierce wrestling of spirit which had torn and wounded them, without consciousness on their part of what they were really contending against, vanished, and left them in perfect peace. Absolute confidence, supreme serenity, now pervaded them, they yielded unhesitatingly to the joy of being together in that lonely nook, so completely hidden from the outside world. They had surrendered themselves to the garden, they awaited in all calmness the behests of that tree of life. It enveloped them in such ecstasy of love that the whole clearing seemed to disappear from before their eyes, and to leave them wrapped in an atmosphere of perfume.

'The air is like ripe fruit,' murmured Albine.

And Serge whispered in his turn: 'The grass seems so full of life and motion, that I could almost think I was treading on your dress.'

It was a kind of religious feeling which made them lower their voices. No sentiment of curiosity impelled them to raise their heads and scan the tree. The consciousness of its majesty weighed heavily upon them. With a glance Albine asked whether she had overrated the enchantment of the greenery, and Serge answered her with two tears that trickled down his cheeks. The joy that filled them at being there could not be expressed in words.

'Come,' she whispered in his ear, in a voice that was softer than a sigh.

And she glided on in front of him, and seated herself at the very foot of the tree. Then, with a fond smile, she stretched out her hands to him; while he, standing before her, grasped them in his own with a responsive smile. Then she drew him slowly towards her and he sank down by her side.

'Ah! do you remember,' he said, 'that wall which seemed to have grown up between us? Now there is nothing to keep us apart—you are not unhappy now?'

'No, no,' she answered; 'very happy.'

For a moment they relapsed into silence whilst soft emotion stole over them. Then Serge, caressing Albine, exclaimed: 'Your face is mine; your eyes, your mouth, your cheeks are mine. Your arms are mine, from your shoulders to the tips of your nails. You are wholly mine.' And as he spoke he kissed her lips, her eyes, her cheeks. He kissed her arms, with quick short kisses, from her fingers to her shoulders. He poured upon her a rain of kisses hot as a summer shower, deluging her cheeks, her forehead, her lips, and her neck.

'But if you are mine, I am yours,' said he; 'yours for ever; for I now well know that you are my queen, my sovereign, whom I must worship on bended knee. I am here only to obey you, to lie at your feet, to anticipate your wishes, to shelter you with my arms, to drive away whatever might trouble your tranquillity. And you are my life's goal. Since I first awoke in this garden, you have ever been before me; I have grown up that I might be yours. Ever, as my end, my reward, have I gazed upon your grace. You passed in the sunshine with the sheen of your golden hair; you were a promise that I should some day know all the mysteries and necessities of creation, of this earth, of these trees, these waters, these skies, whose last secret is yet unrevealed. I belong to you; I am your slave; I will listen to you and obey you, with my lips upon your feet.'

He said this, bowed to the ground, adoring Woman. And Albine, full of pride, allowed herself to be adored. She yielded her hands, her cheeks, her lips, to Serge's rapturous kisses. She felt herself indeed a queen as she saw him, who was so strong, bending so humbly before her. She had conquered him, and held him there at her mercy. With a single word she could dispose of him. And that which helped her to recognise her omnipotence was that she heard the whole garden rejoicing at her triumph, with gradually swelling paeans of approval.

'Ah! if we could fly off together, if we could but die even, in one another's arms,' faltered Serge, scarce able to articulate. But Albine had strength enough to raise her finger as though to bid him listen.

It was the garden that had planned and willed it all. For weeks and weeks it had been favouring and encouraging their passion, and at last, on that supreme day, it had lured them to that spot, and now it became the Tempter whose every voice spoke of love. From the flower-beds, amid the fragrance of the languid blossoms, was wafted a soft sighing, which told of the weddings of the roses, the love-joys of the violets; and never before had the heliotropes sent forth so voluptuous a perfume. Mingled with the soft air which arose from the orchard were all the exhalations of ripe fruit, the vanilla of apricots, the musk of oranges, all the luscious aroma of fruitfulness. From the meadows came fuller notes, the million sighs of the sun-kissed grass, the multitudinous love-plaints of legions of living things, here and there softened by the refreshing caresses of the rivulets, on whose banks the very willows palpitated with desire. And the forest proclaimed the mighty passion of the oaks. Through the high branches sounded solemn music, organ strains like the nuptial marches of the ashes and the birches, the hornbeams and the planes, while from the bushes and the young coppices arose noisy mirth like that of youthful lovers chasing one another over banks and into hollows amid much crackling and snapping of branches. From afar, too, the faint breeze wafted the sounds of the rocks splitting in their passion beneath the burning heat, while near them the spiky plants loved in a tragic fashion of their own, unrefreshed by the neighbouring springs, which themselves glowed with the love of the passionate sun.

'What do they say?' asked Serge, half swooning, as Albine pressed him to her bosom. The voices of the Paradou were growing yet more distinct. The animals, in their turn, joined in the universal song of nature. The grasshoppers grew faint with the passion of their chants; the butterflies scattered kisses with their beating wings. The amorous sparrows flew to their mates; the rivers rippled over the loves of the fishes; whilst in the depths of the forest the nightingales sent forth pearly, voluptuous notes, and the stags bellowed their love aloud. Reptiles and insects, every species of invisible life, every atom of matter, the earth itself joined in the great chorus. It was the chorus of love and of nature—the chorus of the whole wide world; and in the very sky the clouds were radiant with rapture, as to those two children Love revealed the Eternity of Life.

XVI

Albine and Serge smiled at one another.

'I love you, Albine,' said Serge.

'Serge, I love you,' Albine answered.

And never before had those syllables 'I love you' had for them so supreme a meaning. They expressed everything. Joy pervaded those young lovers, who had attained to the fulness of life. They felt that they were now on a footing of equality with the forces of the world; and with their happiness mingled the placid conviction that they had obeyed the universal law. And Serge seemed to have awakened to life, lion-like, to rule the whole far expanse under the free heavens. His feet planted themselves more firmly on the ground, his chest expanded, there was pride and confidence in his gait and demeanour. He took Albine by the hands, she was trembling, and he was obliged to support her.

'Don't be afraid,' he said; 'you are she whom I love.'

It was Albine now who had become the submissive one. She drooped her head upon his shoulder, glancing up at him with anxious scrutiny. Would he never bear her spite for that hour of adoration in which he had called himself her slave? But he smiled, and stroked her hair, while she said to him: 'Let me stay like this, in your arms, for I cannot walk without you. I will make myself so small and light, that you will scarcely know I am there.' Then becoming very serious she added, 'You must always love me; and I will be very obedient and do whatever you wish. I will yield to you in all things if you but love me.'

Serge felt more powerful and virile on seeing her so humble. 'Why are you trembling so?' he asked her; 'I can have no cause to reproach you.'

But she did not answer him, she gazed almost sadly upon the tree and the foliage and the grass around them.

'Foolish child!' he said, laughing; 'are you afraid that I shall be angry with you for your love? We have loved as we were meant to love. Let me kiss you.'

But, dropping her eyelids so that she might not see the tree, she said, in a low whisper, 'Take me away!'

Serge led her thence, pacing slowly and giving one last glance at the spot which love had hallowed. The shadows in the clearing were growing darker, and a gentle quiver coursed through the foliage. When they emerged from the wood and caught sight of the sun, still shining brightly in the horizon, they felt easier. Everything around Serge now seemed to bend down before him and pay homage to his love. The garden was now nothing but an appanage of Albine's beauty, and seemed to have grown larger and fairer amid the love- kisses of its rulers.

But Albine's joy was still tinged with disquietude. She would suddenly pause amid her laughter and listen anxiously.

'What is the matter?' asked Serge.

'Nothing,' she replied, casting furtive glances behind her.

They did not know in what out-of-the-way corner of the park they were. To lose themselves in their capricious wanderings only served to amuse them as a rule; but that day they experienced anxious embarrassment. By degrees they quickened their pace, plunging more and more deeply into a labyrinth of bushes.

'Don't you hear?' asked Albine, nervously, as she suddenly stopped short, almost breathless.

Serge listened, a prey, in his turn, to the anxiety which the girl could no longer conceal.

'All the coppice seems full of voices,' she continued. 'It sounds as though there were people deriding us. Listen! Wasn't that a laugh that sounded from that tree? And over yonder did not the grass murmur something as my dress brushed against it?'

'No, no,' he said, anxious to reassure her, 'the garden loves us; and, if it said anything, it would not be to vex or annoy us. Don't you remember all the sweet words which sounded through the leaves? You are nervous and fancy things.'

But she shook her head and faltered: 'I know very well that the garden is our friend.... So it must be some one who has broken into it. I am certain I hear some one. I am trembling all over. Oh! take me away and hide me somewhere, I beseech you.'

Then they went on again, scanning every tree and bush, and imagining that they could see faces peering at them from behind every trunk. Albine was certain, she said, that there were steps pursuing them in the distance. 'Let us hide ourselves,' she begged.

She had turned quite scarlet. It was new-born modesty, a sense of shame which had laid hold of her like a fever, mantling over the snowy whiteness of her skin, which never previously had known that flush. Serge was alarmed at seeing her thus crimson, her face full of distress, her eyes brimming with tears. He tried to clasp her in his arms again and to soothe her with a caress; but she slipped away from him, and, with a despairing gesture, made sign that they were not alone. And her blushes grew deeper as her eyes fell upon her bare arms. She shuddered when her loose hanging hair stirred against her neck and shoulders. The slightest touch of a waving bough or a passing insect, the softest breath of air, now made her tremble as if some invisible hand were grasping at her.

'Calm yourself,' begged Serge, 'there is no one. You are as crimson as though you had a fever. Let us rest here for a moment. Do; I beg you.'

She had no fever at all, she said, but she wanted to get back as quickly as possible, so that no one might laugh at her. And, ever increasing her pace, she plucked handfuls of leaves and tendrils from the hedges, which she entwined about her. She fastened a branch of mulberry over her hair, twisted bindweed round her arms, and tied it to her wrists, and circled her neck with such long sprays of laurustinus, that her bosom was hidden as by a veil of leaves.

And that shame of hers proved contagious. Serge, who first had jested, asking her if she were going to a ball, glanced at himself, and likewise felt alarmed and ashamed, to a point that he also wound foliage about his person.

Meantime, they could discover no way out of the labyrinth of bushes, but all at once, at the end of the path, they found themselves face to face with an obstacle, a tall, grey, grave mass of stone. It was the wall of the Paradou.

'Come away! come away!' cried Albine.

And she sought to drag him thence; but they had not taken another twenty steps before they again came upon the wall. They then skirted it at a ran, panic-stricken. It stretched along, gloomy and stern, without a break in its surface. But suddenly, at a point where it fringed a meadow, it seemed to fall away. A great breach gaped in it, like a huge window of light opening on to the neighbouring valley. It must have been the very hole that Albine had one day spoken of, which she said she had blocked up with brambles and stones. But the brambles now lay scattered around like severed bits of rope, the stones had been thrown some distance away, and the breach itself seemed to have been enlarged by some furious hand.

XVII

'Ah! I felt sure of it,' cried Albine, in accents of supreme despair. 'I begged you to take me away—Serge, I beseech you, don't look through it.'

But Serge, in spite of himself, stood rooted to the ground, on the threshold of the breach through which he gazed. Down below, in the depths of the valley, the setting sun cast a sheet of gold upon the village of Les Artaud, which showed vision-like amidst the twilight in which the neighbouring fields were already steeped. One could plainly distinguish the houses that straggled along the high road; the little yards with their dunghills, and the narrow gardens planted with vegetables. Higher up, the tall cypress in the graveyard reared its dusky silhouette, and the red tiles on the church glowed brazier-like, the dark bell looking down on them like a human face, while the old parsonage at the side threw its doors and windows open to the evening air.

'For pity's sake,' sobbed Albine, 'don't look out, Serge. Remember that you promised you would always love me. Ah! will you ever love me enough, now? Stay, let me cover your eyes with my hands. You know it was my hands that cured you. You won't push me away.'

But he put her from him gently. Then, while she fell down and clung to his legs, he passed his hands across his face, as though he were wiping from his brow and eyes some last lingering traces of sleep. It was yonder, then, that lay the unknown world, the strange land of which he had never dreamed without vague fear. Where had he seen that country? From what dream was he awakening, that he felt such keen anguish swelling up in his breast till it almost choked him? The village was breaking out into life at the close of the day's work. The men were coming home from the fields with weary gait, their jackets thrown over their shoulders; the women, standing by their doors, were beckoning to them to hasten on; while the children, in noisy bands, chased the fowls about and pelted them with stones. In the churchyard a couple of scapegraces, a lad and a girl, were creeping along under the shelter of the wall in order to escape notice. Swarms of sparrows were retiring to roost beneath the eaves of the church; and, on the steps of the parsonage, a blue calico skirt had just appeared, of such spreading dimensions as to quite block the doorway.

'Oh! he is looking out! he is looking out!' sobbed Albine. 'Listen to me. It was only just now that you promised to obey me. I beg of you to turn round and to look upon the garden. Haven't you been very happy in the garden? It was the garden which gave me to you. Think of the happy days it has in store for us, what lasting bliss and enjoyment. Instead of which it will be death that will force its way through that hole, if you don't quickly flee and take me with you. See, all those people yonder will come and thrust themselves between us. We were so quite alone, so secluded, so well guarded by the trees! Oh! the garden is our love! Look on the garden, I beg it of you on my knees!'

But Serge was quivering. He had began to recollect. The past was re-awakening. He could distinctly hear the stir of the village life. Those peasants, those women and children, he knew them. There was the mayor, Bambousse, returning from Les Olivettes, calculating how much the approaching vintage would yield him; there were the Brichets, the husband crawling along, and the wife moaning with misery. There was Rosalie flirting with big Fortune behind a wall. He recognised also the pair in the churchyard, that mischievous Vincent and that bold hussy Catherine, who were catching big grasshoppers amongst the tombstones. Yes, and they had Voriau, the black dog, with them, helping them and ferreting about in the dry grass, and sniffing at every crack in the old stones. Under the eaves of the church the sparrows were twittering and bickering before going to roost. The boldest of them flew down and entered the church through the broken windows, and, as Serge followed them with his eyes, he recollected all the noise they had formerly made below the pulpit and on the step by the altar rails, where crumbs were always put for them. And that was La Teuse yonder, on the parsonage doorstep, looking fatter than ever in her blue calico dress. She was turning her head to smile at Desiree, who was coming up from the yard, laughing noisily. Then they both vanished indoors, and Serge, distracted with all these revived memories, stretched out his arms.

'It is all over now,' faltered Albine, as she sank down amongst the broken brambles. 'You will never love me enough again.'

She wept, while Serge stood rooted by the breach, straining his ears to catch the slightest sound that might be wafted from the village, waiting, as it were, for some voice that might fully awaken him. The bell in the church- tower had begun to sway, and slowly through the quiet evening air the three chimes of the *Angelus* floated up to the Paradou. It was a soft and silvery summons. The bell now seemed to be alive.

'O God!' cried Serge, falling on his knees, quite overcome by the emotion which the soft notes of the bell had excited in him.

He bent down towards the ground, and he felt the three peals of the *Angelus* pass over his neck and echo through his heart. The voice of the bell seemed to grow louder. It was raised again sternly, pitilessly, for a few moments which seemed to him to be years. It summoned up before him all his old life, his pious childhood, his happy days at the seminary, and his first Masses in that burning valley of Les Artaud, where he had dreamt of a solitary, saintly life. He had always heard it speaking to him as it was doing now. He recognised every inflection of that sacred voice, which had so constantly fallen upon his ears, like the grave and gentle voice of a mother. Why had he so long ceased to hear it? In former times it had promised him the coming of Mary. Had Mary come then and taken him and carried him off into those happy green fastnesses, which the sound of the bell could not reach? He would never have lapsed into forgetfulness if the bell had not ceased to ring. And as he bent his head still lower towards the earth, the contact of his beard with his hands made him start. He could not recognise his own self with that long silky beard. He twisted it and fumbled about in his hair seeking for the bare circle of the tonsure, but a heavy growth of curls now covered his whole head from his brow to the nape of his neck.

'Ah! you were right,' he said, casting a look of despair at Albine. 'It was forbidden. We have sinned, and we have merited some terrible punishment.... But I, indeed, I tried to reassure you, I did not hear the threats which sounded in your ears through the branches.'

Albine tried to clasp him in her arms again as she sobbed out, 'Get up, and let us escape together. Perhaps even yet there is time for us to love each other.'

'No, no; I haven't the strength. I should stumble and fall over the smallest pebble in the path. Listen to me. I am afraid of myself. I know not what man dwells in me. I have murdered myself, and my hands are red with blood. If you took me away, you would never see aught in my eyes save tears.'

She kissed his wet eyes, as she answered passionately, 'No matter! Do you love me?'

He was too terrified to answer her. A heavy step set the pebbles rolling on the other side of the wall. A growl of anger seemed to draw nigh. Albine had not been mistaken. Some one was, indeed, there, disturbing the woodland quiet with jealous inquisition. Then both Albine and Serge, as if overwhelmed with shame, sought to bide themselves behind a bush. But Brother Archangias, standing in front of the breach, could already see them.

The Brother remained for a moment silent, clenching his fists and looking at Albine clinging round Serge's neck, with the disgust of a man who has espied some filth by the roadside.

'I suspected it,' he mumbled between his teeth. 'It was virtually certain that they had hidden him here.'

Then he took a few steps, and cried out: 'I see you. It is an abomination. Are you a brute beast to go coursing through the woods with that female? She has led you far astray, has she not? She has besmeared you with filth, and now you are hairy like a goat…. Pluck a branch from the trees wherewith to smite her on the back.'

Again Albine whispered in an ardent, prayerful voice: 'Do you love me? Do you love me?'

But Serge, with bowed head, kept silence, though he did not yet drive her from him.

'Fortunately, I have found you,' continued Brother Archangias. 'I discovered this hole…. You have disobeyed God, and have slain your own peace. Henceforward, for ever, temptation will gnaw you with its fiery tooth, and you will no longer have ignorance of evil to help you to fight it. It was that creature who tempted you to your fall, was it not? Do you not see the serpent's tail writhing amongst her hair? The mere sight of her shoulders is sufficient to make one vomit with disgust…. Leave her. Touch her not, for she is the beginning of hell. In the name of God, come forth from that garden.'

'Do you love me? Oh! do you love me?' reiterated Albine.

But Serge hastily drew away from her as though her bare arms and shoulders really scorched him.

'In the name of God! In the name of God!' cried the Brother, in a voice of thunder.

Serge unresistingly stepped towards the breach. As soon as Brother Archangias, with rough violence, had dragged him out of the Paradou, Albine, who had fallen half fainting to the ground, with hands wildly stretched towards the love which was deserting her, rose up again, choking with sobs. And she fled, vanished into the midst of the trees, whose trunks she lashed with her streaming hair.

BOOK III

I

When Abbe Mouret had said the *Pater*, he bowed to the altar, and went to the Epistle side. Then he came down, and made the sign of the cross over big Fortune and Rosalie, who were kneeling, side by side, before the altar-rails.

'*Ego conjungo vos in matrimonium, in nomine Patris, et Filii, et Spiritus Sancti.*'

'*Amen,*' responded Vincent, who was serving the mass, and glancing curiously at his big brother out of the corner of his eye.

Fortune and Rosalie bent their heads, affected by some slight emotion, although they had nudged each other with their elbows when they knelt down, by way of making one another laugh. But Vincent went to get the basin and the sprinkler. Fortune placed the ring in the basin, a thick ring of solid silver. When the priest had blessed it, sprinkling it crosswise, he returned it to Fortune, who slipped it upon Rosalie's finger. Her hand was still discoloured with grass-stains, which soap had not been able to remove.

'*In nomine Patris, et Filii, et Spiritus Sancti,*' Abbe Mouret murmured again, giving them a final benediction.

'*Amen,*' responded Vincent.

It was early morning. The sun was not yet shining through the big windows of the church. Outside one could hear the noisy twittering of the sparrows in the branches of the service tree, whose foliage shot through the broken panes. La Teuse, who had not previously had time to clean the church, was now dusting the altar, craning up on her sound leg to wipe the feet of the ochre and lake-bedaubed Christ, and arranging the chairs as quietly as possible; all the while bowing and crossing herself, and following the service, but not omitting a single sweep of her feather broom. Quite alone, at the foot of the pulpit, was mother Brichet, praying in a very demonstrative fashion. She kept on her knees, and repeated the prayers in so loud a whisper that it seemed as if a swarm of bluebottles had taken possession of the nave.

At the other end of the church near the confessional, Catherine held an infant in swaddling clothes. As it began to cry, she turned her back upon the altar, and tossed it up, and amused it with the bell-rope, which dangled just over its nose.

'*Dominus vobiscum,*' said the priest, turning round, and spreading out his hands.

'*Et cum spiritu tuo*,' responded Vincent.

At that moment three big girls came into the church. They were too shy to go far up, though they jostled one another to get a better view of what was going on. They were three friends of Rosalie, who had dropped in for a minute or two on their way to the fields, curious as they were to hear what his reverence would say to the bride and bridegroom. They had big scissors hanging at their waists. At last they hid themselves behind the font, where they pinched each other and twisted themselves about, while trying to choke their bursts of laughter with their clenched fists.

'Well,' whispered La Rousse, a finely built girl, with copper-coloured skin and hair, 'there won't be any scrimmage to get out of church when it's all over.'

'Oh! old Bambousse is quite right,' murmured Lisa, a short dark girl, with gleaming eyes; 'when one has vines, one looks after them. Since his reverence so particularly desired to marry Rosalie, he can very well do it all alone.'

The other girl, Babet, who was humpbacked, tittered. 'There's mother Brichet,' she said; 'she is always here. She prays for the whole family. Listen, do you hear how she's buzzing? All that will mean something in her pocket. She knows very well what she is about, I can tell you.'

'She is playing the organ for them,' retorted La Rousse.

At this all three burst into a laugh. La Teuse, in the distance, threatened them with her broom. At the altar, Abbe Mouret was taking the sacrament. As he went from the Epistle side towards Vincent, so that the water of ablution might be poured upon his thumb and fore-finger, Lisa said more softly: 'It's nearly over. He will begin to talk to them directly.'

'Yes,' said La Rousse, 'and so big Fortune will still be able to go to his work, and Rosalie won't lose her day's pay at the vintage. It is very convenient to be married so early in the morning. He looks very sheepish, that big Fortune.'

'Of course,' murmured Babet. 'It tires him, keeping so long on his knees. You may be sure that he has never knelt so long since his first communion.'

But the girls' attention was suddenly distracted by the baby which Catherine was dangling in her arms. It wanted to get hold of the bell-rope, and was quite blue with rage, frantically stretching out its little hands and almost choking itself with crying.

'Ah! so the youngster is there,' said La Rousse.

The baby now burst into still louder wailing, and struggled like a little Imp.

'Turn it over on its stomach, and let it suck,' said Babet to Catherine.

Catherine lifted up her head, and began to laugh, with the shamelessness of a little minx. 'It's not at all amusing,' she said, giving the baby a shake. 'Be quiet, will you, little pig! My sister plumped it down on my knees.'

'Naturally,' said Babet, mischievously. 'You could scarcely have expected her to give the brat to Monsieur le Cure to nurse.'

At this sally, La Rousse almost fell over in a fit of laughter. She leaned against the wall, holding her sides with her hands. Lisa threw herself against her, and attempted to soothe her by pinching her back and shoulders; while Babet laughed with a hunchback's laugh, which grated on the ear like the sound of a saw.

'If it hadn't been for the little one,' she continued, 'Monsieur le Cure would have lost all use for his holy water. Old Bambousse had made up his mind to marry Rosalie to young Laurent, of Figuieres.'

However, the girls' merriment and their chatter now came to an end, for they saw La Teuse limping furiously towards them. At this the three big hussies felt alarmed, stepped back, and subsided into sedateness.

'You worthless things!' hissed La Teuse. 'You come to talk a lot of filth here, do you? Aren't you ashamed of yourself, La Rousse? You ought to be there, on your knees, before the altar, like Rosalie. I will throw you outside if you stir again. Do you hear?'

La Rousse's copper cheeks were tinged with a rising blush, and Babet glanced at her and tittered.

'And you,' continued La Teuse, turning towards Catherine, 'just you leave that baby alone. You are pinching it on purpose to make it scream. Don't tell me you are not. Give it to me.'

She took the child, hushed it in her arms for a moment, and then laid it upon a chair, where it went to sleep, peacefully like a cherub. The church then subsided into solemn quietness, disturbed only by the chattering of the sparrows on the rowan tree outside. At the altar, Vincent had carried the missal to the right again, and Abbe Mouret had just folded the corporal and slipped it within the burse. He was now saying the concluding prayers with a solemn earnestness, which neither the screams of the baby nor the giggling of the three girls had been able to disturb. He seemed to hear nothing of them, but to be wholly absorbed in the prayers which he was offering up to Heaven for the happiness of the pair whose union he had just blessed. The sky that morning was grey with a hazy heat, which veiled the sun. Through the broken windows a russet vapour streamed into the church, betokening a stormy day. Along the walls the gaudily coloured pictures of the Stations of the Cross displayed their red, blue, and yellow patches; at the bottom of the nave the dry woodwork of the gallery creaked and strained; and under the doorway the tall grass by the steps thrust ripening straw, all alive with little brown grasshoppers. The clock, in its wooden case, made a whirring noise, as though it were some consumptive trying to clear his throat, and then huskily struck half-past six.

'*Ite, missa est,*' said the priest, turning round to the congregation.

'*Deo gratias,*' responded Vincent.

Then, having kissed the altar, Abbe Mouret once more turned round, and murmured over the bent heads of the newly married pair the final benediction: '*Deus Abraham, Deus Isaac, et Deus Jacob vobiscum sit*'—his voice dying away into a gentle whisper.

'Now, he's going to address them,' said Babet to her friends.

'He is very pale,' observed Lisa. 'He isn't a bit like Monsieur Caffin, whose fat face always seemed to be on the laugh. My little sister Rose says that she daren't tell him anything when she goes to confess.'

'All the same,' murmured La Rousse, 'he's not ugly. His illness has aged him a little, but it seems to suit him. He has bigger eyes, and lines at the corners of his mouth which make him look like a man. Before he had the fever, he was too much like a girl.'

'I believe he's got some great trouble,' said Babet. 'He looks as though he were pining away. His face is deadly pale, but how his eyes glitter! When he drops his eyelids, it is just as though he were doing it to extinguish the fire in his eyes.'

La Teuse again shook her broom at them. 'Hush!' she hissed out, so energetically that it seemed as if a blast of wind had burst into the church.

Meantime Abbe Mouret had collected himself, and he began, in a rather low voice:

'My dear brother, my dear sister, you are joined together in Jesus. The institution of marriage symbolises the sacred union between Jesus and His Church. It is a bond which nothing can break; which God wills shall be eternal, so that man may not sever those whom Heaven has joined. In making you flesh of each other's flesh, and bone of each other's bone, God teaches you that it is your duty to walk side by side through life, a faithful couple, along the paths which He, in His omnipotence, appoints for you. And you must love each other with God-like love. The slightest ill-feeling between you will be disobedience to the Creator, Who has joined you together as a single body. Remain, then, for ever united, after the likeness of the Church, which Jesus has espoused, in giving to us all His body and blood.'

Big Fortune and Rosalie sat listening, with their noses peaked up inquisitively.

'What does he say?' asked Lisa, who was a little deaf.

'Oh! he says what they all say,' answered La Rousse. 'He has a glib tongue, like all the priests have.'

Abbe Mouret went on with his address, his eyes wandering over the heads of the newly wedded couple towards a shadowy corner of the church. And by degrees his voice became more flexible, and he put emotion into the words he spoke, words which he had formerly learned by heart from a manual intended for the use of young priests. He had turned slightly towards Rosalie, and whenever his memory failed him, he added sentences of his own:

'My dear sister, submit yourself to your husband, as the Church submits itself to Jesus. Remember that you must leave everything to follow him, like a faithful handmaiden. You must give up father and mother, you must cleave only to your husband, and you must obey him that you may obey God also. And your yoke will be a yoke of love and peace. Be his comfort, his happiness, the perfume of his days of strength, the support of his days of weakness. Let him find you, as a grace, ever by his side. Let him have but to reach out his hand to find yours grasping it. It is thus that you will step along together, never losing your way, and that you will meet with happiness in the carrying out of the divine laws. Oh! my dear sister, my dear daughter, your humility will hear sweet fruit; it will give birth to all the domestic virtues, to the joys of the hearth, and the prosperity that attends a God-fearing family. Have for your husband the love of Rachel, the wisdom of Rebecca, the constant fidelity of Sarah. Tell yourself that a pure life is the source of all happiness. Pray to God each morning that He may give you strength to live as a woman who respects her responsibilities and duties; for the punishment you would otherwise incur is terrible: you would lose your love. Oh! to live loveless, to tear flesh from flesh, to belong no more to the one who is half of your very self, to live on in pain and agony, bereft of the one you have loved! In vain would you stretch out your arms to him; he would turn away from you. You would yearn for happiness, but you would find in your heart nothing but shame and bitterness. Hear me, my daughter, it is in your own conduct, in your obedience, in your purity, in your love, that God has established the strength of your union.'

As Abbe Mouret spoke these words, there was a burst of laughter at the other end of the church. The baby had just woke up on the chair where La Teuse had laid it. But it was no longer in a bad temper. Having kicked itself free of its swaddling clothes, it was laughing merrily, and shaking its rosy little feet in the air. It was the sight of these little feet that made it laugh.

Rosalie, who was beginning to find the priest's address rather tedious, turned her head to smile at the child. But, when she saw it kicking about on the chair, she grew alarmed, and cast an angry look at Catherine.

'Oh! you can look at me as much as you like,' said Catherine. 'I'm not going to take it any more. It would only begin to cry again.'

And she turned aside to ferret in an ant-hole at a corner of one of the stone flags under the gallery.

'Monsieur Caffin didn't talk so long,' now remarked La Rousse. 'When he married Miette, he just gave her two taps on the cheek and told her to be good.'

My dear brother,' resumed Abbe Mouret, turning towards big Fortune, 'it is God who, to-day, gives you a companion, for He does not wish that man should live alone. But, if He ordains that she shall be your servant, He demands from you that you shall be to her a master full of gentleness and love. You will love her, because she is part of your own flesh, of your own blood, and your own bone. You will protect her, because God has given you strong arms only that you may stretch them over her head in the hour of danger. Remember that she is entrusted to you, and that you cannot abuse her submission and weakness without sin. Oh! my dear brother, what proud happiness should be yours! Henceforth, you will no longer live in the selfish egotism of solitude. At all hours you will have a lovable duty before you. There is nothing better than to love, unless it be to protect those whom we love. Your heart will expand; your manly strength will increase a hundredfold. Oh! to be a support and stay, to have a love given into your keeping, to see a being sink her existence in yours and say, "Take me and do with me what you will! I trust myself wholly to you!" And may you be accursed if you ever abandon her! It would be a cowardly desertion which God would assuredly punish. From the moment she gives herself to you, she becomes yours for ever. Carry her rather in your arms, and set her not upon the ground until it be certain that she will be there in safety. Give up everything, my dear brother—'

But here the Abbe's voice faltered, and only an indistinct murmur came from his lips. He had quite closed his eyes, his face was deathly white, and his voice betokened such deep distress that big Fortune himself shed tears without knowing why.

'He hasn't recovered yet,' said Lisa. 'It is wrong of him to fatigue himself. See, there's Fortune crying!'

'Men are softer-hearted than women,' murmured Babet.

'He spoke very well, all the same,' remarked La Rousse. 'Those priests think of a lot of things that wouldn't occur to anybody else.'

'Hush!' cried La Teuse, who was already making ready to extinguish the candles.

But Abbe Mouret still stammered on, trying to utter a few more sentences. 'It is for this reason, my dear brother, my dear sister, that you must live in the Catholic Faith, which alone can ensure the peace of your hearth. Your families have taught you to love God, to pray to Him every morning and evening, to look only for the gifts of His mercy—'

He was unable to finish. He turned round, took the chalice off the altar, and retired, with bowed head, into the vestry, preceded by Vincent, who almost let the cruets and napkin fall, in trying to see what Catherine might be doing at the end of the church.

'Oh! the heartless creature!' said Rosalie, who left her husband to go and take her baby in her arms. The child laughed. She kissed it, and rearranged its swaddling clothes, while threatening Catherine with her fist. 'If it had fallen,' she cried out, 'I would have boxed your ears for you, nicely.'

Big Fortune now came slouching along. The three girls stepped towards him, with compressed lips.

'See how proud he is,' murmured Babet to the others. 'He is sure of inheriting old Bambousse's money now. I used to see him creeping along every night under the little wall with Rosalie.'

Then they giggled, and big Fortune, standing there in front of them, laughed even louder than they did. He pinched La Rousse, and let Lisa jeer at him. He was a sturdy young blood, and cared nothing for anybody. The priest's address had annoyed him.

'Hallo! mother, come on!' he called in his loud voice. But mother Brichet was begging at the vestry door. She stood there, tearful and wizen, before La Teuse, who was slipping some eggs into the pocket of her apron. Fortune didn't seem to feel the least sense of shame. He just winked and remarked: 'She is a knowing old card, my mother is. But then the Cure likes to see people at mass.'

Meanwhile, Rosalie had grown calm again. Before leaving the church, she asked Fortune if he had begged the priest to come and bless their room, according to the custom of the country. So Fortune ran off to the vestry, striding heavily through the church, as if it were a field. He soon reappeared, shouting that his reverence would come. La Teuse, who was scandalised at the noise made by all these people, who seemed to think themselves in a public street, gently clapped her hands, and pushed them towards the door.

'It is all over,' said she; 'go away and get to your work.'

She thought they had all gone, when her eye caught sight of Catherine, whom Vincent had joined. They were bending anxiously over the ants' nest. Catherine was poking a long straw into the hole so roughly, that a swarm of frightened ants had rushed out upon the floor. Vincent declared, however, that she must get her straw right to the bottom if she wished to find the queen.

'Ah! you young imps!' cried La Teuse, 'what are you after there? Can't you leave the poor little things alone? That is Mademoiselle Desiree's ants' nest. She would be nicely pleased if she saw you!'

At this the children promptly took to their heels.

II

Abbe Mouret, now wearing his cassock but still bareheaded, had come back to kneel at the foot of the altar. In the grey light that streamed through the window, his tonsure showed like a large livid spot amidst his hair; and a slight quiver, as if from cold, sped down his neck. With his hands tightly clasped he was praying earnestly, so absorbed in his devotions that he did not hear the heavy footsteps of La Teuse, who hovered around without daring to disturb him. She seemed to be grieved at seeing him bowed down there on his knees. For a moment, she thought that he was in tears, and thereupon she went behind the altar to watch him. Since his return, she had never liked to leave him in the church alone, for one evening she had found him lying in a dead faint upon the flagstones, with icy lips and clenched teeth, like a corpse.

'Come in, mademoiselle!' she said to Desiree, who was peeping through the vestry-doorway. 'He is still here, and he will lay himself up. You know you are the only person that he will listen to.'

'It is breakfast-time,' she replied softly, 'and I am very hungry.'

Then she gently sidled up to the priest, passed an arm round his neck, and kissed him.

'Good morning, brother,' she said. 'Do you want to make me die of hunger this morning?'

The face he turned upon her was so intensely sad, that she kissed him again on both his cheeks. He was emerging from agony. Then, on recognising her, he tried to put her from him, but she kept hold of one of his hands and would not release it. She would scarcely allow him to cross himself, but insisted upon leading him away.

'Come! Come! for I am very hungry. You must be hungry too.'

La Teuse had laid out the breakfast beneath two big mulberry trees, whose spreading branches formed a sheltering roof at the bottom of the little garden. The sun, which had at last succeeded in dissipating the stormy-looking vapours of early morning, was warming the beds of vegetables, while the mulberry-trees cast a broad shadow over the rickety table, on which were laid two cups of milk and some thick slices of bread.

'You see how nice it looks,' said Desiree, delighted at breakfasting in the fresh air.

She was already cutting some of the bread into strips, which she ate with

214

eager appetite. And as she saw La Teuse still standing in front of them, she said, 'Why don't you eat something?'

'I shall, presently,' the old servant answered. 'My soup is warming.'

Then, after a moment's silence, looking with admiration at the girl's big bites, she said to the priest: 'It is quite a pleasure to see her. Doesn't she make you feel hungry, Monsieur le Cure? You should force yourself.'

Abbe Mouret smiled as he glanced at his sister. 'Yes, yes,' he murmured; 'she gets on famously, she grows fatter every day.'

'That's because I eat,' said Desiree. 'If you would eat you would get fat, too. Are you ill again? You look very melancholy. I don't want to have it all over again, you know. I was so very lonely when they took you away to cure you.'

'She is right,' said La Teuse. 'You don't behave reasonably, Monsieur le Cure. You can't expect to be strong, living, as you do, on two or three crumbs a day, as though you were a bird. You don't make blood; and that's why you are so pale. Don't you feel ashamed of keeping as thin as a lath when we are so fat; we who are only women? People will begin to think that we gobble up everything and leave you nothing but the empty plates.'

Then both La Teuse and Desiree, brimful of health and strength, scolded him affectionately. His eyes seemed very large and bright, but empty, expressionless. He was still gently smiling.

'I am not ill,' he said; 'I have nearly finished my milk.' He had swallowed two mouthfuls of it, but had not touched the bread.

'The animals, now,' said Desiree, thoughtfully, 'seem to get on much more comfortably than we do. The fowls never have headaches, have they? The rabbits grow as fat as ever one wants them to be. And you never saw my pig looking sad.'

Then, turning towards her brother, she went on with an air of rapture:

'I have named it Matthew, because it is so like that fat man who brings the letters. It is growing so big and strong. It is very unkind of you to refuse to come and look at it as you always do. You will come to see it some day, won't you?'

While she was thus talking she had laid hold of her brother's share of bread, and was eating away at it. She had already finished one piece, and was beginning the second, when La Teuse became aware of what she was doing.

'That doesn't belong to you, that bread! You are actually stealing his food from him now!'

'Let her have it,' said Abbe Mouret, gently. 'I shouldn't have touched it myself. Eat it all, my dear, eat it all.'

For a moment Desiree fell into confusion, with her eyes fixed upon the bread, whilst she struggled to check her rising tears. Then she began to laugh, and finished the slice.

'My cow,' said she, continuing her remarks, 'is never as sad as you are. You were not here when uncle Pascal gave her to me, on the promise that I would be a good girl, or you would have seen how pleased she was when I kissed her for the first time.'

She paused to listen. A cock crowed in the yard, and a great uproar followed, with flapping of wings and cackling, grunting, and hoarse cries as if the whole yard were in a state of commotion.

'Ah! you know,' resumed Desiree, clapping her hands, 'she must be in calf now. I took her to the bull at Beage, three leagues from here. There are very few bulls hereabouts, you know.'

La Teuse shrugged her shoulders, and glanced at the priest with an expression of annoyance.

'It would be much better, mademoiselle,' said she, 'if you were to go and quiet your fowls. They all seem to be murdering one another.'

Indeed, the uproar in the yard had now become so great that the girl was already hurrying off with a great rustling of her petticoats, when the priest called her back. 'The milk, my dear; you have not finished the milk.'

He held out his cup to her, which he had scarcely touched. And she came back and drank the milk without the slightest scruple, in spite of La Teuse's angry look. Then she again set off for the poultry-yard, where they soon heard her reducing the fowls to peace and order. She had, perhaps, sat down in the midst of them, for she could be heard gently humming as though she were trying to lull them to sleep.

III

'Now my soup is too hot!' grumbled La Teuse, as she returned from the kitchen with a basin, from which a wooden spoon was projecting.

She placed herself just in front of Abbe Mouret, and began to eat very cautiously from the edge of the spoon. She wanted to enliven the Abbe and to draw him out of his melancholy moodiness. Ever since he had returned from the Paradou, he had declared himself well again, and had never complained. Often, indeed, he smiled in so soft and sweet a fashion, that his fever seemed to have increased his saintliness, at least so thought the villagers. But, at intervals, he had fits of gloomy silence, and appeared to be suffering torture which he strove to bear uncomplainingly. It was a mute agony which bore down upon him, and, for hours at a time, left him stupefied, a prey to a frightful inward struggle, the violence of which could only be guessed by the sweat of anguish that streamed down his face.

At such times La Teuse refused to leave him, and overwhelmed him with a torrent of gossip, until he had gradually recovered tranquillity by crushing the rebellion of his blood. On that particular morning, the old servant foresaw a more grievous attack than usual, and poured forth an amazing flood of talk, while continuing her wary manoeuvres with the spoon, which threatened to burn her tongue.

'Well, well,' said she, 'one has to live among a lot of wild beasts to see such goings-on. Would any one ever think in a decent village of being married by candlelight? It shows what a poor sort these Artauds are. When I was in Normandy, I used to see weddings that threw every one into commotion for a couple of leagues round. They would feast for three whole days. The priest would be there, and the mayor, too; and at the marriage of one of my cousins, all the firemen came as well. And didn't they have a fine time of it! But to make a priest get up before sunrise and marry people before even the chickens have left their roost, why, there's no sense in it! If I had been your reverence, I should have refused to do it. You haven't had your proper sleep, and you may have caught cold in the church. It is that which has upset you. Besides which it would be better to marry brute beasts than that Rosalie and her ugly lout. That brat of theirs dirtied one of the chairs.—But you ought to tell me when you feel poorly, and I could make you something warm.—Eh! Monsieur le Cure, speak to me!'

He answered, in a feeble voice, that he was quite well, and only needed a little fresh air. He had just leant against one of the mulberry-trees, and was breathing rather quickly, as if faint.

'Oh! all right,' went on La Teuse, 'do just as you like. Go on marrying people when you haven't the strength for it, and when you know very well that it's bound to upset you. I knew how it would be; I told you so yesterday. And if you took my advice, you wouldn't stay where you are. The smell of the yard is bad for you. It is frightful just now. I can't imagine what Mademoiselle Desiree can be stirring about there. She's singing away, and doesn't seem to mind it at all. Ah! that reminds me of something I want to tell you. You know that I did all I could to keep her from taking the cow to Beage; but she's like you, obstinate, and will go her own way. Fortunately, however, for her, she's none the worse for it. She delights to be amongst the animals and their young ones. But come now, your reverence, do be reasonable. Let me take you to your room. You must lie down and rest a little. What, you don't want to! Well, then, so much the worse for you, if you suffer! Besides, it's absurd to keep one's worries locked up in one's heart till they stifle one.'

Then, in her indignation, she hastily swallowed a big spoonful of soup at the risk of burning her throat. She rattled the handle of the spoon against the bowl, muttering and grumbling to herself.

'There never was such a man,' said she. 'He would die rather than say a word. But it's all very well for him to keep silent. I know quite enough, and it doesn't require much cleverness to guess the rest. Well! well! let him keep it to himself. I dare say it is better.'

La Teuse was jealous. Dr. Pascal had had a tremendous fight with her in order to get her patient away at the time when he had come to the conclusion that the young priest's case would be quite hopeless if he should remain at the parsonage. He had then explained to her that the sound of the bell would aggravate and intensify Serge's fever, that the religious pictures and statuettes scattered about his room would fill his brain with hallucinations, and that entirely new surroundings were necessary if he was to be restored to health and strength and peacefulness of mind. She, however, had vigorously shaken her head, and declared that her 'dear child' would nowhere find a better nurse than herself. Still, she had ended by yielding. She had even resigned herself to seeing him go to the Paradou, though protesting against this selection of the doctor's, which astonished her. But she retained a strong feeling of hatred for the Paradou; and she was hurt by the silence which Abbe Mouret maintained as to the time he had spent there. She had frequently laid all sorts of unsuccessful traps to induce him to talk of it. That morning, exasperated by his ghastly pallor, and his obstinacy in suffering in silence, she ended by waving her spoon about and crying:

'You should go back yonder again, Monsieur le Cure, if you were so happy there—I dare say there is some one there who would nurse you better than I do.'

It was the first time she had ventured upon a direct allusion to her suspicions. The blow was so painful to the priest that he could not check a slight cry, as he raised his grief-racked countenance. At this La Teuse's kindly heart was filled with regret.

'Ah!' she murmured, 'it is all the fault of your uncle Pascal. I told him what it would be. But those clever men cling so obstinately to their own ideas. Some of them would kill you, just for the sake of rummaging in your body afterwards—It made me so angry that I would never speak of it to any one. Yes, Monsieur le Cure, you have me to thank that nobody knew where you were; I was so angry about it. I thought it abominable! When Abbe Guyot, from Saint-Eutrope, who took your place during your absence, came to say mass here on Sundays, I told him all sorts of stories. I said you had gone to Switzerland. I don't even know where Switzerland is.—Well! well! I surely don't want to say anything to pain you, but it was certainly over yonder that you got your trouble. Very finely they've cured you indeed! It would have been very much better if they had left you with me. I shouldn't have thought of trying to turn your head.'

Abbe Mouret, whose brow was again lowered, made no attempt to interrupt her. La Teuse had seated herself upon the ground a few yards away from him, in order if possible to catch his eye. And she went on again in her motherly way, delighted at his seeming complacency in listening to her.

'You would never let me tell you about Abbe Caffin. As soon as I began to speak of him, you always made me stop. Well, well; Abbe Caffin had had his troubles in my part of the world, at Canteleu. And yet he was a very holy man, with an irreproachable character. But, you see, he was a man of very delicate taste, and liked soft pretty things. Well, there was a young party who was always prowling round him, the daughter of a miller, whom her parents had sent to a boarding-school. Well, to put it shortly, what was likely to happen did happen. When the story got about, all the neighbourhood was very indignant with the Abbe. But he managed to escape to Rouen, and poured out his grief to the Archbishop there. Then he was sent here. The poor man was punished quite enough by being made to live in this hole of a place. I heard of the girl afterwards. She had married a cattle-dealer, and was very happy.'

La Teuse, delighted at having been allowed to tell her story, interpreted the priest's silence as an encouragement to continue her gossiping. So she drew a little nearer to him and said:

'He was very friendly with me, was good Monsieur Caffin, and often spoke to me of his sin. It won't keep him out of heaven, I'm sure. He can rest quite peacefully out there under the turf, for he never harmed any one. For my part, I can't understand why people should get so angry with a priest when such a thing unhappily befalls him. Of course it's wrong, and likely to anger God; but then one can confess and repent, and get absolution. Isn't it so, your reverence, that when one truly repents, one is saved in spite of one's sins?'

Abbe Mouret slowly raised his head. By a supreme effort he had overcome his agony, and though his face was still very pale, he exclaimed in a firm voice, 'One should never sin; never! never!'

'Ah! sir,' cried the old servant, 'you are too proud and reserved. It is not a nice thing, that pride of yours.—If I were in your place, I would not harden myself like that. I would talk of what was troubling me, and not try to rend my heart in pieces. You should reconcile yourself to the separation gradually. The worry wears off little by little. But, instead of that, you won't even allow people's names to be uttered. You forbid them to be mentioned. It is as though they were dead. Since you came back, I have not dared to tell you the least bit of news. Well, well, I am going to speak now, and I shall tell you all I know; because I see quite well that it is all this silence that is preying upon your heart.'

He looked at her sternly, and lifted his finger to silence her.

'Yes, yes,' she went on, 'I get news from over yonder, very often indeed, and I am going to tell it to you. To begin with, there is some one there who is no happier than you are.'

'Silence! Silence!' said Abbe Mouret, summoning all his strength to rise and move away.

But La Teuse also rose and barred his way with her bulky figure. She was angry, and cried out:

'There, you see, you want to be off already! But you are going to listen to me. You know quite well that I am not over fond of the people yonder, don't you? If I talk to you about them, it is for your own good. Some people say that I am jealous. Well, one day I mean to take you over there. You would be with me, and you wouldn't be afraid of any harm happening. Will you go?'

He motioned her away from him with his hands, and his face was calm again as he said:

'I desire nothing. I wish to know nothing. There is high mass to-morrow. You must see that the altar is made ready.'

Then, as he walked away, he added, smiling:

'Don't be uneasy, my good Teuse. I am stronger than you imagine. I shall be able to cure myself without any one's assistance.'

With these words he went off, bearing himself sturdily, with his head erect, for he had vanquished his feelings. His cassock rustled very gently against the borders of thyme. La Teuse, who for a moment had remained rooted to the spot where she was standing, sulkily picked up her basin and wooden spoon. Then, shrugging her big shoulders again and again, she mumbled between her teeth:

'That's all bravado of his. He imagines that he is differently made from other men, just because he is a priest. Well, as a matter of fact, he is very firm and determined. I have known some who wouldn't have had to be wheedled so long. And he is quite capable of crushing his heart, just as one might crush a flea. It must be the Almighty who gives him his strength.'

As she returned to the kitchen she saw Abbe Mouret standing by the gate of the farmyard. Desiree had stopped him there to make him feel a capon which she had been fattening for some weeks past. He told her pleasantly that it was very heavy, and the big child chuckled with glee.

'Ah! well,' said La Teuse in a fury, 'that bird has got to crush its heart too. But then it can't help itself.'

IV

Abbe Mouret spent his days at the parsonage. He shunned the long walks which he had been wont to take before his illness. The scorched soil of Les Artaud, the ardent heat of that valley where the vines could never even grow straight, distressed him. On two occasions, in the morning, he had attempted to go out and read his breviary as he strolled along the road; but he had not gone beyond the village. He had returned home, overcome by the perfumes, the heat, the breadth of the landscape. It was only in the evening, in the cool twilight air, that he ventured to saunter a little in front of the church, on the terrace which led to the graveyard. In the afternoons, to fill up his time, and satisfy his craving for some kind of occupation, he had imposed upon himself the task of pasting paper over the broken panes of the church windows, This had kept him for a week mounted on a ladder, arranging his paper panes with great exactness, and laying on the paste with the most scrupulous care in order to avoid any mess.

La Teuse stood at the foot of the ladder and watched him. And Desiree urged that he must not fill up all the windows, or else the sparrows would no longer be able to get through. To please her, the priest left a pane or two in each window unfilled. Then, having completed these repairs, he was seized with the ambition of decorating the church, without summoning to his aid either mason or carpenter or painter. He would do it all himself. This sort of handiwork would amuse him, he said, and help to bring back his strength. Uncle Pascal encouraged him every time he called at the parsonage, assuring him that such exercise and fatigue were better than all the drugs in the world. And so Abbe Mouret began to stop up the holes in the walls with plaster, to drive fresh nails into the disjoined altars, and to crush and mix paints, in order that he might put a new coating on the pulpit and confessional-box. It was quite an event in the district, and folks talked of it for a couple of leagues round. Peasants would come and stand gazing, with their hands behind their backs, at his reverence's work. The Abbe himself, with a blue apron tied round his waist, and his hands all soiled with his labour, became absorbed in it, and used it as an excuse for no longer going out. He spent his days in the midst of his repairs, and was more tranquil than he had been before; almost cheerful, indeed, as he forgot the outer world, the trees and the sunshine and the warm breezes, which had formerly disturbed him so much.

'Monsieur le Cure is free to do as he pleases, since the parish hasn't got to find the money,' said old Bambousse, who came round every evening to see how the work was progressing.

Abbe Mouret spent all his savings on it. Some of his decorations, indeed, were so awkward that they would have excited many people's smiles. The replastering of the stonework soon tired him: so he contented himself with patching up the church walls all round to a height of some six feet from the ground. La Teuse mixed the plaster. When she talked of repairing the parsonage as well, for she was continually fearing that it would topple down on their heads, he told her that he did not think he could manage it, that a regular workman would be necessary; a reply which led to a terrible quarrel between them. La Teuse said it was quite ridiculous to go on ornamenting the church, where nobody slept, while their bedrooms were in such a crazy condition, for she was quite sure they would all be found, one morning, crushed to death by the fallen ceilings.

'I shall end by bringing my bed here, and placing it behind the altar,' she grumbled. 'I feel quite terrified sometimes at night.'

However, when the plaster was all used up, she said no more about repairing the parsonage. The painting which the priest executed quite delighted her. It was the chief charm of the improvements. The Abbe, who had repaired the woodwork everywhere with bits of boards, took particular pleasure in spreading his big brush, dipped in bright yellow paint, over all this woodwork. The gentle, up-and-down motion of the brush lulled him, left him thoughtless for hours whilst he gazed on the oily streaks of paint. When everything was quite yellow, the pulpit, the confessional-box, the altar rails, even the clock-case itself, he ventured to try his hand at imitation marble work by way of touching up the high altar. Then, growing bolder, he painted it all over. Glistening with white and yellow and blue, it was pronounced superb. People who had not been to mass for fifty years streamed into the church to see it.

And now the paint was dry. All that remained for Abbe Mouret to do was to edge the panels with brown beading. So, that afternoon, he set to work at it, wishing to get it done by evening; for on the following day, as he had reminded La Teuse, there would be high mass. She was there ready to arrange the altar. She had already placed on the credence the candlesticks and the silver cross, the porcelain vases filled with artificial roses, and the laced cloth which was only used on great festivals. The beading, however, proved so difficult of execution, that it was not completed till late in the evening. It was growing quite dark as the Abbe finished his last panel.

'It will be really too beautiful,' said a rough voice from amidst the greyish gloom of twilight which was filling the church.

La Teuse, who had knelt down to get a better view of the Abbe's brush as it glided along his rule, started with alarm.

'Ah! it's Brother Archangias,' she said, turning round. 'You came in by the sacristy then? You gave me quite a turn. Your voice seemed to sound from under the floor.'

Abbe Mouret had resumed his work, after greeting the Brother with a slight nod. The Brother remained standing there in silence, with his fat hands clasped in front of his cassock. Then, shrugging his shoulders, as he observed with what scrupulous care the priest sought to make his beading perfectly straight, he repeated:

'It will be really too beautiful.'

La Teuse, who knelt near by in ecstasy, started again.

'Dear me!' she said, 'I had quite forgotten you were there. You really ought to cough before you speak. You have a voice that comes on one so suddenly that one might think it was a voice from the grave.'

She rose up and drew back a little the better to admire the Abbe's work.

'Why too beautiful?' she asked. 'Nothing can be too beautiful when it is done for the Almighty. If his reverence had only had some gold, he would have done it with gold, I'm sure.'

When the priest had finished, she hastened to change the altar-cloth, taking the greatest care not to smudge the beading. Then she arranged the cross, the candlesticks, and the vases symmetrically. Abbe Mouret had gone to lean against the wooden screen which separated the choir from the nave, by the side of Brother Archangias. Not a word passed between them. Their eyes were fixed upon the silver crucifix, which, in the increasing gloom, still cast some glimmer of light on the feet and the left side and the right temple of the big Christ. When La Teuse had finished, she came down towards them, triumphantly.

'Doesn't it look lovely?' she asked. 'Just you see what a crowd there will be at mass to-morrow! Those heathens will only come to God's house when they think He is well-to-do. Now, Monsieur le Cure, we must do as much for the Blessed Virgin's altar.'

'Waste of money!' growled Brother Archangias.

But La Teuse flew into a tantrum; and, as Abbe Mouret remained silent, she led them both before the altar of the Virgin, pushing them and dragging them by their cassocks.

'Just look at it,' said she; 'it is too shabby for anything, now that the high altar is so smart. It looks as though it had never been painted at all. However much I may rub it of a morning, the dust sticks to it. It is quite black; it is filthy. Do you know what people will say about you, your reverence? They will say that you care nothing for the Blessed Virgin; that's what they'll say.'

'Well, what of it?' queried Brother Archangias.

La Teuse looked at him, half suffocated by indignation.

'What of it? It would be sinful, of course,' she muttered. 'This altar is like a neglected tomb in a graveyard. If it were not for me, the spiders would spin their webs across it, and moss would soon grow over it. From time to time, when I can spare a bunch of flowers, I give it to the Virgin. All the flowers in our garden used to be for her once.'

She had mounted the altar steps, and she took up two withered bunches of flowers, which had been left there, forgotten.

'See! it is just as it is in the graveyards,' she said, throwing the flowers at Abbe Mouret's feet.

He picked them up, without replying. It was quite dark now, and Brother Archangias stumbled about amongst the chairs and nearly fell. He growled and muttered some angry words, in which the names of Jesus and Mary recurred. When La Teuse, who had gone for a lamp, returned into the church, she asked the priest:

'So I can put the brushes and pots away in the attic, then?'

'Yes,' he answered. 'I have finished. We will see about the rest later on.'

She walked away in front of them, carrying all the things with her, and keeping silence, lest she should say too much. And as Abbe Mouret had kept the withered bunches of flowers in his hand, Brother Archangias said to him, as they passed the farmyard: 'Throw those things away.'

The Abbe took a few steps more, with downcast head; and then over the palings he flung the flowers upon a manure-heap.

V

The Brother, who had already had his own meal, seated himself astride a chair, while the priest dined. Since Serge's return to Les Artaud, the Brother had thus spent most of his evenings at the parsonage; but never before had he imposed his presence upon the other in so rough a fashion. He stamped on the tiled floor with his heavy boots, his voice thundered and he smote the furniture, whilst he related how he had whipped some of his pupils that morning, or expounded his moral principles in terms as stern, as uncompromising as bludgeon-blows. Then feeling bored, he suggested that he and La Teuse should have a game at cards. They had endless bouts of 'Beggar-my-neighbour' together, that being the only game which La Teuse had ever been able to learn. Abbe Mouret would smilingly glance at the first few cards flung on the table and would then gradually sink into reverie, remaining for hours forgetful of his self-restraint, oblivious of his surroundings, beneath the suspicious glances of Brother Archangias.

That evening La Teuse felt so cross that she had talked of going to bed as soon as the cloth was removed. The Brother, however, wanted his game of cards. So he caught hold of her shoulders and sat her down, so roughly that the chair creaked beneath her. And forthwith he began to shuffle the cards. Desiree, who hated him, had gone off carrying her dessert, which she generally took upstairs with her every evening to eat in bed.

'I want the red cards,' said La Teuse.

Then the struggle began. The old woman at first won some of the Brother's best cards. But before long two aces fell together on the table.

'Here's a battle!' she cried, wild with excitement.

She threw down a nine, which rather alarmed her, but as the Brother, in his turn, only put down a seven, she picked up the cards with a triumphant air. At the end of half an hour, however, she had only gained two aces, so that the chances remained fairly equal. And a quarter of an hour later she lost an ace. The knaves and kings and queens were perpetually coming and going as the battle furiously progressed.

'It's a splendid game, eh?' said Brother Archangias, turning towards Abbe Mouret.

But when he saw him sitting there, so absorbed in his reverie, with such a gentle smile playing unconsciously round his lips, he roughly raised his voice:

'Why, Monsieur le Cure, you are not paying any attention to us! It isn't polite of you. We are only playing on your account. We were trying to amuse you. Come and watch the game. It would do you more good than dozing and dreaming away there. Where were you just now?'

The priest started. He said nothing, but with quivering eyelids tried to force himself to look at the game. The play went on vigorously. La Teuse won her ace back, and then lost it again. On some evenings they would fight in this way over the aces for quite four hours, and often they would go off to bed, angry at having failed to bring the contest to a decisive issue.

'But, dear me! I've only just remembered it!' suddenly cried La Teuse, who greatly feared that she was going to be beaten. 'His reverence has to go out to-night. He promised Fortune and Rosalie that he would go to bless their room, according to the custom. Make haste, Monsieur le Cure! The Brother will go with you.'

Abbe Mouret had already risen from his chair, and was looking for his hat. But Brother Archangias, still holding his cards, flew into a tantrum: 'Oh! don't bother about it,' said he. 'What does it want to be blessed for that pigsty of theirs? It is a custom that you should do away with. I can't see any sense in it. Stay here and let us finish the game. That is much the best thing to do.'

'No,' said the priest, 'I promised to go. Those good people might feel hurt if I didn't. You stay here and play your game out while you are waiting for me.'

La Teuse glanced uneasily at Brother Archangias.

'Well, yes, I will stay here,' cried the Brother. 'It is really too absurd.'

But before Abbe Mouret could open the door, he flung his cards on the table and rose to follow him. Then half turning back he called to La Teuse:

'I should have won. Leave the cards as they are, and we will play the game out to-morrow.'

'Oh! they are all mixed now,' answered the old servant, who had lost no time in shuffling them together. 'Did you suppose that I was going to put your hand away under a glass case? And, besides, I might very well have won, for I still had an ace left.'

A few strides brought Brother Archangias up with Abbe Mouret, who was walking down the narrow path that led to the village. The Brother had undertaken the task of keeping watch over the Abbe's movements. He incessantly played the spy upon him, accompanying him everywhere, or, if he could not go in person, sending some school urchin to follow him. With that terrible laugh of his, he was wont to remark that he was 'God's gendarme.'

And, in truth, the Abbe seemed like a culprit ever guarded by the black shadow of the Brother's cassock; a culprit to be treated distrustfully, since in his weakness he might well lapse into fresh crime were he left free from surveillance for a single moment. Thus he was watched and guarded with all the spiteful eagerness that some jealous old maid might have displayed, the overreaching zeal of a gaoler who might carry precautions so far as to exclude even such rays of light as might creep through the chinks of the prison-house. Brother Archangias was always on the watch to keep out the sunlight, to prevent even a whiff of air from entering, to shut up his prison so completely that nothing from outside could gain access to it. He noted the Abbe's slightest fits of weakness, and by his glance divined his tender thoughts, which with a word he pitilessly crushed, as though they were poisonous vermin. The priest's intervals of silence, his smiles, the paling of his brow, the faint quivering of his limbs, were all noted by the Brother. But he never spoke openly of the transgression. His presence alone was a sufficient reproach. The manner in which he uttered certain words imparted to them all the sting of a whip stroke. With a mere gesture he expressed his utter disgust for the priest's sin. Like one of those betrayed husbands who enjoy torturing their wives with cruel allusions, he contented himself with recalling the scene at the Paradou, in an indirect fashion, by some word or phrase which sufficed to annihilate the Abbe, whenever the latter's flesh rebelled.

It was nearly ten o'clock and most of the villagers of Les Artaud had retired to rest. But from a brightly lighted house at the far end, near the mill, there still came sounds of merriment. While keeping the best rooms for his own use, old Bambousse had given a corner of his house to his daughter and son-in-law. They were all assembled there, drinking a last glass, while waiting for the priest.

'They are drunk,' growled Brother Archangias. 'Don't you hear the row they are making?'

Abbe Mouret made no reply. It was a lovely night and all looked bluish in the moonlight, which lent to the distant part of the valley the aspect of a sleeping lake. The priest slackened his pace that he might the more fully enjoy the charm of that soft radiance, and now and then he even stopped as he came upon some expanse of light, experiencing the delightful quiver which the proximity of fresh water brings one on a hot day. But the Brother continued striding along, grumbling and calling him.

'Come along; come along! It isn't good to loiter out of doors at this time of night. You would be much better in bed.'

All at once, however, just as they were entering the village, Archangias himself stopped short in the middle of the road. He was looking towards the heights, where the white lines of the roads vanished amidst black patches of pine-woods, and he growled to himself, like a dog that scents danger.

'Who can be coming down so late?' he muttered.

But the priest, who neither saw nor heard anything, was now, in his turn, anxious to press on.

'Stay! stay! there he is,' eagerly added Brother Archangias. 'He has just turned the corner. See! he is in the moonlight now. One can see him plainly. It is a tall man, with a stick.'

Then, after a moment's silence, he resumed, in a voice husky with fury: 'It is he, that beggar! I felt sure it was!'

Thereupon, the new-comer having now reached the bottom of the hill, Abbe Mouret saw that it was Jeanbernat. In spite of his eighty years, the old man set his feet down with such force, that his heavy, nailed boots sent sparks flying from the flints on the road. And he walked along as upright as an oak, without the aid of his stick, which he carried across his shoulder like a musket.

'Ah! the villain!' stammered the Brother, still standing motionless. 'May the fiend light all the blazes of hell under his feet!'

The priest, who felt greatly disturbed, and despaired of inducing his companion to come on, turned round to continue his journey, hoping that, by a quick walk to the Bambousses' house, he might yet manage to avoid Jeanbernat. But he had not taken five strides before he heard the bantering voice of the old man close behind him.

'Hie! Cure! wait for me. Are you afraid of me?'

And as Abbe Mouret stopped, he came up and continued: 'Ah! those cassocks of yours are tiresome things, aren't they? They prevent your getting along too quickly. It's such a fine clear night, too, that one can recognise you by your gown a long way off. When I was right at the top of the hill, I said to myself, "Surely that is the little priest down yonder." Oh! yes, I still have very good eyes.... Well, so you never come to see us now?'

'I have had so much to do,' murmured the priest, who had turned very pale.

'Well, well, every one's free to please himself. If I've mentioned the matter, it's only because I want you to know that I don't bear you any grudge for being a priest. We wouldn't even talk about your religion, it's all one and the same to me. But the little one thinks that it's I who prevents your coming. I said to her, "The priest is an idiot," and I think so, indeed. Did I try to eat you during your illness? Why, I didn't even go upstairs to see you. Every one's free, you know.'

He spoke on in the most unconcerned manner, pretending that he did not notice the presence of Brother Archangias; but as the latter suddenly broke into an angry grunt, he added, 'Why, Cure, so you bring your pig out with you?'

'Take care, you bandit!' hissed the Brother, clenching his fists.

Jeanbernat, whose stick was still raised, then pretended to recognise him.

'Hands off!' he cried. 'Ah! it's you, you soul-saver! I ought to have known you by your smell. We have a little account to settle together, remember. I have sworn to cut off your ears in the middle of your school. It will amuse the children you are poisoning.'

The Brother fell back before the raised staff, a flood of abuse rising to his lips; but he began to stammer and went on disjointedly:

'I will set the gendarmes after you, scoundrel! You spat on the church; I saw you. You give the plague to the poor people who merely pass your door. At Saint-Eutrope you made a girl die by forcing her to chew a consecrated wafer which you had stolen. At Beage you went and dug up the bodies of little dead children and carried them away on your back. You are an old sorcerer! Everybody knows it, you scoundrel! You are the disgrace of the district. Whoever strangles you will gain heaven for the deed.'

The old man listened with a sneer, twirling the while his staff between his fingers. And between the Brother's successive insults he ejaculated in an undertone:

'Go on, go on; relieve yourself, you viper. I'll break your back for you by-and-by.'

Abbe Mouret tried to interfere, but Brother Archangias pushed him away, exclaiming: 'You are led by him yourself! Didn't he make you trample upon the cross? Deny it, if you dare!' Then again, turning to Jeanbernat, he yelled: 'Ah! Satan, you must have chuckled and no mistake when you held a priest in your grasp! May Heaven curse those who abetted you in that sacrilege! What was it you did, at night, while he slept? You came and moistened his tonsure with your saliva, eh? so that his hair might grow more quickly. And then you breathed upon his chin and his cheeks that his beard might grow a hand's breadth in a single night. And you rubbed all your philters into his body, and breathed into his mouth the lasciviousness of a dog. You turned him into a brute-beast, Satan.'

'He's idiotic,' said Jeanbernat, resting his stick on his shoulder. 'He quite bores me.'

The Brother, however, growing bolder, thrust his fists under the old man's nose.

'And that drab of yours!' he cried, 'you can't deny that you set her on to damn the priest.'

Then he suddenly sprang backwards, with a shriek, for the old man, swinging his stick with all his strength, had just broken it over his back. Retreating yet a little further, Archangias picked from a heap of stones beside the road a piece of flint twice the size of a man's fist, and threw it at Jeanbernat. It would surely have split the other's forehead open if he had not bent down. He, however, now likewise crossed over to a heap of stones, sheltered himself behind it, and provided himself with missiles; and from one heap to the other a terrible combat began, with a perfect hail of flints. The moon now shone very brightly, and their dark shadows fell distinctly on the ground.

'Yes, yes, you set that hussy on to ruin him!' repeated the Brother, wild with rage. 'Ah! you are astonished that I know all about it! You hope for some monstrous result from it all. Every morning you make the thirteen signs of hell over that minx of yours! You would like her to become the mother of Antichrist. You long for Antichrist, you villain! But may this stone blind you!'

'And may this one bung your mouth up!' retorted Jeanbernat, who was now quite calm again. 'Is he cracked, the silly fellow, with all those stories of his? … Shall I have to break your head for you, before I can get on my way? Is it your catechism that has turned your brain?'

'Catechism, indeed! Do you know what catechism is taught to accursed ones like you? Ah! I will show you how to make the sign of the cross.—This stone is for the Father, and this for the Son, and this for the Holy Ghost. Ah! you are still standing. Wait a bit, wait a bit. Amen!' Then he threw a handful of small pebbles like a volley of grape-shot. Jeanbernat, who was struck upon the shoulder, dropped the stones he was holding, and quietly stepped forwards, while Brother Archangias picked two fresh handfuls from the heap, blurting out:

I am going to exterminate you. It is God who wills it. God is acting through my arm.'

'Will you be quiet!' said the old man, grasping him by the nape of the neck.

Then came a short struggle amidst the dust of the road, all bluish with moonlight. The Brother, finding himself the weaker of the two, tried to bite.

But Jeanbernat's sinewy limbs were like coils of rope which pinioned him so tightly that he could almost feel them cutting into his flesh. He panted and ceased to struggle, meditating some act of treachery.

The old man, having got the other under him, scoffingly exclaimed: 'I have a good mind to break one of your arms. You see that it isn't you who are the stronger, but that it is I who am exterminating you.... Now I'm going to cut your ears off. You have tried my endurance too far.'

Jeanbernat calmly drew his knife from his pocket. But Abbe Mouret, who had several times attempted to part the combatants, now raised such strenuous opposition to the old man's design that he consented to defer the operation till another time.

'You are acting foolishly, Cure,' said he. 'It would do this scoundrel good to be well bled; but, since it seems to displease you, I'll wait a little longer; I shall be meeting him again in some quiet corner.'

And as the Brother broke out into a growl, Jeanbernat cried threateningly: 'If you don't keep still I will cut your ears off at once!'

'But you are sitting on his chest,' said the priest, 'get up and let him breathe.'

'No, no; he would begin his tomfoolery again. I will give him his liberty when I go away, but not before.... Well, I was telling you, Cure, when this good-for-nothing interrupted us, that you would be very welcome yonder. The little one is mistress, you know; I don't attempt to interfere with her any more than I do with my salad-plants. There are only fools like this croaker here who see any harm in it. Where did you see anything wrong, scoundrel? It was yourself who imagined it, villain that you are!'

And thereupon he gave the Brother another shaking. 'Let him get up,' begged Abbe Mouret.

'By-and-by. The little one has not been well for a long time. I did not notice anything myself, but she told me; and now I am on my way to tell your uncle Pascal, at Plassans. I like the night for walking; it is quiet, and, as a rule, one isn't delayed by meeting people.... Yes, yes, the little one is quite ailing.'

The priest could not find a word to say. He staggered, and his head sank.

'It made her so happy to look after you,' continued the old man. 'While I smoked my pipe I used to hear her laugh. That was quite sufficient for me. Girls are like the hawthorns; when they break out into blossom, they do all they can. Well, now, you will come, if your heart prompts you to it. I am sure it would please the little one. Good night, Cure.'

He got up slowly, keeping a firm grasp of the Brother's wrists, to guard against any treacherous attack. Then he proceeded on his way, with swinging strides, without once turning his head. The Brother silently crept to the heap of stones, and waited till the old man was some distance off. Then, with both hands, and with mad violence, he again began flinging stones, but they fell harmlessly upon the dusty road. Jeanbernat did not condescend to notice them, but went his way, upright like a tree, through the clear night.

'The accursed one!—Satan carries him on!' shrieked Brother Archangias, as he hurled his last stone. 'An old scoundrel, that the least touch ought to upset! But he is baked in hell's fire. I smelt his claws.'

The Brother stamped with impotent rage on the scattered flints. Then he suddenly attacked Abbe Mouret. 'It was all your fault,' he cried; 'you ought to have helped me, and, between us, we could have strangled him.'

Meantime, at the other end of the village, the uproar in the Bambousses' house had become greater than ever. The rhythmic tapping of glasses on a table could be distinctly heard. The priest resumed his walk without raising his head, making his way towards the flood of bright light that streamed out of the window like the flare of a fire of vine-cuttings. The Brother followed him gloomily; his cassock soiled with dust, and one of his cheeks bleeding from a stone-cut. And, after a short interval of silence, he asked, in his harsh voice: 'Shall you go?'

Then as Abbe Mouret did not answer, he went on: 'Take care! You are lapsing into sin again. It was sufficient for that man to pass by to send a thrill through your whole body. I saw you by the light of the moon looking as pale as a girl. Take care! take care! Do you hear me? Another time God will not pardon you—you will sink into the lowest abyss! Ah! wretched piece of clay that you are, filth is mastering you!'

Thereupon, the priest at last raised his head. Big tears were streaming from his eyes, and it was in gentle heartbroken accents that he spoke: 'Why do you speak to me like that?—You are always with me, and you know my ceaseless struggles. Do not doubt me, leave me strength to master myself.'

Those simple words, bathed with silent tears, fell on the night air with such an expression of superhuman suffering, that even Brother Archangias, in spite of all his harshness, felt touched. He made no reply, but shook his dusty cassock, and wiped his bleeding cheek. When they reached the Bambousses' house, he refused to go inside. He seated himself, a few yards away, on the body of an overturned cart, where he waited for the Abbe with dog-like patience.

'Ah! here is Monsieur le Cure!' cried all the company of Bambousses and

Brichets as Serge entered.

They filled their glasses once more. Abbe Mouret was compelled to take one, too. There had been no regular wedding-feast; but, in the evening, after dinner, a ten-gallon 'Dame Jane' had been placed upon the table, and they were making it their business to empty it before going to bed. There were ten of them, and old Bambousse was already with one hand tilting over the jar whence only a thread of red liquor now flowed. Rosalie, in a very sportive frame of mind, was dipping her baby's chin into her glass, while big Fortune showed off his strength by lifting up the chairs with his teeth. All the company passed into the bedroom. Custom required that the priest should there drink the glass of wine which had been poured out for him. It brought good luck, and prevented quarrels in the household. In Monsieur Caffin's time, it had always been a very merry ceremony, for the old priest loved a joke. He had even gained a reputation for the skilful way in which he could drain his glass, without leaving a single drop at the bottom of it; and the Artaud women pretended that every drop undrunk meant a year's less love for the newly married pair. But with Abbe Mouret they dare not joke so freely. However, he drank his wine at one gulp, which seemed to greatly please old Bambousse. Mother Brichet looked at the bottom of the glass and saw but a drop or two of the liquid remaining there. Then, after a few jokes, they all returned to the living room, where Vincent and Catherine had remained by themselves. Vincent, standing upon a chair, was clasping the huge jar in his arms, and draining the last drops of wine into Catherine's open mouth.

'We are much obliged to you, Monsieur le Cure,' said old Bambousse, as he escorted the priest to the door. 'Well, they're married now, so I suppose you are satisfied. And they are not likely to complain, I'm sure…. Good night, sleep well, your reverence.'

Brother Archangias had slowly risen from his seat on the old cart.

'May the devil pile hot coals over them, and roast them!' he murmured.

Then without again opening his lips he accompanied Abbe Mouret to the parsonage. And he waited outside till the door was closed. Even then he did not go off without twice looking round to make sure that the Abbe was not coming out again. As for the priest, when he reached his bedroom, he threw himself in his clothes upon his bed, clasping his hands to his ears, and pressing his face to the pillow, in order that he might shut out all sound and sight. And thus stilling his senses he fell into death-like slumber.

VI

The next day was Sunday. As the Feast of the Exaltation of the Holy Cross fell on a high mass day, Abbe Mouret desired to celebrate the festival with especial solemnity. He was now full of extraordinary devotion for the Cross, and had replaced the image of the Immaculate Conception in his bedroom by a large crucifix of black wood, before which he spent long hours in worship. To exalt the Cross, to plant it before him, above all else, in a halo of glory, as the one object of his life, gave him the strength he needed to suffer and to struggle. He sometimes dreamed of hanging there himself, in Jesus's place, his head crowned with thorns, nails driven through his hands and feet, and his side rent by spears. What a coward he must be to complain of an imaginary wound, when God bled there from His whole body, and yet preserved on His lips the blessed smile of the Redemption! And however unworthy it might be, he offered up his wound as a sacrifice, ended by falling into ecstasy, and believing that blood did really stream from his brow and side and limbs. Those were hours of relief, for he fancied that all the impurity within him flowed forth from his wounds. And he then usually drew himself up with the heroism of a martyr, and longed to be called upon to suffer the most frightful tortures, in order that he might bear them without a quiver of the flesh.

At early dawn that day he knelt before the crucifix, and grace came upon him abundantly as dew. He made no effort, he simply fell upon his knees, to receive it in his heart, to be permeated with it to the marrow of his bones in sweetest and most refreshing fulness. On the previous day he had prayed for grace in agony, and it had not come. At times it long remained deaf to his entreaties, and then, when he simply clasped his hands, in quite childlike fashion, it flowed down to succour him. It came upon him that morning like a benediction, bringing perfect serenity, absolute trusting faith. He forgot his anguish of the previous days, and surrendered himself wholly to the triumphant joy of the Cross. He seemed to be cased in such impenetrable armour that the world's most deadly blows would glide off from it harmlessly. When he came down from his bedroom, he stepped along with an air of serenity and victory. La Teuse was astonished, and went to find Desiree, that he might kiss her; and both of them clapped their hands, and said that they had not seen him looking so well for the last six months.

But it was in the church, at high mass, that the priest felt that he had really recovered divine grace. It was a long time since he had approached the altar with such loving emotion; and he had to make a great effort to restrain himself from weeping whilst he remained with his lips pressed to the altar-cloth. It was a solemn high mass. The local rural guard, an uncle of Rosalie, chanted in a deep bass voice which rumbled through the low nave like a hoarse organ. Vincent, robed in a surplice much too large for him, which had formerly belonged to Abbe Caffin, carried an old silver censer, and was vastly amused by the tinkling of its chains; he swung it to a great height, so as to produce copious clouds of smoke, and glanced behind him every now and then to see if he had succeeded in making any one cough. The church was almost full, for everybody wanted to see his reverence's painting. Peasant women laughed with pleasure because the place smelt so nice, while the men, standing under the gallery, jerked their heads approvingly at each deeper and deeper note that came from the rural guard. Filtering through the paper window panes the full morning sun lighted up the brightly painted walls, on which the women's caps cast shadows resembling huge butterflies. The artificial flowers, with which the altar was decorated, almost seemed to possess the moist freshness of natural ones newly gathered; and when the priest turned round to bless the congregation, he felt even stronger emotion than before, as he saw his church so clean, so full, and so steeped in music and incense and light.

After the offertory, however, a buzzing murmur sped through the peasant women. Vincent inquisitively turned his head, and in doing so, almost let the charcoal in his censer fall upon the priest's chasuble. And, wishing to excuse himself, as he saw the Abbe looking at him with an expression of reproof, he murmured: 'It is your reverence's uncle, who has just come in.'

At the end of the church, standing beside one of the slender wooden pillars that supported the gallery, Abbe Mouret then perceived Doctor Pascal. The doctor was not wearing his usual cheerful and slightly scoffing expression. Hat in hand, he stood there looking very grave, and followed the service with evident impatience. The sight of the priest at the altar, his solemn demeanour, his slow gestures, and the perfect serenity of his countenance, appeared to gradually increase his irritation. He could not stay there till the end of the mass, but left the church, and walked up and down beside his horse and gig, which he had secured to one of the parsonage shutters.

'Will that nephew of mine never have finished censing himself?' he asked of La Teuse, who was just coming out of the vestry.

'It is all over,' she replied. 'Won't you come into the drawing-room? His reverence is unrobing. He knows you are here.'

'Well, unless he were blind, he couldn't very well help it,' growled the doctor, as he followed La Teuse into the cold-looking, stiffly furnished chamber, which she pompously called the drawing-room. Here for a few minutes he paced up and down. The gloomy coldness of his surroundings seemed to increase his irritation. As he strode about, flourishing a stick he carried, he kept on striking the well-worn chair-seats of horsehair which sounded hard and dead as stone. Then, tired of walking, he took his stand in front of the mantelpiece, in the centre of which a gaudily painted image of Saint Joseph occupied the place of a clock.

'Ah! here he comes at last,' he said, as he heard the door opening. And stepping towards the Abbe he went on: 'Do you know that you made me listen to half a mass? It is a very long time since that happened to me. But I was bent on seeing you to-day. I have something to say to you.'

Then he stopped, and looked at the priest with an expression of surprise. Silence fell. 'You at all events are quite well,' he resumed, in a different voice.

'Yes, I am very much better than I was,' replied Abbe Mouret, with a smile. 'I did not expect you before Thursday. Sunday isn't your day for coming. Is there something you want to tell me?'

Uncle Pascal did not give an immediate answer. He went on looking at the Abbe. The latter was still fresh from the influence of the church and the mass. His hair was fragrant with the perfume of the incense, and in his eyes shone all the joy of the Cross. His uncle jogged his head, as he noticed that expression of triumphant peace.

'I have come from the Paradou,' he said, abruptly. 'Jeanbernat came to fetch me there. I have seen Albine, and she disquiets me. She needs much careful treatment.'

He kept his eyes fixed upon the priest as he spoke, but he did not detect so much as a quiver of Serge's eyelids.

'She took great care of you, you know,' he added, more roughly. 'Without her, my boy, you might now be in one of the cells at Les Tulettes, with a strait waistcoat on…. Well, I promised that you would go to see her. I will take you with me. It will be a farewell meeting. She is anxious to go away.'

'I can do nothing more than pray for the person of whom you speak,' said Abbe Mouret, softly.

And as the doctor, losing his temper, brought his stick down heavily upon the couch, he added calmly, but in a firm voice:

'I am a priest, and can only help with prayers.'

'Ah, well! Yes, you are right,' said Uncle Pascal, dropping down into an armchair, 'it is I who am an old fool. Yes, I wept like a child, as I came here alone in my gig. That is what comes of living amongst books. One learns a lot from them, but one makes a fool of oneself in the world. How could I guess that it would all turn out so badly?'

He rose from his chair and began to walk about again, looking exceedingly troubled.

'But yes, but yes, I ought to have guessed. It was all quite natural. Though with one in your position, it was bound to be abominable! You are not as other men. But listen to me, I assure you that otherwise you would never have recovered. It was she alone, with the atmosphere she set round you, who saved you from madness. There is no need for me to tell you what a state you were in. It is one of my most wonderful cures. But I can't take any pride, any pleasure in it, for now the poor girl is dying of it!'

Abbe Mouret remained there erect, perfectly calm, his face reflecting all the quiet serenity of a martyr whom nothing that man might do could disturb.

'God will take mercy upon her,' he said.

'God! God!' muttered the doctor below his breath. 'Ah! He would do better not to interfere. We might manage matters if we were left to ourselves.' Then, raising his voice, he added: 'I thought I had considered everything carefully, that is the most wonderful part of it. Oh! what a fool I was! You would stay there, I thought, for a month to recover your strength. The shade of the trees, the cheerful chatter of the girl, all the youthfulness about you would quickly bring you round. And then you, on your side, it seemed to me, would do something to reclaim the poor child from her wild ways; you would civilise her, and, between us, we should turn her into a young lady, for whom we should, by-and-by, find a suitable husband. It seemed such a perfect scheme. And then how was I to guess that old philosophising Jeanbernat would never stir an inch from his lettuce-beds? Well! well! I myself never left my own laboratory. I had such pressing work there…. And it is all my fault! Ah! I am a stupid bungler!'

He was choking, and wished to go off. And he began to look about him for his hat, though, all the while, he had it on his head.

'Good-bye!' he stammered; 'I am going. So you won't come? Do, now— for my sake! You see how miserable, how upset I am. I swear to you that she shall go away immediately afterwards. That is all settled. My gig is here; you might be back in an hour. Come, do come, I beg you.'

The priest made a sweeping gesture; such a gesture as the doctor had seen him make before the altar.

'No,' he said, 'I cannot.'

Then, as he accompanied his uncle out of the room, he added:

'Tell her to fall on her knees and pray to God. God will hear her as He heard me, and He will comfort her as He has comforted me. There is no other means of salvation.'

The doctor looked him full in the face, and shrugged his shoulders.

'Good-bye, then,' he repeated. 'You are quite well now, and have no further need of me.'

But, as he was unfastening his horse, Desiree, who had heard his voice, came running up. She was extremely attached to her uncle. When she had been younger he had been wont to listen to her childish prattle for hours without showing the least sign of weariness. And, even now, he did his best to spoil her, and manifested the greatest interest in her farmyard, often spending a whole afternoon with her amongst her fowls and ducks, and smiling at her with his bright eyes. He seemed to consider her superior to other girls. And so she now flung herself round his neck, in an impulse of affection, and cried:

'Aren't you going to stay and have some lunch with us?'

But having kissed her, he said he could not remain, and unfastened her arms from his neck with a somewhat pettish air. She laughed however, and again clasped her arms round him.

'Oh! but you must,' she persisted. 'I have some eggs that have only just been laid. I have been looking in the nests, and there are fourteen eggs this morning. And, if you will stay, we can have a fowl, the white one, that is always quarrelling with the others. When you were here on Thursday, you know, it pecked the big spotted hen's eye out.'

But her uncle persisted in his refusal. He was irritated to find that he could not unfasten the knot in which he had tied his reins. And then she began to skip round him, clapping her hands and repeating in a sing-song voice: 'Yes! yes! you'll stay, and we will eat it up, we'll eat it up!'

Her uncle could no longer resist her blandishments; he raised his head and smiled at her. She seemed so full of life and health and sincerity; her gaiety was as frank and natural as the sheet of sunlight which was gilding her bare arms.

'You big silly!' he said; and clasping her by the wrists as she continued skipping gleefully about him, he went on: 'No, dear; not to-day. I have to go to see a poor girl who is ill. But I will come some other morning. I promise you faithfully.'

'When? when?' she persisted. 'On Thursday? The cow is in calf, you know, and she hasn't seemed at all well these last two days. You are a doctor, and you ought to be able to give her something to do her good.'

Abbe Mouret, who had calmly remained there, could not restrain a slight laugh.

The doctor gaily got into his gig and exclaimed: 'All right, my dear, I will attend to your cow. Come and let me kiss you. Ah! how nice and healthy you are! And you are worth more than all the others put together. Ah! if every one was like my big silly, this earth would be too beautiful!'

He set his horse off with a cluck of his tongue, and continued talking to himself as the gig rattled down the hill.

'Yes, yes! there should be nothing but animals. Ah! if they were mere animals, how happy and gay and strong they would all be! It has gone well with the girl, who is as happy as her cow; but it has gone badly with the lad, who is in torture beneath his cassock. A drop too much blood, a little too much nerve, and one's whole life is wrecked! ... They are true Rougons and true Macquarts those children there! The tail-end of the stock—its final degeneracy.'

Then, urging on his horse, he drove at a trot up the hill that led to the Paradou.

VII

Sunday was a busy day for Abbe Mouret. He had to think of vespers, which he generally said to empty seats, for even mother Brichet did not carry her piety so far as to go back to church in the afternoon. Then, at four o'clock, Brother Archangias brought the little rogues from his school to repeat their catechism to his reverence. This lesson sometimes lasted until late. When the children showed themselves quite intractable, La Teuse was summoned to frighten them with her broom.

On that particular Sunday, about four o'clock, Desiree found herself quite alone in the parsonage. As she felt a little bored, she went to gather some food for her rabbits in the churchyard, where there were some magnificent poppies, of which rabbits are extremely fond. Dragging herself about on her knees between the grave-stones, she gathered apronfuls of juicy verdure on which her pets fell greedily.

'Oh! what lovely plantains!' she muttered, stooping before Abbe Caffin's tombstone, and delighted with the discovery she had made.

There were, indeed, some magnificent plantains spreading out their broad leaves beside the stone. Desiree had just finished filling her apron with them when she fancied she heard a strange noise behind her. A rustling of branches and a rolling of small pebbles came from the ravine which skirted one side of the graveyard, and at the bottom of which flowed the Mascle, a stream which descended from the high lands of the Paradou. But the ascent here was so rough, so impracticable, that Desiree imagined that the noise could only have been made by some lost dog or straying goat. She stepped quickly to the edge, and, as she looked over, she was amazed to see amidst the brambles a girl who was climbing up the rocks with extraordinary agility.

'I will give you a hand,' she said. 'You might easily break your neck there.'

The girl, directly she saw she was discovered, started back, as though she would rather go down again, but after a moment's hesitation she ventured to take the hand that was held out to her.

'Oh! I know who you are,' said Desiree, with a beaming smile, and letting her apron fall that she might grasp the girl by the waist. 'You once gave me some blackbirds, but they all died, poor little dears. I was so sorry about it.— Wait a bit, I know your name, I have heard it before. La Teuse often mentions it when Serge isn't there; but she told me that I was not to repeat it. Wait a moment, I shall remember it directly!'

She tried to recall the name, and grew quite grave in the attempt. Then, having succeeded in remembering it, she became gay again, and seemingly found great pleasure in dwelling upon its musical sound.

'Albine! Albine!—— What a sweet name it is! At first I used to think you must be a tomtit, because I once had a tomtit with a name very like yours, though I don't remember exactly what it was.'

Albine did not smile. Her face was very pale, and there was a feverish gleam in her eyes. A few drops of blood trickled from her hands. When she had recovered her breath, she hastily exclaimed:

No! no! leave it alone. You will only stain your handkerchief. It is nothing but a scratch. I didn't want to come by the road, as I should have been seen—so I preferred coming along the bed of the torrent—— Is Serge there?'

Desiree did not feel at all shocked at hearing the girl pronounce her brother's name thus familiarly and with an expression of subdued passion. She simply replied that he was in the church hearing the children say their catechism.

'You must not speak at all loudly,' she added, raising her finger to her lips. 'Serge forbade me to talk loudly when he is catechising the children, and we shall get into trouble if we don't keep quiet. Let us go into the stable—shall we? We can talk better there.'

'I want to see Serge,' said Albine, simply.

Desiree cast a hasty glance at the church, and then whispered, 'Yes, yes; Serge will be finely caught. Come with me. We will hide ourselves, and keep quite quiet. We shall have some fine fun!'

She had picked up the herbage which had fallen from her apron, and quitting the graveyard she stole back to the parsonage, telling Albine to hide herself behind her and make herself as little as possible. As they stealthily glided through the farmyard, they caught sight of La Teuse, who was crossing over to the vestry, but she did not appear to notice them.

'There! There!' said Desiree, quite delighted, as they stowed themselves away in the stable; 'keep quiet, and no one will know that we are here. There is some straw there for you to lie down upon.'

Albine seated herself on a truss of straw.

'And Serge?' she asked, persisting in her one fixed idea.

'Listen! You can hear his voice. When he claps his hands, it will be all over, and the children will go away—Listen! he is telling them a tale.'

They could indeed just hear Abbe Mouret's voice, which was wafted to them through the vestry doorway which La Teuse had doubtless left open. It came to them like a solemn murmur, in which they could distinguish the name of Jesus thrice repeated. Albine trembled. She sprang up as though to hasten to that beloved voice whose caressing accents she knew so well, but all sound of it suddenly died away, shut off by the closing of the door. Then she sat down again, to wait, her hands tightly clasped, and her clear eyes gleaming with the intensity of her thoughts. Desiree, who was lying at her feet, gazed up at her with innocent admiration.

'How beautiful you are!' she whispered. 'You are like an image that Serge used to have in his bedroom. It was quite white like you are, with great curls floating about the neck; and the heart was quite bare and uncovered, just in the place where I can feel yours beating—— But you are not listening to me. You are looking quite sad. Let us play at something? Will you?'

Then she stopped short, holding her breath and saying between her teeth: 'Ah! the wretches! they will get us caught!' She still had her apron full of herbage with her, and her pets were taking it by assault. A troop of fowls had surrounded her, clucking and calling each other, and pecking at the hanging green stuff. The goat pushed its head slyly under her arm, and began to eat the longer leaves. Even the cow, which was tethered to the wall, strained at its cord and poked out its nose, kissing her with its warm breath.

'Oh! you thieves!' cried Desiree. 'But this is for the rabbits, not for you! Leave me alone, won't you! You, there, will get your ears boxed, if you don't go away! And you too will have your tail pulled if I catch you at it again. The wretches! they will be eating my hands soon!'

She drove the goat off, dispersed the fowls with her feet, and tapped the cow's nose with her fists. But the creatures just shook themselves, and then came back more greedily than ever, surrounding her, jumping on her, and tearing open her apron. At this she whispered to Albine, as though she were afraid the animals might hear her.

'Aren't they amusing, the dears? Watch them eat.'

Albine looked on with a grave expression.

'Now, now, be good,' resumed Desiree; 'you shall all have some, but you must wait your turns. Now, big Lisa, you first. Eh! how fond you are of plantain, aren't you?'

Big Lisa was the cow. She slowly munched a handful of the juicy leaves which had grown beside Abbe Caffin's tomb. A thread of saliva hung down from her mouth, and her great brown eyes shone with quiet enjoyment.

'There! now it's your turn,' continued Desiree, turning towards the goat. 'You are fond of poppies, I know; and you like the flowers best, don't you? The buds that shine in your teeth like red-hot butterflies! See, here are some splendid ones; they came from the left-hand corner, where there was a burial last year.'

As she spoke, she gave the goat a bunch of scarlet flowers, which the animal ate from her hand. When there was nothing left in her grasp but the stalks, she pushed these between its teeth. Behind her, in the meanwhile, the fowls were desperately pecking away at her petticoats. She threw them some wild chicory and dandelions which she had gathered amongst the old slabs that were ranged alongside the church walls. It was particularly over the dandelions that the fowls quarrelled, so voraciously indeed, with such scratchings and flapping of wings, that the other fowls in the yard heard them. And then came a general invasion. The big yellow cock, Alexander, was the first to appear; having seized a dandelion and torn it in halves, without attempting to eat it, he called to the hens who were still outside to come and peck. Then a white hen strutted in, then a black one, and then a whole crowd of hens, who hustled one another, and trod on one another's tails, and ended by forming a wild flood of feathers. Behind the fowls came the pigeons, and the ducks, and the geese, and, last of all, the turkeys. Desiree laughed at seeing herself thus surrounded by this noisy, squabbling mob.

'This is what always happens,' said she, 'every time that I bring any green stuff from the graveyard. They nearly kill each other to get at it; they must find it very nice.'

Then she made a fight to keep a few handfuls of the leaves from the greedy beaks which rose all round her, saying that something must really be saved for the rabbits. She would surely get angry with them if they went on like that, and give them nothing but dry bread in future. However, she was obliged to give way. The geese tugged at her apron so violently that she was almost pulled down upon her knees; the ducks gobbled away at her ankles; two of the pigeons flew upon her head, and some of the fowls fluttered about her shoulders. It was the ferocity of creatures who smell flesh: the fat plantains, the crimson poppies, the milky dandelions, in which remained some of the life of the dead. Desiree laughed loudly, and felt that she was on the point of slipping down, and letting go of her last two handfuls, when the fowls were panic-stricken by a terrible grunting.

'Ah! it's you, my fatty,' she exclaimed, quite delighted; 'eat them up, and set me at liberty.'

The pig waddled in; he was no longer the little pig of former days—pink as a newly painted toy, with a tiny little tail, like a bit of string; but a fat wobbling creature, fit to be killed, with a belly as round as a monk's, and a back all bristling with rough hairs, that reeked of fatness. His stomach had grown quite yellow from his habit of sleeping on the manure heap. Waddling along on his shaky feet, he charged with lowered snout at the scared fowls, and so left Desiree at liberty to escape, and take the rabbits the few scraps of green stuff which she had so strenuously defended. When she came back, all was peace again. The stupid, ecstatic-looking geese were lazily swaying their long necks about, the ducks and turkeys were waddling in ungainly fashion alongside the wall; the fowls were quietly clucking and peaking at invisible grains on the hard ground of the stable; while the pig, the goat, and the big cow, were drowsily blinking their eyes, as though they were falling asleep. Outside it had just begun to rain.

'Ah! well, there's a shower coming on!' cried Desiree, throwing herself down on the straw. 'You had better stay where you are, my dears, if you don't want to get soaked.'

Then she turned to Albine and added: 'How stupid they all look, don't they? They only wake up just to eat!'

Albine still remained silent. The merry laughter of that buxom girl as she struggled amidst those greedy necks and gluttonous beaks, which tickled and kissed her, and seemed bent on devouring her very flesh, had rendered the unhappy daughter of the Paradou yet paler than she had been before. So much gaiety, so much vitality, so much boisterous health made her despair. She strained her feverish arms to her desolate bosom, which desertion had parched.

'And Serge?' she asked again, in the same clear, stubborn voice.

'Hush!' said Desiree. 'I heard him just now. He hasn't finished yet——We have been making a pretty disturbance; La Teuse must surely have grown deaf this afternoon—— Let us keep quiet now. I like to hear the rain fall.'

The shower beat in at the open doorway, casting big drops upon the threshold. The restless fowls, after venturing out for a moment, had quickly retreated to the far end of the stable; where, indeed, with the exception of three ducks who remained quietly walking in the rain, all the pets had now taken refuge, clustering round the girl's skirts. It was growing very warm amongst the straw. Desiree pulled two big trusses together, made a bed of them, and lay down at full length. She felt extremely comfortable there.

'It is so nice,' she murmured. 'Come and lie down like me. It is so springy and soft, all this straw; and it tickles one so funnily in the neck. Do you roll about in the straw at home? There is nothing I am fonder of—— Sometimes I tickle the soles of my feet with it. That is very funny, too——'

But at that moment, the big yellow cock, who had been gravely stalking towards her, jumped upon her breast.

'Get away with you, Alexander! get away!' she cried. 'What a tiresome creature he is! The idea of his perching himself on me—— You are too rough, sir, and you scratch me with your claws. Do you hear me? I don't want you to go away, but you must be good, and mustn't peck at my hair.'

Then she troubled herself no further about him. The cock still maintained his position, every now and then glancing inquisitively at the girl's chin with his gleaming eye. The other birds all began to cluster round her. After rolling amongst the straw, she was now lying lazily on her back with her arms stretched out.

'Ah! how pleasant it is,' she said; 'but then it makes me feel so sleepy. Straw always makes one drowsy, doesn't it? Serge doesn't like it. Perhaps you don't either. What do you like? Tell me, so that I may know.'

She was gradually dozing off. For a moment she opened her eyes widely, as though she were looking for something, and then her eyelids fell with a tranquil smile of content. She seemed to be asleep, but after a few minutes she opened her eyes again, and said:

'The cow is going to have a calf—— That will be so nice, and will please me more than anything.'

Then she sank into deep slumber. The fowls had ended by perching on her body; she was buried beneath a wave of living plumage. Hens were brooding over her feet; geese stretched their soft downy necks over her legs. The pig lay against her left side, while on the right, the goat poked its bearded head under her arm. The pigeons were roosting and nestling all over her, on her hands, her waist, and her shoulders. And there she lay asleep, in all her rosy freshness, caressed by the cow's warm breath, while the big cock still squatted just below her bosom with gleaming comb and quivering wings.

Outside, the rain was falling less heavily. A sunbeam, escaping from beneath a cloud, gilded the fine drops of water. Albine, who had remained perfectly still, watched the slumber of Desiree, that big, plump girl who found her great delight in rolling about in the straw. She wished that she, too, could slumber away so peacefully, and feel such pleasure, because a few straws had tickled her neck. And she felt jealous of those strong arms, that firm bosom, all that vitality, all that purely animal development which made the other like a tranquil easy-minded sister of the big red and white cow.

However, the rain had now quite ceased. The three cats of the parsonage filed out into the yard one after the other, keeping close to the wall, and taking the greatest precautions to avoid wetting their paws. They peeped into the stable, and then stalked up to the sleeping girl, and lay down, purring, close by her. Moumou, the big black cat, curled itself up close to her cheek, and gently licked her chin.

'And Serge?' murmured Albine, quite mechanically.

What was it that kept them apart? Who was it that prevented them from being happy together? Why might she not love him, and why might she not be loved, freely and in the broad sunlight, as the trees lived and loved? She knew not, but she felt that she had been forsaken, and had received a mortal wound. Yet she was possessed by a stubborn, determined longing, a very necessity, indeed, of once more clasping her love in her arms, of concealing him somewhere, that he might be hers in all felicity. She rose to her feet. The vestry door had just been opened again. A clapping of hands sounded, followed by the uproar of a swarm of children clattering in wooden shoes over the stone flags. The catechising was over. Then Albine gently glided out of the stable, where she had been waiting for an hour amidst the reeking warmth that emanated from Desiree's pets.

As she quietly slipped through the passage that led to the vestry, she caught sight of La Teuse, who was going to her kitchen, and who fortunately did not turn her head. Certain, now, of not being seen and stopped, Albine softly pushed the door which was before her, keeping hold of it in order that it might make no noise as it closed again.

And she found herself in the church.

VIII

At first she could see nobody. Outside, the rain had again begun to fall in fine close drops. The church looked very grey and gloomy. She passed behind the high altar, and walked on towards the pulpit. In the middle of the nave, there were only a number of empty benches, left there in disorder by the urchins of the catechism class. Amidst all this void came a low tic-tac from the swaying pendulum. She went down the church to knock at the confessional-box, which she saw standing at the other end. But, just as she passed the Chapel of the Dead, she caught sight of Abbe Mouret prostrated before the great bleeding Christ. He did not stir; he must have thought that it was only La Teuse putting the seats in order behind him.

But Albine laid her hand upon his shoulder.

'Serge,' she said, 'I have come for you.'

The priest raised his head with a start. His face was very pale. He remained on his knees and crossed himself, while his lips still quivered with the words of his prayer.

'I have been waiting for you,' she continued. 'Every morning and every evening I looked to see if you were not coming. I have counted the days till I could keep the reckoning no longer. Ah! for weeks and weeks—— Then, when I grew sure that you were not coming, I set out myself, and came here. I said to myself: "I will fetch him away with me." Give me your hand and let us go.'

She stretched out her hands, as though to help him to rise. But he only crossed himself, afresh. He still continued his prayers as he looked at her. He had succeeded in calming the first quiver of his flesh. From the Divine grace which had been streaming around him since the early morning, like a celestial bath, he derived a superhuman strength.

'It is not right for you to be here,' he said, gravely. 'Go away. You are aggravating your sufferings.'

'I suffer no longer,' she said, with a smile. 'I am well again; I am cured, now that I see you once more—— Listen! I made myself out worse than I really was, to induce them to go and fetch you. I am quite willing to confess it now. And that promise of going away, of leaving the neighbourhood, you didn't suppose I should have kept it, did you? No, indeed, unless I had carried you away with me on my shoulders. The others don't know it, but you must know that I cannot now live anywhere but at your side.'

She grew quite cheerful again, and drew close to the priest with the caressing ways of a child of nature, never noticing his cold and rigid demeanour. And she became impatient, clapped her hands, and exclaimed:

'Come, Serge; make up your mind and come. We are only losing time. There is no necessity to think so much about it. It is quite simple; I am going to take you with me. If you don't want any one to see you, we will go along by the Mascle. It is not very easy walking, but I managed it all by myself; and, when we are together, we can help each other. You know the way, don't you? We cross the churchyard, we descend to the torrent, and then we shall only have to follow its course right up to the garden. And one is quite at home down there. Nobody can see us, there is nothing but brambles and big round stones. The bed of the stream is nearly dry. As I came along, I thought: "By- and-by, when he is with me, we will walk along gently together and kiss one another." Come, Serge, be quick; I am waiting for you.'

The priest no longer appeared to hear her. He had betaken himself to his prayers again, and was asking Heaven to grant him the courage of the saints. Before entering upon the supreme struggle, he was arming himself with the flaming sword of faith. For a moment he had feared he was wavering. He had required all a martyr's courage and endurance to remain firmly kneeling there on the flagstones, while Albine was calling him: his heart had leapt out towards her, all his blood had surged passionately through his veins, filling him with an intense yearning to clasp her in his arms and kiss her hair. Her mere breath had awakened all the memory of their love; the vast garden, their saunters beneath the trees, and all the joy of their companionship.

But Divine grace was poured down upon him more abundantly, and the torturing strife, during which all his blood seemed to quit his veins, lasted but a moment. Nothing human then remained within him. He had become wholly God's.

Albine, however, again touched him on the shoulder. She was growing uneasy and angry.

'Why do you not speak to me?' she asked. 'You can't refuse; you will come with me? Remember that I shall die if you refuse. But no! you can't; it is impossible. We lived together once; it was vowed that we should never separate. Twenty times, at least, did you give yourself to me. You bade me take you wholly, your limbs, your breath, your very life itself. I did not dream it all. There is nothing of you that you have not given to me; not a hair in your head which is not mine. Your hands are mine. For days and days have I held them clasped in mine. Your face, your lips, your eyes, your brow, all, all are mine, and I have lavished my love upon them. Do you hear me, Serge?'

She stood erect before him, full of proud assertion, with outstretched arms. And, in a louder voice, she repeated:

'Do you hear me, Serge? You belong to me.'

Then Abbe Mouret slowly rose to his feet. He leant against the altar, and replied:

'No. You are mistaken. I belong to God.'

He was full of serenity. His shorn face seemed like that of some stone saint, whom no impulse of the flesh can disturb. His cassock fell around him in straight folds like a black winding-sheet, concealing all the outlines of his body. Albine dropped back at the sight of that sombre phantom of her former love. She missed his freely flowing beard, his freely flowing curls. And in the midst of his shorn locks she saw the pallid circle of his tonsure, which disquieted her as if it had been some mysterious evil, some malignant sore which had grown there, and would eat away all memory of the happy days they had spent together. She could recognise neither his hands, once so warm with caresses, nor his lissom neck, once so sonorous with laughter; nor his agile feet, which had carried her into the recesses of the woodlands. Could this, indeed, be the strong youth with whom she had lived one whole season —the youth with soft down gleaming on his bare breast, with skin browned by the sun's rays, with every limb full of vibrating life? At this present hour he seemed fleshless; his hair had fallen away from him, and all his virility had withered within that womanish gown, which left him sexless.

'Oh! you frighten me,' she murmured. 'Did you think then that I was dead, that you put on mourning? Take off that black thing; put on a blouse. You can tuck up the sleeves, and we will catch crayfishes again. Your arms used to be as white as mine.'

She laid her hand on his cassock, as though to tear it off him; but he repulsed her with a gesture, without touching her. He looked at her now and strengthened himself against temptation by never allowing his eyes to leave her. She seemed to him to have grown taller. She was no longer the playful damsel adorned with bunches of wild-flowers, and casting to the winds gay, gipsy laughter, nor was she the amorosa in white skirts, gracefully bending her slender form as she sauntered lingeringly beside the hedges. Now, there was a velvety bloom upon her lips; her hips were gracefully rounded; her bosom was in full bloom. She had become a woman, with a long oval face that seemed expressive of fruitfulness. Life slumbered within her. And her cheeks glowed with luscious maturity.

The priest, bathed in the voluptuous atmosphere that seemed to emanate from all that feminine ripeness, took a bitter pleasure in defying the caresses of her coral lips, the tempting smile of her eyes, the witching charm of her bosom, and all the intoxication which seemed to pour from her at every movement. He even carried his temerity so far as to search with his gaze for the spots that he had once so hotly kissed, the corners of her eyes and lips, her narrow temples, soft as satin, and the ambery nape of her neck, which was like velvet. And never, even in her embrace, had he tasted such felicity as he now felt in martyring himself, by boldly looking in the face the love that he refused. At last, fearing lest he might there yield to some new allurement of the flesh, he dropped his eyes, and said, very gently:

'I cannot hear you here. Let us go out, if you, indeed, persist in adding to the pain of both of us. Our presence in this place is a scandal. We are in God's house.'

'God!' cried Albine, excitedly, suddenly becoming a child of nature once more. 'God! Who is He? I know nothing of your God! I want to know nothing of Him if He has stolen you away from me, who have never harmed Him. My uncle Jeanbernat was right then when he said that your God was only an invention to frighten people, and make them weep! You are lying; you love me no longer, and that God of yours does not exist.'

'You are in His house now,' said Abbe Mouret, sternly. 'You blaspheme. With a breath He might turn you into dust.'

She laughed with proud disdain, and raised her hands as if to defy Heaven.

'Ah! then,' said she, 'you prefer your God to me. You think He is stronger than I am, and you imagine that He will love you better than I did. Oh! but you are a child, a foolish child. Come, leave all this folly. We will return to the garden together, and love each other, and be happy and free. That, that is life!'

This time she succeeded in throwing an arm round his waist, and she tried to drag him away. But he, quivering all over, freed himself from her embrace, and again took his stand against the altar.

'Go away!' he faltered. 'If you still love me, go away.... O Lord, pardon her, and pardon me too, for thus defiling this Thy house. Should I go with her beyond the door, I might, perhaps, follow her. Here, in Thy presence, I am strong. Suffer that I may remain here, to protect Thee from insult.'

Albine remained silent for a moment. Then, in a calm voice, she said:

'Well, let us stay here, then. I wish to speak to you. You cannot, surely, be cruel. You will understand me. You will not let me go away alone. Oh! do not begin to excuse yourself. I will not lay my hands upon you again, since it distresses you. I am quite calm now as you can see. We will talk quietly, as we used to do in the old days when we lost our way, and did not hurry to find it again, that we might have the more time to talk together.'

She smiled at that memory, and continued:

'I don't know about these things myself. My uncle Jeanbernat used to forbid me to go to church. "Silly girl," he'd say to me, "why do you want to go to a stuffy building when you have got a garden to run about in?" I grew up quite happy and contented. I used to look in the birds' nests without even taking the eggs. I did not even pluck the flowers, for fear of hurting the plants; and you know that I could never torture an insect. Why, then, should God be angry with me?'

'You should learn to know Him, pray to Him, and render Him the constant worship which is His due,' answered the priest.

'Ah! it would please you if I did, would it not?' she said. 'You would forgive me, and love me again? Well, I will do all that you wish me. Tell me about God, and I will believe in Him, and worship Him. All that you tell me shall be a truth to which I will listen on my knees. Have I ever had a thought that was not your own? We will begin our long walks again; and you shall teach me, and make of me whatever you will. Say "yes," I beg of you.'

Abbe Mouret pointed to his cassock.

'I cannot,' he simply said. 'I am a priest.'

'A priest!' she repeated after him, the smile dying out of her eyes. 'My uncle says that priests have neither wife, nor sister, nor mother. So that is true, then. But why did you ever come? It was you who took me for your sister, for your wife. Were you then lying?'

The priest raised his pale face, moist with the sweat of agony. 'I have sinned,' he murmured.

'When I saw you so free,' the girl went on, 'I thought that you were no longer a priest. I believed that all that was over, that you would always remain there with me, and for my sake.—— And now, what would you have me do, if you rob me of my whole life?'

'What I do,' he answered; 'kneel down, suffer on your knees, and never rise until God pardons you.'

'Are you a coward, then?' she exclaimed, her anger roused once more, her lips curving scornfully.

He staggered, and kept silence. Agony held him by the throat; but he proved stronger than pain. He held his head erect, and a smile almost played about his trembling lips. Albine for a moment defied him with her fixed glance; then, carried away by a fresh burst of passion, she exclaimed:

'Well, answer me. Accuse me! Say it was I who came to tempt you! That will be the climax! Speak, and say what you can for yourself. Strike me if you like. I should prefer your blows to that corpse-like stiffness you put on. Is there no blood left in your veins? Have you no spirit? Don't you hear me calling you a coward? Yes, indeed, you are a coward. You should never have loved me, since you may not be a man. Is it that black robe of yours which holds you back? Tear it off! When you are naked, perhaps you will remember yourself again.'

The priest slowly repeated his former words:

'I have sinned. I had no excuse for my sin. I do penitence for my sin without hope of pardon. If I tore off my cassock, I should tear away my very flesh, for I have given myself wholly to God, soul and body. I am a priest.'

'And I! what is to become of me?' cried Albine.

He looked unflinchingly at her.

'May your sufferings be reckoned against me as so many crimes! May I be eternally punished for the desertion in which I am forced to leave you! That will be only just. All unworthy though I be, I pray for you each night.'

She shrugged her shoulders with an air of great discouragement. Her anger was subsiding. She almost felt inclined to pity him.

'You are mad,' she murmured. 'Keep your prayers. It is you yourself that I want. But you will never understand me. There were so many things I wanted to tell you! Yet you stand there and irritate me with your chatter of another world. Come, let us try to talk sensibly. Let us wait for a moment till we are calmer. You cannot dismiss me in this way, I cannot leave you here. It is because you are here that you are so corpse-like, so cold that I dare not touch you. We won't talk any more just now. We will wait a little.'

She ceased speaking, and took a few steps, examining the little church. The rain was still gently pattering against the windows; and the cold damp light seemed to moisten the walls. Not a sound came from outside save the monotonous plashing of the rain. The sparrows were doubtless crouching for shelter under the tiles, and the rowan-tree's deserted branches showed but indistinctly in the veiling, drenching downpour. Five o'clock struck, grated out, stroke by stroke, from the wheezy chest of the old clock; and then the silence fell again, seeming to grow yet deeper, dimmer, and more despairing. The priest's painting work, as yet scarcely dry, gave to the high altar and the wainscoting an appearance of gloomy cleanliness, like that of some convent chapel where the sun never shines. Grievous anguish seemed to fill the nave, splashed with the blood that flowed from the limbs of the huge Christ; while, along the walls, the fourteen scenes of the Passion displayed their awful story in red and yellow daubs, reeking with horror. It was life that was suffering the last agonies there, amidst that deathlike quiver of the atmosphere, upon those altars which resembled tombs, in that bare vault which looked like a sepulchre. The surroundings all spoke of slaughter and gloom, terror and anguish and nothingness. A faint scent of incense still lingered there, like the last expiring breath of some dead girl, who had been hurriedly stifled beneath the flagstones.

'Ah,' said Albine at last, 'how sweet it used to be in the sunshine! Don't you remember? One morning we walked past a hedge of tall rose bushes, to the left of the flower-garden. I recollect the very colour of the grass; it was almost blue, shot with green. When we reached the end of the hedge we turned and walked back again, so sweet was the perfume of the sunny air. And we did nothing else, that morning; we took just twenty paces forward and then twenty paces back. It was so sweet a spot you would not leave it. The bees buzzed all around; and there was a tomtit that never left us, but skipped along by our side from branch to branch. You whispered to me, "How delightful is life!" Ah! life! it was the green grass, the trees, the running waters, the sky, and the sun, amongst which we seemed all fair and golden.'

She mused for another moment and then continued: 'Life 'twas the Paradou. How vast it used to seem to us! Never were we able to find the end of it. The sea of foliage rolled freely with rustling waves as far as the eye could reach. And all that glorious blue overhead! we were free to grow, and soar, and roam, like the clouds without meeting more obstacles than they. The very air was ours!'

She stopped and pointed to the low walls of the church.

'But, here, you are in a grave. You cannot stretch out your hand without hurting it against the stones. The roof hides the sky from you and blots out the sun. It is all so small and confined that your limbs grow stiff and cramped as though you were buried alive.'

'No,' answered the priest. 'The church is wide as the world.'

But she waved her hands towards the crosses, and the dying Christ, and the pictures of the Passion.

'And you live in the very midst of death. The grass, the trees, the springs, the sun, the sky, all are in the death throes around you.'

'No, no; all revives, all grows purified and reascends to the source of light.'

He had now drawn himself quite erect, with flashing eyes. And feeling that he was now invincible, so permeated with faith as to disdain temptation, he quitted the altar, took Albine's hand, and led her, as though she had been his sister, to the ghastly pictures of the Stations of the Cross.

'See,' he said, 'this is what God suffered! Jesus is cruelly scourged. Look! His shoulders are naked; His flesh is torn; His blood flows down His back.... And Jesus is crowned with thorns. Tears of blood trickle down His gashed brow. On His temple is a jagged wound.... Again Jesus is insulted by the soldiers. His murderers have scoffingly thrown a purple robe around His shoulders, and they spit upon His face and strike Him, and press the thorny crown deep into His flesh.'

Albine turned away her head, that she might not see the crudely painted pictures, in which the ochreous flesh of Christ had been plentifully bedaubed with carmine wounds. The purple robe round His shoulders seemed like a shred of His skin torn away.

'Why suffer? why die?' she said. 'O Serge, if you would only remember!... You told me, that morning, that you were tired. But I knew that you were only pretending, for the air was quite cool and we had only been walking for a quarter of an hour. But you wanted to sit down that you might hold me in your arms. Right down in the orchard, by the edge of a stream, there was a cherry tree—you remember it, don't you?—which you never could pass without wishing to kiss my hands. And your kisses ran all up my arms and shoulders to my lips. Cherry time was over, and so you devoured my lips.... It used to make us feel so sad to see the flowers fading, and one day, when you found a dead bird in the grass, you turned quite pale, and caught me to your breast, as if to forbid the earth to take me.'

But the priest drew her towards the other Stations of the Cross.

'Hush! hush!' he cried, 'look here, and here! Bow down in grief and pity —— Jesus falls beneath the weight of His cross. The ascent of Calvary is very tiring. He has dropped down on His knees. But He does not stay to wipe even the sweat from His brow, He rises up again and continues His journey.... And again Jesus falls beneath the weight of His cross. At each step He staggers. This time He has fallen on His side, so heavily that for a moment He lies there quite breathless. His lacerated hands have relaxed their hold upon the cross. His bruised and aching feet leave blood-stained prints behind them. Agonising weariness overwhelms Him, for He carries upon His shoulders the sins of the whole world.'

Albine gazed at the pictured Jesus, lying in a blue shirt prostrate beneath the cross, the blackness of which bedimmed the gold of His aureole. Then, with her glance wandering far away, she said:

'Oh! those meadow-paths! Have you no memory left, Serge? Have you forgotten those soft grassy walks through the meadows, amidst very seas of greenery? On the afternoon I am telling you of, we had only meant to stay out of doors an hour; but we went wandering on and were still wandering when the stars came out above us. Ah! how velvety it was, that endless carpet, soft as finest silk! It was just like a green sea whose gentle waters lapped us round. And well we knew whither those beguiling paths that led nowhere, were taking us! They were taking us to our love, to the joy of living together, to the certainty of happiness.'

With his hands trembling with anguish, Abbe Mouret pointed to the remaining pictures.

'Jesus,' he stammered, 'Jesus is nailed to the cross. The nails are hammered through His outspread hands. A single nail suffices for his feet, whose bones split asunder. He, Himself, while His flesh quivers with pain, fixes His eyes upon heaven and smiles.... Jesus is crucified between two thieves. The weight of His body terribly aggravates His wounds. From His brow, from His limbs, does a bloody sweat stream down. The two thieves insult Him, the passers-by mock at Him, the soldiers cast lots for His raiment. And the shadowy darkness grows deeper and the sun hides himself.... Jesus dies upon the cross. He utters a piercing cry and gives up the ghost. Oh! most terrible of deaths! The veil of the temple is rent in twain from top to bottom. The earth quakes, the stones are broken, and the very graves open.'

The priest had fallen on his knees, his voice choked by sobs, his eyes fixed upon the three crosses of Calvary, where writhed the gaunt pallid bodies of the crucified. Albine placed herself in front of the paintings in order that he might no longer see them.

'One evening,' she said, 'I lay through the long gloaming with my head upon your lap. It was in the forest, at the end of that great avenue of chestnut- trees, through which the setting sun shot a parting ray. Ah! what a caressing farewell He bade us! He lingered awhile by our feet with a kindly smile, as if saying "Till to-morrow." The sky slowly grew paler. I told you merrily that it was taking off its blue gown, and donning its gold-flowered robe of black to go out for the evening. And it was not night that fell, but a soft dimness, a veil of love and mystery, reminding us of those dusky paths, where the foliage arches overhead, one of those paths in which one hides for a moment with the certainty of finding the joyousness of daylight at the other end.

'That evening the calm clearness of the twilight gave promise of a splendid morrow. When I saw that it did not grow dark as quickly as you wished, I pretended to fall asleep. I may confess it to you now, but I was not really sleeping while you kissed me on the eyes. I felt your kisses and tried to keep from laughing. And then, when the darkness really came, it was like one long caress. The trees slept no more than I did. At night, don't you remember, the flowers always breathed a stronger perfume.'

Then, as he still remained on his knees, while tears streamed down his face, she caught him by the wrists, and pulled him to his feet, resuming passionately:

'Oh! if you knew you would bid me carry you off; you would fasten your arms about my neck, lest I should go away without you…. Yesterday I had a longing to see the garden once more. It seems larger, deeper, more unfathomable than ever. I discovered there new scents, so sweetly aromatic that they brought tears into my eyes. In the avenues I found a rain of sunbeams that thrilled me with desire. The roses spoke to me of you. The bullfinches were amazed at seeing me alone. All the garden broke out into sighs. Oh! come! Never has the grass spread itself out more softly. I have marked with a flower the hidden nook whither I long to take you. It is a nest of greenery in the midst of a tangle of brushwood. And there one can hear all the teeming life of the garden, of the trees and the streams and the sky. The earth's very breathing will softly lull us to rest there. Oh! come! come! and let us love one another amidst that universal loving!'

But he pushed her from him. He had returned to the Chapel of the Dead and stood in front of the painted papier-mache Christ, big as a ten-year-old boy, that writhed in such horridly realistic agony. There were real iron nails driven into the figure's limbs, and the wounds gaped in the torn and bleeding flesh.

'O Jesus, Who hast died for us!' cried the priest, 'convince her of our nothingness! Tell her that we are but dust, rottenness, and damnation! Ah! suffer that I may hide my head in a hair-cloth and rest it against Thy feet and stay there, motionless, until I rot away in death. The earth will no longer exist for me. The sun will no longer shine. I shall see nothing more, feel nothing, hear nothing. Nought of all this wretched world will come to turn my soul from its adoration of Thee.'

He was gradually becoming more and more excited, and he stepped towards Albine with upraised hands.

'You said rightly. It is Death that is present here; Death that is before my eyes; Death that delivers and saves one from all rottenness. Hear me! I renounce, I deny life, I wholly refuse it, I spit upon it. Those flowers of yours stink; your sun dazzles and blinds; your grass makes lepers of those that lie upon it; your garden is but a charnel-place where all rots and putrefies. The earth reeks with abomination. You lie when you talk of love and light and gladsome life in the depths of your palace of greenery. There is nought but darkness there. Those trees of yours exhale a poison which transforms men into beasts; your thickets are charged with the venom of vipers; your streams carry pestilence in their blue waters. If I could snatch away from that world of nature, which you extol, its kirtle of sunshine and its girdle of greenery, you would see it hideous like a very fury, a skeleton, rotting away with disease and vice.

'And even if you spoke the truth, even if your hands were really filled with pleasures, even if you should carry me to a couch of roses and offer me the dreams of Paradise, I would defend myself yet the more desperately from your embraces. There is war between us; war eternal and implacable. See! the church is very small; it is poverty-stricken; it is ugly; its confessional-box and pulpit are made of common deal, its font is merely of plaster, its altars are formed of four boards which I have painted myself. But what of that? It is yet vaster than your garden, greater than the valley, greater, even, than the whole earth. It is an impregnable fortress which nothing can ever break down. The winds, the sun, the forests, the ocean, all that is, may combine to assault it; yet it will stand erect and unshaken for ever!

'Yes, let all the jungles tower aloft and assail the walls with their thorny arms, let all the legions of insects swarm out of their holes in the ground and gnaw at the walls; the church, ruinous though it may seem, will never fall before the invasion of life. It is Death, Death the inexpugnable!... And do you know what will one day happen? The tiny church will grow and spread to such a colossal size, and will cast around such a mighty shadow, that all that nature, you speak of, will give up the ghost. Ah! Death, the Death of everything, with the skies gaping to receive our souls, above the curse- stricken ruins of the world!'

As he shouted those last words, he pushed Albine forcibly towards the door. She, extremely pale, retreated step by step. When he had finished in a gasping voice she very gravely answered:

'It is all over, then? You drive me away? Yet, I am your wife. It is you who made me so. And God, since He permitted it, cannot punish us to such a point as this.'

She was now on the threshold, and she added:

'Listen! Every day, at sunset, I go to the end of the garden, to the spot where the wall has fallen in. I shall wait for you there.'

And then she disappeared. The vestry door fell back with a sound like a deep sigh.

IX

The church was perfectly silent, except for the murmuring sound of the rain, which was falling heavily once more. In that sudden change to quietude the priest's anger subsided, and he even felt moved. It was with his face streaming with tears, his frame shaken by sobs, that he went back to throw himself on his knees before the great crucifix. A torrent of ardent thanksgiving burst from his lips.

'Thanks be to Thee, O God, for the help which Thou hast graciously bestowed upon me. Without Thy grace I should have hearkened unto the promptings of my flesh, and should have miserably returned to my sin. It was Thy grace that girded my loins as with armour for battle; Thy grace was indeed my armour, my courage, the support of my soul, that kept me erect, beyond weakness. Oh! my God, Thou wert in me; it was Thy voice that spoke in me, for I no longer felt the cowardice of the flesh, I could have cut asunder my very heart-strings. And now, O God, I offer Thee my bleeding heart. It no longer belongs to any creature of this world; it is Thine alone. To give it to Thee I have wrenched it from all worldly affection. But think not, O God, that I take any pride to myself for this victory. I know that without Thee I am nothing; and I humbly cast myself at Thy feet.'

He sank down upon the altar steps, unable to utter another word, while his breath panted incense-like from his parted lips. The divine grace bathed him in ineffable ecstasy. He sought Jesus in the recesses of his being, in that sanctuary of love which he was ever preparing for His worthy reception. And Jesus was now present there. The Abbe knew it by the sweet influences which permeated him. And thereupon he joined with Jesus in that spiritual converse which at times bore him away from earth to companionship with God. He sighed out the verse from the 'Song of Solomon,' 'My beloved is mine, and I am his; He feedeth his flock among the lilies, until the day be cool, and the shadows flee away.' He pondered over the words of the 'Imitation:' 'It is a great art to know how to talk with Jesus, and it requires much prudence to keep Him near one.' And then, with adorable condescension, Jesus came down to him, and spoke with him for hours of his needs, his happiness, and his hopes. Their confidences were not less affectionate and touching than those of two friends, who meet after long separation and quietly retire to converse on the bank of some lonely stream; for during those hours of divine condescension Jesus deigned to be his friend, his best, most faithful friend, one who never forsook him, and who in return for a little love gave him all the treasures of eternal life. That day the priest was eager to prolong the sweet converse, and indeed, when six o'clock sounded through the quiet church, he was still listening to the words which echoed through his soul.

On his side there was unreserved confession, unimpeded by the restraints of language, natural effusion of the heart which spoke even more quickly than the mind. Abbe Mouret told everything to Jesus, as to a God who had come down in all the intimacy of the most loving tenderness, and who would listen to everything. He confessed that he still loved Albine; and he was surprised that he had been able to speak sternly to her and drive her away, without his whole being breaking out into revolt. He marvelled at it, and smiled as though it were some wonderful miracle performed by another. And Jesus told him that he must not be astonished, and that the greatest saints were often but unconscious instruments in the hands of God. Then the Abbe gave expression to a doubt. Had he not lost merit in seeking refuge in the Cross and even in the Passion of his Saviour? Had he not shown that he possessed as yet but little courage, since he had not dared to fight unaided? But Jesus evinced kindly tolerance, and answered that man's weakness was God's continual care, and that He especially loved those suffering souls, to whose assistance He went, like a friend to the bedside of a sick companion.

But was it a sin to love Albine, a sin for which he, Serge, would be damned? No; if his love was clean of all fleshly taint, and added another hope to his desire for eternal life. But, then, how was he to love her? In silence; without speaking a word to her, without taking a step towards her; simply allowing his pure affection to breathe forth, like a sweet perfume, pleasing unto heaven. And Jesus smiled with increasing kindliness, drawing nearer as if to encourage confession, in such wise that the priest grew bolder and began to recapitulate Albine's charms. She had hair that was fair and golden as an angel's; she was very white, with big soft eyes, like those of the aureoled saints. Jesus seemed to listen to this in silence, though a smile still played upon His face. And the priest continued: She had grown much taller. She was now like a queen, with rounded form and splendid shoulders. Oh! to clasp her waist, were it only for a second, and to feel her shoulders drawn close by his embrace! But the smile on the divine countenance then paled and died away, as a star sinks and falls beneath the horizon. Abbe Mouret now spoke all alone. Ah! had he not shown himself too hard-hearted? Why had he driven her away without one single word of affection, since Heaven allowed him to love her?

'I do love her! I do love her!' he cried aloud, in a distracted voice, that rang through the church.

He thought he saw her still standing there. She was stretching out her arms to him; she was beautiful enough to make him break all his vows. He threw himself upon her bosom without thought of the reverence due to his surroundings, he clasped her and rained kisses upon her face. It was before her that he now knelt, imploring her mercy, and beseeching her to forgive him his unkindness. He told her that, at times a voice which was not his own spoke through his lips. Could he himself ever have treated her harshly? It was the strange voice that had repulsed her. It could not, surely, be he himself, for he would have been unable to touch a hair of her head without loving emotion. And yet he had driven her away. The church was really empty! Whither should he hasten to find her again, to bring her back, and wipe her tears away with kisses? The rain was streaming down more violently than ever. The roads must be rivers of mud. He pictured her to himself lashed by the downpour, tottering alongside the ditches, her clothes soaked and clinging to her skin. No! no! it could not have been himself; it was that other voice, the jealous voice that had so cruelly sought to slay his love.

'O Jesus!' he cried in desperation, 'be merciful and give her back to me!'

But his Lord was no longer there. Then Abbe Mouret, awaking with a start, turned horribly pale. He understood it all. He had not known how to keep Jesus with him. He had lost his friend, and had been left defenceless against the powers of evil. Instead of that inward light, which had shone so brightly within him as he received his God, he now found utter darkness, a foul vapour that irritated his senses. Jesus had withdrawn His grace on leaving him; and he, who since early morning had been so strong with heaven-sent help, now felt utterly miserable, forsaken, weak and helpless as an infant. How frightful was his fall! How galling its bitterness! To have straggled so heroically, to have remained unshaken, invincible, implacable, while the temptress actually stood before him, with all her warm life, her swelling bosom and superb shoulders, her perfume of love and passion; and then to fall so shamefully, to throb with desire, when she had disappeared, leaving behind her but the echo of her skirts, and the fragrance diffused from her white neck! Now, these mere recollections sufficed to make her all powerful, her influence permeated the church.

'Jesus! Jesus!' cried the priest, once more, 'return, come back to me; speak to me once again!'

But Jesus remained deaf to his cry. For a moment Abbe Mouret raised his arms to heaven in desperate entreaty. His shoulders cracked and strained beneath the wild violence of his supplications. But soon his hands fell down again in discouragement. Heaven preserved that hopeless silence which suppliants at times encounter. Then he once more sat down on the altar steps, heart-crushed and with ashen face, pressing his elbows to his sides, as though he were trying to reduce his flesh to the smallest proportions possible.

'My God! Thou deserted me!' he murmured. 'Nevertheless, Thy will be done!'

He spoke not another word, but sat there, panting breathlessly, like a hunted beast that cowers motionless in fear of the hounds. Ever since his sin, he had thus seemed to be the sport of the divine grace. It denied itself to his most ardent prayers; it poured down upon him, unexpectedly and refreshingly, when he had lost all hope of winning it for long years to come.

At first he had been inclined to rebel against this dispensation of Heaven, complaining like a betrayed lover, and demanding the immediate return of that consoling grace, whose kiss made him so strong. But afterwards, after unavailing outbursts of anger, he had learned to understand that humility profited him most and could alone enable him to endure the withdrawal of the divine assistance. Then, for hours and for days, he would humble himself and wait for comfort which came not. In vain he cast himself unreservedly into the hands of God, annihilated himself before the Divinity, wearied himself with the incessant repetition of prayers. He could not perceive God's presence with him; and his flesh, breaking free from all restraint, rose up in rebellious desire. It was a slow agony of temptation, in which the weapons of faith fell, one by one, from his faltering hands, in which he lay inert in the clutch of passion, in which he beheld with horror his own ignominy, without having the courage to raise his little finger to free himself from the thraldom of sin.

Such was now his life. He had felt sin's attacks in every form. Not a day passed that he was not tried. Sin assumed a thousand guises, assailed him through his eyes and ears, flew boldly at his throat, leaped treacherously upon his shoulders, or stole torturingly into his bones. His transgression was ever present, he almost always beheld Albine dazzling as the sunshine, lighting up the greenery of the Paradou. He only ceased to see her in those rare moments when the divine grace deigned to close his eyes with its cool caresses. And he strove to hide his sufferings as one hides those of some disgraceful disease. He wrapped himself in the endless silence, which no one knew how to make him break, filling the parsonage with his martyrdom and resignation, and exasperating La Teuse, who, at times, when his back was turned, would shake her fist at heaven.

This time he was alone now, and need take no care to hide his torment. Sin had just struck him such an overwhelming blow, that he had not strength left to move from the altar steps, where he had fallen. He remained there, sighing, and groaning, parched with agony, incapable of a single tear. And he thought of the calm unruffled life that had once been his. Ah! the perfect peace, the full confidence of his first days at Les Artaud! The path of salvation had seemed so straight and easy then! He had smiled at the very mention of temptation. He had lived in the midst of wickedness, without knowledge of it, without fear of it, certain of being able to withstand it. He had been a model priest, so pure and chaste, so inexperienced and innocent in God's sight, that God had led him by the hand like a little child.

But now, all that childlike innocence was dead, God visited him in the morning, and forthwith tried him. A state of temptation became his life on earth. Now that full manhood and sin had come upon him, he entered into the everlasting struggle. Could it be that God really loved him more now than before? The great saints have all left fragments of their torn flesh upon the thorns of the way of sorrow. He tried to gather some consolation from this circumstance. At each laceration of his flesh, each racking of his bones, he tried to assure himself of some exceeding great reward. And then, no infliction that Heaven might now cast upon him could be too heavy. He even looked back with scorn on his former serenity, his easy fervour, which had set him on his knees with mere girlish enthusiasm, and left him unconscious even of the bruising of the hard stones. He strove also to discover pleasure in pain, in plunging into it, annihilating himself in it. But, even while he poured out thanks to God, his teeth chattered with growing terror, and the voice of his rebellious blood cried out to him that this was all falsehood, and that the only happiness worth desiring was in Albine's arms, amongst the flowers of the Paradou.

Yet he had put aside Mary for Jesus, sacrificing his heart that he might subdue his flesh, and hoping to implant some virility in his faith. Mary disquieted him too much, with her smoothly braided hair, her outstretched hands, and her womanly smile. He could never kneel before her without dropping his eyes, for fear of catching sight of the hem of her dress. Then, too, he accused her of having treated him too tenderly in former times. She had kept him sheltered so long within the folds of her robe, that he had let himself slip from her arms to those of a human creature without being conscious even of the change of his affection. He thought of all the roughness of Brother Archangias, of his refusal to worship Mary, of the distrustful glances with which he had seemed to watch her. He himself despaired of ever rising to such a height of roughness, and so he simply left her, hiding her images and deserting her altar. Yet she remained in his heart, like some love which, though unavowed, is ever present. Sin, with sacrilege whose very horror made him shudder, made use of her to tempt him.

Whenever he still invoked her, as he did at times of irrepressible emotion, it was Albine who showed herself beneath the white veil, with the blue scarf knotted round her waist and the golden roses blooming on her bare feet. All the representations of the Virgin, the Virgin with the royal mantle of cloth-of-gold, the Virgin crowned with stars, the Virgin visited by the Angel of the Annunciation, the peaceful Virgin poised between a lily and a distaff, all brought him some memory of Albine, her smiling eyes or her delicately curved mouth or her softly rounded cheeks.

Thereupon, by a supreme effort, he drove the female element from his worship, and sought refuge in Jesus, though even His gentle mildness sometimes proved a source of disquietude to him. What he needed was a jealous God, an implacable God, the Jehovah of the Old Testament, girded with thunder and manifesting Himself only to chastise the terrified world. He had done with the saints and the angels and the Divine Mother; he bowed down before God Himself alone, the omnipotent Master, who demanded from him his every breath. And he felt the hand of this God laid heavily upon him, holding him helpless at His mercy through space and time, like a guilty atom. Ah! to be nothing, to be damned, to dream of hell, to wrestle vainly against hideous temptations, all that was surely good.

From Jesus he took but the cross. He was seized with that passion for the cross which has made so many lips press themselves again and again to the crucifix till they were worn away with kissing. He took up the cross and followed Jesus. He sought to make it heavier, the mightiest of burdens; it was great joy to him to fall beneath its weight, to drag it on his knees, his back half broken. In it he beheld the only source of strength for the soul, of joy for the mind, of the consummation of virtue and the perfection of holiness. In it lay all that was good; all ended in death upon it. To suffer and to die, those words ever sounded in his ears, as the end and goal of mortal wisdom. And, when he had fastened himself to the cross, he enjoyed the boundless consolation of God's love. It was no longer, now, upon Mary that he lavished filial tenderness or lover's passion. He loved for love's mere sake, with an absolute abstract love. He loved God with a love that lifted him out of himself, out of all else, and wrapped him round with a dazzling radiance of glory. He was like a torch that burns away with blazing light. And death seemed to him to be only a great impulse of love.

But what had he omitted to do that he was thus so sorely tried? With his hand he wiped away the perspiration that streamed down his brow, and reflected that, that very morning, he had made his usual self-examination without finding any great guilt within him. Was he not leading a life of great austerity and mortification of the flesh? Did he not love God solely and blindly? Ah! how he would have blessed His Holy Name had He only restored him his peace, deeming him now sufficiently punished for his transgression! But, perhaps, that sin of his could never be expiated. And then, in spite of himself, his mind reverted to Albine and the Paradou, and all their memories.

At first he tried to make excuses for himself. He had fallen, one evening, senseless upon the tiled floor of his bedroom, stricken with brain fever. For three weeks he had remained unconscious. His blood surged furiously through his veins and raged within him like a torrent that had burst its banks. His whole body, from the crown of his head to the soles of his feet, was so scoured and renewed and wrought afresh by the mighty labouring of his ailment, that in his delirium he had sometimes thought he could hear the very hammer blows of workmen that nailed his bones together again. Then, one morning, he had awakened, feeling like a new being. He was born a second time, freed of all that his five-and-twenty years of life had successively implanted in him. His childish piety, his education at the seminary, the faith of his early priesthood, had all vanished, had been carried off, and their place was bare and empty. In truth, it could be hell alone that had thus prepared him for the reception of evil, disarming him of all his former weapons, and reducing his body to languor and softness, through which sin might readily enter.

He, perfectly unconscious of it all, unknowingly surrendered himself to the gradual approach of evil. When he had reopened his eyes in the Paradou, he had felt himself an infant once more, with no memory of the past, no knowledge of his priesthood. He experienced a gentle pleasure, a glad feeling of surprise at thus beginning life afresh, as though it were all new and strange to him and would be delightful to learn. Oh! the sweet apprenticeship, the charming observations, the delicious discoveries! That Paradou was a vast abode of felicity; and hell, in placing him there, had known full well that he would be defenceless. Never, in his first youth, had he known such enjoyment in growing. That first youth of his, when he now thought of it, seemed quite black and gloomy, graceless, wan and inactive, as if it had been spent far away from the sunlight.

But at the Paradou, how joyfully had he hailed the sun! How admiringly had he gazed at the first tree, at the first flower, at the tiniest insect he had seen, at the most insignificant pebble he had picked up! The very stones charmed him. The horizon was a source of never-ending amazement. One clear morning, the memory of which still filled his eyes, bringing back a perfume of jasmine, a lark's clear song, he had been so affected by emotion that he felt all power desert his limbs. He had long found pleasure in learning the sensations of life. And, ah! the morning when Albine had been born beside him amidst the roses! As he thought of it, an ecstatic smile broke out upon his face. She rose up like a star that was necessary to the very sun's existence. She illumined everything, she made everything clear. She made his life complete.

Then in fancy he once again walked with her through the Paradou. He remembered the little curls that waved behind her neck as she ran on before him. She exhaled delicious scent, and the touch of her warm swaying skirts seemed like a caress. And when she clasped him with her supple curving arms, he half expected to see her, so slight and slender she was, twine herself around him. It was she who went foremost. She led him through winding paths, where they loitered, that their walk might last the longer. It was she who instilled into him love for nature; and it was by watching the loves of the plants that he had learned to love her, with a love that was long, indeed, in bursting into life, but whose sweetness had been theirs at last. Beneath the shade of the giant tree they had reached their journey's goal. Oh! to clasp her once again—yet once again!

A low groan suddenly came from the priest. He hastily sprang up and then flung himself down again. Temptation had just assailed him afresh. Into what paths were his recollections leading him? Did he not know, only too well, that Satan avails himself of every wile to insinuate his serpent-head into the soul, even when it is absorbed in self-examination? No! no! he had no excuse. His illness had in no wise authorised him to sin. He should have set strict guard upon himself, and have sought God anew upon recovering from his fever. And what a frightful proof he now had of his vileness: he was not even able to make calm confession of his sin. Would he never be able to silence his nature? He wildly thought of scooping his brains out of his skull that he might be able to think no more, and of opening his veins that his blood might no longer torment him. For a moment he buried his face within his hands, shuddering as though the beasts that he felt prowling around him might infect him with the hot breath of temptation.

But his thoughts strayed on in spite of himself, and his blood throbbed wildly in his very heart. Though he held his clenched fists to his eyes, he still saw Albine, dazzling like a sun. Every effort that he made to press the vision from his sight only made her shine out before him with increased brilliancy. Was God, then, utterly forsaking him, that he could find no refuge from temptation? And, in spite of all his efforts to control his thoughts, he espied every tiny blade of grass that thrust itself up by Albine's skirts; he saw a little thistle-flower fastened in her hair, against which he remembered that he had pricked his lips. Even the perfumed atmosphere of the Paradou floated round him, and well-remembered sounds came back, the repeated call of a bird, then an interval of hushed silence, then a sigh floating through the trees.

Why did not Heaven at once strike him dead with its lightning? That would have been less cruel. It was with a voluptuous pang, like the pangs which assail the damned, that he recalled his transgression. He shuddered when he again heard in his heart the abominable words that he had spoken at Albine's feet. Their echoes were now accusing him before the throne of God. He had acknowledged Woman as his sovereign. He had yielded to her as a slave, kissing her feet, longing to be the water she drank and the bread she ate. He began to understand now why he could no longer recover self-control. God had given him over to Woman. But he would chastise her, scourge her, break her very limbs to force her to let him go! It was she who was the slave; she, the creature of impurity, to whom the Church should have denied a soul. Then he braced himself, and shook his fists at the vision of Albine; but his fists opened and his hands glided along her shoulders in a loving caress, while his lips, just now breathing out anger and insult, pressed themselves to her hair, stammering forth words of adoration.

Abbe Mouret opened his eyes again. The burning apparition of Albine vanished. It was sudden and unexpected solace. He was able to weep. Tears flowed slowly and refreshingly down his cheeks, and he drew a long breath, still fearing to move, lest the Evil One should again grip him by the neck, for he yet thought that he heard the snarl of a beast behind him. And then he found such pleasure in the cessation of his sufferings that his one thought was to prolong the enjoyment of it.

Outside the rain had ceased falling. The sun was setting in a vast crimson glow, which spread across the windows like curtains of rose-coloured satin. The church was quite warm and bright in the parting breath of the sinking luminary. The priest thanked God for the respite He had been pleased to vouchsafe to him. A broad ray of light, like a beam of gold-dust, streamed through the nave and illumined the far end of the building, the clock, the pulpit, and the high altar. Perhaps the Divine grace was returning to him from heaven along that radiant path. He watched with interest the atoms that came and went with prodigious speed through the ray, like a swarm of busy messengers ever hastening with news from the sun to the earth. A thousand lighted candles would not have filled the church with such splendour. Curtains of cloth-of-gold seemed to hang behind the high altar; treasures of the goldsmith's art covered all the ledges; candle-holders arose in dazzling sheaves; censers glowed full of burning gems; sacred vases gleamed like fiery comets; and around all there seemed to be a rain of luminous flowers amidst waving lacework—beds, bouquets, and garlands of roses, from whose expanding petals dropped showers of stars.

Never had Abbe Mouret desired such magnificence for his poor church. He smiled, and dreamt of how he might retain all that splendour there, and then arrange it most effectively. He would have preferred to see the curtains of cloth-of-gold hung rather higher; the vases, too, needed more careful arrangement; and he thought that the bouquets of flowers might be tied up more neatly, and the garlands be more regularly shaped. Yet how wondrously magnificent it all was! He was the pontiff of a church of gold. Bishops, princes, princesses, arrayed in royal mantles, multitudes of believers, bending to the ground, were coming to visit it, encamping in the valley, waiting for weeks at the door until they should be able to enter. They kissed his feet, for even his feet had turned to gold, and worked miracles. The bath of gold mounted to his knees. A golden heart was beating within his golden breast, with so clear a musical pulsation that the waiting crowds could hear it from outside. Then a feeling of overweening pride seized upon him. He was an idol. The golden beam mounted still higher, the high altar was all ablaze with glory, and the priest grew certain that the Divine grace must be returning to him, such was his inward satisfaction. The fierce snarl behind him had now grown gentle and coaxing, and he only felt on his shoulder a soft velvety pressure, as though some giant cat were lightly caressing him.

He still pursued his reverie. Never before had he seen things under such a favourable light. Everything seemed quite easy to him now that he once more felt full of strength. Since Albine was waiting for him, he would go and join her. It was only natural. On the previous morning he had married Fortune and Rosalie. The Church did not forbid marriages. He saw that young couple again as they knelt before him, smiling and nudging each other while his hands were held over them in benediction. Then, in the evening, they had shown him their room. Each word that he had spoken to them echoed loudly in his ear. He had told Fortune that God had sent him a companion, because He did not wish man to live alone; and he had told Rosalie that she must cleave to her husband, never leaving him, but always acting as his obedient helpmate. But he had said these things also for Albine and himself. Was she not his companion, his obedient helpmate, whom God had sent to him that his manhood might not wither up in solitude? Besides, they had been joined the one to the other. He felt surprised that he had not understood and recognised it at once; that he had not gone away with her, as his duty plainly required that he should have done. But he had quite made up his mind now; he would certainly join her in the morning. He could be with her in half an hour. He would go through the village, and take the road up the hill; it was much the shortest way. He could do what he pleased; he was the master, and no one would presume to say anything to him. If any one looked at him, a wave of his hand would force them to bend their heads. He would live with Albine. He would call her his wife. They would be very happy together.

The golden stream mounted still higher, and played amongst his fingers. Again did he seem to be immersed in a bath of gold. He would take the altar-vases away to ornament his house, he would keep up a fine establishment, he would pay his servants with fragments of chalices which he could easily break with his fingers. He would hang his bridal-bed with the cloth-of-gold that draped the altar; and he would give his wife for jewels the golden hearts and chaplets and crosses that hung from the necks of the Virgin and the saints. The church itself, if another storey were added to it, would supply them with a palace. God would have no objection to make since He had allowed them to love each other. And, besides, was it not he who was now God, with the people kissing his golden miracle-working feet?

Abbe Mouret rose. He made that sweeping gesture of Jeanbernat's, that wide gesture of negation, that took in everything as far as the horizon.

'There is nothing, nothing, nothing!' he said. 'God does not exist.'

A mighty shudder seemed to sweep through the church. The terrified priest turned deadly pale and listened. Who had spoken? Who was it that had blasphemed? Suddenly the velvety caress, whose gentle pressure he had felt upon his shoulder, turned fierce and savage: sharp talons seemed to be rending his flesh, and once more he felt his blood streaming forth. Yet he remained on his feet, struggling against the sudden attack. He cursed and reviled the triumphant sin that sniggered and grinned round his temples, whilst all the hammers of the Evil One battered at them. Why had he not been on his guard against Satan's wiles? Did he not know full well that it was his habit to glide up softly with gentle paws that he might drive them like blades into the very vitals of his victim?

His anger increased as he thought how he had been entrapped, like a mere child. Was he destined, then, to be ever hurled to the ground, with sin crouching victoriously on his breast? This time he had actually denied his God. It was all one fatal descent. His transgression had destroyed his faith, and then dogma had tottered. One single doubt of the flesh, pleading abomination, sufficed to sweep heaven away. The divine ordinances irritated one; the divine mysteries made one smile. Then came other temptations and allurements; gold, power, unrestrained liberty, an irresistible longing for enjoyment, culminating in luxuriousness, sprawling on a bed of wealth and pride. And then God was robbed. His vessels were broken to adorn woman's impurity. Ah! well, then, he was damned. Nothing could make any difference to him now. Sin might speak aloud. It was useless to struggle further. The monsters who had hovered about his neck were battening on his vitals now. He yielded to them with hideous satisfaction. He shook his fists at the church. No; he believed no longer in the divinity of Christ; he believed no longer in the Holy Trinity; he believed in naught but himself, and his muscles and the appetites of his body. He wanted to live. He felt the necessity of being a man.

Oh! to speed along through the open air, to be lusty and strong, to owe obedience to no jealous master, to fell one's enemies with stones, to carry off the fair maidens that passed upon one's shoulders. He would break out from that living tomb where cruel hands had thrust him. He would awaken his manhood, which had only been slumbering. And might he die of shame if he should find that it were really dead! And might the Divinity be accursed if, by the touch of His finger, He had made him different from the rest of mankind.

The priest stood erect, his mind all dazed and scared. He fancied that, at this fresh outburst of blasphemy, the church was falling down upon him. The sunlight, which had poured over the high altar, had gradually spread and mounted the walls like ruddy fire. Flames soared and licked the rafters, then died away in a sanguineous, ember-like glow. And all at once the church became quite black. It was as though the fires of the setting sun had burst the roof asunder, pierced the walls, thrown open wide breaches on every side to some exterior foe. The gloomy framework seemed to shake beneath some violent assault. Night was coming on quickly.

Then, in the far distance, the priest heard a gentle murmur rising from the valley of Les Artaud. The time had been when he had not understood the impassioned language of those burning lands, where writhed but knotted vine-stocks, withered almond-trees, and decrepit olives sprawling with crippled limbs. Protected by his ignorance, he had passed undisturbed through all that world of passion. But, to-day, his ear detected the slightest sigh of the leaves that lay panting in the heat. Afar off, on the edge of the horizon, the hills, still hot with the sinking luminary's farewell, seemed to set themselves in motion with the tramp of an army on the march. Nearer at hand, the scattered rocks, the stones along the road, all the pebbles in the valley, throbbed and rolled as if possessed by a craving for motion. Then the tracts of ruddy soil, the few fields that had been reduced to cultivation, seemed to heave and growl like rivers that had burst their banks, bearing along in a blood-like flood the engenderings of seeds, the births of roots, the embraces of plants. Soon everything was in motion. The vine-branches appeared to crawl along like huge insects; the parched corn and the dry grass formed into dense, lance-waving battalions; the trees stretched out their boughs like wrestlers making ready for a contest; the fallen leaves skipped forward; the very dust on the road rolled on. It was a moving multitude reinforced by fresh recruits at every step; a legion, the sound of whose coming went on in front of it; an outburst of passionate life, sweeping everything along in a mighty whirlwind of fruitfulness. And all at once the assault began. From the limits of the horizon, the whole countryside, the hills and stones and fields and trees, rushed upon the church. At the first shock, the building quivered and cracked. The walls were pierced and the tiles on the roof were thrown down. But the great Christ, although shaken, did not fall.

A short respite followed. Outside, the voices sounded more angrily, and the priest could now distinguish human ones amongst them. The Artauds, those bastards who sprang up out of the rocky soil with the persistence of brambles, were now in their turn blowing a blast that reeked of teeming life. They had planted everywhere forests of humanity that swallowed up all around them. They came up to the church, they shattered the door with a push, and threatened to block up the very nave with the invading scions of their race. Behind them came the beasts; the oxen that tried to batter down the walls with their horns, the flocks of asses, goats, and sheep, that dashed against the ruined church like living waves, while swarms of wood-lice and crickets attacked the foundations and reduced them to dust with their sawlike teeth. Yet again, on the other side, there was Desiree's poultry-yard, where the dunghill reeked with suffocating fumes. Here the big cock, Alexander, sounded the assault, and the hens loosened the stones with their beaks, and the rabbits burrowed under the very altars; whilst the pig, too fat to stir, grunted and waited till all the sacred ornaments should be reduced to warm ashes in which he might wallow at his ease.

A great roar ascended, and a second assault was delivered. The villagers, the animals, all that overflowing sea of life assailed the church with such impetuosity that the rafters bent and curved. This time a part of the walls tottered and fell down, the ceiling shook, the woodwork of the windows was carried away, and the grey mist of the evening streamed in through the frightful gaping breaches. The great Christ now only clung to His cross by the nail that pierced His left hand.

A mighty shout hailed the downfall of the block of wall. Yet the church still stood there firmly, in spite of the injuries it had received. It offered a stern, silent, unflinching resistance, clutching desperately to the tiniest stones of its foundations. It seemed as though, to keep itself from falling, it required only the support of its slenderest pillar, which, by some miracle of equilibration, held up the gaping roof. Then Abbe Mouret beheld the rude plants of the plateau, the dreadful-looking growths that had become hard as iron amidst the arid rocks, that were knotted like snakes and bossy with muscles, set themselves to work. The rust-hued lichens gnawed away at the rough plasterwork like fiery leprosy. Then the thyme-plants thrust their roots between the bricks like so many iron wedges. The lavenders insinuated hooked fingers into the loosened stonework, and by slow persistent efforts tore the blocks asunder. The junipers, the rosemaries, the prickly holly bushes, climbed higher and battered the walls with irresistible blows; and even the grass, the grass whose dry blades slipped beneath the great door, stiffened itself into steel-like spears and made its way down the nave, where it forced up the flagstones with powerful levers. It was a victorious revolt, it was revolutionary nature constructing barricades out of the overturned altars, and wrecking the church which had for centuries cast too deep a shadow over it. The other combatants had fallen back, and let the plants, the thyme and the lavender and the lichens, complete the overthrow of the building with their ceaseless little blows, their constant gnawing, which proved more destructive than the heavier onslaught of the stronger assailants.

Then, suddenly, the end came. The rowan-tree, whose topmost branches had already forced their way through the broken windows under the vaulted roof, rushed in violently with its formidable stream of greenery. It planted itself in the centre of the nave and grew there monstrously. Its trunk expanded till its girth became so colossal that it seemed as though it would burst the church asunder like a girdle spanning it too closely. Its branches shot out in knotted arms, each one of which broke down a piece of the wall or thrust off a strip of the roof, and they went on multiplying without cessation, each branch ramifying, till a fresh tree sprang out of each single knot, with such impetuosity of growth that the ruins of the church, pierced through and through like a sieve, flew into fragments, scattering a fine dust to the four quarters of the heavens.

Now the giant tree seemed to reach the stars; its forest of branches was a forest of legs, arms, and breasts full of sap; the long locks of women streamed down from it; men's heads burst out from the bark; and up aloft pairs of lovers, lying languid by the edges of their nests, filled the air with the music of their delights.

A final blast of the storm which had broken over the church swept away the dust of its remains: the pulpit and the confessional-box, which had been ground into powder, the lacerated holy pictures, the shattered sacred vessels, all the litter at which the legion of sparrows that had once dwelt amongst the tiles was eagerly pecking. The great Christ, torn from the cross, hung for a moment from one of the streaming women's curls, and then was whirled away into the black darkness, in the depths of which it sank with a loud crash. The Tree of Life had pierced the heavens; it overtopped the stars.

Abbe Mouret was filled with the mad joy of an accursed spirit at the sight before him. The church was vanquished; God no longer had a house. And thenceforward God could no longer trouble him. He was free to rejoin Albine, since it was she who triumphed. He laughed at himself for having declared, an hour previously, that the church would swallow up the whole earth with its shadow. The earth, indeed, had avenged itself by consuming the church. The mad laughter into which he broke had the effect of suddenly awakening him from his hallucination. He gazed stupidly round the nave, which the evening shadows were slowly darkening. Through the windows he could see patches of star-spangled sky; and he was about to stretch out his arms to feel the walls, when he heard Desiree calling to him from the vestry-passage:

'Serge! Serge! Are you there? Why don't you answer? I have been looking for you for this last half-hour.'

She came in; she was holding a lighted lamp; and the priest then saw that the church was still standing. He could no longer understand anything, but remained in a horrible state of doubt betwixt the unconquerable church, springing up again from its ashes, and Albine, the all-powerful, who could shake the very throne of God by a single breath.

X

Desiree came up to him, full of merry chatter.

'Are you there? Are you there?' she cried. 'Why are you playing at hide-and-seek? I called out to you at the top of my voice at least a dozen times. I thought you must have gone out.'

She pried into all the gloomy corners with an inquisitive glance, and even stepped up to the confessional-box, as though she had expected to surprise some one hiding there. Then she came back to Serge, disappointed, and continued:

'So you are quite alone? Have you been asleep? What amusement do you find in shutting yourself up all alone in the dark? Come along; it is time we went to dinner.'

The Abbe drew his feverish hands across his brow to wipe away the traces of the thoughts which he feared were plain for all the world to read. He fumbled mechanically at the buttons of his cassock, which seemed to him all disarranged. Then he followed his sister with stern-set face and never a sign of emotion, stiffened by that priestly energy which throws the dignity of sacerdotalism like a veil over the agonies of the flesh. Desiree did not even suspect that there was anything the matter with him. She simply said as they entered the dining-room:

'I have had such a good sleep; but you have been talking too much, and have made yourself quite pale.'

In the evening, after dinner, Brother Archangias came in to have his game of cards with La Teuse. He was in a very merry mood that night; and, when the Brother was merry, it was his habit to prod La Teuse in the sides with his big fists, an attention which she returned by heartily boxing his ears. This skirmishing made them both laugh, with a laughter that shook the very ceiling. The Brother, too, when he was in these gay humours, would devise all kinds of pranks. He would try to smash plates with his nose, and would offer to wager that he could break through the dining-room door in battering-ram fashion. He would also empty the snuff out of his box into the old servant's coffee, or would thrust a handful of pebbles down her neck. The merest trifle would give rise to these noisy outbursts of gaiety in the very midst of his wonted surliness. Some little incident, at which nobody else laughed, often sufficed to throw him into a state of wild hilarity, make him stamp his feet, twirl himself round like a top, and hold in his splitting sides.

'What is it that makes you so gay to-night?' La Teuse inquired.

He made no reply, bestriding a chair and galloping round the table on it.

'Well! well! go on making a baby of yourself!' said the old woman; 'and, my gracious, what a big baby you are! If the Lord is looking at you, He must be very well pleased with you!'

The Brother had just slipped off the chair and was lying on the floor, with his legs in the air.

'He does see me, and is pleased to see me as I am. It is His wish that I should be gay. When He wishes me to be merry for a time, He rings a bell in my body, and then I begin to roll about; and all Paradise smiles as it watches me.'

He dragged himself on his back to the wall, and then, supporting himself on the nape of his neck, he hoisted up his body as high as he could and began drumming on the wall with his heels. His cassock slipped down and exposed to view his black breeches, which were patched at the knees with green cloth.

'Look, Monsieur le Cure,' he said, 'you see how high I can reach with my heels. I dare bet that you couldn't do as much. Come! look amused and laugh a little. It is better to drag oneself along on one's back than to think about a hussy as you are always doing. You know what I mean. For my part, when I take to scratching myself I imagine myself to be God's dog, and that's what makes me say that all Paradise looks out of the windows to smile at me. You might just as well laugh too, Monsieur le Cure. It's all done for the saints and you. See! here's a turn-over for Saint Joseph; here's another for Saint Michael, and another for Saint John, and another for Saint Mark, and another for Saint Matthew——'

So he went on, enumerating a whole string of saints, and turning somersaults all round the room.

Abbe Mouret, who had been sitting in perfect silence, with his hands resting on the edge of the table, was at last constrained to smile. As a rule, the Brother's sportiveness only disquieted him. La Teuse, as Archangias rolled within her reach, kicked at him with her foot.

'Come!' she said, 'are we to have our game to-night?'

His only reply was a grunt. Then, upon all fours, he sprang towards La Teuse as if he meant to bite her. But in lieu thereof he spat upon her petticoats.

'Let me alone! will you?' she cried. 'What are you up to now? I begin to think you have gone crazy. What it is that amuses you so much I can't conceive.'

'What makes me gay is my own affair,' he replied, rising to his feet and shaking himself. 'It is not necessary to explain it to you, La Teuse. However, as you want a game of cards, let us have it.'

Then the game began. It was a terrible struggle. The Brother hurled his cards upon the table. Whenever he cried out the windows shook sonorously. La Teuse at last seemed to be winning. She had secured three aces for some time already, and was casting longing eyes at the fourth. But Brother Archangias began to indulge in fresh outbursts of gaiety. He pushed up the table, at the risk of breaking the lamp. He cheated outrageously, and defended himself by means of the most abominable lies, 'Just for a joke,' said he. Then he suddenly began to sing the 'Vespers,' beating time on the palm of his left hand with his cards. When his gaiety reached a climax, and he could find no adequate means of expressing it, he always took to chanting the 'Vespers,' which he repeated for hours at a time. La Teuse, who well knew his habits, cried out to him, amidst the bellowing with which he shook the room:

'Make a little less noise, do! It is quite distracting. You are much too lively to-night.'

But he set to work on the 'Complines.' Abbe Mouret had now seated himself by the window. He appeared to pay no attention to what went on around him, apparently neither hearing nor seeing anything of it. At dinner he had eaten with his ordinary appetite and had even managed to reply to Desiree's everlasting rattle of questions. But now he had given up the struggle, his strength at an end, racked, exhausted as he was by the internal tempest that still raged within him. He even lacked the courage to rise from his seat and go upstairs to his own room. Moreover, he was afraid that if he turned his face towards the lamplight, the tears, which he could no longer keep from his eyes, would be noticed. So he pressed his face close to the window and gazed out into the darkness, growing gradually more drowsy, sinking into a kind of nightmare stupor.

Brother Archangias, still busy at his psalm-singing, winked and nodded in the direction of the dozing priest.

'What's the matter?' asked La Teuse.

The Brother replied by a yet more significant wink.

'Well, what do you mean? Can't you speak? Ah! there's a king. That's capital!—so I take your queen.'

The Brother laid down his cards, bent over the table, and whispered close to La Teuse's face: 'That hussy has been here.'

'I know that well enough,' answered La Teuse. 'I saw her go with mademoiselle into the poultry-yard.'

At this he gave her a terrible look, and shook his fist in her face.

'You saw her, and you let her come in! You ought to have called me, and we would have hung her up by the feet to a nail in your kitchen.'

But at this the old woman lost her temper, and, lowering her voice solely in order that she might not awaken Abbe Mouret, she replied: 'Don't you go talking about hanging people up in my kitchen! I certainly saw her, and I even kept my back turned when she went to join his reverence in the church when the catechising was over. But all that was no business of mine. I had my cooking to attend to! As for the girl herself, I detest her. But if his reverence wishes to see her—why, she is welcome to come whenever she pleases. I'd let her in myself!'

'If you were to do that, La Teuse,' retorted the Brother ragefully, 'I would strangle you, that I would.'

But she laughed at him.

'Don't talk any of your nonsense to me, my man! Don't you know that it is forbidden you to lay your hands upon a woman, just as it's forbidden for a donkey to have anything to do with the *Pater Noster*? Just you try to strangle me and you'll see what I'll do! But do be quiet now, and let us finish the game. See, here's another king.'

But the Brother, holding up a card, went on growling:

'She must have come by some road that the devil alone knows for me to have missed her to-day. Every afternoon I go and keep guard up yonder by the Paradou. If ever I find them together again, I will acquaint the hussy with a stout dogwood stick which I have cut expressly for her benefit. And I shall keep a watch in the church as well now.'

He played his card, which La Teuse took with a knave. Then he threw himself back in his chair and again burst into one of his loud laughs. He did not seem to be able to work himself up into a genuine rage that evening.

'Well, well,' he grumbled, 'never mind, even if she did see him, she had a smacking fall on her nose. I'll tell you all about it, La Teuse. It was raining, you know. I was standing by the school-door when I caught sight of her coming down from the church. She was walking along quite straight and upright, in her stuck-up fashion, in spite of the pouring rain. But when she got into the road, she tumbled down full length, no doubt because the ground was so slippery. Oh! how I did laugh! How I did laugh! I clapped my hands, too.

When she picked herself up again, I saw she was bleeding at the wrist. I shall feel happy over it for a week. I cannot think of her lying there on the ground without feeling the greatest delight.'

Then, turning his attention to the game, he puffed out his cheeks and began to chant the *De profundis*. When he had got to the end of it, he began it all over again. The game came to a conclusion in the midst of this dirge. It was he who was beaten, but his defeat did not seem to vex him in the least.

When La Teuse had locked the door behind him, after first awakening Abbe Mouret, his voice could still be heard, as he went his way through the black night, singing the last verse of the psalm, *Et ipse redimet Israel ex omnibus iniquitatibus ejus*, with extraordinary jubilation.

XI

That night Abbe Mouret slept very heavily. When he opened his eyes in the morning, later than usual, his face and hands were wet with tears. He had been weeping all through the night while he slept. He did not say his mass that day. In spite of his long rest, he had not recovered from his excessive weariness of the previous evening, and he remained in his bedroom till noon, sitting in a chair at the foot of his bed. The condition of stupor into which he more and more deeply sank, took all sensation of suffering away from him. He was conscious only of a great void and blank as he sat there overpowered and benumbed. Even to read his breviary cost him a great effort. Its Latin seemed to him a barbarous language, which he would never again be able to pronounce.

Having tossed the book upon his bed he gazed for hours through his open window at the surrounding country. In the far distance he saw the long wall of the Paradou, creeping like a thin white line amongst the gloomy patches of the pine plantations to the crest of the hills. On the left, hidden by one of those plantations, was the breach. He could not see it, but he knew it was there. He remembered every bit of bramble scattered among the stones. On the previous night he would not have thus dared to gaze upon that dreaded scene. But now with impunity he allowed himself to trace the whole line of the wall, as it emerged again and again from the clumps of verdure which here and there concealed it. His blood pulsed none the faster for this scrutiny. Temptation, as though disdaining his present weakness, left him free from attack. Forsaken by the Divine grace, he was incapable of entering upon any struggle, the thought of sin could no longer even impassion him; it was sheer stupor alone that now rendered him willing to accept that which he had the day before so strenuously refused.

At one moment he caught himself talking aloud and saying that, since the breach in the wall was still open, he would go and join Albine at sunset. This decision brought him a slight feeling of worry, but he did not think that he could do otherwise. She was expecting him to go, and she was his wife. When he tried to picture her face, he could only imagine her as very pale and a long way off. Then he felt a little uneasy as to their future manner of life together. It would be difficult for them to remain in the neighbourhood; they would have to go away somewhere, without any one knowing anything about it. And then, when they had managed to conceal themselves, they would need a deal of money in order to live happily and comfortably. He tried a score of times to hit upon some scheme by which they could get away and live together like happy lovers, but he could devise nothing satisfactory. Now that he was no longer wild with passion, the practical side of the situation alarmed him. He found himself, in all his weakness, face to face with a complicated problem with which he was incompetent to grapple.

Where could they get horses for their escape? And if they went away on foot, would they not be stopped and detained as vagabonds? Was he capable of securing any employment by which he could earn bread for his wife? He had never been taught any kind of trade. He was quite ignorant of actual life. He ransacked his memory, and he could remember nothing but strings of prayers, details of ceremonies, and pages of Bouvier's 'Instruction Theologique,' which he had learned by heart at the seminary. He worried too over matters of no real concern. He asked himself whether he would dare to give his arm to his wife in the street. He certainly could not walk with a woman clinging to his arm. He would surely appear so strange and awkward that every one would turn round to stare at him. They would guess that he was a priest and would insult Albine. It would be vain for him to try to obliterate the traces of his priesthood. He would always wear that mournful pallor and carry the odour of incense about with him. And what if he should have children some day? As this thought suddenly occurred to him, he quite started. He felt a strange repugnance at the very idea. He felt sure that he should not care for any children that might be born to him. Suppose there were two of them, a little boy and a little girl. He could never let them get on his knees; it would distress him to feel their hands clutching at his clothes. The thought of the little girl troubled him the most; he could already see womanly tenderness shining in the depths of her big, childish eyes. No! no! he would have no children.

Nevertheless he resolved that he would flee with Albine that evening. But when the evening came, he felt too weary. So he deferred his flight till the next morning. And the next morning he made a fresh pretext for delay. He could not leave his sister alone with La Teuse. He would prepare a letter, directing that she should be taken to her uncle Pascal's. For three days he was ever on the point of writing that letter, and the paper and pen and ink were lying ready on the table in his room. Then, on the third day, he went off, leaving the letter unwritten. He took up his hat quite suddenly and set off for the Paradou in a state of mingled stupor and resignation, as though he were unwillingly performing some compulsory task which he saw no means of avoiding. Albine's image was now effaced from his memory; he no longer beheld her, but he was driven on by old resolves whose lingering influence, though they themselves were dead, still worked upon him in his silence and loneliness.

He took no pains to escape notice when he set foot out of doors. He stopped at the end of the village to talk for a moment to Rosalie. She told him that her baby was suffering from convulsions; but she laughed, as she spoke, with the laugh that was natural to her. Then he struck out through the rocks, and walked straight on towards the breach in the wall. By force of habit he had brought his breviary with him. Finding the way long, he opened the book and read the regulation prayers. When he put it back again under his arm, he had forgotten the Paradou. He went on walking steadily, thinking about a new chasuble that he wished to purchase to replace the old gold-broidered one, which was certainly falling into shreds. For some time past he had been saving up twenty-sous pieces, and he calculated that by the end of seven months he would have got the necessary amount of money together. He had reached the hills when the song of a peasant in the distance reminded him of a canticle which had been familiar to him at the seminary. He tried to recall the first lines of it, but his recollection failed him. It vexed him to find that his memory was so poor. And when, at last, he succeeded in remembering the words, he found a soothing pleasure in humming the verses, which came back to his mind one by one. It was a hymn of homage to Mary. He smiled as though some soft breath from the days of his childhood were playing upon his face. Ah! how happy he had then been! Why shouldn't he be as happy again? He had not grown any bigger, he wanted nothing more than the same old happiness, unruffled peace, a nook in the chapel, where his knees marked his place, a life of seclusion, enlivened by the delightful puerilities of childhood. Little by little he raised his voice, singing the canticle in flutelike tones, when he suddenly became aware of the breach immediately in front of him.

For a moment he seemed surprised. Then, the smile dying from his face, he murmured quietly:

'Albine must be expecting me. The sun is already setting.'

But just as he was about to push some stones aside to make himself a passage, he was startled by a snore. He sprang down again: he had only just missed setting his foot upon the very face of Brother Archangias, who was lying on the ground there sleeping soundly. Slumber had overtaken him while he kept guard over the entrance to the Paradou. He barred the approach to it, lying at full length before its threshold, with arms and legs spread out. His right hand, thrown back behind his head, still clutched his dogwood staff, which he seemed to brandish like a fiery sword. And he snored loudly in the midst of the brambles, his face exposed to the sun, without a quiver on his tanned skin. A swarm of big flies was hovering over his open mouth.

Abbe Mouret looked at him for a moment. He envied the slumber of that dust-wallowing saint. He wished to drive the flies away, but they persistently returned, and clung around the purple lips of the Brother, who was quite unconscious of their presence. Then the Abbe strode over his big body and entered the Paradou.

XII

Albine was seated on a patch of grass a few paces away from the wall. She sprang up as she caught sight of Serge.

'Ah! you have come!' she cried, trembling from head to foot.

'Yes,' he answered calmly, 'I have come.'

She flung herself upon his neck, but she did not kiss him. To her bare arms the beads of his neckband seemed very cold. She scrutinised him, already feeling uneasy, and resuming:

'What is the matter with you? Why don't you kiss my cheeks as you used to do? Oh! if you are ill, I will cure you once again. Now that you are here, all our old happiness will return. There will be no more wretchedness.... See! I am smiling. You must smile, too, Serge.'

But his face remained grave.

'I have been troubled, too,' she went on. 'I am still quite pale, am I not? For a whole week I have been living on that patch of grass, where you found me. I wanted one thing only, to see you coming back through the breach in the wall. At every sound I sprang up and rushed to meet you. But, alas! it was not you I heard. It was only the leaves rustling in the wind. But I was sure that you would come. I should have waited for you for years.'

Then she asked him:

'Do you still love me?'

'Yes,' he answered, 'I love you still.'

They stood looking at each other, feeling rather ill at ease. And deep silence fell between them. Serge, who evinced perfect calmness, did not attempt to break it. Albine twice opened her mouth to speak, but closed it immediately, surprised at the words that rose to her lips. She could summon up nothing but expressions tinged with bitterness. She felt tears welling into her eyes. What could be the matter with her that she did not feel happy now that her love had come back?

'Listen to me,' she said at last. 'We must not stay here. It is that hole that freezes us! Let us go back to our old home. Give me your hand.'

They plunged into the depths of the Paradou. Autumn was fast approaching, and the trees seemed anxious as they stood there with their yellowing crests from which the leaves were falling one by one. The paths were already littered with dead foliage soaked with moisture, which gave out a sound as of sighing beneath one's tread. And away beyond the lawns misty vapour ascended, throwing a mourning veil over the blue distance. And the whole garden was wrapped in silence, broken only by some sorrowful moans that sounded quiveringly.

Serge began to shiver beneath the avenue of tall trees, along which they were walking.

'How cold it is here!' said he in an undertone.

'You are cold indeed,' murmured Albine, sadly. 'My hand is no longer able to warm you. Shall I wrap you round with part of my dress? Come, all our love will now be born afresh.'

She led him to the parterre, the flower-garden. The great thicket-like rosary was still fragrant with perfume, but there was a tinge of bitterness in the scent of the surviving blossoms, and their foliage, which had expanded in wild profusion, lay strewn upon the ground. Serge displayed such unwillingness to enter the tangled jungle, that they lingered on its borders, trying to detect in the distance the paths along which they had passed in the spring-time. Albine recollected every little nook. She pointed to the grotto where the marble woman lay sleeping; to the hanging screens of honeysuckle and clematis; the fields of violets; the fountain that spurted out crimson carnations; the steps down which flowed golden gilliflowers; the ruined colonnade, in the midst of which the lilies were rearing a snowy pavilion. It was there that they had been born again beneath the sunlight. And she recapitulated every detail of that first day together, how they had walked, and how fragrant had been the air beneath the cool shade. Serge seemed to be listening, but he suddenly asked a question which showed that he had not understood her. The slight shiver which made his face turn pale never left him.

Then she led him towards the orchard, but they could not reach it. The stream was too much swollen. Serge no longer thought of taking Albine upon his back and lightly bounding across with her to the other side. Yet there the apple-trees and the pear-trees were still laden with fruit, and the vines, now with scantier foliage, bent beneath the weight of their gleaming clusters, each grape freckled by the sun's caress. Ah! how they had gambolled beneath the appetising shade of those ancient trees! What merry children had they then been! Albine smiled as she thought of how she had clambered up into the cherry-tree that had broken down beneath her. He, Serge, must at least remember what a quantity of plums they had eaten. He only answered by a nod. He already seemed quite weary. The orchard, with its green depths and chaos of mossy trunks, disquieted him and suggested to his mind some dark, dank spot, teeming with snakes and nettles.

Then she led him to the meadow-lands, where he had to take a few steps amongst the grass. It reached to his shoulders now, and seemed to him like a swarm of clinging arms that tried to bind his limbs and pull him down and drown him beneath an endless sea of greenery. He begged Albine to go no further. She was walking on in front, and at first she did not stop; but when she saw how distressed he appeared, she halted and came back and stood beside him. She also was growing gradually more low-spirited, and at last she shuddered like himself. Still she went on talking. With a sweeping gesture she pointed out to him the streams, the rows of willows, the grassy expanse stretching far away towards the horizon. All that had formerly been theirs. For whole days they had lived there. Over yonder, between those three willows by the water's edge, they had played at being lovers. And they would then have been delighted if the grass had been taller than themselves so that they might have lost themselves in its depths, and have been the more secluded, like larks nesting at the bottom of a field of corn. Why, then, did he tremble so to-day, when the tip of his foot just sank into the grass?

Then she led him to the forest. But the huge trees seemed to inspire Serge with still greater dread. He did not know them again, so sternly solemn seemed their bare black trunks. Here, more than anywhere else, amidst those austere columns, through which the light now freely streamed, the past seemed quite dead. The first rains had washed the traces of their footsteps from the sandy paths, the winds had swept every other lingering memorial into the underbrush. But Albine, with grief at her throat, shot out a protesting glance. She could still plainly see their lightest footprints on the sandy gravel, and, as they passed each bush, the warmth with which they had once brushed against it surged to her cheeks. With eyes full of soft entreaty, she still strove to awaken Serge's memory. It was along that path that they had walked in silence, full of emotion, but as yet not daring to confess that they loved one another. It was in that clearing that they had lingered one evening till very late watching the stars, which had rained upon them like golden drops of warmth. Farther, beneath that oak they had exchanged their first kiss. Its fragrance still clung to the tree, and the very moss still remembered it. It was false to say that the forest had become voiceless and bare.

Serge, however, turned away his head, that he might escape the gaze of Albine's eyes, which oppressed him.

Then she led him to the great rocks. There, perhaps, he would no longer shudder with that appearance of debility which so distressed her. At that hour the rocks were still warm with the red glow of the setting sun. They still wore an aspect of tragic passion, with their hot ledges of stone whereon the fleshy plants writhed monstrously. Without speaking a word, without even turning her head, Albine led Serge up the rough ascent, wishing to take him ever higher and higher, far up beyond the springs, till they should emerge into the full light on the summit. They would there see the cedar, beneath whose shade they had first felt the thrill of desire, and there amidst the glowing stones they would assuredly find passion once more. But Serge soon began to stumble pitiably. He could walk no further. He fell a first time on his knees. Albine, by a mighty effort, raised him and for a moment carried him along, but afterwards he fell again, and remained, quite overcome, on the ground. In front of him, beneath him, spread the vast Paradou.

'You have lied!' cried Albine. 'You love me no longer!'

She burst into tears as she stood there by his side, feeling that she could not carry him any higher. There was no sign of anger in her now. She was simply weeping over their dying love. Serge lay dazed and stupefied.

'The garden is all dead. I feel so very cold,' he murmured. But she took his head between her hands, and showed him the Paradou.

'Look at it! Ah! it is your eyes that are dead; your ears and your limbs and your whole body. You have passed by all the scenes of our happiness without seeing them or hearing them or feeling their presence. You have done nothing but slip and stumble, and now you have fallen down here in sheer weariness and boredom.... You love me no more.'

He protested, but in a gentle, quiet fashion. Then, for the first time, she spoke out passionately.

'Be quiet! As if the garden could ever die! It will sleep for the winter, but it will wake up again in May, and will restore to us all the love we have entrusted to its keeping. Our kisses will blossom again amongst the flower- beds, and our vows will bud again with the trees and plants. If you could only see it and understand it, you would know that it throbs with even deeper passion, and loves even more absorbingly at this autumn-time, when it falls asleep in its fruitfulness.... But you love me no more, and so you can no longer understand.'

He raised his eyes to her as if begging her not to be angry. His face was pinched and pale with an expression of childish fear. The sound of her voice made him tremble. He ended by persuading her to rest a little while by his side. They could talk quietly and discuss matters. Then, with the Paradou spreading out in front of them, they began to speak of their love, but without even touching one another's fingers.

'I love you; indeed I love you,' said Serge, in his calm, quiet voice. 'If I did not love you, I should not be here: I should not have come. I am very weary, it is true. I don't know why. I thought I should find that pleasant warmth again, of which the mere memory was so delightful. But I am cold, the garden seems quite black. I cannot see anything of what I left here. But it is not my fault. I am trying hard to be as you would wish me and to please you.'

'You love me no longer!' Albine repeated once more.

'Yes, I do love you. I suffered grievously the other day after I had driven you away.... Oh! I loved you with such passion that, had you come back and thrown yourself in my arms, I should almost have crushed you to death.... And for hours your image remained present before me. When I shut my eyes, you gleamed out with all the brightness of the sun and threw a flame around me.... Then I trampled down every obstacle, and came here.'

He remained silent for a moment, as if in thought. Then he spoke again:

'And now my arms feel as though they were broken. If I tried to clasp you, I could not hold you; I should let you fall.... Wait till this shudder has passed away. Give me your hands, and let me kiss them again. Be gentle and do not look at me with such angry eyes. Help me to find my heart again.'

He spoke with such genuine sadness, such evident longing to begin the past anew, that Albine was touched. For a moment all her wonted gentleness returned to her, and she questioned him anxiously:

'What is the matter with you? What makes you so ill?'

'I do not know. It is as though all my blood had left my veins. Just now, as I was coming here, I felt as if some one had flung a robe of ice around my shoulders, which turned me into stone from head to foot.... I have felt it before, but where I don't remember.'

She interrupted him with a kindly laugh.

'You are a child. You have caught cold, that's all. At any rate, it is not I that you are afraid of, is it? We won't stop in the garden during the winter, like a couple of wild things. We will go wherever you like, to some big town. We can love each other there, amongst all the people, as quietly as amongst the trees. You will see that I can be something else than a wilding, for ever bird's-nesting and tramping about for hours. When I was a little girl, I used to wear embroidered skirts and fine stockings and laces and all kinds of finery. I dare say you never heard of that.'

He was not listening to her. He suddenly gave vent to a little cry, and said: 'Ah! now I recollect!'

She asked him what he meant, but he would not answer her. He had just remembered the feeling he had long ago experienced in the chapel of the seminary. That was the icy robe enwrapping his shoulders and turning him to stone. And then his life as a priest took complete possession of his thoughts. The vague recollections which had haunted him as he walked from Les Artaud to the Paradou became more and more distinct and assumed complete mastery over him. While Albine talked on of the happy life that they would lead together, he heard the tinkling of the sanctuary bell that signalled the elevation of the Host, and he saw the monstrance trace gleaming crosses over the heads of kneeling multitudes.

'And for your sake,' Albine was saying, 'I will put on my broidered skirts again.... I want you to be bright and gay. We will try to find something to make you lively. Perhaps you will love me better when you see me looking beautiful and prettily dressed, like a fine lady. I will wear my comb properly and won't let my hair fall wildly about my neck any more. And I won't roll my sleeves up over my elbows; I will fasten my dress so as to hide my shoulders. I still know how to bow and how to walk along quite properly. Yes, I will make you a nice little wife, as I walk through the streets leaning on your arm.'

'Did you ever go to church when you were a little girl?' he asked her in an undertone, as if, in spite of himself, he were continuing aloud the reverie which prevented him from hearing her. 'I could never pass a church without entering it. As soon as the door closed silently behind me, I felt as though I were in Paradise itself, with the angels whispering stories of love in my ears and the saints caressing me with their breath. Ah! I would have liked to live there for ever, in that absorbing beatitude.'

She looked at him with steady eyes, a passing blaze kindling in her loving glance. Nevertheless, submissive still, she answered:

'I will do as you may fancy. I learned music once. I was quite a clever young lady and was taught all the accomplishments. I will go back to school and start music again. If there is any tune you would like to hear me play, you will only have to tell me, and I will practise it for months and months, so as to play it to you some evening in our own home when we are by ourselves in some snug little room, with the curtains closely drawn. And you will pay me with just one kiss, won't you? A kiss right on the lips, which will awaken all your love again!'

'Yes, yes,' he murmured, answering his own thoughts only; 'my great pleasure at first was to light the candles, prepare the cruets, and carry the missal. Then, afterwards, I was filled with bliss at the approach of God, and felt as though I could die of sheer love. Those are my only recollections. I know of nothing else. When I raise my hand, it is to give a benediction. When my lips protrude it is to kiss the altar. If I look for my heart, I can no longer find it. I have offered it to God, and He has taken it.'

Albine grew very pale and her eyes gleamed like fire. In a quivering voice she resumed:

'I should not like my little girl to leave me. You can send the boy to college, if you wish, but the little girl must always keep with me. I myself will teach her to read. Oh! I shall remember everything, and if indeed there be anything that I find I have forgotten, I will have masters to teach me.... Yes, we will keep our dear little ones always about our knees. You will be happy so, won't you? Speak to me; tell me that you will then feel warm again, and will smile, and feel no regrets for anything you have left behind.'

But Serge continued:

'I have often thought of the stone-saints that have been censed in their niches for centuries past. They must have become quite saturated with incense; and I am like one of them. I have the fragrance of incense in the inmost parts of my being. It is that embalmment that gives me serenity, deathlike tranquillity of body, and the peace which I enjoy in no longer living.... Ah! may nothing ever disturb my quiescence! May I ever remain cold and rigid, with a ceaseless smile on my granite lips, incapable of descending among men! That is my one, my only desire!'

At this Albine sprang to her feet, exasperated, threatening. She shook Serge and cried:

'What are you saying? What is it you are dreaming aloud? Am I not your wife? Haven't you come here to be my husband?'

He recoiled, trembling yet more violently.

'No! Leave me! I am afraid!' he faltered.

'But our life together, our happiness, the children we shall have?'

'No, no; I am afraid.' And he broke out into a supreme cry: 'I cannot! I cannot!'

For a moment Albine remained silent, gazing at the unhappy man who lay shivering at her feet. Her face flared. She opened her arms as if to seize him and strain him to her breast with wild angry passion. But another idea came to her, and she merely took him by the hand and raised him to his feet.

'Come!' said she.

She led him away to that giant tree, to the very spot where their love had reigned supreme. There was the same bliss-inspiring shade, there was the same trunk as of yore, the same branches spreading far around, like sheltering and protecting arms. The tree still towered aloft, kindly, robust, powerful, and fertile. As on the day of their nuptials, languorous warmth, the glimmer of a summer's night fading on the bare shoulder of some fair girl, a sob of love dying away into passionate silence, lingered about the clearing as it lay there bathed in dim green light. And, in the distance, the Paradou, in spite of the first chills of autumn, sighed once more with passion, again becoming love's accomplice. From the parterre, from the orchard, from the meadow-lands, from the forest, from the great rocks, from the spreading heavens, came back a ripple of voluptuous joy. Never had the garden, even on the warmest evenings of spring-time, shown such deep tenderness as now, on this fair autumn evening, when the plants and trees seemed to be bidding one another goodnight ere they sank to sleep. And the scent of ripened germs wafted the intoxication of desire athwart the scanty leaves.

'Do you hear? Do you hear?' faltered Albine in Serge's ear, when she had let him slip upon the grass at the foot of the tree.

Serge was weeping.

'You see that the Paradou is not dead,' she added. 'It is crying out to us to love each other. It still desires our union. Oh, do remember! Clasp me to your heart!'

Serge still wept.

Albine said nothing more. She flung her arms around him; she pressed her warm lips to his corpse-like face; but tears were still his only answer.

Then, after a long silence, Albine spoke. She stood erect, full of contempt and determination.

'Away with you! Go!' she said, in a low voice.

Serge rose with difficulty. He picked up his breviary, which had fallen upon the grass. And he walked away.

'Away with you! Go!' repeated Albine, in louder tones, as she followed and drove him before her.

Thus she urged him on from bush to bush till she had driven him back to the breach in the wall, in the midst of the stern-looking trees. And there, as she saw Serge hesitate, with lowered head she cried out violently:

'Away with you Go!'

And slowly she herself went back into the Paradou, without even turning her head. Night was fast falling, and the garden was but a huge bier of shadows.

XIII

Brother Archangias, aroused from his slumber, stood erect in the breach, striking the stones with his stick and swearing abominably.

'May the devil break their legs for them! May he drag them to hell by their feet, with their noses trailing in their abomination!'

But when he saw Albine driving away the priest, he stopped for a moment in surprise. Then he struck the stones yet more vigorously, and burst into a roar of laughter.

'Good-bye, you hussy! A pleasant journey to you! Go back to your mates the wolves! A priest is no fit companion for such as you.'

Then, looking at Abbe Mouret, he growled:

'I knew you were in there. I saw that the stones had been disturbed.... Listen to me, Monsieur le Cure. Your sin has made me your superior, and God tells you, through my mouth, that hell has no torments severe enough for a priest who lets himself succumb to the lusts of the flesh. If He were to pardon you now, He would be too indulgent, it would be contrary to His own justice.'

They slowly walked down the hill towards Les Artaud. The priest had not opened his lips; but gradually he raised his head erect: he was no longer trembling. As in the distance he caught sight of the Solitaire looming blackly against the purplish sky, and the ruddy glow of the tiles on the church, a faint smile came to his lips, while to his calm eyes there rose an expression of perfect serenity.

Meantime the Brother was every now and then giving a vicious kick at the stones that came in his way. Presently he turned to his companion:

'Is it all over this time?' he asked. 'When I was your age I was possessed too. A demon was ever gnawing at me. But, after a time, he grew weary of it, and took himself off. Now that he has gone I live quietly enough.... Oh! I knew very well that you would go. For three weeks past I have been keeping watch upon you. I used to look into the garden through the breach in the wall. I should have liked to cut the trees down. I have often hurled stones at them; it was delightful to break the branches. Tell me, now, is it so very nice to be there?'

He made Abbe Mouret stop in the middle of the road, and glared at him with a terrible expression of jealousy. The thought of the priest's life in the Paradou tortured him. But the Abbe kept perfect silence, so Archangias set off again, jeering as he went. Then, in a louder voice, he said:

'You see, when a priest behaves as you have done, he scandalises every other priest. I myself felt sullied by your conduct. However, you are now behaving more sensibly. There is no need for you to make any confession. I know what has happened well enough. Heaven has broken your back for you, as it has done for so many others. So much the better! So much the better!'

He clapped his hands triumphantly. But Abbe Mouret, immersed in deep reverie, with a smile spreading over his whole face, did not even hear him. When the Brother quitted him at the parsonage door, he went round and entered the church. It was grey and gloomy, as on that terrible rainy evening when temptation had racked him so violently. And it still remained poverty- stricken and meditative, bare of all that gleaming gold and sighing passion that had seemed to him to sweep in from the countryside. It preserved solemn silence. But a breath of mercy seemed to fill it.

Kneeling before the great Christ and bursting into tears, which he let flow down his cheeks as though they were so many blessings, the priest murmured:

'O God, it is not true that Thou art pitiless. I know it, I feel it: Thou hast already pardoned me. I feel it in the outpouring of Thy grace, which, for hours now, has been flowing through me in a sweet stream, bringing me back, slowly but surely, perfect peace and spiritual health. O God, it was at the very moment when I was about to forsake Thee that Thou didst protect me most effectually. Thou didst hide Thyself from me, the better to rescue me from evil. Thou didst allow my flesh to run its course, that I might be convinced of its nothingness. And now, O God, I see that Thou hast for ever marked me with Thy seal, that awful seal, pregnant with blessings, which sets a man apart from other men, and whose mark is so ineffaceable that, sooner or later, it makes itself manifest even upon those who sin. Thou hast broken me with sin and temptation. Thou hast ravaged me with Thy flames. Thou hast willed that there should be nought left of me save ruins wherein Thou mightest safely descend. I am an empty tabernacle wherein Thou may'st dwell. Blessed art Thou, O God!'

He prostrated himself and continued stammering in the dust. The church triumphed. It remained firm and unshaken over the priest's head, with its altars and its confessional, its pulpit, its crosses, and its holy images. The world had ceased to exist. Temptation was extinguished like a fire that was henceforth unnecessary for the Abbe's purification. He was entering into supernatural peace. And he raised this supreme cry:

'To the exclusion of life and its creatures and of everything that be in it, I belong to Thee, O God; to Thee, Thee alone, through all eternity!'

XIV

At that moment Albine was still wandering about the Paradou with all the mute agony of a wounded animal. She had ceased to weep. Her face was very white and a deep crease showed upon her brow. Why did she have to suffer that deathlike agony? Of what fault had she been guilty, that the garden no longer kept the promises it had held out to her since her childhood's days? She questioned herself as she walked along, never heeding the avenues through which the gloom was slowly stealing. She had always obeyed the voices of the trees. She could not remember having injured a single flower. She had ever been the beloved daughter of the greenery, hearkening to it submissively, yielding to it with full belief in the happiness which it promised to her. And when, on that supreme day, the Paradou had cried to her to cast herself beneath the giant-tree, she had done so in compliance with its voice. If she then had nothing to reproach herself with, it must be the garden which had betrayed her; the garden which was torturing her for the mere sake of seeing her suffer.

She halted and looked around her. The great gloomy masses of foliage preserved deep silence. The paths were blocked with black walls of darkness. The distant lawns were lulling to sleep the breezes that kissed them. And she thrust out her hands with a gesture of hopelessness and raised a cry of protest. It could not all end thus. But her voice choked beneath the silent trees. Thrice did she implore the Paradou to answer her, but never an explanation fell from its lofty branches, not a leaf seemed to be moved with pity for her. Then she resumed her weary wandering, and felt that she was entering into the fatal sternness of winter. Now that she had ceased to rebelliously question the earth, she caught sound of a gentle murmur speeding along the ground. It was the farewell of the plants, wishing one another a happy death. To have drunk in the sunshine for a whole season, to have lived ever blossoming, to have breathed continual perfume, and then, at the first blast, to depart, with the hope of springing up again elsewhere, was not that sufficiently long and full a life which obstinate craving for further existence would mar? Ah! how sweet death must be; how sweet to have an endless night before one, wherein to dream of the short days of life and to recall eternally its fugitive joys!

She stayed her steps once more; but she no longer protested as she stood there amidst the deep stillness of the Paradou. She now believed that she understood everything. The garden doubtless had death in store for her as a supreme culminating happiness. It was to death that it had all along been leading her in its tender fashion. After love, there could be nought but death.

And never had the garden loved her so much as it did now; she had shown herself ungrateful in accusing it, for all the time she had remained its best beloved child. The motionless boughs, the paths blocked up with darkness, the lawns where the breezes fell asleep, had only become mute in order that they might lure her on to taste the joys of long silence. They wished her to be with them in their winter rest, they dreamt of carrying her off, swathed in their dry leaves with her eyes frozen like the waters of the springs, her limbs stiffened like the bare branches, and her blood sleeping the sleep of the sap. And, yes, she would live their life to the very end, and die their death. Perhaps they had already willed that she should spring up next summer as a rose in the flower-garden, or a pale willow in the meadow-lands, or a tender birch in the forest. Yes, it was the great law of life; she was about to die.

Then, for the last time, she resumed her walk through the Paradou in quest of death. What fragrant plant might need her sweet-scented tresses to increase the perfume of its leaves? What flower might wish the gift of her satinlike skin, the snowy whiteness of her arms, the tender pink of her bosom? To what weakly tree should she offer her young blood? She would have liked to be of service to the weeds vegetating beside the paths, to slay herself there so that from her flesh some huge greenery might spring, lofty and sapful, laden with birds at May-time, and passionately caressed by the sun. But for a long while the Paradou still maintained silence as if it had not yet made up its mind to confide to her in what last kiss it would spirit away her life. She had to wander all over it again, seeking, pilgrim-like, for her favourite spots. Night was now more swiftly approaching, and it seemed to her as if she were being gradually sucked into the earth. She climbed to the great rocks and questioned them, asking whether it was upon their stony beds that she must breathe her last breath. She crossed the forest with lingering steps, hoping that some oak would topple down and bury her beneath the majesty of its fall. She skirted the streams that flowed through the meadows, bending down at almost every step she took so as to peep into the depths and see whether a couch had not been prepared for her amongst the water lilies. But nowhere did Death call her; nowhere did he offer her his cold hands. Yet, she was not mistaken. It was, indeed, the Paradou that was about to teach her to die, as, indeed, it had taught her to love. She again began to scour the bushes, more eagerly even than on those warm mornings of the past when she had gone searching for love. And, suddenly, just as she was reaching the parterre, she came upon death, amidst all the evening fragrance. She ran forward, breaking out into a rapturous laugh. She was to die amongst the flowers.

First she hastened to the thicket-like rosary. There, in the last flickering of the gloaming, she searched the beds and gathered all the roses that hung languishing at the approach of winter. She plucked them from down below, quite heedless of their thorns; she plucked them in front of her, with both hands; she plucked them from above, rising upon tip-toes and pulling down the boughs. So eager was she, so desperate was her haste, that she even broke the branches, she, who had ever shown herself tender to the tiniest blades of grass. Soon her arms were full of roses, she tottered beneath her burden of flowers. And having quite stripped the rose trees, carrying away even the fallen petals, she turned her steps to the pavilion; and when she had let her load of blossoms slip upon the floor of the room with the blue ceiling, she again went down to the garden.

This time she sought the violets. She made huge bunches of them, which she pressed one by one against her breast. Then she sought the carnations, plucking them all, even to the buds; massing them together in big sheaves of white blossoms that suggested bowls of milk, and big sheaves of the red ones, that seemed like bowls of blood. Then, too, she sought the stocks, the patches of mirabilis, the heliotropes and the lilies. She tore the last blossoming stocks off by the handful, pitilessly crumpling their satin ruches; she devastated the beds of mirabilis, whose flowers were scarcely opening to the evening air; she mowed down the field of heliotropes, piling her harvest of blooms into a heap; and she thrust bundles of lilies under her arms like handles of reeds. When she was again laden with as much as she could carry, she returned to the pavilion to cast the violets, the carnations, the lilies, the stocks, the heliotrope, and the mirabilis by the side of the roses. And then, without stopping to draw breath, she went down yet again.

This time she repaired to that gloomy corner which seemed like the graveyard of the flower-garden. A warm autumn had there brought on a second crop of spring flowers. She raided the borders of tuberoses and hyacinths; going down upon her knees, and gathering her harvest with all a miser's care, lest she should miss a single blossom. The tuberoses seemed to her to be extremely precious flowers, which would distil drops of gold and wealth and wondrous sweetness. The hyacinths, beaded with pearly blooms, were like necklets, whose every pearl would pour forth joys unknown to man. And although she almost buried herself beneath the mass of tuberoses and hyacinths which she plucked, she next stripped a field of poppies, and even found means to crop an expanse of marigolds farther on. All these she heaped over the tuberoses and hyacinths, and then ran back to the room with the blue ceiling, taking the greatest care as she went that the breeze should not rob her of a single pistil. And once more did she come downstairs.

But what was she to gather now? She had stripped the parterre bare. As she rose upon the tips of her shoes in the dim gloom, she could only see the garden lying there naked and dead, deprived of the tender eyes of its roses, the crimson smile of its carnations, and the perfumed locks of its heliotropes. Nevertheless, she could not return with empty arms. So she laid hands upon the herbs and leafy plants. She crawled over the ground, as though she would have carried off the very soil itself in a clutch of supreme passion. She filled her skirt with a harvest of aromatic plants, southernwood, mint, verbenas. She came across a border of balm, and left not a leaf of it unplucked. She even broke off two big fennels which she threw over her shoulders like a couple of trees. Had she been able, she would have carried all the greenery of the garden away with her between her teeth. When she reached the threshold of the pavilion, she turned round and gave a last look at the Paradou. It was quite dark now. The night had fully come and cast a black veil over everything. Then for the last time she went up the stairs, never more to step down them.

The spacious room was quickly decked. She had placed a lighted lamp upon the table. She sorted out the flowers heaped upon the floor and arranged them in big bunches, which she distributed about the room. First she placed some lilies behind the lamp on the table, forming with them a lofty lacelike screen which softened the light with its snowy purity. Then she threw handfuls of carnations and stocks over the old sofa, which was already strewn with red bouquets that had faded a century ago, till all these were hidden, and the sofa looked like a huge bed of stocks bristling with carnations. Next she placed the four armchairs in front of the alcove. On the first one she piled marigolds, on the second poppies, on the third mirabilis, and on the fourth heliotrope. The chairs were completely buried in bloom, with nothing but the tips of their arms visible. At last she thought of the bed. She pushed a little table near the head of it, and reared thereon a huge pile of violets. Then she covered the whole bed with the hyacinths and tuberoses she had plucked. They were so abundant that they formed a thick couch overflowing all around, so that the bed now looked like one colossal bloom.

The roses still remained. And these she scattered chancewise all over the room, without even looking to see where they fell. Some of them dropped upon the table, the sofa, and the chairs; and a corner of the bed was inundated with them. For some minutes there was a rain of roses, a real downpour of heavy blossoms, which settled in flowery pools in the hollows of the floor. But as the heap seemed scarcely diminished, she finished by weaving garlands of roses which she hung upon the walls. She twined wreaths around the necks and arms and waists of the plaster cupids that sported over the alcove. The blue ceiling, the oval panels, edged with flesh-coloured ribbon, the voluptuous paintings, preyed upon by time, were all hung with a mantle, a drapery of roses. The big room was fully decked at last. Now she could die there.

For a moment she remained standing, glancing around her. She was looking to see if death was there. And she gathered up the aromatic greenery, the southernwood, the mint, the verbenas, the balm, and the fennel. She broke them and twisted them and made wedges of them with which to stop up every little chink and cranny about the windows and the door. Then she drew the white coarsely sewn calico curtains and, without even a sigh, laid herself upon the bed, on all the florescence of hyacinths and tuberoses.

And then a final rapture was granted her. With her eyes wide open she smiled at the room. Ah! how she had loved there! And how happily she was there going to die! At that supreme moment the plaster cupids suggested nothing impure to her; the amorous paintings disturbed her no more. She was conscious of nothing beneath that blue ceiling save the intoxicating perfume of the flowers. And it seemed to her as if this perfume was none other than the old love-fragrance which had always warmed the room, now increased a hundredfold, till it had become so strong and penetrating that it would surely suffocate her. Perchance it was the breath of the lady who had died there a century ago. In perfect stillness, with her hands clasped over her heart, she continued smiling, while she listened to the whispers of the perfumes in her buzzing head. They were singing to her a soft strange melody of fragrance, which slowly and very gently lulled her to sleep.

At first there was a prelude, bright and childlike; her hands, that had just now twisted and twined the aromatic greenery, exhaled the pungency of crushed herbage, and recalled her old girlish ramblings through the wildness of the Paradou. Then there came a flutelike song, a song of short musky notes, rising from the violets that lay upon the table near the head of the bed; and this flutelike strain, trilling melodiously to the soft accompaniment of the lilies on the other table, sang to her of the first joys of love, its first confession, and first kiss beneath the trees of the forest. But she began to stifle as passion drew nigh with the clove-like breath of the carnations, which burst upon her in brazen notes that seemed to drown all others. She thought that death was nigh when the poppies and the marigolds broke into a wailing strain, which recalled the torment of desire. But suddenly all grew quieter; she felt that she could breathe more freely; she glided into greater serenity, lulled by a descending scale that came from the throats of the stocks, and died away amidst a delightful hymn from the heliotropes, which, with their vanilla-like breath, proclaimed the approach of nuptial bliss. Here and there the mirabilis gently trilled. Then came a hush. And afterwards the roses languidly made their entry. Their voices streamed from the ceiling, like the strains of a distant choir. It was a chorus of great breadth, to which she at first listened with a slight quiver. Then the volume of the strain increased, and soon her whole frame vibrated with the mighty sounds that burst in waves around her. The nuptials were at hand, the trumpet blasts of the roses announced them. She pressed her hands more closely to her heart as she lay there panting, gasping, dying. When she opened her lips for the kiss which was to stifle her, the hyacinths and tuberoses shot out their perfume and enveloped her with so deep, so great a sigh that the chorus of the roses could be heard no more.

And then, amidst the final gasp of the flowers, Albine died.

XV

About three o'clock the next afternoon, La Teuse and Brother Archangias, who were chatting on the parsonage-steps, saw Doctor Pascal's gig come at full gallop through the village. The whip was being vigorously brandished from beneath the lowered hood.

'Where can he be off to at that rate?' murmured the old servant. 'He will break his neck.'

The gig had just reached the rising ground on which the church was built. Suddenly, the horse reared and stopped, and the doctor's head, with its long white hair all dishevelled appeared from under the hood.

'Is Serge there?' he cried, in a voice full of indignant excitement.

La Teuse had stepped to the edge of the hill. 'Monsieur le Cure is in his room,' she said. 'He must be reading his breviary. Do you want to speak to him? Shall I call him?'

Uncle Pascal, who seemed almost distracted, made an angry gesture with his whip hand. Bending still further forward, at the risk of falling out, he replied:

'Ah! he's reading his breviary, is he? No! no! don't call him. I should strangle him, and that would do no good. I wanted to tell him that Albine was dead. Dead! do you hear me? Tell him, from me, that she is dead!'

And he drove off, lashing his horse so fiercely that it almost bolted. But, twenty paces away, he pulled up again, and once more stretching out his head, cried loudly:

'Tell him, too, from me, that she was *enceinte*! It will please him to know that.'

Then the gig rolled on wildly again, jolting dangerously as it ascended the stony hill that led to the Paradou. La Teuse was quite dumbfounded. But Brother Archangias sniggered and looked at her with savage delight glittering in his eyes. She noticed this at last, and thrust him away from her, almost making him fall down the steps.

'Be off with you!' she stammered, full of anger, seeking to relieve her feelings by abusing him. 'I shall grow to hate you. Is it possible to rejoice at any one's death? I wasn't fond of the girl, myself; but it is very sad to die at her age. Be off with you, and don't go on sniggering like that, or I will throw my scissors in your face!'

It was only about one o'clock that a peasant, who had gone to Plassans to sell vegetables, had told Doctor Pascal of Albine's death, and had added that Jeanbernat wished to see him. The doctor now was feeling a little relieved by what he had just shouted as he passed the parsonage. He had gone out of his way expressly to give himself that satisfaction. He reproached himself for the death of the girl as for a crime in which he had participated. All along the road he had never ceased overwhelming himself with insults, and though he wiped the tears from his eyes that he might see where to guide his horse, he ever angrily drove his gig over heaps of stones, as if hoping that he would overturn himself and break one of his limbs. However, when he reached the long lane that skirted the endless wall of the park, a glimmer of hope broke upon him. Perhaps Albine was only in a dead faint. The peasant had told him that she had suffocated herself with flowers. Ah! if he could only get there in time, if he could only save her! And he lashed his horse ferociously as though he were lashing himself.

It was a lovely day. The pavilion was all bathed in sunlight, just as it had been in the fair spring-time. But the leaves of the ivy which mounted to the roof were spotted and patched with rust, and bees no longer buzzed round the tall gilliflowers. Doctor Pascal hastily tethered his horse and pushed open the gate of the little garden. All around still prevailed that perfect silence amidst which Jeanbernat had been wont to smoke his pipe; but, to-day, the old man was no longer seated on his bench watching his lettuces.

'Jeanbernat!' called the doctor.

No one answered. Then, on entering the vestibule, he saw something that he had never seen before. At the end of the passage, below the dark staircase, was a door opening into the Paradou, and he could see the vast garden spreading there beneath the pale sunlight, with all its autumn melancholy, its sere and yellow foliage. The doctor hurried through the doorway and took a few steps over the damp grass.

'Ah! it is you, doctor!' said Jeanbernat in a calm voice.

The old man was digging a hole at the foot of a mulberry-tree. He had straightened his tall figure on hearing the approach of footsteps. But he promptly betook himself to his task again, throwing out at each effort a huge mass of rich soil.

'What are you doing there?' asked Doctor Pascal.

Jeanbernat straightened himself again and wiped the sweat off his face with the sleeve of his jacket. 'I am digging a hole,' he answered simply. 'She always loved the garden, and it will please her to sleep here.'

The doctor nearly choked with emotion. For a moment he stood by the edge of the grave, incapable of speaking, but watching Jeanbernat as the other sturdily dug on.

'Where is she?' he asked at last.

'Up there, in her room. I left her on the bed. I should like you to go and listen to her heart before she is put away in here. I listened myself, but I couldn't hear anything at all.'

The doctor went upstairs. The room had not been disturbed. Only a window had been opened. There the withered flowers, stifled by their own perfumes, exhaled but the faint odour of dead beauty. Within the alcove, however, there still hung an asphyxiating warmth, which seemed to trickle into the room and gradually disperse in tiny puffs. Albine, snowy-pale, with her hands upon her heart and a smile playing over her face, lay sleeping on her couch of hyacinths and tuberoses. And she was quite happy, since she was quite dead. Standing by the bedside, the doctor gazed at her for a long time, with a keen expression such as comes into the eyes of scientists who attempt to work resurrections. But he did not even disturb her clasped hands. He kissed her brow, on the spot where her latent maternity had already set a slight shadow. Below, in the garden, Jeanbernat was still driving his spade into the ground in heavy, regular fashion.

A quarter of an hour later, however, the old man came upstairs. He had completed his work. He found the doctor seated by the bedside, buried in such a deep reverie that he did not seem conscious of the heavy tears that were trickling down his cheeks.

The two men only glanced at each other. Then, after an interval of silence, Jeanbernat slowly said:

'Well, was I not right? There is nothing, nothing, nothing. It is all mere nonsense.'

He remained standing and began to pick up the roses that had fallen from the bed, throwing them, one by one, upon Albine's skirts.

'The flowers,' he said, 'live only for a day, while the rough nettles, like me, wear out the very stones amidst which they spring.... Now it's all over; I can kick the bucket; I am nearly distracted. My last ray of sunlight has been snuffed out. It's all nonsense, as I said before.'

He threw himself upon one of the chairs in his turn. He did not shed a tear; he bore himself with rigid despair, like some automaton whose mechanism is broken. Mechanically he reached out his hand and took a book that lay on the little table strewn with violets. It was one of the books stored away in the loft, an odd volume of Holbach,* which he had been reading since the morning, while watching by Albine's body. As the doctor still remained silent, buried in distressful thought, he began to turn its pages over. But a sadden idea occurred to him.

* Doubtless Holbach's now forgotten *Catechism of Nature*, into
  which M. Zola himself may well have peeped whilst writing this
  story.—ED.

'If you will help me,' he said to the doctor, 'we will carry her downstairs, and bury her with all her flowers.'

Uncle Pascal shuddered. Then he explained to the old man that it was not allowed for one to keep the dead in that fashion.

'What! it isn't allowed!' cried Jeanbernat. 'Well, then, I will allow it myself! Doesn't she belong to me? Isn't she mine? Do you think I am going to let the priests walk off with her? Let them try, if they want to get a shot from my gun!'

He sprang to his feet and waved his book about with a terrible gesture. But the doctor caught hold of his hands and clasped them within his own, beseeching him to be calm. And for a long time he talked to him, saying all that he had upon his mind. He blamed himself, made fragmentary confessions of his fault, and vaguely hinted at those who had killed Albine.

'Listen,' he said in conclusion, 'she is yours no longer; you must give her up.'

But Jeanbernat shook his head, and again waved his hand in token of refusal. However, his obstinate resolution was shaken; and at last he said:

'Well, well, let them take her, and may she break their arms for them! I only wish that she could rise up out of the ground and kill them all with fright.... By the way. I have a little business to settle over there. I will go to- morrow.... Good-bye, then, doctor. The hole will do for me.'

And, when the doctor had left, he again sat down by the dead girl's side, and gravely resumed the perusal of his book.

XVI

That morning there was great commotion in the yard at the parsonage. The Artaud butcher had just slaughtered Matthew, the pig, in the shed. Desiree, quite enthusiastic about it all, had held Matthew's feet, while he was being bled, kissing him on the back that he might feel the pain of the knife less, and telling him that it was absolutely necessary that he should be killed, now that he had got so fat. No one could cut off a goose's neck with a single stroke of the hatchet more unconcernedly than she could, or gash open a fowl's throat with a pair of scissors. However much she loved her charges, she looked upon their slaughter with great equanimity. It was quite necessary, she would say. It made room for the young ones who were growing up. And that morning she was very gay.

'Mademoiselle,' grumbled La Teuse every minute, 'you will end by making yourself ill. There is no sense in working yourself up into such a state, just because a pig has been slaughtered. You are as red as if you had been dancing a whole night.'

But Desiree only clapped her hands and turned away and bustled about again. La Teuse, for her part, complained that her legs were sinking under her. Since six o'clock in the morning her big carcass had been perpetually rolling between the kitchen and the yard, for she had black puddings to make. It was she who had whisked the blood in two large earthenware pans, and she had thought that she would never get finished, since mademoiselle was for ever calling her away for mere nothings.

It must be admitted that, at the very moment when the butcher was bleeding Matthew, Desiree had been thrilled with wild excitement, for Lisa, the cow, was about to calve. And the girl's delight at this had quite turned her head.

'One goes and another comes!' she cried, skipping and twirling round. 'Come here, La Teuse! come here!'

It was eleven o'clock. Every now and then the sound of chanting was wafted from the church. A confused murmur of doleful voices, a muttering of prayers could be heard amidst scraps of Latin pronounced in louder and clearer tones.

'Come! oh, do come!' repeated Desiree for the twentieth time.

'I must go and toll the bell, now,' muttered the old servant. 'I shall never get finished really. What is it that you want now, mademoiselle?'

But she did not wait for an answer. She threw herself upon a swarm of fowls, who were greedily drinking the blood from the pans. And having angrily kicked them away, and then covered up the pans, she called to Desiree:

'It would be a great deal better if, instead of tormenting me, you only came to look after these wretched birds. If you let them do as they like there will be no black-pudding for you. Do you hear?'

Desiree only laughed. What of it, if the fowls did drink a few drops of the blood? It would fatten them. Then she again tried to drag La Teuse off to the cow, but the old servant refused to go.

'I must go and toll the bell. The procession will be coming out of church directly. You know that quite well.'

At this moment the voices in the church rose yet more loudly, and a sound of steps could be distinctly heard.

'No! no!' insisted Desiree, dragging La Teuse towards the stable. 'Just come and look at her, and tell me what ought to be done.'

La Teuse shrugged her shoulders. All that the cow wanted was to be left alone and not bothered. Then she set off towards the vestry, but, as she passed the shed, she raised a fresh cry:

'There! there!' she shrieked, shaking her fist. 'Ah! the little wretch!'

Matthew was lying at full length on his back, with his feet in the air, under the shed, waiting to be singed.* The gash which the knife had made in his neck was still quite fresh, and was beaded with drops of blood. And a little white hen was very delicately picking off these drops of blood one by one.

* In some parts of France pigs, when killed, are singed, not scalded, as is, I think, the usual practice in England.—ED.

'Why, of course,' quietly remarked Desiree, 'she's regaling herself.' And the girl stooped and patted the pig's plump belly, saying: 'Eh! my fat fellow, you have stolen their food too often to grudge them a wee bit of your neck now!'

La Teuse hastily doffed her apron and threw it round Matthew's neck. Then she hurried away and disappeared within the church. The great door had just creaked on its rusty hinges, and a burst of chanting rose in the open air amidst the quiet sunshine. Suddenly the bell began to toll with slow and regular strokes. Desiree, who had remained kneeling beside the pig patting his belly, raised her head to listen, while still continuing to smile. When she saw that she was alone, having glanced cautiously around, she glided away into the cow's stable and closed the door behind her.

The little iron gate of the graveyard, which had been opened quite wide to let the body pass, hung against the wall, half torn from its hinges. The sunshine slept upon the herbage of the empty expanse, into which the funeral procession passed, chanting the last verse of the *Miserere*. Then silence fell.

'*Requiem ternam dona ei, Domine,*' resumed Abbe Mouret, in solemn tones.

'*Et lux perpetua luceat ei,*' Brother Archangias bellowed.

At the head walked Vincent, wearing a surplice and bearing the cross, a large copper cross, half the silver plating of which had come off. He lifted it aloft with both his hands. Then followed Abbe Mouret, looking very pale in his black chasuble, but with his head erect, and without a quiver on his lips as he chanted the office, gazing into the distance with fixed eyes. The flame of the lighted candle which he was carrying scarcely showed in the daylight. And behind him, almost touching him, came Albine's coffin, borne by four peasants on a sort of litter, painted black. The coffin was clumsily covered with too short a pall, and at the lower end of it the fresh deal of which it was made could be seen, with the heads of the nails sparkling with a steely glitter. Upon the pall lay flowers: handfuls of white roses, hyacinths, and tuberoses, taken from the dead girl's very bed.

'Just be careful!' cried Brother Archangias to the peasants, as they slightly tilted the litter in order to get it through the gateway. 'You will be upsetting everything on to the ground!'

He kept the coffin in its place with one of his fat hands. With the other—as there was no second clerk—he was carrying the holy-water vessel, and he likewise represented the choirman, the rural guard, who had been unable to come.

'Come in, too, you others,' he exclaimed, turning round.

There was a second funeral, that of Rosalie's baby, who had died the previous day from an attack of convulsions. The mother, the father, old mother Brichet, Catherine, and two big girls, La Rousse and Lisa, were there. The two last were carrying the baby's coffin, one supporting each end.

Suddenly all voices were hushed again, and there came another interval whilst the bell continued tolling in slow and desolate accents. The funeral procession crossed the entire burial-ground, going towards the corner which was formed by the church and the wall of Desiree's poultry-yard. Swarms of grasshoppers leaped away at the approaching footsteps, and lizards hurried into their holes. A heavy warmth hung over this corner of the loamy cemetery. The crackling of the dry grass beneath the tramp of the mourners sounded like choking sobs.

'There! stop where you are!' cried the Brother, barring the way before the two big girls who were carrying the baby's coffin. 'Wait for your turn. Don't be getting in our legs here.'

The two girls laid the baby on the ground. Rosalie, Fortune, and old mother Brichet were lingering in the middle of the graveyard, while Catherine slyly followed Brother Archangias. Albine's grave was on the left hand of Abbe Caffin's tomb, whose white stone seemed in the sunshine to be flecked with silvery spangles. The deep cavity, freshly dug that morning, yawned amidst thick tufts of grass. Big weeds, almost uprooted, drooped over the edges, and a fallen flower lay at the bottom, staining the dark soil with its crimson petals. When Abbe Mouret came forward, the soft earth crumbled and gave way beneath his feet; he was obliged to step back to keep himself from slipping into the grave.

'*Ego sum*—' he began in a full voice, which rose above the mournful tolling of the bell.

During the anthem, those who were present instinctively cast furtive glances towards the bottom of the empty grave. Vincent, who had planted the cross at the foot of the cavity opposite the priest, pushed the loose earth with his foot, and amused himself by watching it fall. This drew a laugh from Catherine, who was leaning forward from behind him to get a better view. The peasants had set the litter on the grass and were stretching their arms, while Brother Archangias prepared the sprinkler.

'Come here, Voriau!' called Fortune.

The big black dog, who had gone to sniff at the coffin, came back sulkily.

'Why has the dog been brought?' exclaimed Rosalie.

'Oh! he followed us,' said Lisa, smiling quietly.

They were all chatting together in subdued tones round the baby's coffin. The father and mother occasionally forgot all about it, but on catching sight of it again, lying between them at their feet, they relapsed into silence.

'And so old Bambousse wouldn't come?' said La Rousse. Mother Brichet raised her eyes to heaven.

'He threatened to break everything to pieces yesterday when the little one died,' said she. 'No, no, I must say that he is not a good man. Didn't he nearly strangle me, crying out that he had been robbed, and that he would have given one of his cornfields for the little one to have died three days before the wedding?'

'One can never tell what will happen,' remarked Fortune with a knowing look.

'What's the good of the old man putting himself out about it? We are married, all the same, now,' added Rosalie.

Then they exchanged a smile across the little coffin while Lisa and La Rousse nudged each other with their elbows. But afterwards they all became very serious again. Fortune picked up a clod of earth to throw at Voriau, who was now prowling about amongst the old tombstones.

'Ah! they've nearly finished over there, now!' La Rousse whispered very softly.

Abbe Mouret was just concluding the *De profundis* in front of Albine's grave. Then, with slow steps, he approached the coffin, drew himself up erect, and gazed at it for a moment without a quiver in his glance. He looked taller, his face shone with a serenity that seemed to transfigure him. He stooped and picked up a handful of earth, and scattered it over the coffin crosswise. Then, in a voice so steady and clear that not a syllable was lost, he said:

'*Revertitur in terrain suam unde erat, et spiritus redit ad Deum qui dedit illum.*'

A shudder ran through those who were present. Lisa seemed to reflect for a moment, and then remarked with an expression of worry: 'It is not very cheerful, eh, when one thinks that one's own turn will come some day or other.'

But Brother Archangias had now handed the sprinkler to the priest, who took it and shook it several times over the corpse.

'*Requiescat in pace*,' he murmured.

'*Amen*,' responded Vincent and the Brother together, in tones so respectively shrill and deep that Catherine had to cram her fist into her mouth to keep from laughing.

'No, indeed, it is certainly not cheerful,' continued Lisa. 'There really was nobody at all at that funeral. The graveyard would be quite empty without us.'

'I've heard say that she killed herself,' said old mother Brichet.

'Yes, I know,' interrupted La Rousse. 'The Brother didn't want to let her be buried amongst Christians, but Monsieur le Cure said that eternity was for everybody. I was there. But all the same the Philosopher might have come.'

At that very moment Rosalie reduced them all to silence by murmuring: 'See! there he is, the Philosopher.'

Jeanbernat was, indeed, just entering the graveyard. He walked straight to the group that stood around Albine's grave; and he stepped along with so lithe, so springy a gait, that none of them heard him coming. When he was close to them, he remained for a moment behind Brother Archangias and seemed to fix his eyes, for an instant, on the nape of the Brother's neck. Then, just as the Abbe Mouret was finishing the office, he calmly drew a knife from his pocket, opened it, and with a single cut sliced off the Brother's right ear.

There had been no time for any one to interfere. The Brother gave a terrible yell.

'The left one will be for another occasion,' said Jeanbernat quietly, as he threw the ear upon the ground. Then he went off.

So great and so general was the stupefaction that nobody followed him. Brother Archangias had dropped upon the heap of fresh soil which had been thrown out of the grave. He was staunching his bleeding wound with his handkerchief. One of the four peasants who had carried the coffin, wanted to lead him away, conduct him home; but he refused with a gesture and remained where he was, fierce and sullen, wishing to see Albine lowered into the pit.

'There! it's our turn at last!' said Rosalie with a little sigh.

But Abbe Mouret still lingered by the grave, watching the bearers who were slipping cords under Albine's coffin in order that they might let it down gently. The bell was still tolling; but La Teuse must have been getting tired, for it tolled irregularly, as though it were becoming a little irritated at the length of the ceremony.

The sun was growing hotter and the Solitaire's shadow crept slowly over the grass and the grave mounds. When Abbe Mouret was obliged to step back in order to give the bearers room, his eyes lighted upon the marble tombstone of Abbe Caffin, that priest who also had loved, and who was now sleeping there so peacefully beneath the wild-flowers.

Then, all at once, even as the coffin descended, supported by the cords, whose knots made it strain and creak, a tremendous uproar arose in the poultry-yard on the other side of the wall. The goat began to bleat. The ducks, the geese, and the turkeys raised their loudest calls and flapped their wings. The fowls all cackled at once. The yellow cock, Alexander, crowed forth his trumpet notes. The rabbits could even be heard leaping in their hutches and shaking their wooden floors. And, above all this lifeful uproar of the animal creation, a loud laugh rang out. There was a rustling of skirts. Desiree, with her hair streaming, her arms bare to the elbows, and her face crimson with triumph, burst into sight, her hands resting upon the coping of the wall. She had doubtless climbed upon the manure-heap.

'Serge! Serge!' she cried.

At that moment Albine's coffin had reached the bottom of the grave. The cords had just been withdrawn. One of the peasants was throwing the first shovelful of earth into the cavity.

'Serge! Serge!' Desiree cried, still more loudly, clapping her hands, 'the cow has got a calf!'

THE END